Drink

ALLYSON K.
ABBOTT

KENSINGTON BOOKS

http://www.kensingtonbooks.com

KENSINGTON BOOKS are published by

Kensington Publishing Corp.
119 West 40th Street
New York, NY 10018

All Kensington titles, imprints and distributed lines are available at special quantity discounts for bulk purchases for sales promotion, premiums, fund-raising, educational or institutional use. Special book excerpts or customized printings can also be created to fit specific needs. For details, write or phone the office of the Kensington Special Sales Manager: Kensington Publishing Corp., 119 West 40th Street, New York, NY, 10018. Attn. Special Sales Department. Phone: 1-800-221-2647.

Kensington and the K logo Reg. U.S. Pat. & TM Off.

ISBN-13: 978-0-7582-8019-0
ISBN-10: 0-7582-8019-X
First Kensington Mass Market Edition: August 2015

ISBN-13: 978-0-7582-8020-6
ISBN-10: 0-7582-8020-3
First Kensington Electronic Edition: August 2015

10 9 8 7 6 5 4 3 2 1

Printed in the United States of America

For Aleah, Lindsay, Cameron, Lincoln,
Nicholas, and Renna . . .
you guys inspire me and make me proud.

Acknowledgments

I can never say enough about the key people involved with creating these books: my editor, Peter Senftleben, for his wisdom, understanding, insight, and humor; my agent, Adam Chromy, for his tireless efforts on my behalf and his unfailing belief in me and my work; and all those behind the scenes at Kensington Books who help to make my books a success. It is a pleasure and an honor to work with all of you. Thank you.

With that said, the biggest thanks of all go to my readers, because without all of you none of this would be possible. You have brought joy into my life, and I hope that in some small way I can return the favor by bringing a small measure of joy into yours. Cheers!

Chapter 1

Dear Ms. Dalton,

It is my understanding from all the hype I've heard and read recently in the local media that you are some kind of crime-solving savant who can literally sniff out clues. I find this claim both intriguing and highly suspect, and frankly I don't believe your ability—whatever it is—can beat out a brilliant mind. Therefore, I would like to put you to a series of tests. If you pass the first test you will move on to the next phase, and so on.

Fail it and I will leave a body for you somewhere here in the city. It won't be a random death. It will be someone you know, someone who is close to you, someone who is a significant part of your life. Should this occur, perhaps you will be able to interpret the clues I will provide and figure out who I am. I rather doubt you can do these things, but I do value a good challenge and I'm eager to see what you can accomplish.

I do have a few rules. You must figure things out using your wits and your "special ability" without any help from the police. That means

*your friend—or is he a boyfriend?—Detective
Albright cannot be involved in any way. If I get
wind of his involvement, there will be dire
consequences. I do hope you understand how
strict I will be if you opt to cheat because the lives
of many people will depend on your willingness to
play by my rules.*

*Each phase of this test will be timed. If you do
not achieve the goals I lay out for you within the
time parameters I have set, I will kill someone else
and the game will go on. I do hope that the added
stress of knowing your failure will cost someone
their life won't interfere with your supposed
abilities. But if it does, so be it. Let us begin.*

*The letter you now hold in your hand is your
first clue. There is something very unique about
this letter and if you can figure out what that is,
it will lead you to the second clue. You must
achieve this by nine P.M. on December twelfth or
experience the consequences.*

*I doubt you will succeed. In fact, I'm counting
on your failure. And lest you think this is a
prank, I have left something for you to prove there
are no "happy days" ahead if you fail to take me
seriously. I will be watching you.*

Good luck.

An intrigued fan

I read the letter three times in a row, slower
each time, unwilling to believe what I was seeing.
Then I picked up the envelope, convinced
there had been a mix-up and I wasn't the intended recipient. But there was no mix-up. It
was addressed to Mackenzie Dalton and the

address of my bar appeared below the name. There was no return address—hardly surprising given the contents and nature of the letter—but there was a Milwaukee postage meter stamp.

With shaking hands I set both the letter and the envelope down on my desk, realizing too late that I had contaminated both by touching them. I studied the letter some more, this time focusing on the structure and design as opposed to the words. The handwritten letters were done in a simple calligraphic style with varying widths in the strokes, suggesting the use of a fountain pen. The paper was basic and white, the kind sold in hundreds of stores for use in copiers, printers, and the like. The envelope was equally as generic. In fact, I had identical ones in my own desk: business-sized, plain white, with an adhesive strip on the flap covered by a removable piece of paper. This eliminated the need to lick an envelope, and based on what I had learned watching the occasional crime show, it also eliminated a potential source for DNA.

I read the letter again, stopping when I reached the imposed deadline. I glanced at my watch, saw that it was just past four in the afternoon, and cursed under my breath. Since it was Friday the eleventh of December, I had less than thirty hours to figure things out. Another look at the meter stamp told me that the letter had been posted three days ago, meaning it had likely been sitting on my desk for two. I might have had more time if I hadn't procrastinated on opening my mail, but I'd received way more than the usual amount of late. That's because I was getting a lot of personal letters and cards mixed in among the bills and sale flyers that made up my usual deliveries.

The sudden spate of personal mail was from people who had heard about me in the news over the past few weeks when my involvement with the local police during a recent high-profile kidnapping and murder case had become known. While many of the letters were supportive, some had been skeptical, and a few had been downright mean. As a result, I'd stopped opening them after the first couple of weeks and began tossing them into a pile instead. Today was the day I'd decided to tackle them, though for one brief moment I considered simply throwing all of them away unopened. Fortunately, or unfortunately—I wasn't sure yet—I hadn't done that.

I ran my hands through my hair and then immediately regretted doing so as one long fiery-red strand fell onto the offending letter.

Way to go, Mack. Like you haven't contaminated this thing enough already.

I leaned back in my chair, distancing myself—at least physically—from the letter, and indulging in a moment of self-pity. Why this? Why now? Wasn't my life stressful enough already? I wished I could climb into a time machine and go back a year, knowing what I knew now. Maybe then I could fix things, prevent things, change the future. Maybe my father would still be alive, and his girlfriend, Ginny, would still be alive, and the man I considered both a blessing and a curse wouldn't have entered my life yet. Then again, maybe he wouldn't have entered it at all. Would that have been a good thing?

The man is Duncan Albright, a homicide

detective here in Milwaukee. He entered my life around two months ago when I found Ginny's body in the alley behind the bar I own, the bar my father bought back before I was born. My father named it after himself—Mack's Bar—and then gave me the name Mackenzie so I could carry on the legacy. Some might have been annoyed by such presumptuousness, but I was always content with the assumption that I would carry on both the name and the business. This was made easier by the fact that I literally grew up in the bar; my father and I lived in an apartment above it. But the legacy became a little harder to bear when the bar became mine alone last January after my father was murdered in that same back alley where I found Ginny.

Duncan wasn't involved with the investigation into my father's murder because he didn't live or work in Milwaukee then. When I met him he was relatively new in town, having arrived only months before Ginny's murder, a fact that came into play while he was investigating the crime. Because he was not well-known in town, he decided to do a little undercover work by pretending to be an employee in my bar. I wasn't very keen on the idea at first, but Duncan's threats to shut me down if I didn't cooperate helped me decide to go along. Still, I didn't like it for several reasons. For one, he was convinced the killer was one of my employees or customers, and to me that idea was unfathomable. My employees and some of my long-term customers were like family to me. The idea that one of them might be a cold-blooded killer was an idea I could hardly bear to consider.

Another reason I wasn't too keen on having a

homicide detective watching my every move was because of my disorder. I'm a synesthete, which sounds worse than it is . . . at least most of the time. Synesthesia is a neurological disorder in which the senses are cross-wired. I don't experience the world around me the way most people do. Every sense I experience is multifaceted and complex. For instance, I may taste or see things that I hear, or I may experience a smell or tactile sensation when I look at certain things or people. Both smells and tastes are typically accompanied by sounds or some sort of physical sensation. In addition to this cross-wiring, my senses are also highly acute and I'm able to smell things others can't, or hear things others can't, presumably because of my synesthesia.

I'm not alone in having this condition. There are a number of people in the general population who have it, though there are varying degrees of the disorder. People with artistic inclinations seem to have a higher incidence of synesthesia than other groups of people, and there are theories that the synesthesia plays a role in artistic ability. For instance, there are musicians who not only hear music but see it in their minds as colors, shapes, or some combination of these. The "rightness" of the colors and shapes helps the musician sense when the music is right. I have a similar experience with numbers and letters. They all appear to me with colors attached, and the rightness of those colors makes me very good at both math and spelling. Defining the "rightness," however, is something I'm not good at. It's an intuitive thing, something I know but can't seem to explain to other people.

I've spent most of my life trying to hide my synesthesia. There was a time when members of the medical profession thought my sensory experiences were manifestations of a severe psychological disorder, and I started getting slapped with labels like schizophrenia. When I was a child, my classmates and friends would often tease me, calling me weird or crazy whenever I said things like *this music appears too green,* or *this apple tastes like a blaring trumpet.* It didn't take me long to realize I was different, and when you're a kid, different is the kiss of death. So I learned to keep my experiences to myself.

For many years I was perfectly content to maintain my secret, sharing it only with my father. Over time I told a few close friends about it, but for the most part no one knew. Then Duncan Albright came into my life and everything changed. I was forced to tell him about my synesthesia and try to explain how it worked because my experiences were a key element in solving Ginny's murder. And since I was a suspect, solving Ginny's murder became my main focus. In some ways my synesthesia made things more difficult, but for the most part it not only aided the investigation, it helped to solve it.

I was impressed by the fact that Duncan didn't have the same skeptical attitude many people have when they first hear me describe my synesthesia. Not that he bought into it right away, but he didn't dismiss it immediately either. Nor did he declare me crazy. And by the time we solved the case, he was beginning to think my synesthesia might be of some use to him in his job. He spent several weeks testing me, setting up scenarios and asking me to identify a certain smell from something he would briefly bring into a room and then remove, or having me enter a room and tell him if something had recently been moved or changed. I'd been playing such parlor tricks with my father most of my life, so I passed this part of Duncan's test with flying colors. And I mean this literally. The happiness I felt whenever Duncan praised my efforts made me see swirling, floating bands of color.

Parlor tricks don't solve crimes, however, so some of the customers in my bar decided to help me develop my deductive reasoning. They did this by forming a crime-solving group dubbed the Capone Club that discussed and analyzed both real and made-up riddles and crimes. The group has proven to be quite popular and it, combined with some of the publicity surrounding Ginny's murder, attracted a lot of new clientele to my bar. I thought the increased business might be transitory—the latest gimmick for people's entertainment until something more interesting came along—but so far both my business and the Capone Club have grown.

Following Ginny's murder, the secret of my synesthesia became known by more and more people, and for a while I was okay with that. For the first time in my life, it didn't feel like something I had to hide or be embarrassed about. Many people found it fascinating, and Duncan's interest in using it to help him solve real crimes made me feel like it was a valuable trait, something that could be used for good. After several weeks of Duncan's test scenarios, I was given the chance to prove my mettle with some real crimes. Unfortunately, the last one I helped him with became a top news item. It was the headline story for days, and through some incidental events and careless slips of the tongue, my participation in helping to solve the crime became public knowledge.

This did not sit well with Duncan's bosses, particularly after the press and the newscasters claimed the local police were using voodoo, fortune-tellers, witchcraft, and hocus-pocus to help them solve their cases. In addition to the embarrassing public relations nightmare, Duncan was chastised for putting a civilian—namely me—in harm's way. He was placed on suspension for two weeks while the powers decided his fate, and then their two-week decision stretched into three. I'd begun to fear Duncan would lose his job, but this past Monday he was finally allowed to return to work. Because of his suspension, Duncan had deemed it wise for us to keep our distance until the furor died down, so I haven't seen him for several weeks, though we've spoken on the phone a handful of times. It's been hard for me because Duncan and I were starting to explore a more intimate relationship when all this happened, and the sudden separation left me with some emotional baggage. It was also hard for me because the local reporters were determined to get a story highlighting the strange barkeep with the weird ability, and for the past two weeks they have stalked me relentlessly. Some of them have been professional enough to be up-front about the reason they were hounding me, but others have come into the bar pretending to be customers, hoping to pry a story loose from me, or from some of my employees, close friends, and patrons. Fortunately, those folks in the know are devoted and reliable, and as far as I know no one has discussed me, my synesthesia, or my involvement with the police with anyone. I thought the press would quickly lose interest, and that their inability to get anything out of anyone in the bar would deter them from writing their stories, but that wasn't the case. What they didn't know they made up, sensationalizing and speculating along the way. They turned me into a Milwaukee freak show.

So while I'm normally a very present and hands-on owner when it comes to running my bar, the recent publicity storm has forced me into hiding either in my office or my apartment much of the time. Fortunately I have a group of capable and dependable employees who can run things just fine without me, though I'm rarely more than one locked door or text message away.

Unfortunately, this need to hide coincided with the grand opening of my new expansion. After Ginny's death, I learned I was the sole beneficiary in her will. I went from counting pennies and barely scraping by, wondering from one day to the next if I was going to be able to keep the bar open, to a degree of financial independence. I bought an empty building that shared a wall with my bar, and doubled the size of my place. It was a risky move, but one I felt I needed to make to stay competitive and keep the bar alive. In an ironic twist, all the publicity helped because it kept a steady stream of curiosity seekers coming in, hoping for a glimpse of the crime-solving, psychic fortune-teller who also happened to own a bar. So while I hated all the media attention focused on me, the weeks since the mediafest began have been the busiest ever at Mack's Bar. I know some of the traffic might be transient, but I hope that once things do finally die down, there will continue to be enough business to maintain a healthy bottom line.

I was hugely relieved that Duncan didn't lose his job, but his return to work didn't help our personal relationship any. He was brought back on duty with the caveat that he wasn't to get any help with his cases from "that woman." This edict upset Duncan because he genuinely believed my synesthesia was an asset that could help him solve cases. I wanted to think it also upset him because of the strain it put on our relationship, but our last few phone conversations had been blandly polite and benignly social with little to no hint of romance or intimacy. I told myself it was because Duncan was distracted and worried about his job, but I'd harbored a fear from day one that his interest in me was more because of what I could do for him and his career than it was anything he liked about me personally. Not that there wasn't a genuine attraction between us; there was. But I wasn't convinced it was strong enough on his end to keep him interested if I was no longer of any use to him careerwise. Time would tell, I supposed, so I kept reminding myself to be patient.

But now I had this letter to deal with. If it was real—and I had no reason to think it wasn't—it was going to complicate my relationship with Duncan even more. My gut told me to tell him about the letter regardless of the writer's warning.

Handling it alone was out of the question, and I had faith in Duncan's ability to help me sort it out while keeping it secret. But before I took that leap, I wanted to run it by a few other people who were among my core group of regulars, people who were the heart and soul of the Capone Club: my makeshift, substitute family.

Chapter 2

I peeked out of my office door and did a quick scan of the customers I could see. The place was bustling with business, and most of the tables were full. I didn't see any obvious reporters among the mix, but some of them had been so clever and clandestine in carrying out their business that I couldn't be sure.

I thought back to one of the last lines of the letter: *I will be watching you.* I scanned the unknown faces in the bar, wondering if the letter writer was one of them. Would he or she be brazen enough to patronize my place? I thought about that for a moment and decided that anyone cheeky enough to write such a letter in the first place would have no qualms about coming into the bar to watch me. And if the letter was serious in its threat—meaning the writer would kill someone for what amounted to sport—then anything was possible.

One of my waitresses, Debra Landers, a no-nonsense mother of two teenage boys, saw me and made her way over. I thought about asking her to fetch the people I wanted and bring them to me, but I was feeling claustrophobic and trapped. I needed to get out of the dark recesses of my office and into the open air. I missed my bar, my customers, my life.

"I think you're safe," Debra said, interpreting part of my hesitation correctly. "I've been watching and listening closely to most of the customers in this section and I don't think any of them are reporters."

Most of my employees had been doing watch duty for me these past weeks, and Debra, who had an uncanny ability to sniff out people's true motives—a trait that had earned her the nickname Ann Landers—was the best of the bunch.

"I can't be sure about the customers in Missy's or Linda's sections," she added. "So depending on where you're headed, I'd either avoid the new section or hurry through it."

"I'm going upstairs to the Capone Club room," I told her.

"Then just walk fast and avoid eye contact," Debra said. "If anyone tries to make a move on you, I'll run interference."

"Thanks." I stepped out of my office and hurried through the crowd toward the new section of the bar. Here the tables were less full, and a large portion of the area was taken up by a stage that I had yet to use. I hoped to bring in some live music for the weekends, and maybe even a DJ during the week, in which case part of the area around the stage that was currently occupied by tables would become a dance floor.

Despite Debra's advice, I continued scanning the faces of my customers. Most of them appeared oblivious to my presence and very involved with their tablemates, but there were a few people who watched my progress with unmasked curiosity. It was hard to interpret the motives behind those watchers. I became something of a local celebrity thanks to the recent news coverage, and my picture had appeared on the news for the better part of a week. As a result, there were people who now recognized me and called to me by name even though I'd never met them before. The media has a way of creating a false sense of intimacy.

I had almost reached the stairs on the far wall when I was waylaid. But it wasn't a reporter or a curiosity seeker who nabbed me; it was another one of my waitresses, Missy Channing. With her silky blond hair, milky skin, big blue eyes, and curvaceous body, Missy was an attraction for many of my male customers. She was also a hard and dependable worker with an uncanny ability to associate a face with a drink. If you ordered something once, Missy would remember it the next time she saw you. Unfortunately, Missy's cerebral attributes ended there. She wasn't very bright when it came to general knowledge or simple, everyday common sense, which is why, at the age of twenty-two, she was a single mother of two kids and living with her parents.

Missy grabbed me by the arm just as I was about to start up the stairs to the second level. Her face was flushed red and her hairline was damp with sweat. "Mack, we need to do something about that new girl, Linda. She's slow as molasses! Debra put her in this new section because it has fewer tables and customers, but even with the smaller crowd she can't keep up. I'm having to carry half of her section along with my own. And running up and down these stairs is killing me."

"Okay," I told her. "I'll talk to Debra and see if we can expand Linda's training time. In the meantime, do the best you can for tonight because I don't think we have anyone extra we can bring in on such short notice."

Missy's shoulders sagged and she looked like she wanted to cry.

"I know this transition hasn't been easy," I told her, reaching up and giving her shoulder a reassuring squeeze. "And I appreciate everything you do. Just get through tonight and I promise you I'll make it better."

"I'll do what I can," Missy said with a sigh, swiping the back of her hand over the beads of sweat on her forehead.

"I know you will. I'll ask Debra to help Linda out as much as she can, too. And to make it up to you, I'll pay you time and a half for tonight to compensate you for all the extra work you have to do."

That brought a smile to Missy's face. Her current goal in life was to be able to afford to move out of her parents' house, and that meant money talked. She was a good employee so I considered the time and a half a wise investment to keep her happy. With Missy placated, I headed upstairs, making a mental note to tell Debra to pair Linda up with another waitress for more training after tonight.

Linda Manko was one of several new hires I had brought on to help staff the expanded bar areas. She was twenty-one, single, and starting school in the spring with hopes of becoming a dental hygienist. I almost didn't hire her because of her quiet, shy demeanor and mousy, bespectacled appearance. She also had no previous experience, and while waiting tables isn't exactly rocket science, it does require some social and organizational skills, skills I wasn't sure Linda possessed. But there was something about her, an underlying sadness or pensiveness that pulled at me and made me want to give her a chance. My father had always told me not to let my emotions rule my decisions when it came to hiring or firing staff, but that was a lesson I never quite learned. I didn't know if Linda was going to work out, but I was willing to give her a little more time to prove herself.

I climbed the stairs two at a time, eager to move on. The second floor in the original portion of the building above the bar was my apartment, but I decided to use the second floor in the new section for some special rooms. The first one I came to was the game room, or what many of my customers had dubbed the Man Cave. It was equipped with a pool table, two large-screen TVs, a foosball table, a dartboard, a putting green, computers with gaming systems, and some comfy recliner chairs. Not surprisingly, this room had been a big hit so far. What did surprise me was how many women used it. At first I thought the women were in there because they were single and looking, and figured that's where they could find the men. But at least half the women in the room on any given day or night were married or playing games with other women, simply enjoying a girls' night out.

Just past the game room was the room that had been taken over by the Capone Club. There was a third room, as well, but at the moment it was closed off. I intended to use it for extra-busy nights as simple overflow seating, and for special group functions. There was also a second bar on this level, one that could be locked behind a drop-down, garage door when I didn't need to use it. I had opened it a handful of times in the preceding weeks, mostly on Thursday nights and weekends—my busiest times—and twice when the third room was being used for some specialty events: a retirement party for an employee of a local company and a bridal shower. My original intent was to keep the second bar closed the rest of the time, but both the Capone Club room and the Man Cave were being used steadily, and my staff started to complain about having to climb the stairs to serve people on the second level. So I made the decision last night to staff both bars for now and provide dedicated waitstaff for the second floor to see how it played out. It wasn't a perfect solution because the kitchen was on the first floor and that meant there was still plenty of stair climbing involved whenever there were food orders. Tonight the second-floor bar was manned by Curtis Donovan, a new bartender I'd recently hired. Curtis was in his mid-thirties and came with several years of experience. He was a big guy with a big personality, soulful brown eyes, and a dimpled chin. He was also refreshingly and un-apologetically gay. There was a group of women crowded around his bar, watching as Curtis entertained them with a mixing show worthy of Tom Cruise in *Cocktail*. He winked at me as I walked by and headed for the Capone Club room.

The Capone Club room was by far my favorite part of the additional space. The walls were wood paneled like an old-fashioned library or den, and there were bookshelves where I had placed a sampling of both novels and nonfiction books that could be swapped out using an honor system. It had taken less than a week for those shelves to be filled in by my customers with all manner of mystery novels and crime-related texts: forensic books, true crime novels, reference books on poisons, guns, crime scene analysis, and police procedures, and the requisite smattering of Sherlock Holmes tales. Scattered about the room were a dozen small round tables and an assortment of cozy chairs that could be pulled into a conversation circle, or hauled into a corner if someone wanted some privacy. A combination of recessed lighting and table lamps gave the room a warm feel while still providing enough light to read by. The star feature of the room at the time, given that it was mid-December, was the gas fireplace. Its heat and ambience made it a magnet for anyone who came into the room, so it wasn't too surprising to see that most of the Capone Club group was gathered around it. I did a quick scan, looking for any new or suspicious faces that might be reporters or crazed murderers in disguise, but everyone in the room at that moment was someone I knew.

Cora Kingsley was the first to see and greet me. "Mack!" she hollered, waving me into the room. "It's about time you ventured out of that cave you call an office." Cora was forty-something, single, and an incurable flirt. She had a saucy personality, hair almost the same flaming color as mine— although hers came from a bottle—and a bosom that most men couldn't resist staring at. Cora didn't discourage such leers or ogles; in fact she seemed to invite and enjoy them. Her voluptuous build and flirty personality were mere window dressing for a very sharp mind and business acumen. The temptation to label Cora as a femme fatale was a big one, but the fact that she was a computer geek didn't quite fit into this mold. She owned her own company, which offered development and troubleshooting services for both computer hardware and software. One of her pet projects of late was a program she and one of her employees were working on that would help solve crimes. It operated much like the game Clue, and while it had so far proven to be too flawed to be of any real use, the Capone Club group enjoyed using it to come up with crime riddles they would then try to solve.

Back when we were investigating Ginny's murder, and I was trying to understand and interpret my synesthetic reactions to help solve it, Cora offered to be in charge of cataloging my reactions. They tend to be consistent and repeatable, but there are so many of them, and I've spent so many years trying to ignore them, that it was hard at times for me to accurately interpret them. Cora has built and maintained a searchable database of my crosswired reactions to things. It has helped immensely because I can tell her what type of reaction I have to something and often as not she can look it up and tell me what it means if I don't already know. Though now, with the kibosh put on my services by the police department, the database might not serve much of a purpose.

Tad Amundsen followed up Cora's chastising greeting with "Given the way the press has been hounding Mack, can you blame her for hiding?"

Tad, like Cora, was a long-standing patron and

member of the Capone Club. He was a financial advisor who owned his own company, though most of his revenue these days came from the friends of his very wealthy wife. Tad was a trophy husband and his ambivalence about it—he wasn't happy in his marriage, but was unwilling to give up the money—had him frequenting my bar often under the pretense of working late.

"I'm hoping my hiding days are almost over," I told the group. "Sooner or later the press will find a new story to move on to."

"I'm truly sorry about all dat," said Tiny Gruber, an ironically nicknamed, huge hulk of a man whose real first name was Jürgen. Tiny was a construction worker and Cora's latest beau. He was new to both the group and my bar a few weeks ago when the publicity firestorm started. In fact, it was Tiny who started it. His younger sister Lori and her best friend, Anna Hermann, had disappeared and been found murdered twelve years ago when they were both fourteen years old. The crime had never been solved, and when Tiny saw what I was doing for the police, and the involvement and success the Capone Club had in helping to solve both real and made-up crimes, he went to the press and told them about it, not knowing the complications it would cause. He didn't do it maliciously; he merely wanted to generate some interest in his sister's long-cold case. It was a sentiment I understood all too well given that my father's murder went unsolved for many months, so I couldn't begrudge him his actions.

"It's okay, Tiny," I assured him. "I think the press is starting to lose interest in me."

"Oh, good," he said. "It made me mad because

dat dere woman I talked to told me she would highlight Lori's case and she never did." Despite Tiny's towering size and his age, which I guessed to be in his mid- to late thirties, he seemed child-like with his ponytailed blond hair, big blue eyes, and cherubic cheeks. And when he pouted, like he was doing now, he looked even younger.

"Just don't share anything else with them unless you run it by the group here, okay?" I cautioned him.

He nodded vigorously, still pouting, and said, "I won't talk to dem dere newspeople ever again."

Cora looked over at me and winked. "I have him reined in," she said. "And we're going to start looking into his sister's case, so that's made him happy."

"Any progress yet?" I asked.

"Not really," Cora said. "We're just getting started and so far all we've done is go over some of the info Tiny has in his own file. It's kind of limited and it would help if we could get our hands on the official police file, or at least some tidbits of official information, but I don't suppose Duncan or anyone else over there is going to be very amenable to such sharing right now."

"No, I suppose not."

The Signoriello brothers, Joe and Frank, were kicked back in cushy chairs pushed up as close to the fireplace as they could get without combusting from the heat. They each had a beer in hand and two empty sandwich plates sat on the table in front of them. A hint of a smile graced both faces and it made me smile, too, seeing how comfortable, cozy, and relaxed they looked. They weren't as spry as they used to be, given that their combined ages hit just shy of one-fifty, though their grizzled, wrinkled faces and salt-and-pepper hair hadn't changed much in the past twenty years. Now that my father was gone, Frank and Joe were the closest thing to family I had. My mother died shortly after giving birth to me, not from the birth, but from a head injury she sustained in a traffic accident weeks before I was born. She was kept alive on machines until I could safely be delivered, and then the machines were removed and she was allowed to die. My father raised me, and given that the bar was his life, it became mine as well. A number of women served as temporary, surrogate mothers as I grew up, offering me advice on girly stuff like bras, clothing, hairstyles, menstruation, and dating . . . subjects my father didn't feel comfortable discussing or was hopelessly uninformed on. But over time most of them moved on. The Signoriello brothers, however, have been there since before I was born, and they're like two kindly, doting uncles, offering advice, watching out for my interests, even screening potential boyfriends for me, something they've been doing since my high school days. Since they are both retired insurance salesmen, they are also a great asset for the Capone Club.

Cora had become like a sister to me in recent months, and thanks to the nature of her business and her independent employees, she could work anywhere she wanted to as long as she had a laptop with Internet access. She had set up a Wi-Fi Internet system in the bar several years ago, and this allowed her to spend a good portion of her day—sometimes her entire day—in my bar rather than in her office, which was just around the corner.

It was Cora and the Signoriello brothers whom

I wanted to pull aside; they were my family, my
most trusted confidantes, and the people I hoped
would have the wisdom to tell me what to do about
that letter in my office. But I didn't want anyone to
know the reason why I was about to summon them
to my office, so I made up some stories.

"Cora, I'm having some problems with the Wi-
Fi access. Can you come down to my office and
look at it?"

"I sure can," she said, picking up the laptop she
never went anywhere without.

"Joe, Frank, I need to talk to both of you, too, if
you don't mind. I need you to go over my new insurance policy on the bar. I'm worried that I don't
have enough coverage, what with the new expansion."

"We'll be right down," Joe said, stretching and
then slowly easing out of his chair. "Though I hate
to leave this fireplace," he added. "That heat feels
awful good on these cranky old joints."

"That it does," Frank said, mimicking his brother's
slow movements.

Cora and I headed for my office, leaving the
brothers to come along at their own pace. Normally, I would have waited and escorted the brothers down the stairs but I wanted a minute or two to
talk to Cora in private.

I led the way, scurrying across the main floor,
keeping my head down to avoid any eye contact
with the customers, and breathing a sigh of relief
as soon as we were safe and secure behind my
office door.

"What's the real reason you called me in here?'
Cora asked.

"Am I that transparent?"

"To me you are. I know you well enough by now to know when something is bothering you. And besides, the Wi-Fi is working just fine. Is it Duncan?"

"Sort of," I said with a shrug and a little waggle of my head.

"Still no hint of romance in your discussions?"

"Not much. He returned to work this week and I hoped he might pop in to say hi, but he hasn't."

"Maybe he feels like they're still watching him."

"Plenty of other cops come in here every day. Several of them even participate in the Capone Club."

"Those other cops didn't get a suspension. Give him a little more time."

I nodded, frowning. I wasn't convinced that more time would make any difference. "That's not the main reason I wanted to talk to you," I said. "This is." I pointed to the letter, which was still sitting on top of my desk where I'd left it. "Read it but please don't touch it."

Cora set down her laptop in a nearby chair and walked around to my side of the desk to read the letter. I watched her facial expressions change as she did so, from disbelief to skepticism, horror, and finally fear.

"Do you think this is legit?" she asked.

"If it's a practical joke, it's not a very funny one."

The Signoriello brothers walked in at that point, and I explained the real reason I'd asked them into my office and repeated the instructions I'd given to Cora. She joined me on the opposite side of the desk and watched along with me as the brothers read the letter, their facial expressions mirroring the ones Cora had exhibited moments ago.

When they were done, Joe shot me a worried look while Frank simply looked skeptical.

"It came in the mail yesterday or maybe the day before," I told the others. "I thought it was going to be another fan letter." The skepticism in my voice when I said the word *fan* was heavy.

All three of them looked at me questioningly, not surprising since I hadn't yet told anyone other than Duncan about the letters. So I explained. "Ever since that big media storm three weeks ago, I've been receiving letters from folks in and around the Milwaukee area that have seen or read the news reports about me. Many of the letter writers have been supportive or at least neutral, and a few even asked if I would provide private fortune-telling services for them. Two letters came with checks and questions the senders wanted me to answer. I returned those, along with the money and an explanation that I'm not a fortune-teller. Those were amusing, but several other letters I've received have been anything but. For instance, I got one last week from a religious fanatic who calls himself Apostle Mike. He thinks I'm an abomination in desperate need of saving and redemption if I'm to have any hope of ascending to heaven. Another letter that came a few days ago accused me of being a charlatan who's trying to sucker poor unsuspecting people into paying money so I can scam them with some made-up prophecies."

"Geez," Cora said, frowning. "Why didn't you tell us about these letters?"

"I didn't see any reason to. I've discussed them with Duncan, though only in general terms, and he feels they're harmless. I haven't told him about this one yet, though," I said, pointing to the latest letter. "Do you think I should?"

Frank said, "Do you think it's real? It could be nothing more than a practical joke, a sick one, I'll grant you, but still . . ."

"I don't think she can ignore it," Joe said. "The stakes are too high."

"I'm with Joe," Cora said. "I think we should run it by Duncan."

Part of me was glad they felt Duncan needed to be involved, if only because I wanted so badly to see him.

Frank frowned and shook his head. "I'm not convinced it's real. It's probably someone's perverted idea of a joke. Or maybe it's someone in the Capone Club, trying out a new crime puzzle on us."

"I don't think anyone in our group would be this twisted," Joe said. "Real or not."

"Do *you* think it's legit?" Cora asked me.

I thought a minute before I answered. "I do, mainly because there *is* something unusual about the letter. And that makes me think that whoever wrote it is serious about testing me. If they're crazy enough to do that, who's to say what else they might do?"

"What's unusual about it?" Joe asked.

"It's written by hand in a fancy, calligraphic style, but the ink sounds unusual."

"It sounds unusual?" Cora said, settling onto the couch and opening her laptop.

"Yes," I said. "All inks come with sounds for me. For instance, when I look at a typed-out letter of any sort, I can tell if the ink is from an ink jet printer or a laser printer because the ink sounds different. I think it's because they smell different.

The ink used in the majority of pens is distinctive, too, and they all have underlying associated sounds. But this ink doesn't sound like any I've ever heard before."

Cora started tapping the keys on her laptop. "I don't think we've cataloged any of your reactions related to ink or paper before, but let me search through what we've recorded in the database so far to make sure."

"In the meantime, you should call Duncan," Joe said.

"But the letter makes it clear I shouldn't do that. If I do, it puts all of you in danger."

"*If* it's serious," Frank said. "I suspect it's a lot of bluff and blunder. Besides, Joe and I can take care of ourselves. And I suspect Cora here can, too."

"I can't risk that on a guess. What if the sender targets someone else, like one of my employees, or someone else in the Capone Club?" I shook my head. "I couldn't live with that."

Cora said, "If you don't involve Duncan, your chances of figuring this out on your own are much slimmer, even with our help. And if you don't figure it out and it's legit, someone will die anyway."

I looked at all of them with a pleading expression. "So what should I do? If I don't involve Duncan, someone might die, and if I do involve him someone might die. I can't win."

"Then we should find a way to involve Duncan without anyone knowing," Joe said. "What if you call him, read him the letter, and then arrange to meet him somewhere on the sly?"

Cora brightened up then and said, "And in the meantime, maybe we can use all this press attention you've been getting to your advantage."

"How so?" I asked, curious.

"The next time one of them comes into the bar, mention that you and Duncan are a thing of the past, and that you don't want anything more to do with him. Don't make it obvious. Just let them overhear a discussion you have with someone."

Joe said, "If we're careful about it, maybe we can use some of the other cops who come in here as secret go-betweens for you and Duncan. There should be a couple of cops you can trust to do that, right?"

"Maybe," I said, not sure if I liked the idea. "Though it seems to me that the more people we involve in this, the more likely it is something will leak. That's why I decided to share this with you three only and not the rest of the group. I trust you guys to keep it to yourselves, at least for now."

"And you know we will," Joe said. "But I think we're overlooking an even more important issue here." He paused to see if anyone could guess what he was referring to but we all stared blankly at him. "*Your* safety," he said. "Clearly this nut-job has a bone to pick with you. He's fixated on you, and that means you're in jeopardy."

I frowned at this, staring at the letter. "I suppose," I said. "But I don't get a sense of imminent danger toward me. Instead I feel like whoever wrote this wants to hurt me in other ways, by killing people, people I know and care about. It feels like it's a game to him . . . or her, because I suppose it could be a woman who wrote it."

"Statistics don't bear that out," Cora said, "but you're right. We shouldn't harbor any biases or jump to any conclusions that might blind us to the facts."

"I'm all for involving Duncan," Frank said. "I'm still not convinced this isn't some kind of sick prank, but I agree that the stakes are too high for us to simply shrug it off or ignore it."

I nodded my agreement. "If we can involve Duncan and keep it from being known, that would be my preference, too. I could have him come down here and enter through the back door in the alley behind the new section. There's no way to be sure it isn't being watched, but I think if Duncan understands the need to be secretive, he can pull it off."

"That works for me," Cora said, and the two brothers nodded their agreement.

"Then we're agreed," I said. I took out my cell phone and after a deep, bracing breath, I added, "Here goes nothing."

Chapter 3

I hit the speed dial number for Duncan. He answered two rings later, and his voice triggered a sweet burst of chocolate in my mouth, though the taste was also fizzy and slightly metallic as a result of hearing it through the phone. The metal taste and fizziness always infiltrate the flavor of voices when I hear them over the phone.

"Hey, Mack," he said. "I was just about to call you."

"You were? Why?"

"I'm off duty tonight and I'm about to leave the station. I was wondering if you might be able to escape the bar for a while and have dinner with me."

Though I was delighted to hear him suggest some personal time together, I wanted to cry over the bad timing. "I don't think that will work. And here's why."

I then told him about the letter and read it to him over the phone, letting him know that the words *happy days* were in quotes. When I was done, there was a disturbing silence on his end that lasted so long I thought the call had been dropped.

"Are you there?" I asked.

"I am. Sorry."

Assured I still had his ear, I told him about my discussion with Cora, Frank, and Joe, and my concerns about not following the instructions in the letter. "I don't want to be responsible for anything happening to someone," I concluded. "But we're all wondering if this might be some kind of stupid prank."

"I'm truly sorry I got you involved in any of this, Mack."

"I'm a big girl who made her own decisions. I went into it willingly and with my eyes wide open. Besides, what's done is done and it can't be undone, so all we can do is move forward from here."

"You're right, but it still irks me that this has turned into such a nightmare for you. That was never my plan."

"We can talk more about that later if you want. Right now the clock is ticking on this letter and I could really use your advice and thoughts on how to proceed. Do you think we should take it seriously?"

"I'm afraid we have to," he said with a sigh. "The squad on duty this afternoon got an anonymous tip earlier, and they found the body of a man who had been stabbed to death. The body was on an ice ledge under the east side RiverWalk bridge area. It was wrapped in garbage bags so it looked like trash someone had tossed over the railing."

"That's sad," I said, "but what's that got to do with this? Just because someone was killed doesn't mean it's connected to this letter. It could be a coincidence."

"I don't think so," Duncan said, sounding grim.

"The body was located directly underneath the *Bronze Fonz*."

The *Bronze Fonz* was exactly what it sounded like. Back in 2008, a tourism group in Milwaukee raised money to commission a bronze statue of Arthur Fonzarelli, the character made popular in the Milwaukee-based sitcom, *Happy Days*. The statue features Fonzie in his characteristic leather jacket and jeans, and he's posed in the character's iconic thumbs-up stance. Its creation and placement was a controversial topic for the city, but it has proven to be a popular tourist attraction. Given where the body Duncan just mentioned was found, the "happy days" reference in the letter I received clearly wasn't a coincidence.

"Who is the victim?" I asked, bracing myself for the answer. I feared it would be someone I knew, someone I cared about. Even if it wasn't, I felt the guilt start building inside me. Whoever the victim was, he was dead because of me, however indirectly.

"I don't know," Duncan said. "They hadn't ID'd the guy yet last I heard."

I winced and felt icy cold fingers traipse down my spine—literally. I felt weak in the knees and dropped into the chair behind my desk. "This is all my fault," I said in a tone of disbelief.

"It is *not* your fault," Duncan said, and Joe said the same thing a split second later. Duncan must have heard him because he said, "Who's there with you?"

"Joe, Frank, and Cora. They know not to discuss it with anyone." I glanced at the faces of the others in the room and they all nodded.

Duncan said, "The letter said there was something unique about it. Any idea what it is?"

"I think it's the ink. It's unusual."

"You mean it looks different?"

"No, it smells different."

"It smells different literally, or synesthetically?" Duncan asked.

"Literally, I think. Ink smells trigger specific sounds for me, but this ink doesn't sound like any I've encountered before."

"I need to see it." After a pause, he added, "And I need to see you. I've missed you, Mack."

I squeezed my eyes closed and pivoted in my chair, turning my back on the others, hoping to hide my smile and relief. It seemed callous and cold, under the circumstances, but I couldn't help myself.

After a few seconds I said, "You can't be seen here. The letter is pretty explicit about what will happen if the writer thinks you're involved or helping me in any way."

"Just because I come by the bar, it doesn't mean I'm helping you with this. I'm entitled to drop by for a drink or a meal like anyone else."

"No!" I said, emphasizing my adamancy with a firm shake of my head even though Duncan couldn't see it. "I won't risk anyone else's life that way. There's no way to know how closely I'm being watched. For all I know, the writer of this letter could be sitting out in the bar right now, drinking my booze and eating my food. We can't risk anyone seeing you come here, or seeing the two of us together. But I have an idea on how we might be able to get around that."

I then told him my thoughts about him entering through the alley door in the original section of the bar, which is located at the end of a hallway right next to both the basement access and the door leading to my apartment. Unfortunately, that hallway also provides access to the bar restrooms, so it tends to get a lot of traffic. The alley door is locked on the outside but opens from the inside with a simple push. It's alarmed and there are signs on it warning people of that fact and instructing them not to use it as an exit unless it's an emergency. "I can disable the alarm long enough to let you in and then reset it," I told Duncan. "If we time it carefully and have the door to my apartment open, you should be able to slip inside without anyone seeing, even if someone happens to come down that hallway to use the restrooms. You'll just have to be careful to make sure no one sees you entering the alley and coming in through the door."

"I can make that work. I'm going to set up a bit of a decoy before I come over there, so give me an hour or so. Six sound okay?"

"It does."

"See you then."

"Duncan?"

"Yeah?"

"Can you do me one more favor before you come by?"

"What?"

"Can you bring me something from the police file on Lori Gruber, Tiny's sister? Anything that might help?"

There was a long silence on the other end, and I knew Duncan was debating the risks involved with doing that.

"It's not an active case," I urged, hoping to sway him. "It's been cold for years."

"I'll see what I can do."

"Thanks." I quickly disconnected the call so he couldn't renege, then I updated Cora and the brothers on the plan.

"We need to be extremely careful," Cora said. "The writer of that letter could be anyone."

"I know, which is why I think it would be best if you guys return to the group right away and stay there while I meet with Duncan. I don't want to rouse suspicion by keeping the three of you separate from the others for too long. Cora, I'd appreciate it if you'd stick by your cell phone in case I need to call you and have you look something up. Just pretend it's someone from your office calling so no one knows it's me you're talking to."

The three of them nodded and then, as a group, they left the office and headed back upstairs to the Capone Club room. I stayed behind, once again imprisoned in my office. I stared at the letter, breathing in deep. I wanted to pick it up and touch it some more, run my fingers over the letters, but I didn't. I'd already messed things up just by holding it while I read it, and in case Duncan might be able to do something more with it, I didn't want to contaminate it any further.

After staring at the page for a while, I closed my eyes, leaned forward, and sniffed. The ink was definitely not your standard variety stuff.

I realized then that I was going to have to transport the letter from my office to my apartment somehow, and that meant touching it again . . . or maybe not. I left the office and went into the kitchen where my new cook, Jon, was busy at work. I offer a number of food items in addition to drinks, mostly typical bar fare such as deep-fried cheese curds, fries, burgers, sandwiches, and pizzas. While the variety might not be anything unique, I do try to add my own spin to many of the food items to make them stand out.

Still keenly aware that someone might be in the bar watching my every move, after greeting Jon and telling him for the umpteenth time what a great job he was doing, I spent the next ten minutes or so pretending to inventory supplies, something I'd already done this morning before the bar opened. But I needed to hang in the kitchen for the amount of time it would take to fix a pizza. Once my requisite time had passed, I grabbed one of the empty pizza boxes that I use when customers want to take their leftovers home with them, found a clean pair of tongs and dropped them into the box when Jon wasn't looking. Then I added two large plastic baggies with zip closures. After closing the box, I also grabbed a plain brown bag, tossed a box of gloves into the bottom of it, and added a few empty containers on top of that to give it some bulk before rolling the top of it closed. I carried both items back to my office, hoping that any onlookers would assume there was food inside them.

As soon as I was inside my office with the door closed and locked, I emptied the pizza box, picked up the letter using the tongs, and slipped it inside one of the baggies. I then did the same thing with the envelope it came in. When I was done I sealed the baggie, placed it back inside the pizza box, and closed the lid. Next, I took the containers out of the paper bag and gathered up the rest of the "fan mail" I had received over the past few weeks and put all of it in there instead. Finally, after glancing at the clock, I walked over to the alarm control board and disabled the one on the back door to the alley in the original part of the building.

At two minutes to six, I again stepped out of my office, carrying the closed paper bag in one hand and the pizza box in the other. I made my way down the back hall to where the doors to both my apartment and the basement were located, right next to the alarmed exit to the alley. This next part of my little subterfuge was the riskiest. The back hallway wasn't visible to the main area of the bar, though anyone going in or out of the kitchen could see down it. It was also where the restrooms were located and if anyone went in or out of those, they would see me. I had to hope for the best and try to time Duncan's entrance and the opening of the two doors so that anyone entering into the hallway wouldn't see him or what I was doing. I glanced at my watch, saw it was seconds away from six o'clock, and set down the bag so I could unlock my apartment door and have it ready. Just as I inserted the key in the lock, two female figures entered the hallway headed for the women's bathroom.

"Hey, Mack!" one of the girls hollered down the hall, and as I looked, both of them waved at me. I recognized them as locals who had been in the bar before a few times, though I couldn't remember either one's name. I waved back with the hand that had been holding the key, which now dangled from the lock, and balanced the pizza box in my other hand.

"Do you need a hand?" one of the girls asked.

"No!" I said, and immediately wished I could have a do-over. I knew I'd sounded too hurried, too desperate. "I got it, but thanks." The two of them looked at me with bemused expressions for a few seconds while I silently prayed that they would heed my dismissal and go on about their business. Finally, one of the girls shrugged and pushed open the door to the bathroom. Both of them disappeared inside and I let out a sigh of relief, watching the shadow of light on the hallway floor disappear as the bathroom door closed behind them. I unlocked my apartment door and propped it open with the bag of mail, then after one more glance down the hall to be sure it was empty, I pushed open the alley door, hoping Duncan would be there.

Chapter 4

He was there all right, and he wasn't alone. There was a woman with him, a woman wearing a faux fur coat, a miniskirt, fishnet stockings, and stiletto heels. Her hair was teased, her makeup was way overdone, and the smell of her perfume made me hear a sound like rattling chains. I recognized the sound—and hence the smell that triggered it—as Calvin Klein's Eternity. I was given a small bottle of it as a gift by my ex-boyfriend, who had a hard time understanding why I never wore it. I don't wear any fragrances and I use only fragrance-free shampoos and soaps whenever possible. Otherwise, the resultant cacophony of sound and visual sensations makes it difficult for me to function. It's hard enough dealing with other people's smells without adding any of my own.

Duncan was dressed in a bulky winter coat, which was open at the moment because the weather that day had been warmer than usual. Beneath the coat he was wearing a flannel shirt and loose-fitting bib overalls. His feet were clad in heavy work boots, and he had a stocking cap on his head, pulled down so low that none of his hair was visible. On his face was a pair of black-rimmed, big-lensed eyeglasses. He had the woman who was with him pushed up against the wall beside the door, his body against hers, their faces nearly touching. Had he not looked directly at me when I opened the door, I wouldn't have known it was him, and even then I had to look twice to be sure.

My jaw dropped, but before I could utter a word I heard the woman say just above a whisper, "I haven't seen anyone. I think you're clear."

With that, Duncan pushed himself away from her, said, "Thanks, Libby," and stepped inside. The woman turned and sashayed down the alley toward the street.

I closed the door, gaping at Duncan in disbelief.

"What?" he said, with a mischievous grin. "I told you I was going to create a cover."

"That's your cover? Some hot tamale you picked up somewhere?"

"That tamale would be quite offended to hear you speak of her in that manner. Libby happens to be one of the best undercover cops in our district. I asked her if she would pretend to be my drunken girlfriend while we walked the streets to get here so that if anyone was watching, they wouldn't suspect it was me."

I glared at him, too stymied to say anything. The sound of laughter from the women's restroom down the hall brought me back to reality. "We can discuss this more later. Grab that bag," I said, pointing to the paper sack I had set on the floor and holding the apartment door open. "Let's get upstairs and out of sight."

Still holding on to the pizza box, I let Duncan

slide past me into the foyer at the base of the stairs. "Go on upstairs," I told him. "I need to go turn the alarm back on and then I'll meet you up there."

I went to hand him the pizza box and he said, "You didn't have to provide me with dinner."

"I didn't. The letter is in there." Duncan looked momentarily horrified until I added, "The box is clean. It was never used."

I stepped out into the hallway, returned to my office, and switched the alarm back on. Then I headed upstairs to my apartment. A man and a woman both entered the hallway at the same time I did, but now that Duncan was safely ensconced upstairs, I didn't care who saw me. As soon as I was inside the foyer at the base of my stairs, I pulled the door closed and locked it on the inside with the slide bolt.

Duncan was waiting for me at the top of the stairs and as soon as I reached him, he pulled me into his arms. "Man, have I missed you, Mack Dalton," he said in a half whisper. I was about to say I'd missed him, too, but he didn't give me a chance. Instead we reunited with a long, heated kiss that said it all. Things progressed to a point where I knew we would end up in my bedroom if we didn't stop so, reluctantly, I pushed myself away from him.

"I want to be with you, believe me I do," I said, a bit breathless. "But the clock is ticking and I can't focus on anything else with this letter-writing whacko thing hanging over my head."

"I'm betting I can alter your focus," Duncan said, his eyes dark and deliciously dangerous.

"I'm sure you could," I countered, "which is why I pushed away."

Duncan sighed, nodded slowly, and turned his attention to the dining room table where he had set the pizza box and the bag of letters. He went for the box first, opened it, and removed the baggie with the letter.

"Nice job," he said, holding the baggie by one corner.

"Not really. I didn't know what it was until after I'd read it, so I'd already touched and held it before I put it in the baggie."

"That couldn't be helped," he said. "What you've done here is the best you could. It's what the cops would have done." He held the page up then so he could read it through the plastic. I watched his facial expression change, from mild curiosity to worry, and then anger.

"What's in the paper bag?" he asked when he was done.

"All the letters I've gotten since the media storm started. Most of them are either friendly or neutral, but there are some that are not so friendly. Of those, most are simply critical but a few are downright mean. I thought we might want to go through them to see if there are any connections between this letter and any of those."

"Excellent idea," Duncan said, bestowing me with a smile. "You're getting better at this crime stuff."

"Yeah, now that I can't use it."

"We'll see about that," he said, piquing my curiosity. Then he switched his focus back to the baggie and said, "This is the envelope the letter came in?"

"It is. It's one of those peel and stick business-sized envelopes you can buy anywhere. In fact, I have a whole box of the same ones in my office. I put it in a baggie even though I don't know what good it will do. Between the post office and here, who knows how many people have handled it? And since it's a self-stick envelope, there won't be any DNA."

"Don't be so sure," Duncan said. "Those adhesive strips can sometimes catch skin cells, hairs, or other debris. Same thing with the stamp; in fact, it might even have a partial print on it."

"That's all fine, but what good does it do if we can't run it?"

Duncan looked puzzled. "Why can't we run it?"

"Because the writer of that letter made it very clear that if I involved you in this, someone would die as a result."

"Someone has already died."

"Yes, but I couldn't stop that death. I can, however, stop any others from happening if I play by the rules outlined in that letter."

"You've already broken the rules by contacting me. So what difference does it make if we run some stuff through the lab? I have some connections there. We can keep it as secret as my being here."

"I don't know," I said, shaking my head. "The more people who get involved, the greater the odds are the writer will find out. I don't want to risk that."

"Trust me on this, okay? I promise you I can keep what I do off the record, at least for now. And if you don't want me to provide some investigative assistance, why did you ask me here?"

"Well, for one, I wanted to see you." That got me

a wink and a smile. "And for another, we both know that I'm not very good at this deductive reasoning stuff. I've played at it when the Capone Club presents their puzzle cases and with one or two exceptions that were more accident than anything, I can't make my mind work that way. I may have unique abilities with the synesthesia thing, but I don't have the ability to think like a detective. Maybe it's *because* of my synesthesia that I can't seem to think that way. Whatever the reason, I suck at it. And that's why I need you."

"Okay, so where do you want to start?"

"The body you found, has it been on the news yet?"

Duncan nodded and glanced at his watch. "The first news report should have aired at five."

"Good. That means my knowing about it didn't have to come from you. I'm guessing the killer counted on me hearing about it on the news, otherwise the "happy days" reference would have been for naught, assuming the newscasts announce where the body was found."

"They not only announced it, they shot their segment right in front of the statue."

"Good, I guess."

Duncan nodded thoughtfully, staring at the letter. "You said this ink smelled different . . . unusual. Can you be more specific?"

"I'll try. Each type of ink has certain sounds that go with it. For instance, inkjet printer inks sound like random low notes on a piano. In contrast, the toner from a laser printer triggers a crackling sound, kind of like a fire. The inks used in ballpoint pens all smell more or less the same, very similar to the inkjet printer but they trigger higher notes. Gel pen inks have a distinct odor, too, different from regular ink. They also sound like high notes on a piano, but with a tinnier sound, as if it they're being played on a child's piano. I've always assumed that the subtle differences in the smells and sounds the inks trigger are due to slightly different ingredients, but they all have something in common. They all have a squeaky underlying sound. But whatever ink was used in this letter triggers a totally different sound, sort of a deep bass thrum mixed in with some watery sounds, like sloshing waves. And there's no squeak."

"Okay," Duncan said, frowning. "How can you be sure the smell is from the ink as opposed to something infused into the paper?"

"Because if something was added to the paper it would feel different, and I'd see something different as a result. The paper used for the letter appears to be generic copier/printer stuff. When I was holding it, the feel of it made me see white fibers with the ends unraveling. That's the exact same thing I see when I hold the printer paper I use in my office. When I hold the morning newspaper, the feel of it makes me see more of a mesh than a fiber, and it's gray, not white. Once, when I spilled my coffee on the morning newspaper and let it dry, it felt different to me when I picked it up, and the mesh I typically see looked more like a piece of brown paper bag."

"Could it have been the smell of the coffee that made it different in that case?"

I considered this for a second or two. "I don't think so. Smells don't trigger visual manifestations. Sounds, touch, and emotions do."

"Maybe you were upset that you spilled the coffee?" Duncan posed with a wry grin. I cocked my head and gave him a give-me-a-break look. He shrugged. "Just exploring all the possibilities."

"Besides," I went on, "if there was something on or in the paper to make it smell different, the envelope would pick it up, and I didn't get any sense that the envelope was affected at all. In fact, I'm pretty sure the address on the envelope was done with an inkjet printer."

"If so, it might be a lucky break for us. We might be able to track it."

I looked askance at him. "Seriously? That sounds like sci-fi, Big Brother stuff to me."

"I know, but it's true. Some printers are set up so that they will leave a series of small yellow dots on every page it prints. If you can see them and know how to interpret them, it will give you the date and time the page was printed, and the serial number of the printer."

"That is scary," I said.

"I suppose, but if you aren't doing anything wrong, it shouldn't be a problem."

"I guess. But it still seems like an invasion of privacy."

"I suppose it is," Duncan agreed. "But it helps make my job easier. Mostly it's the laser printers that leave the dots behind, but there are some inkjet manufacturers that are starting to do it now, too."

I took the baggie with the envelope from him and held it up close to my eyes, scrutinizing the surface. "I don't see any dots."

"They can't be seen with the naked eye. You have to use a special light and sometimes you need a magnifying glass or even a microscope. Don't you have a black light down in the bar?"

"I do. Want me to get it?"

Duncan thought a moment and then said, "Maybe it would be best to have the professionals look at it. There are other things that might be useful. For instance, inkjet printers sometimes create tiny defects in the printing, defects that are visible under magnification and caused by an uneven spray from one of the jets. It can prove as specific as a fingerprint, though if a cartridge is changed between when the original was printed and when the sample is printed, all bets are off because the spray is often altered by the realignment and cleaning of the jets. Plus we'd have to have a specific suspect printer first."

"My dad has an old microscope in his office. It's one he used in college but I think it still works. And I have this," I said, grabbing my key ring. On it was a small flashlight, a promotional giveaway I got from one of my beer suppliers. The light it gave out was an ultrabright blue. "Think this would work to show up the yellow dots?"

"It might," Duncan admitted.

I handed him the little flashlight and then went into my father's office to get the microscope. I had to blow some dust off it, and before I gave it to Duncan I went into the kitchen and got a paper towel to wipe off the lenses. By the time I returned to the dining room table, Duncan was scrutinizing the envelope with the flashlight.

"Find anything?" I asked.

"Nope, but I'll look at it again under the microscope." He placed the envelope, still inside the baggie, on the microscope's platform while I plugged in the cord to a wall outlet. Duncan flipped a switch and the microscope's light source came on. He spent the next several minutes adjusting the focus and moving the envelope back and forth, up and down beneath the lens. At one point he took my key ring light and shined it down on top of the envelope. Finally he looked at me and shook his head. "Nothing," he announced. "Let's try a different tack. Let's say you're right about the letter ink being unique or different—"

"I am."

Duncan smiled. "If there is something odd or different about it, what is it and what does it mean?"

"Well, the letter is handwritten using calligraphy. That's something that usually requires a special pen, right? Does it require a special type of ink, too?"

"Good question. Let's look it up on the computer."

I grabbed my laptop and brought it to the table. After a few minutes of exploring various sites and reading up on calligraphy, we came up with a list of facts that might or might not be a clue as to why it was used to write the letter: Greek origins, the need for a more water-based ink, the special types of paper that can be used, special types of pens that can be used, and the types of strokes needed to make the various letters.

When we were done with our research, Duncan said, "Where do we start? How do we know what's relevant? How can we even be sure the calligraphy is a clue?"

"We can't be one hundred percent sure," I

admitted. "But it makes sense to me because the calligraphy is unusual and everything else about the letter is ordinary and generic. Though I have to admit I'm not sure if it's the fact that calligraphy was used that's significant, or if it's the ink used to create it."

"We can't just dismiss the content of the letter, either," Duncan said. "The *happy days* reference might be more than a clue to where the body was found."

"You're right," I said with an exasperated sigh. "There are too many variables here."

"We should pick a path and stick with it for now. Let's go with the idea that the calligraphy is the significant thing. I would think the pens and ink used would be found in an art supply store. We could start by canvasing them, beginning with the ones closest to where we found the body."

"You mean *I* should start by canvasing them."

"No, *we* should."

"Duncan, it has to be me . . . me alone. You can't be a part of this, at least not in any obvious or apparent way. Your involvement has to stay behind the scenes."

"All right then, let's divide and conquer. You look up art supply stores in the area and either call or visit them to see if anything pops up. Get Cora to research any Greek references related to Milwaukee to see if anything comes up that seems relevant. Have her research the phrase *happy days,* too, to see what other locations or items might come up."

I glanced at my watch. "It's almost six-thirty already. I wonder how many art supply stores are still open."

"I don't know. You might have to wait until morning to hit them up."

"That's too long. The clock is ticking on this." I felt panic rising inside me and the need to do something, anything, now. "Can you check to see if there is any new information about the man who was killed that might help?"

"It's not my case, but let me make some phone calls to see what I can find out."

"Don't tell anyone why you're asking," I cautioned, garnering an eye roll from Duncan. "And while you do that, I'll make some calls to see if I can get a head start on these art stores." Duncan nodded, punched a number into his cell phone, and wandered off into the kitchen. I got back on my laptop and did a Google search of art supply stores in the area. When the list came up, I located the one closest to the Fonz statue, which was also the one closest to my bar. It was a little over a mile away, in the Historic Third Ward. I dialed the number, praying they would still be open. They were.

"Collier Art Supply, this is Jim."

"Hi, Jim. I'm interested in learning how to do calligraphy but I wasn't sure how to get started. Someone said I need a special ink and pen for that. Is that something you would sell?"

"It is. Are you going to be taking a class? Because sometimes the instructors work out discounts for materials with specific stores."

"No, no formal class. Just something I want to look into as a hobby. I've always been interested."

"I should be able to get you started with anything you want."

"How late are you open tonight?"

"Until nine." I glanced at my watch, seeing that I had a little over two hours. And I didn't miss the fact that his closing time coincided with the time deadline mentioned in the letter.

"Thanks." I hung up the phone and looked over at Duncan who was coming out of the kitchen and also disconnecting his call. "I'm going to start with a visit to this art store," I told him, showing him the Web page for the shop. "Did you find out anything about the guy who was killed?"

"I did," he said, looking grim.

"Anything that might help us, like some trace evidence?"

"Not yet, but I'm sure they'll find something by the time they conclude the autopsy. I can tell you that the body was wrapped in two layers. The outside was plastic sheeting like you can find in any home improvement store. It might be good for prints but we won't know if there are any until the lab processes it. Inside the plastic sheeting was a large canvas tarp. Again, until the lab can analyze it we don't know if it will offer anything."

"Was any of that revealed to the news media?"

Duncan nodded. "I didn't ask for specifics, but I do know that the news reports I heard earlier mentioned both the plastic sheeting and the canvas tarp because both of them were visible at the site when the body was retrieved."

"Then that's it!" I said excitedly. "I don't think it's a coincidence that the body was wrapped in a *canvas* tarp." Duncan stared at me with a confused expression. "Don't you see?" I said. "The calligraphy, the unusual ink, canvas . . . it all points to an art store."

"Maybe," Duncan said, sounding unconvinced.

"I'm going to head for this art store to see if I'm right. Do you want to stay here while I'm gone?"

"You can't go alone."

"Duncan, we've been over this. I can't be seen with you."

"I know that. But I'm not letting you go traipsing about on your own, Mack. For all we know this whack-job could be trying to lure you out to hurt or kill you."

"I don't think so," I said. "It's a game, and whoever is writing those letters wants to play it out."

"So now you've suddenly developed deductive reasoning well enough that you're willing to risk your life on it?"

I gave him an exasperated look.

"There's something else you need to know about the body they found earlier," he said, and the gravity in his tone stopped me from making any additional objections or arguments. I sensed he was about to tell me something awful and I braced myself for it. Good thing I did because what he said next made me weak in the knees.

"They have a tentative ID on the victim and it's someone you know, someone from the Capone Club."

I collapsed into one of the dining room chairs. "Who?" I asked, not sure I could bear to hear the answer.

"It's Lewis Carmichael."

Chapter 5

"Oh, no." I felt sick to my stomach. I swallowed down the bile that was threatening to come up and took a few deep breaths to try to center myself.

"I'm sorry, Mack," Duncan said, walking over and gently massaging my shoulders.

"It's Lewis Carmichael? Are they sure?"

"Sure enough," Duncan said. "They haven't informed next of kin yet so it's not official, but he's been identified by ID he had on him, fingerprints, and some unique scars he had on one of his legs."

Lewis Carmichael was a nurse who worked at a nearby hospital and a frequent patron of my bar as well as a member of the Capone Club. The letter writer had kept his or her promise, striking close to home. The sick, frightened feeling I'd had a moment ago faded and an intense anger took its place. I literally saw red, something that always happens when I'm really mad. "Damn it," I seethed. I squeezed my eyes closed and massaged my temples. "What now?"

"I have an idea," Duncan said. "Give me a minute." Once again he retreated to the kitchen and dialed a number on his phone. I tried to eavesdrop, but he spoke in a low voice and all I could make out was a word here and there. After several minutes he disconnected the call and came back out to the dining area.

"Okay, here's the plan. We have a guy who's been working undercover for the past month with a construction company that we think might be operating a sophisticated burglary ring using some of its workers. He's likely to have to maintain his undercover status for a while as we think only the long-term hires that the boss comes to trust get let in on the alternate business. His name is Malachi O'Reilly and he's your date."

"My *what?*"

"Date," Duncan said grinning. "Think about it. It solves several problems. You can have police protection while you're looking into this letter and no one will know. Just tell anyone who asks that you and he are a couple. Parade him around to the Capone Club and others in the bar. Once everyone sees that you and Malachi are an item, it will make it clear that you and I are no longer together."

"Wait a minute," I said, narrowing my eyes at him. "How much time are we talking here?"

"As much as we need. Malachi isn't seeing anyone right now, so we won't be interfering with his social life. He'll need to be at his construction job during the day of course, but he's free every evening and every weekend."

I stared at Duncan with disbelief. "You want me to pretend I'm dating someone else?"

"Basically, yeah," Duncan said with a shrug.

"What about us?"

"We'll still be us. We just have to do it behind closed doors and without anyone knowing for now."

"And what happens if I need to go out and look into something during the daytime hours when Malachi is at work?"

That gave him pause. After a few seconds he shrugged. "We'll just have to try to avoid that as much as possible."

I didn't like the idea of having anyone with me because of what the letter said, but I also liked the idea of knowing I wouldn't be out there completely on my own. After weighing the pros and cons for a few seconds, I nodded. "Okay. I'm fine with that, for now."

"Good," Duncan said, leaning down and kissing me on the cheek, "because Malachi will be here in about ten minutes. While we're waiting, we need to come up with a backstory for the two of you . . . how you met, how long you've been together, some shared history, that sort of thing."

"That isn't going to work. The regulars here are going to know something is up. They know I've been hiding out for the past few weeks so how could I have met anyone?"

"Tell them he's an old friend from the past."

I gave Duncan my best skeptic look. "We already used that one with you when you went undercover in my bar during the investigation into Ginny's murder, remember?"

"Oh, right." He thought for a moment and then said, "Why don't you tell them it's a blind date someone arranged for you?"

"Who would do that?"

Duncan thought for a moment. "Cora?"

He had a point. It sounded like something Cora

would do. And Cora, more than anyone else, except perhaps the Signoriello brothers, would eventually know the truth anyway, so we might as well involve her right up front. "Okay, let's see if she'll play along."

I texted Cora on my phone and asked her to come upstairs to my apartment. Then I went down to the foyer door to meet her. She showed up barely a minute later, carrying her laptop.

"What's going on?" she asked, looking worried. "Did Duncan break up with you or something?"

"Not exactly," I said. "He's here. We need your help with something."

I led her upstairs and we filled her in. A few minutes into it, Duncan's phone rang and after answering the call, he informed us that Malachi was outside the bar waiting for instructions.

Five minutes later we had a plan in place and Cora went back to the bar. After a few minutes I joined her, leaving Duncan alone in my apartment. Cora hadn't gone back upstairs to the Capone Club room; she had stayed at the bar in the main area instead, chatting with my bartender, Billy Hughes.

The place was busy and I scanned the tables. Anxiety struck me as I recognized a face sitting at a table near the bar. It was Clay Sanders, a balding, forty-something, particularly pushy reporter with the local paper who had badgered me in the past for details about my involvement with Duncan. His presence now was a good thing, considering what was about to happen, but that didn't ease my nerves any. I avoided looking at him as I walked to the bar.

"I don't know about this," I said to Cora, sidling

up next to her and speaking loud enough for Clay to overhear. "I never should have let you talk me into this."

"Talk you into what?" Billy said, drying a glass and smiling quizzically.

"I fixed Mack up with a blind date," Cora said. "He should be here any minute now." Though she spoke in a normal conversational tone, she made no effort to keep her voice low. In the bar, where the ambient noise level was fairly loud when it was full like it was now, many people had to speak louder than usual in order to converse. I knew Clay Sanders was no dummy but hoped he wouldn't be smart enough to figure out that we were purposefully speaking louder so he could hear.

Billy shot me a look. "A blind date? I thought you and Duncan were . . ." He left the conclusion hanging, which struck me as disturbingly apt.

"Duncan and I have gone our separate ways," I announced. "Things didn't work out."

"That's too bad," Billy said. "You two seemed like a good fit."

"Sometimes what seems like the right thing isn't," I said.

This statement had special meaning for me with Billy, who was dating someone I felt was all wrong for him, particularly since he could have his pick of women. He was movie-star handsome with his café au lait colored skin, emerald green eyes, and tall, lanky build. His whip-smart mind, good sense of humor, and charismatic smile rounded out the package. He was in law school and would finish in another year—an event I would approach with mixed emotions since I would be happy for him but sad for me—and I had no doubt he'd make a superb trial lawyer. Despite the number of women who flirted with Billy, he had stayed true to his girl-friend, Whitney, for the past two years. At first blush, Whitney seemed like a good match for Billy. She was a dark-skinned, dark-eyed beauty from a wealthy family and was also enrolled in law school. But once you got past the beauty on the outside, there was some ugliness beneath. I'd met Whitney a few times when she came into the bar to drop something off for Billy. With each visit she made it very clear that she considered the bar milieu be-neath her, and Billy's job there beneath him. By association, anyone in the bar, and me, for owning it, were beneath her as well. Her distaste with us and the place was screamingly obvious whenever she came in, in the look of disgust on her face, in her cross-armed body language, and in the snobby, condescending tones she used whenever she talked to anyone.

Whitney had been trying to talk Billy out of his job ever since she met him. Billy, however, liked bartending and was good at it. He made far more in tips than any of my other bartenders. It was a good fit with his amiable nature, his school hours, and his lifestyle, so I was glad to see that he had resisted Whitney's attempts to shame him out of the job, at least so far. I just wished he could resist the rest of Whitney along with it.

"You and Duncan broke up?" said a woman seated two stools away. It was Alicia Maldonado, a woman in her late twenties who worked at a bank near the bar. Alicia was from a mixed Hispanic and African American background and had coal dark eyes and long, wavy, dark hair. She enjoyed participating in the Capone Club's crime games, but if Billy wasn't nearby, she would usually drift away from the club regulars to be near him. Alicia had a major crush on Billy, and despite getting nothing more than friendly banter and smiles from him, she refused to be discouraged. Her flirtations with him were shameless and obvious.

"We did," I said to Alicia's inquiry. I was about to embellish the story but Cora spoke up before I could.

"Malachi's here," she said, waving at someone across the room. I saw Clay Sanders turn and look toward the door.

Cora knew what Malachi looked like because Duncan had shown her a picture of him on his phone, a picture he wouldn't let me see, claiming it would add some legitimacy to the blind date story. I couldn't help but wonder if there was something else behind his reluctance. Was it the way Malachi looked? Did Duncan think I was shallow enough to balk at claiming someone for a boyfriend if he was less than perfect?

Malachi knew what Cora looked like because Duncan had also taken her picture and sent it to Malachi's phone. I had no idea if Malachi knew what I looked like. My face had been on the news at times over the past few weeks but I didn't know if Malachi had seen it. When I realized I was nervous and fretting over this as if it was a real blind date, I forced myself to take a deep breath and relax. Then I turned and looked at the man who waved back at Cora.

Malachi O'Reilly was about six feet tall, very muscular, with even features, black wavy hair, and brilliant blue eyes. As he smiled at Cora—revealing deep dimples in both cheeks—and made his way over to us, I found myself feeling relieved. Maybe I was a little bit shallow after all.

"Hi, Malachi," Cora said. "Good to see you, as always."

"You get lovelier every time I see you, Cora," Malachi said, and his voice triggered a burst of sweet mint flavor in my mouth with just a hint of chocolate. It was a little startling. No other voice had ever triggered a taste like that. I watched as Malachi leaned over and gave Cora a buss on the cheek as if he really was the old friend he was pretending to be. I had to admit that both of them were frighteningly good at this last-minute deception. They had me convinced they knew one another, so I had no doubt others would believe so, too.

After Malachi's quick kiss, Cora turned her blushing attention to me. "Malachi O'Reilly, this is Mackenzie Dalton."

Malachi looked at me with those startling blue eyes and I felt mesmerized. "Wow, you weren't kidding when you said she was lovely, Cora," he said, and the minty chocolate taste intensified. I looked around and realized our little tête-à-tête was the focus of attention for half the people in the bar, including Clay Sanders. I felt both relieved—goal achieved—and embarrassed.

Malachi cocked his arm and proffered it to me. "Shall we? I've made dinner reservations for us."

I took his arm and the touch made me see a crackling fire—hot, comforting, yet sizzling. "Sure," I said. "Just let me grab my coat." I walked Malachi over to my office, unlocked it, grabbed my coat from the coatrack, and shrugged it on. After zipping it up, I again took Malachi's arm and let him escort me from the bar as dozens of eyes watched us leave.

Once we were outside, he said, "My car is parked a couple of blocks over." With that out of the way, he started up with typical blind date chatter. "Cora tells me you've lived in the bar all your life."

"True, well, not in the bar per se, but in the apartment above it."

"You must like what you do to live and breathe it every day like that."

"I love my work. I love the bar, I love meeting all the different people who come in, I love experimenting with drink recipes, I love being a part of the downtown milieu. It suits me."

"That's nice, loving what you do."

There were other people out walking around, and I couldn't help looking at each and every one of them, wondering if they were eavesdropping on our conversation and watching my every move.

"How about you?" I said. I was still hanging on to Malachi's crooked arm, and I let it go long enough to unzip my coat. The temperature outside was surprisingly warm. "Cora tells me you're in construction," I continued, taking his arm again. "Do you enjoy it?"

"It's not my life's dream," he said with a shrug. "I hope to someday move into something different. But I do love the building aspects, the creation of a bigger something from pieces and parts. I'm hoping to go to school to become an architect one of these days, just as soon as I get settled."

"Are you from Milwaukee originally?"

He shook his head. "I'm from Washington State.Yakima to be exact."

"How did you end up here in Milwaukee?" As I

asked, I wondered how much of what he was telling me was true and how much of it was made up on the fly.

"I hate to sound clichéd, but it was a girl. Her name is Sabrina." He gave me a sheepish, apologetic look. "She works for a brewery here in Milwaukee, and I met her while she was in Yakima on business, shopping for a new hops supplier. That supplier just happened to be a friend of mine. Sabrina came out there four different times and we seemed to hit it off. After that we tried the long distance thing for a few months to see if there was really something there, but it's too hard to tell when you're that far apart. So I bit the bullet, packed everything up, and made the move to Milwaukee. We lasted all of a month before we both agreed that whatever we had was little more than a flash in the pan."

"So are you planning on staying here, or going back to Yakima?"

"I like Milwaukee. I'm planning on staying for now."

We had reached his car and he proceeded to unlock and open the passenger side door for me. As he did so, I said, "I wonder if you could do me a favor. There is an art supply store I wanted to hit today before it closes. It's not too far from here, over in the Historic Third Ward. Would it be possible to stop there before we go to dinner?"

"Sure. I do some drawing and wouldn't mind picking up a few things myself."

As soon as he had climbed in on his side and shut the door, he said, "What's the address of the store?" I gave it to him and he started the car and pulled out into the evening traffic. "Duncan clued me in on what you want to do," he said once we were underway, "but I'm not sure how you want to play this once we get to the art store. Do you want me to come in with you? That would be my preference since I can keep a better eye on you that way."

"To be honest, I'd feel better, too, if you came in with me. I don't want to jeopardize things, but the letter didn't specifically say I couldn't seek help from someone other than the cops. I think if you can be convincing enough on this blind date thing and no one fingers you for a cop, it would be all right for you to come in with me. In fact, if we really were on a blind date, I think it would seem odd if you didn't."

"Then come along I will," he said.

"So how much of that backstory you just gave me was true and how much was made up?"

"The story is true enough. I find it's best to stick to the truth as much as possible in these cases. The fewer lies you have to keep track of the better. I really did work construction back in the day before I became a cop. I also really like architecture, but I like the cop work more."

"Well, I appreciate you doing this, even though it isn't part of your normal cop stuff."

"Actually, it works for me. You can be a part of my cover story as much as I'm a part of yours. If my bosses are watching me, it would look funny to them if I didn't have some sort of personal life."

"Glad to be of help," I said, somewhat facetiously.

"Duncan said you knew the man they found downtown beneath the RiverWalk."

I nodded, my throat tightening. "I did," I managed to say. "He was a regular customer, and seemed like a nice guy. He sure as hell didn't deserve to die because of me."

From the corner of my eye I saw Malachi shoot me a look. "He didn't die because of you," he said with a scowl. "He died because there are some twisted people in this world. In no way is this your fault."

I wasn't sure I agreed with him, but my throat had tightened enough that speech was momentarily impossible. I stared out the windshield as a minute or two of silence passed and willed myself to let it go . . . for now.

"Do you like seafood?" Malachi asked.

The sudden change of topic threw me. "Um, sure. Why?"

"Because I made reservations for us at Harbor House. They have other stuff on the menu of course, but they're known for their seafood."

"You mean we're really going to dinner?"

"Sure, why not? We have to eat, right? And if we're going to make this dating thing look convincing, we should start it off on the right foot."

"I suppose so," I said.

I must have sounded a little hesitant because next he said, "If you don't like seafood, Harbor House has steaks and chicken, too. Or if you want we can go somewhere else."

"No, that won't be necessary. Harbor House will be fine. I've never eaten there but I've heard good things about it." My hesitation had nothing to do with going to Harbor House, but rather with going anywhere with Malachi at all. This felt uncomfortably real to me, and uncomfortably . . . well, comfortable.

We pulled up in front of the art supply store and

Malachi found a parking space on the street two doors down. We got out and walked together to the store, Malachi once again offering his arm. I felt uncomfortable, but I wasn't sure if it was the situation with the letter and the art store that had me feeling that way, or if it was the situation with Malachi. Maybe it was both. It wasn't that I didn't like Malachi, I did. In fact, I liked him a lot. He felt . . . right.

As if things weren't confusing enough for me already.

Chapter 6

The art store had a bell that rang as we entered, though it wasn't needed to announce our arrival. The place was small, and there was a young man behind the counter, which was right next to the door.

"Hi. Can I help you folks find something?" he asked.

"You can," I said, taking the lead. "I called just a bit ago. I'm interested in learning how to do calligraphy and wondered if you could direct me to the appropriate supplies. I own a bar downtown and I'm thinking of redoing my menus and using the calligraphy to fancy them up."

The young man, whose name tag read ADAM, nodded and said, "Sure." Then he looked at Malachi with a curious expression. "Are you interested in calligraphy, too?"

Malachi held up a hand and shook his head. "No, I'm just along for the ride. She wanted to stop here before we go to dinner. But as long as I'm here, I could use some new leads for my mechanical pencil."

Adam nodded. "Those would be in aisle three, over there." He pointed off to the left, and then shifted his attention to me. "If you come with me, I'll show you some stuff for the calligraphy."

Malachi wandered off in the direction of aisle three while I followed Adam toward the back of the store.

"You'll want to start off with some pens and ink," Adam said as we walked, "and there are special types of paper, too, if you want, though they aren't absolutely necessary."

"What's so special about the inks?"

"They tend to be more water based than the usual inks," Adam explained. "It helps with the flow. I have lots of the premade stuff, or if you prefer being a bit more hardcore, I can provide you with a recipe for making your own and the necessary supplies to do so."

I thought about the unusual smell present in the ink used in the letter and figured a recipe was the more likely avenue. Perhaps the smell of one of the ingredients in the recipe would trigger a connection for me between it and the smell of the letter. "I'm thinking hardcore," I said. "It sounds like fun and I am a mixologist of sorts. Is it a complicated process?"

"Not if you stick to the basics, though there are some professional calligraphers who get crazy mixing up their own stuff."

We had reached the back of the store and Malachi was no longer in view, off in his own section. Adam pointed to a shelf on the back wall that held an assortment of fountain pens, nibs, and ink wells. "This is the most popular pen here," he said, grabbing one. "It has interchangeable nibs but comes equipped with a basic one."

"Sold," I said, smiling.

He handed me the packaged pen and then took down a recipe box from another shelf. He opened it and I saw it was filled with index cards. He grabbed one from the front. "This is the most popular black ink recipe," he said. I started to take it but he pulled it back at the last second and cocked his head. "What's your name?" he asked.

"Mackenzie Dalton."

"I thought so," he said, his voice dropping to just above a whisper. "I received a package the other day that had some money and instructions in it. It said I was supposed to deliver a message if a woman named Mackenzie with fiery red hair came in asking about calligraphy or inks."

My heart began to race.

"But the instructions said you were supposed to be alone," Adam added.

"I would have been, but I had a friend fix me up with this blind date and I didn't have a way to get out of it gracefully. Plus, I'm in a bit of a time crunch." I gave him my best charming smile.

"So you were expecting a message?"

"I was hoping for one, yes. Was it a man or a woman who gave you these instructions?"

"Neither, technically. The instructions were typed out and they came by courier along with a hundred bucks. I have to say, the whole thing is kind of . . . odd."

"I'm sure it seems so," I said, thinking fast. "But it's just a game I play with some online friends, sort of a treasure hunt thing, you know? I haven't met the other players, but one of the objectives is to garner clues about the person who is staging your hunt, to try to figure out who they are. Sometimes knowing the person helps in figuring out the clues."

Adam smiled and visibly relaxed. "Okay, now I get it," he said. "That actually sounds like fun. Can anyone join and play?"

I hadn't anticipated that question, so once again I had to scramble to come up with an answer. "Um, geez, I don't know. I got into it by invitation from a friend. If you want, I can ask her. Give me your e-mail address."

Adam flipped the index card he was holding and took a pen from his shirt pocket. "Here you go," he said, scribbling something on the back of the card and handing to me. "I'm supposed to gather up all the ingredients in this ink recipe for you, and I have something else to give you before you leave. It's a sealed envelope I have up at the register. The instructions included a deadline and said I should destroy the envelope if no one came in by then. But you made it in plenty of time. I'll slip it into the bag when I ring up your stuff."

"That will be great," I said, hoping my voice wasn't betraying the nervous excitement I felt. "Do you still have the courier envelope that held these instructions?"

"It's in the trash up at the front counter," he said. He had turned to another shelf and was gathering supplies.

"Can I have that, too?"

Adam shrugged. "I guess so. The instructions didn't say I couldn't give it to you."

"Were there any other instructions?" I asked. "For instance, were you given a means for communicating that your task was carried out?"

Adam nodded. "If you show up and get the supplies as directed, I'm supposed to put a paint palette with a glob of green acrylic paint on it in the display window and leave it there for two nights."

I realized how smart this was. Even if someone staked out the store 24-7, there would be no way to know which of the hundreds of people driving or walking by were looking for a sign in the art store window.

Adam finished rounding up his supplies and handed them to me one at a time. "You start with lamp black," he said as he handed me a small jar filled with a black powdery substance. "It used to be made by collecting the soot from oil lamps. You can make your own if you want by holding a plate over a candle and collecting the soot that accumulates on the plate, but most people just prefer to buy it like this." Next he handed me two small bottles, both of which were filled with a pale yellow liquid. The first one was labeled HONEY, the second was labeled GUM ARABIC. "The honey is the same stuff you buy in the grocery store," Adam explained. "The gum arabic is made out of hardened sap from acacia trees. It gives the ink gloss and consistency, to help it spread more evenly."

"This is all I need?" I asked.

"If you read the recipe you'll see you have to add an egg yolk. You mix all the ingredients together the way the recipe says and you'll end up with a thick paste that you can store in a jar or any other container with a tight lid. When you want to make your ink, you add a small amount of water to the paste until you get the right consistency."

"How will I know what the right consistency is?"

"Trial and error. And it may vary from one project to another depending on the type of paper you use."

"That's it?"

"That's it," Adam echoed. "I have some instructional booklets up by the register."

Malachi came walking up to us carrying a box of pencil leads, a straight edge, a compass, and a large tablet of drafting paper. "Got what you need?" he asked me.

I nodded. "I think so, yes."

We headed up front and Adam talked me into buying two calligraphy instructional booklets that I was pretty sure I didn't need. He then proceeded to check us out, ringing up Malachi's purchases first, then mine. I watched as he bagged my supplies and saw him slip in the sealed envelope he'd mentioned. Then he reached down below the desk and came up with a standard cardboard delivery flat that had been ripped open, slipping that into my bag, too. After we had paid, we bid Adam a good night and headed back to the car.

"How did it go?" Malachi asked once we were settled inside the car. He had tossed his purchases into the backseat but I had mine in my lap.

"Okay, I think." I glanced out my window, watching the passing cars and the pedestrians who were out, wondering if any of them were watching us. I then told him about my conversation with Adam.

"Interesting," he said when I was done. "Are you going to open the letter?"

I shook my head. "Not yet. I want to let Duncan do it in case there's any trace evidence on it."

Malachi looked over at me with an amused expression.

"What?"

"You sound like a cop."

"Duncan has taught me a lot. Between him and the Capone Club, I sometimes feel like a cop."

"I've heard rumors about this Capone Club. It's some type of crime-solving game group, isn't it?"

"Sort of, though they don't just do games. They also work at solving real crimes. It's quite an eclectic group of people from various walks of life with varied experiences and knowledge. When you put them all together, it can be quite useful in figuring things out."

"Sounds interesting," Malachi said.

"It is. If you want, we can go back to the bar after dinner and I'll introduce you to them."

"I'd like that. Besides, I've also heard that both your food and your drinks are rather good, particularly your coffee."

"I am a bit of a coffee snob," I admitted.

We arrived at the Harbor House restaurant and I carried my bag of purchases inside with me, unwilling to risk leaving them in the car. The contents practically screamed at me to examine them, and I feared I would be a distracted and boring companion for dinner. But Malachi, or Mal as he said he preferred to be called, turned out to be an interesting and entertaining date. We enjoyed a four-course meal—a steak and lobster main course for him and sea scallops for me—and the time flew by. I kept the bag of items at my feet throughout the meal, and despite my eagerness to examine the items more closely, by the time we were done I had nearly forgotten about them.

Mal and I shared more of our life stories in typical first-date fashion. I learned that his father was Irish but his mother was Jewish, and their union had caused a great deal of strife on both sides of the family. His first name had been chosen as a placating measure to the Jewish side of the family, though it hadn't had the effect his parents had hoped. And while each parent had stayed true to their respective cultures and religions as much as they could, Mal was brought up with exposure to both sides so he could choose his own path. Both Christmas and Hanukkah were celebrated. He attended both a Catholic Church and a synagogue. He learned the history and cultural traditions of both the Jews and Irish Catholics, and participated in the rituals and celebrations held by both sides of the family. The battle for his heart and soul waged on through most of his life, with his parents serving as mediators and objective guides, determined to let their son choose his own path. Apparently, no one anticipated him choosing the path he did. When he declared himself an agnostic and refused to honor any of the traditions, holidays, or tenets that went with either religion or culture, it triggered a great deal of head-shaking disbelief.

In the end, his family learned to accept him for who he was, and while he said the efforts to make him see the light still continued at times, his relationship with his extended family had remained amiable and loving. My story in contrast with his seemed pathetic and destitute. While I never felt as if I was lacking in any way, or missing anything important, I had to admit that his relationship with his large, loving, extended family left me feeling a bit envious. It felt almost sacrilegious to feel this way, as if I was somehow dishonoring my father, or undermining the way he raised me.

We were very different, Mal and I, but not once during our meal did I feel as if things were awkward or uncomfortable between us. The dinner proved to be a welcome and enjoyable respite from the gritty reality of what those bagged items at my feet were about, and when it came time to leave, I found myself not wanting it to end.

I was glad Mal wanted to come back to the bar and meet some of the others, though I also felt a sudden awkwardness about having Duncan there. I realized Duncan's little plan might have backfired in an unexpected way. I was attracted to Mal O'Reilly, and given the uncertainty I'd been feeling regarding my relationship with Duncan, this could prove to be a dangerous arrangement.

Chapter 7

We left our coats open during the trip back in deference to the unusually warm weather. When we arrived back at the bar, I led Mal upstairs to the Capone Club room. It was a little after ten—not that late for a Friday night—so most of the regulars were there. The Signoriello brothers were in their usual spot, chairs pulled up close to the fireplace. Our resident novelist wannabe and part-time waiter, Carter Fitzpatrick, was there, along with his friend, Sam Warner, a psych grad student. Carter's girlfriend, Holly, who worked with Alicia at a nearby bank, was also present, but Alicia was still downstairs making moon eyes at Billy. Cora was there, of course—these days she practically lived in my bar—and with her was Tiny. Tad Amundsen was also with the group, as was Kevin Baldwin, a local trash collector, though he preferred the title Sanitation Engineer. I made the necessary introductions and then asked the group what they were up to.

"We were looking at the case involving Tiny's sister, Lori," Cora explained.

"I'd like to have someone bring me up to speed on where you guys are with that," I said. "But I have to tend to a couple of things with the bar first."

"That's fine," Cora said, one of the few people in the group who had a clue what those things were. "Why don't you go do that and we'll give Mal here an introduction to the group by testing him on our case of the day."

"A test?" Mal said, tossing his coat over the back of an empty chair. He held his hands up in a defensive motion. "You guys are tough on newcomers."

Cora laughed; she had a rich, throaty laugh that was both sexy and engaging. "It's fun," she said. "You'll see. They're mostly riddles designed to challenge your deductive reasoning and thinking skills."

"I'm going to throw you to these wolves," I said to Mal, "but I'll be back before they eat you alive. I'll send you up a drink to help you along." I looked at the group and added, "Be kind to him. I think he's one of the good guys."

With that I left the group and headed back downstairs. After checking in with Billy to order a drink for Mal and make sure everything was running smoothly with the bar, I made my way to the back hallway and entered the door to my apartment. I didn't know if Duncan would still be there, and I felt torn as I climbed the stairs, unsure if I would be relieved or disappointed if he was gone.

He was there. I found him sitting at the dining room table, the letters I had collected in the bag earlier, spread out around him.

"Hey, Mack," he said when he saw me at the top of the stairs. "How did it go?"

"It went well, I think," unsure if he meant my visit to the art shop or my date with Mal, though I assumed it was the former. "I have something new for us to look at, several somethings, in fact."

I tossed my coat on my couch, and then proceeded to tell him how the art store visit had gone, and my conversation with Adam. I donned a pair of gloves and removed the items from my bag as I talked, laying them out on the table.

Duncan, who was already wearing gloves, zeroed in on the courier envelope. I, on the other hand, grabbed the bottles of honey and gum arabic and opened each one. I went for the honey first, sniffed it, and closed my eyes. The smell made me hear a faint low hum, or thrum. I resealed it, gave myself a moment to let my nose clear, and did the same with the gum arabic. It made me hear a very faint rustling noise. When I was done with that, I removed the lid on the bottle of lamp black and waved my hand over the opening to get a whiff of it. The bass sound I'd heard from the letter came through loud and clear.

"None of these triggers the exact sound I heard when I held and sniffed the letter," I told Duncan, "but there are components that might join together to make that sound. Maybe if I make the ink the way the recipe says, it will help."

"Does it matter?" Duncan said. "We know we hit the right spot and you got another letter, so it might not matter how the ink is made."

"The instructions given to the guy at the store specifically said to give me the recipe, so it might be important somehow."

Duncan shrugged. "I guess it can't hurt to make

it." He dropped the courier envelope back onto the table. "I'll get this envelope analyzed and I'll follow up with the courier service to see what I can find out."

"Maybe *I* should do that," I told him. "If you do it and the writer finds out, it will negate the rules of this nasty game."

Duncan sighed and frowned. "At least let me dust it for prints first. If we can find something that will lead us to this sicko, you might not have to do anything more. In fact, we should dust that first letter for prints, too." He took a pen out of his shirt pocket, held it as if he was going to write something, and then pretended to do so on top of my table with the point of the pen retracted. "The writer would likely have rested his hand on the paper," he said, demonstrating. Then he lifted his own hand away and pointed to the faint hand print that had been left on the table's surface. "We might get a partial from the side of the hand of whoever wrote it, like this."

"I have a feeling that whoever is behind this isn't stupid enough to leave prints on anything."

"Perhaps, but can we afford to not check?" he countered. "I wouldn't want someone else to die because we made an erroneous assumption and credited this person with more cleverness than he or she actually has."

His words stung and I felt another pang of guilt over Lewis Carmichael's death. "I suppose, but I have to say again that we need to keep it unofficial, off the books."

Duncan nodded, looking a little perturbed by my insistence. I turned away from this look of disapproval and my eyes settled on the unopened envelope that Adam had slipped into my bag. I picked it up and examined it. It looked the same as the one the original letter had come in. "I suppose we should open this first and see what it offers before we decide on anything else?"

Duncan nodded and held out his hand. I gave him the envelope and after examining it for a few seconds, he went to the kitchen, got a knife from a drawer, and slit the envelope open. "Do you have a piece of plain white paper?" he asked.

I nodded and fetched one from my father's office. "Why the paper?" I asked, handing it to him.

"In case there's any trace inside the envelope or the letter . . . a piece of dirt, a grain of salt . . . anything that might help." He set the paper down on the table and then held the envelope over it. He squeezed the edges together and caught a one-page letter as it slid out. As if he'd known somehow, a small, dark hair also fell out of the envelope and onto the paper.

"We got something!" I said, excited.

Duncan's expression looked less enthusiastic. "I suspect we were meant to get this something. That hair is too obvious to be in there by accident."

I bent down and studied the hair. It was coarse and dark and there was a faint odor to it. Then I heard heavy breathing, or rather panting, and it made me turn and look at Duncan. I expected to find him bent down close to me, breathing in an odd, panting way for some reason, but he was still standing, just watching me. His breathing appeared normal. I realized then what the sound was but, to verify my suspicion, I bent down again and took a big sniff. The panting sound, sort of a repetitive *chuff,* grew louder.

"I'm pretty sure it isn't human," I said, straightening up. "It's some sort of animal hair."

"Like a dog, perhaps?"

I wrinkled my face in thought, and in doubt. "I don't think so, but I can't be sure. I haven't spent a lot of time around animals and never had any pets other than a couple of goldfish when I was growing up. But whenever I've encountered animals, like the cats that hang out in the back alley, or the occasional service dog in the bar, their smell makes me hear a rapid breathing sound, like the way a dog pants. This hair does that, too, but the sound is different. It's harder, more grunting. I suppose it could be a different breed of dog, but I get a sense that it's another animal all together." I paused, frowned, and shook my head. "I don't know. What does the letter say?"

It was folded in thirds, and after Duncan carefully unfolded it, I stood beside him to read it along with him.

Deer Ms. Dalton,

Congratulations on "sniffing" out your first clue. But bear with me for the game is far from done. Now you must find the next clue and do so by two-thirty P.M. on Monday, December 14th. If you fail to meat this deadline, someone close to you will die. Don't waste any time, but take care of yourself. I would hate for our game to end too soon. Remember to eat, but don't wolf your food down.

"Look at the misspellings," I said. "I don't think those are accidental. We have the word *deer* instead of *dear*, and *meat* instead of *meet*. Plus there are the words *wolf*, and *bear*. I don't think that's a coincidence given the hair that was enclosed."

"I'm inclined to agree," Duncan said. "Maybe the word *game* has a double meaning, too."

"Where would we find all of those animals? Where would we find meat and game?"

We looked at one another and came up with the answer at the same time.

"The zoo," we said in stereo.

"I assume it's the Milwaukee County Zoo," I said. "But what part?"

"The letter mentions eating. Aren't there animals there that visitors are allowed to feed?"

I nodded. "Yes, the giraffes, I think. I remember reading an article about it in the paper not too long ago."

Duncan glanced at his watch. "We have some time, at least. But we should probably plan on a trip to the zoo tomorrow."

"*I* should plan on a trip to the zoo, not we," I reminded him.

"Let me think about it," Duncan said with a frown. Then he reached over and rubbed my arm. "In the meantime, what should we do with the rest of our night?"

"I should go rescue Mal from the Capone Club if I'm going to keep up this charade. Maybe he can go to the zoo with me."

"That's not a bad idea," Duncan said. I wasn't sure I agreed. "Why don't you go do whatever you need to with Mal and the bar and see if he can go with you to the zoo tomorrow. If it's okay with you, I'll wait here for you to finish for the night."

"Make yourself at home," I said, smiling warmly. "I'm not sure how long I'll be. The club was going to test Mal on a crime puzzle, but they are also working on Tiny's case. Which reminds me—"

"Right." Duncan walked over to his coat and took a roll of papers out of an inside pocket. "These are copies of the spec sheets for the primary suspects from the initial investigation. You can use the information on them, but the sheets themselves can't be distributed or my ass will be on the line. And if we're going to continue our little charade we need to find a way to present the information to the group members without them knowing you're in touch with me."

I thought about that. "What if I give them to Cora and have her present the information in an entirely different format and tell the group she dug up the info on her own using her computer skills?"

Duncan nodded. "I suppose that could work. Cora is trustworthy, but I wouldn't extend that trust to too many other people. Have you considered that the author of these letters might be someone who frequents your bar? Maybe even someone in the Capone Club?"

I nodded, feeling a shiver of fear and uncertainty race down my spine. "I have. I'll be careful."

"Please do."

He moved closer then, pulling me into his arms and giving me a long, deep kiss that made me rethink my plan to leave. But duty called, so with a sigh of regret, I whispered, "Wait for me," and left.

I went downstairs to my office and sent Cora a

text message to meet me there as soon as possible. She tapped at the door a mere two minutes later and when I opened it she hurried in, laptop in hand.

"How are things going?" she asked. "Is everything okay?"

"Everything is fine as far as the letter is concerned." I filled her in on what had happened at the art store and the contents of the second letter. "We were going to have you research some stuff for the first letter, things like other *happy days* references or Greek connections in the city. But we don't need that now that we have the second clue. Duncan and I agree that it has something to do with the zoo, though we're not sure how or what. So the plan is for me to head to the zoo tomorrow."

"What can I do to help?" Cora asked, setting her laptop down on my desk.

"I don't think there's anything you can do with the zoo thing, but I have something else you can help with." I then showed her the papers Duncan had given me regarding the suspects in Tiny's case and explained what we wanted her to do.

"No problem," Cora said. "I can tell folks I dug this stuff up on my own. I'll retype it and print it out to make it look like something I found on my computer. I'll give it to them tomorrow since it's getting late tonight."

"Thanks."

"How did things go with Mal?"

"They went fine," I said with a smile. "He seems like a nice guy." Since Cora was supposed to be an acquaintance of his, I then filled her in on some of the history he had shared with me about his family, his love life, and his interests.

When I was done, Cora cocked her head to one side and narrowed her eyes at me. "Oh, my," she said after a few seconds. "You like him, don't you?"

I shrugged. "Like I said, he seems like a nice guy, but we've only had one dinner together. That's hardly enough time to determine much of anything."

Cora arched an eyebrow, assumed a crooked smile, and shook her head. "Boy, did Duncan dig himself a hole with this one."

"What do you mean?"

"I mean, he managed to find the one guy out there that can give him a run for his money."

"Don't be ridiculous."

"Mack Dalton, I can read you pretty well and I can tell you are more than a little interested in Mal O'Reilly. Don't insult my intelligence by denying it. You may have the extrasensory stuff with other things, but when it comes to matters of the heart, I've got you beat."

I smiled at her and caved. "Okay, yes, I'm a bit interested in Mal. He was very easy to get along with and not once did we have one of those awkward moments one might expect on a first date."

"He's not exactly hard on the eyes, either," Cora said slyly.

"No," I said with a sigh. "He's not."

"Is Duncan still upstairs?"

I nodded. "He's going to wait until I come up. I think he plans to spend the night."

"So things seem to be going okay with that for now?"

"If sneaking around as if we're in high school is going okay, then yes."

"Interesting," Cora said. "I'll be curious to see how all this plays out."

"You're jumping the gun, don't you think? Mal is only pretending to be my date. I may not even be his type."

Cora arched a skeptical eyebrow at me. "Based on the expression I saw on his face when he first set eyes on you, I'm pretty sure you're his type."

"Whatever," I said, though secretly I was glad to hear it. I turned to head out of my office, but Cora stopped me. "I'm curious about something, Mack. Do you taste chocolate when you hear Mal's voice?"

My abashed expression told her all she needed to know.

"Oh, yes," she said, rubbing her hands together with glee. "This is definitely going to be interesting."

When we returned to the Capone Club room, we discovered that Billy had asked Gary Gunderson to cover the bar for him and had headed upstairs to the Capone Club group. Gary was a bouncer and bartender who had been working at the bar since before my father was killed. He had to take a leave of absence for health reasons nearly two months ago, but had recently returned to his job.

Of course, now that Billy was hanging out upstairs with the club members, Alicia had followed along. Mal looked comfortable sitting at one end of several tables that had been pushed together, and he was drinking the Irish coffee I'd ordered for him. I figured it was a fitting drink for a man with the last name of O'Reilly. Plus I've put my own spin on the original classic to make it extraspecial. I use a mix of espresso and chilled coffee, and always make it with brown sugar instead of white. Then I top it off with a pinch of nutmeg.

"Your guy here is a natural," Tad announced. "He figured out today's riddle."

I looked over at Mal, feeling anxious. The last thing I needed was for him to give himself away by demonstrating better than average sleuthing skills.

He seemed to sense my concern and said, "They're making it sound like more than it was. I had a bit of an advantage."

"How so?" I asked.

"Don't tell her," Frank said. "Let's run it by her and see if she can figure it out."

I walked over and grabbed an empty chair, dragging it up next to Mal's. Cora settled in across from us. I looked over at Mal with a sad expression and said, "Don't expect much. I suck at most of these."

Mal leaned toward me and spoke in a voice that was low but could still be heard by others nearby, "Just remember our conversation tonight and I think you'll figure it out." Then he proffered his glass and added, "Dynamite coffee, by the way."

"Thanks."

Frank said. "Sam came up with tonight's riddle. He said it's designed to see who the lateral thinkers are, whatever the hell that means. Personally I think he's running some secret psychotherapy experiment on us for one of his classes. So watch out. The men in the white coats are probably right around the corner, and given some of the personalities in this group, I suspect they'll be busy for quite a while."

I smiled at that, but on the inside I quaked a little. My past relationships with shrinks hadn't been pleasant ones, thanks to my synesthesia.

"Okay," I said. "Fire away and make me look bad in front of my date."

Sam leaned forward, elbows on his knees, hands laced together. He looked directly into my eyes and said, "Listen carefully, because all the information you need is in what I'm about to say. In a small town, police are called to the home of a wealthy man where there has been a break-in, murder, and robbery. There is a witness of sorts, the rich man's wife, who was upstairs when the break-in occurred. Her husband was downstairs and she heard him yell at the intruder, heard sounds of a struggle, and then a shot. When she heard someone climbing the stairs to her level, she hid under a bed in a guest bedroom. She could tell from the way the person walked that it wasn't her husband who had come up the stairs, so she stayed as quiet and still as she could. She was never able to see anything, but at one point the perpetrator's cell phone rang and she heard a man's voice answer. Then she heard him say, 'Got it. Poker game in thirty minutes at 5731 Sunset Drive. See you there.'

"The police immediately head for the address the woman gave them and when they enter the house they find there is indeed a poker game going on. Seated at the poker table are five people the cops know: a fireman, a police officer, a construction worker, a mechanic, and a golf pro. Without asking any questions or even speaking to any of the players, the police immediately walk over and arrest the fireman. How did they know he was the culprit?"

Sam sat back in his chair and smiled. Everyone in the group stared at me, waiting. I ran back over Sam's words as carefully as I could, and then I tried to recall the conversational topics earlier in the evening with Mal. He had talked about his family mostly, his parents, his sisters, his cousins, aunts, uncles, and such. Did family play a role in this? If so, I didn't see the connection. We'd also talked some about his work as a cop, and his work in construction. His father owned a construction company and the whole family was involved in the business. Then I remembered something else he had mentioned, something that amused him about his family and their business. A mental light-bulb turned on, and oddly enough I saw an accompanying flash of light with it. I replayed Sam's words and his list of suspects: a fireman, a police officer, a construction worker, a mechanic, and a golf pro. And with that, I thought I had it figured it out.

"Is it because the fireman was the only male member of the group at the poker table?" I posed.

The group exploded with a chorus of exclamations and Mal gave my arm a squeeze and said, "Atta girl!"

"You're definitely getting better at this," Joe said, looking like a proud uncle.

"Not necessarily. Mal was right when he said he had an advantage. You see, his family owns a construction company and they all work in it. He has two sisters. One of them is a master carpenter and the other is a master plumber. At dinner tonight he was telling me how amusing the reactions are when his sisters show up to do their jobs. The stereotype of men holding those jobs is so ingrained that when a woman shows up, the reactions run from disbelief and worry about their ability to do the job to over-the-top feminist affirmation. So the idea of gender role reversal was planted in my brain earlier, and Mal helped me remember it."

"We make a good team," Mal said, smiling at me.

I smiled back. "Yes, we do." From the corner of my eye I saw Joe give Frank a nudge in the ribs with his elbow and the two of them exchanged a look.

Cora said, "I do believe Mal has earned himself a free drink."

Mal shook his head. "I'm happy to accept but I'll have to take a rain check. This is enough for me," he said, holding up his nearly empty glass. "I have an early day tomorrow." He drained the last of his drink, got up from his chair, grabbed his coat, and looked down at me. "Walk me out?" he asked.

"Sure."

The group bade Mal good night, invited him to return at any time, and then the two of us headed downstairs. I saw him to the door and stepped outside with him so we could speak with some level of public privacy. Once I made sure no one was close enough to eavesdrop, I leaned in close to him and said, "I need to make a trip to the zoo."

"Something in that letter you got at the art store?" he said just above a whisper.

I nodded.

"Are you planning on going tomorrow?"

Again I nodded.

"Need someone to come along?"

"That would be nice."

"I offered to put in some OT tomorrow . . . cuddling up to the boss, you know. But I only have to work until eleven. Give me some time for travel, a shower, and a change of clothes, and I can be here around noon. So if you can wait until then, I'd be happy to go with you."

"The zoo is open until four-thirty on the weekends, so that should give us enough time," I told him, hoping it was true. I knew we could easily cover the zoo area in the amount of time we had if we didn't dawdle at any of the exhibits, but I was basically going on a scavenger hunt where I didn't know what I was looking for, or if I was looking for it in the right place. I had to hope that my intuition—and Duncan's—was on target, and something at the zoo was the answer to the latest letter. And that I'd somehow figure out what that something was once we got there.

"Great," Mal said. "Shall I pick you up here around noon?"

"Sure."

"Then it's a date," he said with a smile. "And speaking of dates, we should make this look official, so brace yourself."

With that he took me by the shoulders, leaned down, and gave me a kiss on the lips. It wasn't a deep or romantic kiss, just a basic peck really, but the feel of his lips on mine set off a visual display of fireworks.

When he was done, he stood there, staring at me with an odd expression. Several seconds ticked by, and then he suddenly turned me toward the door. "Go inside and tend to your customers," he said, giving me a nudge. "I'll see you tomorrow."

I felt rather than saw him turn away, and I started to open the door to the bar to go inside. But instead I turned and watched him walk down the sidewalk, hands in his pockets, a light wind whipping his dark hair. Warmth had flared in my chest with that chaste and brief little kiss, but by the time Mal turned the corner and disappeared from my view, it had cooled, leaving me feeling strangely hollow inside. I finally opened the door and headed back inside. I made my way to the bar, asked Gary if he and Billy would close things up for me later, and headed upstairs.

Mal's kiss had unsettled me, and I felt an almost desperate need to be with Duncan, to reaffirm our relationship, even though I wasn't sure what kind of relationship we had. Regardless, I felt certain that once I was with him, things would seem right again and everything would make sense. But when I got upstairs, I discovered Duncan was gone, along with both of the letters and the envelopes they had come in, and some of the other letters he'd been looking at. In their place was a note that said: *Something came up and I had to sneak out. Sorry . . . I will miss you . . . will call you later.* He had signed it off with a capital letter *D*, no heartfelt closing, no words of love, not even his full name.

I crumpled the note in my hand, walked into the kitchen, and tossed it in the trash. For some reason I felt a hot ball of anger building inside me, but I wasn't sure what, or who, I was angry with. I had no reason to be mad at Duncan. After all, I was the one who had put him off first tonight. Maybe I was mad at the lunatic who was writing the letters, the nut-job who had set my life atilt, the whacko who seemed to be manipulating me as if I were a marionette.

I desperately needed to unwind and relax, to get my head straight. So I opened a bottle of wine and ran myself a hot bath. As I sank down into the water and felt the warmth seep into my muscles and bones, another thought occurred to me.

I realized that Duncan must have left through the bar. If he had used the alley exit, it would have set off the alarm, something Billy or Gary would have told me about. Had Duncan disabled the alarm? I got out of the tub, dried off, and re-dressed. Then I went back downstairs and into my office to check. The alarm was still on, so he had gone out through the bar. Had his disguise been good enough? Had someone recognized him? And if so, was someone else going to pay for it with their life?

Chapter 8

I decided I might as well take advantage of my staff closing shop for me, and I headed for bed around one, hoping to snag a few extra hours of sleep. But my internal clock—and my racing mind—wouldn't allow it. After an hour or two of tossing and turning, I finally fell asleep around three when all the noises downstairs had died out. I awoke the next morning at a little after nine and settled in at the dining room table with a cup of coffee and the newspaper online. The body that had been found beneath the *Bronze Fonz* was the top story of the day and the identity of the victim had been released. The article gave some details about Lewis's life, some of which I hadn't known. What I did know was that he was an ICU nurse at a local hospital, single, and not from the Milwaukee area originally. What I hadn't known was that his family currently lived in Minnesota: his parents, a brother, and a sister.

The article ended with a plea to the public to call a hotline number if anyone had any information they thought might be relative to the case. I had plenty, but nothing I was willing to share with anyone other than Duncan, Cora, Mal, and the Signoriello brothers.

I knew that Lewis's death would be the topic of the day in the bar, particularly with the Capone Club members. Even though I had had time to process the fact, I would have to act as if the news was as much a surprise to me as it was to the others. I spent a few minutes over my coffee, mentally rehearsing my reactions.

Just before ten, Duncan called.

"Morning, Sunshine," he said, and his words made me taste fizzy chocolate that blended nicely with the lingering taste of my coffee. "Sorry I had to leave last night."

"Me, too. What came up that was so important?" I heard the slight tone of resentment in my voice and wondered if Duncan could, too. "And how did you leave?"

"Something came up on one of my cases that couldn't wait," he said vaguely. "And I borrowed a scarf from you. Between that, my wool cap, and the bulky coat, my face was well hidden. I walked straight out through the bar. No one noticed."

I said nothing, too miffed to speak, so he went on. "I did manage to get a little work done on our shared, secret case last night. I dusted the envelopes and the letter for prints, and had a friend run them for me on the sly. I told her it was for something personal. We came up with several prints on the envelopes, but the only one that produced anything in AFIS was the art store guy, who has a record. He had a prior arrest for burglary."

"Do you think he might be behind this?"

"I don't. The burglary rap was six years ago

when he was in his early twenties and it was a friend he robbed. Claimed the stuff was his originally, but the jury didn't believe him. He did ninety days in jail and a year of probation. Other than that, his record is clean."

"That doesn't mean he couldn't have written the letters."

"True, but I did some checking and he owns and runs that art store. He's there every day from when he opens until he closes. I don't think his schedule is very conducive to what the letter suggests and there are witnesses who say he was in the store around the time that Lewis Carmichael was killed."

"So it's a dead end," I said, resisting an urge I had to add that I'd told him so.

"That part is, but after reading through a couple of the other letters you had, I zeroed in on one in particular, the one from Apostle Mike. He sounds like a zealot, so I thought it would be worth it to take a deeper look into him and his so-called mission."

"And?"

"Well, he's a fringe lunatic, but I'm guessing you figured that out on your own. He is also clearly not a fan of yours and he has a record for felony assault. He pistol whipped a couple ten years ago who were the landlords of the house he was living in. He did two years in prison and another five on probation."

"Anything since then?"

"Yeah, plenty. He started this right wing group of militant conservatives who protest against the government interfering in any way with individual rights, particularly the right to bear arms. There is a possibility he has connections to some militant groups in upper Michigan who are known to have huge stockpiles of weapons and a belief that such stockpiles are necessary to protect them against a police-run state. So given your prior connections to me and the department, it's quite possible that this guy and some of his compatriots see you as part of the Big Brother enemy."

This revelation made me taste fear. The idea that I was facing one lunatic was bad enough. The thought that it might be an entire group of fanatics was almost more than I could stand. "How do we find that out?"

"We need to have a chat with him."

"But if you do, and he is involved, it would let him and anyone he might be working with know that I involved you in this against his explicit instructions. I don't think I could bear to live with the consequences if he carries out his threat. I've already got one death on my shoulders. I can't handle another one."

"Lewis's death is not your fault, Mack. And I thought you might balk at the idea of me questioning this guy, so I thought I'd have someone else question him about something unrelated to you and your letters. I can have one of the other guys bring him in and question him while you and I secretly observe."

"You mean, at the police station?"

"Yes."

"But if I'm seen even going to the police station . . ." I let the implication hang, knowing he would guess what I meant.

"We can figure ways around that," he assured me. "And I have one or two guys I can trust to help us out with this and keep it under wraps."

"Is Jimmy one of them?" Jimmy Patterson was Duncan's partner and someone who had eyed me with skepticism and a degree of distrust from the first day I met him. The distrust part was mutual. Whenever he was around, I sensed the level of dislike and discomfort he felt with me.

"He is," Duncan said. "I know the two of you haven't seen eye to eye on things all the time, and I know he's been skeptical of you and your abilities, but it doesn't mean he dislikes you. And regardless of whether or not he believes in you, he's someone I trust."

"I don't agree with you about him not disliking me, but I'll accept your judgment of his trustworthiness," I said, thinking *at least for now, since I don't have much of a choice.*

"I'll let you know when we find Apostle Mike and we'll figure out a way to sneak you in here to listen in when we talk to him."

"Just don't do it today. I'm going to the zoo, remember?"

"Yeah, about that . . ." He sighed. "I don't like the idea of you traipsing around to these places alone. We don't know what this person has in mind. Maybe it's not a game they want to play. Maybe they're trying to lure you out somewhere so they can kidnap you, or worse."

"The zoo is a public place," I said with more conviction than I felt. I didn't want Duncan to sense how afraid I really was. "Besides, I'm not going alone. I'm taking Mal."

"Okay. That's good," Duncan said, though the tone in his voice suggested otherwise. Why, I wondered? Was he worried about my safety, or was he starting to feel a prickle of jealousy? "I'll try to arrange for Apostle Mike to be brought in some other time then, maybe tomorrow. That might be better anyway since there are fewer people around here on a Sunday."

"Let me know," I said. "In the meantime, I'm more or less free until Mal comes at noon. Can I interest you in sneaking over here for brunch?"

"That sounds great, and I do want to see you, but I don't think I can get away. Jimmy and I pulled a drug-related double homicide and right now I've got more work than I can handle. Can I take a rain check?"

"Anytime," I said, trying to disguise the disappointment I felt.

After hanging up, I headed downstairs to start my morning bar prep. As I entered the bar I saw my daytime bartender, Pete, was already in and busy cutting up fruit for the bar. Debra had just walked in and was shedding her coat, a lighter weight one than her usual.

"Good morning," I said to the two of them, eyeing the brilliant sunshine beaming in through the windows. I knew that at this time of the year that sunshine can be deceptive, shining bright in the midst of bitter, brittle cold. "What's it like outside? The paper said we were in for a bit of a warm spell for a couple of days."

"It's nice," Debra said. "It's in the upper thirties now and I think it's supposed to hit the mid- to high fifties later on."

Given that we'd just had a two-week stretch of temperatures in the teens and twenties, the fifties sounded heavenly.

"Did you see the news this morning?" Debra asked.

I nodded solemnly. "Lewis, you mean?"

She nodded just as solemnly. "What a horrible thing. It's scary to think that someone we know has been murdered. Makes me wish you and Duncan were still close so you could get the scoop."

"Maybe some of the other cops who come in can give us some info," Pete suggested. "I didn't know the guy real well, but he seemed nice enough."

"He was," I agreed.

With that topic out of the way, Debra started quizzing me relentlessly on my date with Mal last night. "Did you like him?" she asked. "Are you going to see him again? Did he hold your hand? Did he kiss you?"

Pete's questions were more fatherly in nature. "Did he treat you well? Did he act like a gentleman? Did he pay for your dinner? Have you checked into his background?"

I fielded their inquiries with honest answers—at least mostly honest—until Debra hit me with "So what happened with you and Duncan?"

Pete echoed this question with one of his own before I could answer. "Yeah, what's the deal with you and Duncan?"

I didn't want to lie to them, and even though I felt I could trust both of them, I didn't want to tell them the truth, either. Sometimes people let things slip unintentionally when their guards are down, or they are otherwise distracted. And I wasn't willing to risk a life on someone else's careless slip of the tongue. Based on that, I figured the fewer people who knew the truth, the better. So I opted for evasion instead.

"I don't want to talk about Duncan," I said, trying to look wounded and hurt. "Let's just say that for now I'm content to see where things go with Mal."

With that, I disappeared into the kitchen, leaving the two of them behind and putting an end to the interrogation. But I did look out through the door window once I was in the kitchen and saw Pete and Debra exchange a look between them. I had no doubt that speculation about what had happened between me and Duncan would be the second most popular topic of gossip in the bar for a while, but like most gossip, it would eventually grow old and be replaced with something juicier, more current, and more interesting. Hopefully, it wouldn't be the murder of someone else we all knew.

We opened the doors at eleven and the usual group of regulars came in. The Signoriello brothers ate lunch at my bar nearly every day of the week. They were very punctual and always arrived within a minute or two of eleven. Cora was less driven by the clock, but she typically showed up within the first couple of hours and then spent most of the day in the bar. Today she arrived at five minutes after eleven with Tiny in tow.

"I have some exciting news about Tiny's sister's case," she announced to us. "Send anyone who's interested upstairs to the Capone Club room."

Over the next ten minutes, Carter, Holly, Tad, and Alicia arrived and headed upstairs to join the brothers and Cora. By eleven-thirty, Sam and

Kevin had joined the fray. Saturdays were always the busiest day for the Capone Club since most of the members were off work on the weekends. One exception to this rule was Karen Tannenbaum, or Dr. T as we called her, who worked various shifts in the ER at the same hospital where Lewis Carmichael had worked. As it turned out, Dr. T was off for the day, and she showed up at eleven-thirty for lunch. I was curious to see how folks in the group would react to the news about Lewis, and also curious to see how they would react to Cora's news about Tiny's case, so I ventured upstairs to listen in.

Just as I'd thought, Lewis's murder was the hot topic. Everyone looked a little shell-shocked over it, and several folks were consoling Dr. T, who had known Lewis better than any of us.

"Have you heard any rumors about what happened?" Cora asked her.

Dr. T shook her head. "The cops haven't said anything, though they've been talking to a bunch of us. I imagine they'll be around to talk to you guys, too. So far they're keeping mum on the subject, and if they know anything they aren't sharing. No one knows of anyone who had it out for Lewis so the speculation for now is that he was the unfortunate victim of a robbery gone wrong. If I hear anything more concrete, I'll let you guys know."

The group spent ten minutes or so holding a mini memorial for Lewis, sharing some memories and anecdotes of him, but his involvement with the group had been hit and miss for the most part, so aside from Dr. T, the mourning remained on a somewhat distant, superficial level. Cora, Frank, and Joe shot me meaningful looks several times, and I knew they were making the connection between Lewis's murder and the letter. They looked troubled and worried, but not particularly frightened, and I made a mental note to talk to them later and caution them to be extra-wary and careful.

None of the others seemed to feel particularly threatened by the proximity of Lewis's murder to our group, and I felt some relief over that. But I also felt guilty hiding the knowledge I had. Was I endangering them more by keeping the information I had to myself? Or was it better to let them live on in blissful ignorance? Only time would tell, and I prayed that I was making the right decision.

Once the topic of Lewis petered out, Cora said, "No disrespect meant to Lewis, but I have some news on another topic that I think you'll all find interesting. I dug up some info on the primary suspects in Lori Gruber's case."

I could see that Cora had written up her own version of the suspect sheets that included pictures, bios, and pertinent facts about each of the suspects. I wondered how much of the info had been included in the sheets Duncan had obtained and how much of it Cora had dug up on her own using her many databases and hacking skills. She had a stack of pages stapled together and she handed them out to everyone in the room.

There were four men listed on the pages: a local homeless man named Lonnie Carlisle who had a sex offender history; Erik Hermann, the older brother of Lori's friend, Anna Hermann, who had been abducted and killed along with Lori; a man named William Schneider, who had lived in the same neighborhood as Lori and Anna, and who had a reputation for being "strange" according to his neighbors; and a plumber named Timothy Johnson, who went by the moniker TJ, and who had visited the Gruber household the day before the two girls disappeared.

The pages also revealed that while investigating TJ, the cops had found a large stash of kiddie porn in his house, for which he was arrested. He worked a deal with the DA and did two years of jail time along with four years of probation, and earned himself a spot on the sex offenders' list as a result.

A picture of each man was included, along with a summary of their statements, and their alibis if they had one. The strange neighbor, the plumber, and the homeless man had no alibis, but Erik had a friend named Dylan Cochran who swore that the two of them were out driving around in the country together at the time of the girls' disappearance.

Three of the men still lived in Milwaukee. Lonnie Carlisle was the exception and he was no longer homeless. He was currently residing at the Waupun Correctional Institute after being convicted of attempted murder, attempted child molestation, and attempted sexual assault.

"Interesting collection of suspects," I said. "Was there any DNA evidence to connect any of them?"

Tiny, managing to look both sad and hopeful, shook his head. "Da bodies were found two mont's after dey disappeared. Dey were in da Little Menomonee River in a wooded area by da Oak Leaf Trail," he said, referencing a bike path that circles in and around the city through its parklands. "Dey went missing at da end of Christmas break after dey went out on a bike ride. We had a weird warm spell dat year between Christmas and New Year's—kinda like what we're having now—but da wedder turned bitterly cold later dat night. Da bodies didn't surface until early March when t'ings warmed up enough to t'aw the river water. My parents were told dat da bodies were well preserved t'anks to da cold." His face scrunched up and his jaw muscles twitched as he paused, and after a deep, bracing breath he went on. "Da cops said Lori showed evidence of sexual assault but dere was no usable DNA found because of da water."

It was obvious from the pain on Tiny's face that the subject still left him feeling raw even after twelve years. I noticed that his emotions deepened at the end of his summary when he finally said his sister's name instead of referring to her and Anna as *the bodies*. I understood that form of detachment all too well. I had used a similar dodge whenever I talked about my father's murder, finding it much easier to discuss certain aspects of the event without breaking down if I referred to his body rather than him personally.

I ached for Tiny and leaned over to pat him on the shoulder. "I'm so sorry, Tiny," I said, and others in the group murmured similar condolences.

Once the murmurs died down, Cora said, "Do you have a favorite suspect in this group, Tiny? Or someone else that's not on the list who you thought might be involved?"

He nodded. "I do t'ink it's one of dem guys. But I'd radder not say who just yet. I want to see what udder people t'ink first."

"It makes sense to start with the ones the cops

were most focused on," Sam said. He looked over at Tiny. "But if they don't pan out, we should look into your sister's life a little deeper, hers and Anna's, to see if there are some other suspects out there that the cops might have overlooked."

Everyone nodded their agreement and a murmur of assent filled the room.

"Okay, then," I said, looking at the sheet in front of me and then at Tiny. "What's the story behind Lonnie Carlisle's conviction?"

"I heard he tried to attack two girls da summer after Lori and Anna died," Tiny explained. "Dey rebuffed his sexual advances and he beat one of da girls so bad she ended up in a coma. She's still alive but she's got severe brain damage. Lonnie said da girls attacked him for no reason, and he swore he didn't do anyt'ing to eeder one of dem. He said she musta fallen and hit her head. He said he didn't do anyt'ing except try to get away from dem, and dat he acted in self-defense."

A couple of people in the room rolled their eyes, and others harrumphed at Lonnie's reported explanation. Based on their reactions it wasn't hard to imagine which version of events the cops and jury had believed.

"Do you know why he was on the sex offenders' list before your sister's disappearance?" I asked.

Tiny shook his head and started to say something, but before he could, Cora piped up with an answer. "According to the court records it was a case of statutory rape. Lonnie was in love with a girl who was only sixteen when he was eighteen. Apparently the girl's parents didn't approve and they filed the charges."

"So no history of any other sexual offenses?" Sam asked.

Cora shook her head. "Not that I could find. His main issue seemed to be with booze. The girl, by the way, committed suicide a couple of months after Lonnie's conviction. About a year after that, he started racking up DUIs. He dropped out of college, did some job hopping for several years, and eventually did jail time for a DUI accident that injured someone else. After doing two years he got out, but apparently he wasn't able to turn his life around. He spent some time in a halfway house but left after a few months and then dropped off the radar. No taxes paid, no jobs that I could find. I'm guessing that's when he became homeless. It was two years after that when Lori Gruber disappeared and he became a suspect."

"That's a tragic tale," I said.

Most of the group nodded, though I noticed that Tiny didn't.

"Damn alcohol," Carter said. "It ruins a lot of lives."

Everyone looked at their drink, then at me. Realizing what he'd just said, Carter blushed and added, "Nothing personal, Mack. I'm talking about people who abuse the stuff. Not anyone here."

Despite his disclaimer, both of the Signoriello brothers and Tad set their drinks down.

"No offense taken," I said in an effort to ease everyone's minds. "Moderation is the key."

"What got Lonnie on the cops' radar in your sister's case?" Sam asked. "A statutory rape charge isn't the sort of sex offense that typically segues into regular rape and murder. And based on the history, it sounds like he and the girl were truly in love. Was he a suspect right from the beginning, or only after the other two girls were attacked? "

Tiny fielded this one. "He was a suspect right from da start. The cops said dey found witnesses who saw Lori talking to da guy. Lonnie didn't deny it. He said he knew her because he saw her walking home from school all da time and one day she started talking to him, trying to get him to go to church wit' her. We used to attend da Lutheran Church in our neighborhood and dey funded a program for homeless people. Lonnie said Lori befriended him and gave him money a couple of times so he could get somet'ing to eat."

"Did you believe him?" I asked Tiny.

He shrugged. "Lori woulda done somet'ing like dat. She was always bringing home stray animals, and sticking up for kids at school who were bullied, dat dere sorta stuff. She had a big heart. But the cops said Lori resembled da girl he used to date, da one whose parents filed da charges. Dey t'ought maybe he confused Lori for her, tried to do somet'ing to her, and when she resisted, he killed her."

I made a mental note to try to arrange a visit to Waupun and Lonnie in the near future. I wanted to talk to the man, to hear his side of the story. I'm pretty good at detecting when people are lying about something. Their voices change in subtle ways, ways that I can see or taste.

"What do you know about this neighbor guy, William Schneider?" Dr. T asked. "The one who everyone said was strange."

Once again Cora beat Tiny to the punch. "He has some mental health issues. Based on the court records I could find, he's been in and out of mental facilities and doesn't take his meds like he's supposed to. His background is another tragic story."

This made Tiny frown and I imagined he didn't take kindly to anyone feeling sorry in any way for the suspects in his sister's murder.

"He lost his wife and daughter in a house fire twenty years ago and never remarried. He was home at the time, and the fire was found to have been caused by a pile of gasoline-soaked rags that had been left in the garage. William was a mechanic and he had an old car he was trying to restore, so you can probably guess who left the rags in there."

Sam said, "Again I have to ask, what got him on the cops' radar with Lori and Anna's case?"

Tiny finally had a chance to speak. "He used to call out to young girls when dey walked by his house, asking dem to come inside and join him for some cookies and milk. Lori was nice to him; she often waved or said hi when she walked by his house. So I t'ink the cops t'ought she mighta gone inside."

"Was there any other evidence connecting him to Lori and Anna?" I asked.

Tiny shrugged. Cora said, "Not that I've been able to find. Maybe one of the cops who come in here from time to time can shed some more light on it for us by sneaking a peek at the files."

Everyone nodded and I mentally put William Schneider at the bottom of my list for now.

"How about the plumber?" Alicia asked.

"I like TJ for it," Cora said. "The cops found that collection of kiddie porn and when they searched his computer, they found a bunch of Web sites that he visited regularly that either had illegal kiddie porn on them or were hangouts for other pedophiles. Based on the porn he had, the stuff he said, and what he watched online, he liked young girls who were around Lori's age. He did some time and went to a court-mandated treatment facility when he got out, but he was arrested again a year later when he was caught sitting in his car by the high school and flogging his dog while he was watching some girls play soccer."

Tiny looked over at Cora with a shocked expression. "He was beating up on his dog?" he said, sounding angry.

There was a cacophony of awkward sniggers, grunts, and giggles as the others shifted nervously in their seats.

"Um, not exactly," Cora said to Tiny. Then she leaned over and whispered in his ear.

He said, "Oh," and turned as red as the maraschino cherry garnish in his chocolate-covered cherry martini.

"I agree that he sounds like the most likely suspect so far," Sam said.

I agreed as well, and moved TJ to the top of my list.

"And that leaves us with Anna's brother, Erik Hermann," Cora said.

"Would he have killed and raped his own sister?" I said, feeling a little squeamish. It was sickening to think there were all these twisted people in the world.

"Anna wasn't raped," Tiny reminded us. "Only Lori was. And Erik had da hots for my sister."

"Having the hots for a girl when you're in high school doesn't make you a killer," Tad said.

"Except Lori didn't like Erik back," Tiny said angrily. "He made advances on her da day before she disappeared, and when she told him no he got real mad and slapped her. She didn't tell me or my parents about it. Da police found out because Anna kept a diary and had written about it da night before."

"A diary? That could be helpful," Carter said. "I don't suppose you have a copy of it?"

"I don't," Tiny said. "But da cops gave it back to her parents after dey copied everyt'ing in it."

"Is there any way we can get a copy of it?" Carter asked.

Cora threw up her hands and said, "My computer skills won't help with that."

"Would Anna's parents let you have a copy of it?" Sam asked Tiny.

"I don't t'ink so," he said, shaking his head and frowning. "Dey got pretty mad when dere son became a suspect. And I said some bad t'ings about Erik."

"If the police made a copy of it, maybe we can get a copy from them," I posed. "Nick and Tyrese come in here a lot," I said, naming two of the local cops who frequented my bar both off duty for some R&R, and while on duty for my coffee. My brew was a hit with the local police. "Why don't you guys ask one of them if they can get it?"

"You're the one with the cop connection," Tad said. "Why don't you ask them?"

"I'm persona non grata with the PD right now. Besides," I added, glancing at my watch, "I've got a date who will be here any minute, so I might not see them."

"I doubt there's much help to be had with the diary anyway," Cora said. "If there was anything useful in there, the cops would have looked into it already."

"You never know," Sam said. "And it doesn't hurt to ask. All they can do is say no."

"I might have a better idea," Carter said. "What if I approached Anna's parents and told them I'm working on a true crime book based on the case? If I make it sound like I'm trying to exonerate their son, maybe they'd let me have a look at it."

"Like I said, it doesn't hurt to ask," Sam repeated, giving his friend a nod of approval.

"What about talking to the friend Erik used as an alibi?" Joe suggested. "Mack could talk to him and use that special talent she has to see if he's telling the truth."

"I don't know," I said, frowning. "I'm not always right when it comes to that sort of stuff."

"You could at least give it a try," Joe persisted. "What have we got to lose?"

Everyone looked at me expectantly, awaiting my answer. Had it not been for the pleading expression of sad desperation on Tiny's face, I probably would have said no. But I understood all too well how he felt since I'd been there myself with my father's murder. "Okay," I said, caving to the pressure. "I'll give it a shot."

"T'ank you," Tiny said with a huge smile.

"Don't thank me yet, and don't get your hopes up too soon. I can't promise anything."

"I know," Tiny said. "I know we may never find da answer but at least we're trying. I want all of you to know dat I appreciate what you're doing." With that, he reached over and picked up one of the many papers that were spread out on the table next to him. He flipped it around to show it to me, revealing a smiling blond girl who had Tiny's features. "Lori would say t'ank you, too, if she could," he added.

As I stared at the face in the picture, so full of youthful life, young innocence, and hope for the future, I knew I wouldn't rest until I'd done all I could to help Tiny find the culprit who had murdered his sister.

Chapter 9

Mal arrived then and after greeting the group and being introduced to the members he hadn't met the night before, he and I left to head for the zoo. When I mentioned grabbing a coat, he said, "Make it a light one. It's beautiful outside."

I ran upstairs to my apartment to grab my fall jacket, and when I returned, Mal and I headed out under a hail of good-byes and edicts to have fun. The weather was warming rapidly, and I realized that even the lightweight jacket might turn out to be unnecessary. Like most Wisconsinites, I adjust to the cold temperatures pretty quickly. While fifty degrees might make some people shiver, on the heels of the near-zero temps we'd had recently, it felt like summer. Also like most Wisconsinites, I never take unexpected warmth and sunshine for granted, and, as we walked to Mal's car, I tipped my face toward the sun a few times, relishing the feel of it on my skin.

As soon as we were inside the car, I filled Mal in on what the letter had said and contained.

"That doesn't narrow things down much," he

said when I was done. "And that's assuming the zoo is even the right place to go."

"Do you have any other ideas?"

He thought a moment and shrugged. "Can't say that I do. So we might as well operate under the assumption that the zoo is where we need to go and play it by ear from there."

With that topic out of the way, I quizzed Mal about his undercover construction job assignment.

"Duncan said you were hoping to get an invite into the inner sanctum from the boss," I said. "Any idea how long that will take? And how do you know it will happen at all?"

"I don't," he said. "But I've dropped some hints by discussing some of my prior jobs and how my family's business wasn't strictly on the up-and-up in some of their dealings. I'm hoping that word will get back to the boss based on that."

"Is that true? Does your family business operate on the shady side of things?"

"Not my father's portion. He's an honest man and he'd never jeopardize the business or the family name that way. But one of my uncles also owns a segment of the business and his dealings have come under scrutiny a time or two. He likes to cut corners, we think he's paid graft to some building inspectors, and he's been known to run the occasional side business as a bookie. My father and he don't get along too well."

"I have to admit I'm a little relieved to find a flaw in your family structure," I told him. "I was starting to feel very deprived and inadequate when I compared my family history and structure to yours."

He gave me a funny look. "How so?"

"Well, you have this wonderful extended family with some very big differences in their beliefs, and yet you all manage to set that aside in the name of peace, love, happiness, and harmony. I, on the other hand, have no one anymore. For the first thirty-four years of my life it was just me and my father, and now I have no one."

"What about your mother?"

"She died right after I was born, though I suppose technically she died before I was born. A car accident left her brain dead when she was a little over seven months pregnant with me, but the doctors were able to keep her alive on machines until she got close enough to term to deliver me. Then they took the machines away and let her die."

"Wow. I'm so sorry. That couldn't have been easy for you."

I shrugged. "It wasn't like I had a mother and then lost her. Sure, I've grieved for her, but since I never knew life any other way, I didn't experience the sort of grief a child might if they lost a parent later on, one they came to know."

"Did you have any grandparents, aunts, or cousins who could have filled in?"

"Nope. Both of my mother's parents and my father's mother died before I was born. My father never knew who his father was, so I suppose it's possible I have a grandfather out there somewhere. My mother had a sister and as far as I know she's still in France. But she didn't like my father, blamed him for my mother's death, and has never had any contact with us."

"So your father raised you by himself?"

"Yes, he did, right there in the bar. It's been my home all my life."

"It sounds kind of lonely."

"I imagine it does to someone from a family like yours. But to be honest, I never felt lonely. Between my father, our employees, and some of the regulars who frequent the bar, I've always felt like I had plenty of family around. It's a different definition of family perhaps, but it's worked for me."

We arrived at the entrance to the zoo and Mal pulled in behind another car at the gate. When our turn came, he pulled up and took an informational brochure from the attendant, handing it to me. As Mal paid our fee, I opened up the brochure and started reading. One of the first things I noticed was the zoo hours. I'd looked them up last night online in anticipation of today's' visit, but had focused only on the weekend hours. Now I saw what the weekday hours were and felt a tiny trill of excitement.

"Mal, look," I said as we pulled away from the gate and into the parking lot. "The zoo closes at two-thirty on Monday and that was the deadline in the letter. That's significant, don't you think?"

"Maybe," he said with a glimmer of hope. "But it could also be a coincidence." He pulled into a parking spot, shut off the engine, and turned to me. "Listen, about the conversation we were having a moment ago, I just want to say that your definition of family must work well enough because you certainly turned out fine."

He smiled at me, and after thanking him, I smiled back. Our gazes held a second or two longer than they should have and after an awkward few seconds, he turned away, cleared his throat, and got out of the car. I briefly debated waiting for him to come around and open my door, and then decided not to. But when he proffered his arm, I took it and let him lead me through the main entry building and out the back to start our tour.

In the zoo proper area, we stopped and consulted the map contained in the brochure we'd been given at the gate. "I think I'd like to focus on a couple of exhibits to start with," I said, pointing them out on the map. "The letter misspelled the word *dear* in the salutation so I want to check out any deer exhibits. Also the bears and the wolves since both of those words were in the letter. And since we know that they sometimes allow people to feed the giraffes and the letter mentioned not forgetting to eat, that might be worth checking out, too. Besides, it's near the wolves and one of the bear exhibits."

"What exactly are we looking for?" Mal asked.

"I wish I knew. Let's just hit up those spots and see if anything strikes us, okay?"

We walked at a brisk pace, occasionally consulting the map and the directional signs, dodging the multitude of strollers and scampering kids. I was surprised to see so many people there given the time of year, but figured the unusual weather had drawn people out to enjoy the unexpected warmth and sunshine.

We arrived at the giraffe exhibit first, and saw the platform that was used to allow visitors to feed them, but it was closed, either for the day or for the season. After watching the animals for several minutes, and looking around to see if anyone was paying particular attention to us, I said, "Let's move on and check out the wolves."

They were located a short walk away, just across the tarmac, though we had to meander along a wooden walkway to reach a position where we could see the animals. There was a small wooden observation nook and from there we could see two small mounds of gray fur huddled beneath some trees at the back of the fenced-in area.

"It doesn't look like they want to be sociable," Mal said.

Again I glanced around to see if anyone was watching us. There were several families walking toward or away from us on the boardwalk, but no one stood out, or seemed interested in us in any way. Another idea occurred to me, and I bent down, looked beneath the wooden structure, and ran my hands along the underside of the railings. All I got for my efforts was a splinter in one of my fingers.

"Ow!" I said, pulling back and shaking my hand.

Mal reached over and took my hand in his, examining the tiny wood shard whose end was poking out at the base of my index finger. He reached into his pocket with his other hand and pulled out a Swiss Army knife. With the fingers of that hand he deftly exposed a tiny pair of tweezers. Seconds later, the splinter was history.

"I'm guessing you've done that before," I said, impressed with how fast and ably he had accomplished the task.

"I work in construction, remember? It's one of the hazards of the job, a very common one in fact." He folded the tweezers back into the knife handle with one hand and returned it to his pocket. That's when I realized his thumb was gently rubbing over the area where the splinter had been. His hand was warm and his touch triggered a blanket of tiny sparkling lights along the periphery of my vision.

"You should probably wash this well with some soap and water at the first restroom we come to," he said, his thumb still rubbing.

I shifted my gaze from my hand to his face and found him looking back at me. His thumb movement slowed, and then stopped. And once again our eyes held for a second or two longer than was comfortable. I pulled my hand loose from his and shoved it in my pocket. I resurrected the map in my mind, a nifty little trick I suspect I can do because of my synesthesia. "There's a restaurant with bathrooms just beyond the polar bear exhibit," I said, looking away from him and down the boardwalk. Then I started to babble out of nervousness. "If we go around this building we'll see the kangaroos and emu, and the brown bear is next to them. Then we pass the moose and cross over to the polar bear."

I took off in the direction I'd indicated, leaving Mal to follow behind me. The kangaroos, like the wolves, were hard to see as they were all huddled against the building, far back from the surrounding fence. We didn't see the emu at all but the brown bears were out, sprawled and enjoying an afternoon nap in the warm sunshine. We stood side by side, watching the magnificent creatures as they ignored the gawking humans pointing and staring at them. It struck me as a little sad seeing them penned in like that. Granted the enclosure was large and done up to be "natural" but it was still a far cry from the wildlife they should have known.

The moose looked as bored as I was starting to

feel, and I worried that the entire trip had been a huge waste of time.

"It's a little sad seeing them trapped and on display here, isn't it?" Mal said, echoing my thoughts.

"It is," I agreed. "Though it's the only way many people will ever get to see most of these animals. And I don't suppose their lives here are all that horrible."

"The ones that bother me the most are the single animals that don't have any other members of their species here. That seems like such a lonely existence."

"Kind of like me, you mean?" I said, experiencing a surprising sting—both physically and emotionally—at the feelings his words triggered.

We had started walking again, heading for the polar bear exhibit, and he grabbed my arm and spun me around.

"Mack, I'm very sorry if what I said sounded like a judgment on you. It certainly wasn't meant as such."

"No apology necessary," I said, feeling horrible when I saw how sincerely concerned he looked. "I'm overly sensitive on the subject, I think. It's been less than a year since my father died, and I'm still feeling the loss."

"Of course you are. It was an insensitive comment for me to have made. Again, I'm sorry."

"Don't worry about it. Let's move on. I have a feeling this trip is going to be a bust and I want to get back so I can consider some other options."

We had arrived in front of the polar bear exhibit and after standing in front of it as we had the others, studying the faces and demeanors of those around us, I said, "I'm hungry. Let's grab a bite to eat at the café over there."

I led the way and, once we were inside, we stopped to survey the menu. It was a fast food type setup and after telling Mal I wanted a cheeseburger and fries, I left him in line to place the order while I hit up the bathroom to wash my hands.

When I came back out, Mal already had a tray bearing our food items in hand. We made our way to a table and settled in to eat.

"We should have grabbed a bite at my bar before we came here," I said in a low voice. "My food is much better than this."

"Are you inviting me on a lunch date?" Mal asked with a smile.

"I suppose I am. I'd be interested in seeing what you think of some of the stuff on my menu. I make a mean cheese curd."

He laughed at that, and as I stuffed a couple of fries into my mouth, a young girl who worked inside the café walked over to our table carrying a tray.

"Is your name Mack Dalton by any chance?" she asked me.

My heart skipped a beat as I nodded. Then it hit me. I was the one who was supposed to eat, not the animals. The animal clues had simply been a clue to which of the eateries within the zoo I was supposed to go to. I gave myself a mental slap upside the head for being so stupid and not realizing this before.

"I thought so," the girl said with a smile. "You look like the picture."

"Picture?" I said once I swallowed. The fries didn't go down easy. My throat had tightened up, turning them into a pulpy mass that felt as if it was stuck halfway down.

The girl picked up a paper from her tray and showed it to me. It was a newspaper clipping from a week or so ago with a picture of me, highlighting my involvement with the PD.

"That article arrived at my apartment this morning. I found it outside my door. It was in a big envelope and with it were instructions to give you something if you came in here before my next day off."

"When is your next day off?" I asked.

"Tuesday," she said. "I work every Saturday, Sunday, and Monday from open to close."

"Who would know that?" Mal asked her.

She thought a moment and then said, "Anyone, I suppose. Our schedule is posted on the wall over there behind the cash register." She pointed to the area where the orders were taken and I could see the schedule on the back wall. "But in my case it doesn't really matter. I work the same days every week and have since school started in order to fit my work hours in around my school schedule." She then picked up another item from her tray and handed it to me. I recognized it right away. It was another of the plain, white, business-sized envelopes. I took it from her and laid it on the table.

"Was there a payment in the big envelope for you as well?" I asked her.

The girl nodded and glanced around nervously as if looking to see if anyone was listening or nearby. "It's not anything illegal, is it?" she asked.

"No," I lied with a smile. "It's fine. Thank you."

"This isn't some kind of drug deal or something like that?"

"Don't worry," I reassured her. "It's just a game, a scavenger hunt."

The girl nodded, but still looked wary. She started to turn away, but I stopped her. "Do you still have the big envelope this came in?"

She shook her head, her eyes wide with worry. "It's at home in my trash. Why?"

"It's no big deal," I said. "I just thought that if you did have it I could take it. Tell me, are you supposed to let the sender know somehow that the package was delivered?"

She nodded. "My instructions said to leave a picture of one of the brown bears in my front window at home."

"Where do you live?"

"Lake Summit Apartments. I have a second-story unit overlooking Summit Avenue. I'm a student at UW Milwaukee and it's close by."

"And did the instructions tell you what to do if I didn't show up?"

"Yeah, it was very specific. The note said the deadline was an absolute one and at exactly two-thirty on Monday I should destroy the letter by shredding it. Our boss has a shredder in his office so I figured I'd use that if it came down to it."

I glanced at the name badge she was wearing, saw it said HEATHER, and said, "Thanks, Heather. You've been a big help."

This time when she turned to leave, I let her go. I looked at Mal, my eyes wide with caution. I could tell he wanted to say something, or to ask about the letter, but I needed him to remember that someone might be watching or listening.

He gave me a very slight nod of his head to indicate he understood and then proceeded to play along. "So what's this scavenger hunt you're doing?" he asked with a smile. "I didn't realize you were such an adventurous type."

"It's nothing really. Just a silly online game I play to help pass the time and get me out of the bar on occasion."

"So you had an ulterior motive when you suggested we come to the zoo today?"

"Busted," I said with a sheepish smile, holding my hands up in surrender. "It's something I've been wanting to do anyway ever since my father died because he used to bring me here a lot when I was a little girl. I have a lot of fond memories of him associated with this place. I've been putting it off because I wasn't quite ready emotionally, and the bar has been keeping me so busy. But then you came along. My schedule has eased up, and the scavenger hunt clues pointed to the zoo, so it seemed like fate."

"Well, I'm happy to oblige," Mal said with a warm smile. "If I'm going to be used by a woman, this isn't a bad way to do it."

I marveled at how well he was handling our little game. We played off one another nicely, communicating so easily and often with few words. Had it not been for the very dire reason we were here, it truly would have been an enjoyable, nearly perfect date.

"I know there's stuff we haven't seen yet," I said, "but I should get back to the bar. I've been neglecting it lately, abusing this sudden free time I have. But this has been fun. And I'd love to come back again with you to see the rest of it. That is if you'll forgive my subterfuge this time."

He reached across the table, took my hand, and

held it in his. His hand was surprisingly warm, and the calluses I could feel along his palm made me taste popcorn. "I'm happy to go anywhere and do anything with you," he said, and if the taste of his voice was any indication, he meant it.

Reluctantly, I withdrew my hand from his, picked up the envelope, and stuffed it in my purse. I knew that doing so would contaminate it, but if history was any indication, it wouldn't matter. We carried our trays over to a trash bin, cleaned them off, and added them to a stack of other dirty trays. Then we went back outside and headed toward the main entrance. We didn't talk at all as we walked, but Mal took hold of my hand and held it the entire way.

When we reached the car and he finally let go of my hand I was disappointed. It was an exciting but scary emotion, and even though I've always considered myself a pretty together person, at that moment I was as confused as I've ever been.

Chapter 10

"Are you going to open that letter?" Mal asked once we were under way.

I shook my head. "Not yet. I've contaminated it enough already just by stuffing it inside my purse. The last letter had that single animal hair tucked inside. If this one has any sort of similar clue, I don't want to risk losing it. Besides, I'm sure Duncan wants to examine it himself."

We were stopped at a red light, and I sensed Mal wanted to say something but was hesitant to do so. My first thought was that his curiosity was killing him and he was trying to figure out a way to talk me into giving him a peek at the letter. But it turned out I was wrong . . . very wrong.

"So you and Duncan are business associates?"

I turned to look at him, but he kept his focus forward out the windshield. "We're not business associates, not really," I said. "I did help him out with a couple of cases a few weeks back, but I'm sure you heard all the media crap that came out as a result."

"I saw a few news reports and read something in the paper. They were saying that you're some kind of psychic or something?" His voice was rife with skepticism. "You're not, are you?"

I shook my head. "No, I'm not a psychic. I can't foretell the future, I don't speak with dead people, and I can't read your mind."

"Phew!" he said, swiping the back of his hand across his forehead. "That mind-reading stuff might get me into trouble." The light changed to green and he hit the gas.

"Your thoughts are safe from me," I said with a laugh.

"So what exactly did you do for Duncan to help him solve these cases?"

"Didn't Duncan tell you about me, about my . . . little talent as he calls it?"

Mal gave me a puzzled look. "What little talent?"

I sighed. I had assumed Mal knew about my synesthesia. Now that I realized he didn't, I was reluctant to tell him about it, not wanting him to see me in a different, potentially weird light. But now that the subject had been raised, I knew there was no avoiding it.

"I have a neurological disorder called synesthesia," I began. And during the rest of our drive, I filled him in as best I could, explaining how it affected me, a brief synopsis of the childhood issues I'd had with it, and how Duncan had used it—and me—to help him solve cases. By the time I was finished we had arrived back at the bar. Mal parked his car in a spot two blocks away, the closest one he could find.

"I had no idea," he said as he turned off the engine.

"Really? Don't you guys down at the station share in the latest scuttlebutt?"

"We do, but when you're undercover the way I am now, you don't go to the station for long periods of time in order to keep up the façade. Besides, I'm in a different district than Duncan. And I don't hang out or talk with the other cops all that much. It helps keep me in character, you know, kind of like an actor immersing himself in a role he's playing by staying in character even when he's not acting."

"So how is it you know Duncan? Or maybe I should ask how he knows you?"

"We met at the gun range. The two of us happened to show up at the same one at the same time and we got to talking. We discovered we were both cops, and that we were both recovering from broken hearts, although Duncan's was worse than mine. He got left at the altar."

"Yeah, he briefly mentioned something about that." I had wanted to ask Duncan more about it at the time, but couldn't figure out a way to do so without being rude. And I didn't feel our relationship at the time gave me any proprietary rights, so I let it go.

"Anyway," Mal went on, "we bonded over our shared miseries and went out for a few brews. We've remained friends ever since. So when he called and said he needed some help, I didn't mind pitching in, particularly since it involves the kind of sicko who is behind this letter crap."

"Well, however you got here, know that I appreciate your help." I turned to open my door and get out of the car, but Mal grabbed me by the arm. It was a gentle, staying touch, but it sent an electric shock of warmth all the way up my arm to my chest.

"Can I ask you something?" he said.

"Sure." That touch flustered me. I looked back at him but kept my hand on the door handle. I'm not sure why. It wasn't like I was going to have to flee, but something about the touch of that handle, the cool, smooth feel of it, steadied me.

"You and Duncan . . . are you more than just business associates?"

"Um, I suppose we are," I told him. "But right now things are kind of strange with the constraints he's had placed on him by his boss, all the media hype, and now this." I pointed to the envelope sticking out of my purse. "The first letter made it very clear that I was not to consult with Duncan in any way. If I do, someone else will die. So if we do get together at all, it has to be very clandestine."

"Hunh," Mal said with an arch of his brows. "That can't make for an easy relationship."

"No, it doesn't."

"Well, I wish you two the best." He turned and opened his door to get out, and this time I was the one who stopped him.

"Why did you ask me that?"

His door was open and he had one foot on the ground. He froze where he was, but he didn't look back at me when he answered. "I like you, Mack. But I don't want to step on anyone's toes, particularly Duncan's."

He got out then, shut his door, and this time he came around to open mine. We fell into step, side by side, walking down the street toward the bar.

After half a block I said, "I like you, too, Mal. I'm not sure where things are going with Duncan, but I'm not in a position right now to move on to something else."

"I understand totally," Mal said with a warm smile. "I figured it couldn't hurt to ask. Thanks for letting me know where things stand."

"You won't stop helping me out with these letters because of it, will you?"

"Of course not," he said. "You can't get rid of me that easily. If we figure this letter thing out and catch this moron, I suppose you and I will have to stage some sort of breakup. But until then, I'll keep up the façade and keep coming around the bar, both to hang with you and to hang with your group. I kind of like them and what they do."

"Good, because I think they like you, too." *I know I do.*

We walked the rest of the way in silence. It wasn't quite a comfortable silence, but it wasn't completely awkward either. We'd established a relaxed rhythm and camaraderie quickly, and I liked how easy it felt to be with him. Being in his company energized me; I felt daring, adventurous, and exquisitely alive. I knew in my mind that our relationship was something of a façade, a secret to be kept hidden, and maybe that lent it a spice that appealed to me. But in my heart I suspected it might be more than that.

The truth of our relationship, at least on the surface, made me realize something by the time we reached the bar. I stopped before opening the door, turned to him, and said, "Before we go in we need to discuss something." I looked around to see if anyone was close enough to be eavesdropping on our conversation, but the nearest people were far enough away that I felt safe as long as I lowered my voice. "There are several cops who come into my bar on a regular basis, including some who hang with the Capone Club. Do we need to do something, or tell them anything to give them a heads-up about you? I don't want to blow your cover . . . *our* cover."

Mal shook his head, looking confident and unworried. "I think we'll be fine. I've only been here in Milwaukee for a year and I've been undercover almost the entire time. I had a six-month assignment in narcotics before this current job. You would have loved me on that one. I had hair down to my shoulders and a full beard. I was pretty scruffy and looked a lot different. Most of the guys in my own district don't know me, much less Duncan's cronies."

With that potential obstacle eliminated, we headed inside. After fielding greetings from my staff and a few customers on the main floor, the two of us headed upstairs to my apartment. I took the envelope out of my purse and laid it on top of the dining room table. Then I took out my cell phone and called Duncan.

He answered after only one ring. "Hey, Mack, how did it go?"

"It went as well as can be expected, I guess." I gave him a brief—and sterile—summary of our trip to the zoo and how we had finally ended up getting the next envelope.

"Did you open it?" Duncan asked.

"No, I thought you might want to do that."

"Is Mal still with you?"

"He is."

"Are the two of you alone?"

"We are," I said, and for some reason, I felt myself start to blush.

"Put me on speaker then."

I did so and set my phone down on top of the dining room table, a ways away from the envelope.

"Hey, Mal," Duncan said.

"Hi, Duncan."

"Any insight you can give me on this thing?"

"Not really. It sounds like whoever is sending this stuff has all the bases covered. Mack said you already looked at the envelopes and letters. Find anything?"

"I found a bunch of prints on the courier envelope. We didn't get any hits in AFIS, but I'm betting they belong to the delivery guy and other employees from the company. The envelope from the first letter had a bunch of prints and partials, too, but since it came via the mail, I'm sure it was handled by any number of people. The inside envelope from the second letter had two sets of prints on it—Mack's and the guy from the art store. When we got to the actual letters, the first one had Mack's prints on it, but the second one didn't have any."

"It sounds like we're dealing with a smart guy here. But even the smart ones trip up eventually. What do you want us to do with this envelope? I can bring it to you if you like."

"Not until I open it," I said quickly. "I need to see what it says."

There was a moment of silence while I waited for either man to say something. It was Duncan who went first. "Do you remember how I handled the last one?" he asked.

"I do," I said. "Plain piece of paper beneath it, open it slowly and carefully, and wear gloves of course."

"You got it," Duncan said. "And get some baggies from your kitchen to put stuff in when you're done."

"I already have them here on the table from last time."

"You're in your apartment?"

"Yes. Why?"

"No reason," Duncan said, but even over the phone's speaker I sensed he was lying. "I had pictured you in your office, is all. Go ahead when you're ready."

I put on some gloves, and then went into my father's office to fetch a sheet of clean white paper from the printer. I set it on the dining room table and then used a clean steak knife to carefully slice the envelope open. Holding the envelope over the paper, I removed the folded letter. I peeked inside the envelope for anything else and turned it upside down, shaking it just to be sure. Nothing came out, so I switched my attention to the letter.

Like the others, it was folded in thirds. I carefully unfolded it and stared at the page.

It was blank.

Chapter 11

"There's nothing," I said, my disappointment— and a tinge of fear—clear in my voice. "Wait, there is something." In the bottom right corner printed in very small letters was a date and time: Tuesday, December 15, 5:00 P.M. I showed it to Mal and then told Duncan what it said.

"No trace this time?" Duncan asked.

"No anything," I told him. "Just a folded sheet of paper that's completely blank except for that deadline."

Several seconds of silence ticked by as the three of us contemplated the meaning of the essentially blank page.

"Wait a minute . . ." I said, staring at the sheet and sorting through my senses. "There's something off about the paper. The color and texture are both wrong. And there's a smell, an odd out-of-place smell. I think the paper was soaked in something because it looks slightly rippled, as if it might have been wet at one time."

Mal looked at the paper, then at me. I held the paper close to my nose and inhaled. I heard faint strains of classical string music and knew what the odor was—or rather what the odors were, because there were two of them. The music I heard was a mix of high-pitched violin and the deep base sounds of a cello.

"It's champagne . . . and beer," I said. "This paper has been soaked in champagne and beer."

"Are you sure?" Duncan said. Then, without waiting for me to answer, he added, "What the hell is that supposed to mean?"

Mal, who had also gloved up, reached over, took the paper from me, and repeated my actions by holding it under his own nose.

"I don't know what it means," I said, watching as Mal sniffed, shrugged, and then shook his head. He handed the sheet back to me, eyeing me with a curious expression.

My body felt as if it was vibrating all over, a common thing that happens when I'm frightened. "I'm certain of the beer and champagne thing, but I don't have any idea what it means. With no other clues, how am I supposed to figure this out?" I said to no one in particular, feeling panicky. "This is getting out of hand."

"Take a deep breath," Duncan said. "Let's give it some thought and regroup on it in the morning."

I didn't want to wait until morning. Lives literally hung in the balance. But at the moment I didn't have any choice. "I have to tell you, this whole thing has me more than a little spooked," I said. "Everywhere I go, everything I do, I can't help but wonder if this sicko is somewhere nearby, watching me." I could feel the panic growing inside me and heard it in my voice. Normally, my own voice has no taste for me, but when I experience strong emotions, it sometimes does. The taste it had now, the taste of panic and fear, was cold and bitter, like sucking on a Popsicle made from unsweetened chocolate.

"This whole thing *is* twisted," Mal said, placing a reassuring hand on my arm. "But don't let it get the better of you. We need to keep our heads on straight to make sure we're thinking clearly. It appears that whoever is behind this wants to play a mental game, so we have to stay mentally tough." He paused, frowned, and then added, "Though to be on the safe side, I don't think you should be staying here alone at night."

Duncan agreed. "Mal is right, Mack. You should have someone there with you, just in case. I don't think this psycho is trying to come after you in any physical sense, at least not yet, but we can't be sure." My heart leapt with anticipation, thinking Duncan intended to come and spend the night with me, but his next words were a cold shock of reality. "I wish I could be there with you tonight, Mack," he said. "But this case Jimmy and I are working on is sucking up every spare minute I have."

"That's okay," I said, feeling my heart sink. "I'm always careful to make sure I lock everything up tight at night. I'll be okay."

"Even so, I'd feel better if there was someone there with you," Duncan insisted. "Mal, is there any chance you can stay there for a night or two and keep an eye on her?"

Mal and I glanced at one another but he quickly looked away. "I don't see why not," he said with a shrug. "After all, we *are* supposed to be dating."

I didn't know how to feel about this latest development. On the one hand, I was relieved to have someone stay with me, though I was disappointed it wasn't going to be Duncan. On the other hand, I was happy to have Mal there, and I felt comfortable with the idea for the most part, though after our earlier discussion, I feared things might get awkward.

I finally decided to just go with the flow, though I felt a need to clarify things up front. "Thanks, Mal. You can sleep in my dad's bedroom if you want."

"I'll be fine on the couch," he said. "It's a more central location."

"Suit yourself," I said.

Duncan thanked Mal and then I picked up my phone, took it off speaker, and meandered into my kitchen for some privacy. "It's just you and me now," I said to Duncan. "Am I ever going to get to see you again?"

I heard him sigh and it saddened me. "Of course you will," he said. "I'm just not sure when. Between this case I'm working and the need to be so secretive . . ."

"It isn't always going to be like this though, right?"

"Man, I hope not. But in the meantime, watch your back, even with the people you think you can trust. And that reminds me, have you made any progress with Tiny's sister's case?"

"A little." I told him about the discussion we'd had earlier and how Carter was going to try to get a copy of Anna Hermann's diary. "I'm thinking I might go and talk to some of the suspects, just to get a feel for what they have to say, to determine if I think they're telling the truth, and to see if anything unusual jumps out at me. Though given the time span since the crime, I don't know if my synesthesia will be of much use other than to get a feel for whether or not someone is lying."

"Mack, you can't just go around and start chatting up people who might have committed a murder—make that two murders—in the past. Who knows what they've done since then and who knows what they're capable of doing now if they feel like someone is breathing down their neck? Don't you have enough stress right now with this psycho letter writer?"

"Yes, I do have stress," I said, my tone a bit more irritable than I intended. I was angry, not with Duncan per se, but with the way our relationship seemed to be evolving . . . or devolving. "That's why I need something else to focus on. Plus, I can't help but empathize with Tiny and his situation. I know what it feels like to lose someone you love to murder, and to wonder if the culprit will ever be caught. I feel compelled to help him if I can."

"It's not your job, Mack."

"You didn't feel that way when I was helping you. Then you were all about making it my job."

"That was different. You had police protection and processes working with you. Doing this alone isn't the same."

"Then I won't do it alone. I'll take Tiny along with me. Or maybe Mal. And if neither of them can come along, I'll take Gary. Now that he's back at work, I can make good use of him as a bodyguard."

"I really wish you wouldn't do this, Mack, not without me."

"Yeah, well, you're not here, are you? And the fact that I even want to do it is largely your fault."

"My fault? How do you figure?"

"You're the one who got me started on this

crime-solving stuff. You're the one who showed me that I can make a difference. You're the one who made me see that something I once thought was a curse could be put to use to help other people."

I heard him sigh again, and could see him in my mind's eye, running his hand through his hair the way he did whenever he got exasperated. He muttered something that sounded like "Frigging hot-tempered redheads," though I couldn't be sure. Then he said, "Okay, I know when I'm beat. And I know you well enough to know that when you're this determined about something, you're going to do what you want regardless of what I say. So all I'm going to ask is that you be careful and use good sense."

"I will."

"I want you to keep me abreast of what's going on. Call me every day."

"Is there a time that's best?"

"Just call me when you can. Any time will do. And please be careful, Mack. I don't want anything to happen to you."

"I will."

"Promise?"

"I promise."

"I need to get back to work, so I'll say good-bye for now. But if anything else comes up today, tonight, tomorrow, whenever, you call me."

"I said I will."

With that I ended the call. I felt annoyed and irritated, and I wasn't sure why. Duncan's statement that he didn't want anything to happen to me might have been his way of saying he cared, but on what level? It was hardly a declaration of love—not that we were at that stage in our relationship yet—

and that wasn't what I was after. I felt a very strong attraction to the man, and as such I wanted to know if we had a potential future together as a couple. Was he romantically interested in me over the long term, or had he been stringing me along so he could use me and my synesthesia to help him in his job?

Then I recalled what both Duncan and Mal had said about Duncan being left at the altar in his last relationship. Certainly that had to have been a crushing blow, not to mention humiliating. Given that, I supposed it made sense that he was being slow and cautious now. But it did give me pause. Was I simply a rebound relationship, someone he could use to bide his time until he recovered from his last one?

Agonizing over it was making me crazy, so I shoved my thoughts to the back of my mind and returned to Mal. "Thanks for offering to stay with me."

"My pleasure. My place is pretty lonely and, to be honest, it's also kind of a dump. So this is a move up in the world for me."

"Do you need to go to your place to get some extra clothes and stuff?"

Mal shook his head. "I always keep an overnight bag in my trunk that has some basic toiletries in it along with a couple of changes of clothes."

"Duncan does that, too," I said. "Must be a cop thing."

"It is. You never know in this business when you're going to be up all night on a stakeout or something."

"Okay, then," I said, seeing that he had bagged the latest letter and envelope. "I was planning on checking in with the Capone Club to see what's new with Tiny's case. Want to come along?"

"I'd love to. But only if you promise to treat me to one of those cheese curds you were bragging about."

"I'll fix you up something special," I said. "Cheese curds and one of my famous BLT sandwiches. If that combo doesn't satisfy your appetite and harden your arteries, nothing will."

"Hell, we only live once," he said. With that, he crooked one arm and waved the other toward the stairs. "Shall we?"

I took his proffered arm and let him lead the way.

Chapter 12

We stopped at the bar to order our food and get some drinks to take with us. Mal told me to surprise him with the drinks, so I whipped us up a couple of cocktails my father called a Frustration. It seemed appropriate, given the way things were going, and my father said it was one of those drinks that would make all your frustrations disappear.

As I was mixing up our concoctions, Debra came over to talk to us. "How was your afternoon at the zoo?"

"It was nice," I said. "The weather cooperated and the trip brought back a lot of fond memories."

Mal excused himself to hit up the men's room and, as soon as he was gone, Debra leaned into me and her questions turned interrogative. "So, how's it going with Mal? I have to give Cora credit. He's pretty hot, don't you think? And he seems to really like you. Do you like him? Have you kissed him yet?"

Debra's voice was low, but not low enough that Billy didn't hear. He smiled and shook his head.

"It's going fine," I said. "Slow but steady, and yes, yes, and yes."

"I'm happy for you, Mack," Debra said. "I thought you and Duncan were going to work out, but if not, I'm glad you found someone else."

"Thanks," I said, wondering if Duncan and I ever were going to work out.

Mal returned, and as soon as Billy handed us our drinks, we headed upstairs to the Capone Club room. The group had changed some since our last visit. Carter and Holly, his girlfriend, were gone, as was Tad. And both of the Signoriello brothers were gone as well. Alicia was in the bar, but she was downstairs hanging around Billy as usual. There were two additions to the group: Nick and Tyrese, both of whom were local cops from Duncan's district.

"Welcome back, you two," Cora said as Mal and I walked in.

"Thanks." I greeted Tyrese and Nick and then introduced them to Mal, watching closely for any signs of recognition. If they knew him, they didn't let on.

"What have you two been up to?" Nick asked. Though his question sounded innocent and friendly on the surface, I sensed, and tasted, an undercurrent of something in his voice. During one of the cases I'd worked with Duncan a few weeks ago, Nick had hinted that he was interested in dating me, and I wondered if that might be the cause. Or maybe he thought I was two-timing Duncan.

"We went to the zoo," I said. "It's something I've wanted to do for a while now and given what an unusually nice day it was weatherwise, Mal and I decided to make an afternoon of it."

I saw a frown flit across Nick's face, but it was there and gone in a flash. I made a mental note to take him aside later and talk to him about it.

Cora said, "We have some exciting updates on Tiny's case to report."

"Fill us in," I said, settling into one of the empty chairs. Mal took the one next to me.

"Carter just called me," Cora continued. "He and Holly went to talk to Anna Hermann's parents. They gave them that spiel we cooked up about him working on a true crime story highlighting Lori and Anna's case, and they agreed to let him copy Anna's diary. I also found out where Anna's brother, Erik, is living and got some updates on his status. He's married now, has a degree in chemistry, and he's teaching at UW Milwaukee." Cora handed me a piece of paper with two addresses written on it. "That first address is his residence, and the second is his office on campus."

"That's great," I said. "I'll see if I can go and talk to him either tomorrow or Monday. Maybe Carter can come with me and we can continue with the pretense of the book thing."

Cora then handed me another piece of paper. "This one is the address of William Schneider, the so-called strange neighbor who lived in Lori's neighborhood. He still lives there, in the same house."

"I'll add him to my itinerary," I said, hoping I'd be able to do it all. Depending on whether or not we were able to interpret the latest letter, my time might be otherwise occupied. I looked around at the faces in the room. If I didn't figure out this last letter, one of them might turn up dead. I felt the panic start to build again and forced it deep down inside me somewhere, mentally locking it away.

"Maybe you should let the cops do what they do," Mal said. "Something like this is their territory. They have cold case squads, don't they?"

"Ya," Tiny said. "But dey told me dey don't have any new leads in my sister's case so dey aren't working it."

Mal frowned. "But if the cops don't have any leads, what do all of you hope to accomplish? Certainly their resources are better than yours." I began to wonder if he and Duncan were in cahoots together on this matter.

Cora said, "We have a few tricks up our sleeves. I can access information with my computer that isn't strictly legal. And then we have Mack here, and her special powers."

"Special powers?" Mal said, looking at me and arching his brows.

"You didn't tell him?" Cora said.

"I told him," I said, "though I didn't go into a lot of detail."

"Are you referring to this disorder you have?" Mal asked.

"More of a gift than a disorder," Cora countered. "She can sniff out stuff ordinary people, including the cops, can't. And I mean that both figuratively and literally."

Dr. T, who up until now had remained quiet, said, "Mack does have a rather unique ability with her synesthesia. I've done a little research on it and while her case is a rather extreme one, it's a legitimate disorder. Mack's senses are not only cross-wired—a typical finding among synesthetes—they are also extrasensitive. She is able to pick up on things normal humans can't." She shot me a look then and added, "Sorry, I don't mean to imply that you're abnormal, but you are kind of unique."

"No offense taken," I said. "But Mal does raise a valid point. My abilities are very time sensitive. I may be able to pick up on something that was moved within the last hour, or the remnants of a smell from something that was here within the last day or so, but we're talking about a twelve-year-old murder case here. I don't know how useful my senses are going to be in that situation."

"Yeah, but you can do your lie detector t'ing," Tiny said.

"Lie detector thing?" Mal echoed, giving me a questioning look.

"Yeah, I can often tell when someone is lying about something because I can pick up on subtle changes in their voice."

"Good to know," Mal said, looking a little wary. Considering that he and I had already had this discussion a short time ago, I had to admire his acting skill. "But I'm still concerned about you messing with potential murderers. I mean, this crime-solving stuff you guys do here is interesting and fun when you're sitting in this cozy room and doing it from a safe distance, but going out and stirring up an old case that's never been solved could be dangerous. At the very least, you should have someone go with you."

"You're welcome to come along," I said.

"You should have a cop go with you," Nick said. "Both to protect yourself and any evidence you might dig up."

I was a millisecond away from slipping and saying that Mal *was* a cop when Mal saved me. "Nick is right," he said. "I don't mind coming along with you when I can, but I won't always be able to do it because I've got to work during the week. So you should probably take Nick or Tyrese along with you."

"What about Duncan?" Nick asked.

"What about him?" I countered.

"Why wouldn't you take him with you?"

"Things are a bit strained between us right now, both personally and, for him, professionally."

Tyrese gave Nick an elbow in the ribs and said, "Dude, you know what the chief said about Duncan using Mack and what he called her voodoo magic. Hell, the guy nearly lost his job over it."

"That's true," I said. "And I don't want to put either of you in the same position, so maybe it's better if you don't come with me."

Tyrese considered this a moment, shrugged, and then said to me, "What we choose to do on our off hours is our own business. We're allowed to look into cold cases on our own time so if you turn up something useful, we can find a way to make it look like we dug it up ourselves so your involvement won't be known. Mal is right; you really shouldn't be doing this alone, Mack. I'm willing to help you out during my off hours."

I looked at the papers Cora had given me with the addresses on them, and thought about the latest letter. I had no idea what the letter meant and didn't think sitting around agonizing over it would help. Sometimes doing something else and letting my subconscious figure out a problem works best. So I might as well spend Sunday following up on Tiny's case. "Okay," I said to the three men who seemed determined to help me. "Who's free tomorrow?"

Nick frowned and said, "I'm off work but tomorrow is my sister's birthday and I promised I'd come by her place for lunch."

Tyrese said, "I'm free."

"As am I," Mal added.

"So which one should we tackle first?" I asked. "Maybe we should go up to Waupun and pay a visit to Lonnie Carlisle."

"I can arrange that," Tyrese offered. "I can tell the prison officials that I want to talk to him regarding a case we're investigating. Essentially, that's the truth."

I considered this, and nodded. "See if you can set something up for tomorrow. Shoot for a time around one in the afternoon." Then I turned and looked at Mal. "Would you be willing to come with me to talk to Erik Hermann in the morning?"

"Absolutely," Mal said. "What time?"

"Let's do it around ten. That should give us enough time to talk to him and still drive up to Waupun and get there around one."

"Sounds like a plan," Mal said. "Can I come along for the Waupun trip, too?"

I looked at Tyrese and he shrugged his indifference. "Sure," I said. Once again Nick frowned.

Cora reached over and set a hand on Tyrese's arm. "Can you guys tell us anything about Lewis?"

Now it was Tyrese's turn to frown. Nick shook his head and said, "It's an ongoing investigation and we can't tell you anything more than what you'll hear on the news. Though many of you should expect to be questioned at some point since you knew him." Tyrese got up from his chair and grabbed his coat. "It was a crappy thing that happened to him," he said, looking around the room. "I know it's going to be hard on all of you."

"You don't think his death had anything to do with the group, do you?" Sam asked.

"I highly doubt it. It looks to be an isolated thing as far as I know. I'm not directly involved with the case, but I can't imagine anyone trying to pick off you guys simply because you spend time trying to solve crimes." Tyrese chuffed a laugh at the apparent absurdity of the idea, but in the next second his expression turned grim. "Look, I know you guys are going to want to look into Lewis's death to see if you can figure out what happened and who did it. But I'm going to urge you to stay out of it for now. If you start mucking around with the case by tipping off witnesses or messing with evidence, you might screw up the official investigation." This was met with mixed emotions judging from the expressions in the room. There was some agreement, some consternation, and Dr. T looked downright rebellious.

Tyrese turned his attention to me. "I'm going to head home now, but I'll give the prison a call and set things up for around one tomorrow. It's a little over an hour drive, give it an hour and a half. Should I plan to pick you and Mal up here around eleven-thirty?"

I looked over at Mal, who nodded. "That will be great, Tyrese," I said. "Thanks."

As Tyrese was leaving, Carter and Holly came walking in. Carter was sporting a huge grin and carrying a large manila envelope.

"I got Anna's diary," he said, holding up the envelope.

"Fantastic!" I said. "Have you had a chance to read it yet?"

Carter shook his head. "We've been busy copying it and returning the original to her family."

Cora asked, "Did you talk to Anna's parents about the case?"

"Some," Carter said. "We spent about an hour with them. They're still pretty raw on the subject, which I guess is to be expected."

"Ya," Tiny said, "da pain never really goes away."

"They did put one caveat on letting me have the diary to copy," Carter said. "They made me promise I wouldn't shed their son, Erik, in a bad light in the book."

"Well, since you aren't actually writing a book, that shouldn't be a problem," Sam said.

Carter flashed a guilty smile. "Except I'm thinking I might actually do it. I haven't had much luck with my fiction, so maybe it's not a bad idea to switch to true crime. It's a hot selling genre, and with the help of all of you I should be able to investigate any number of cases, both current and cold."

There was silence and another mix of expressions as the group contemplated this. I had mixed feelings myself. And I couldn't help but wonder how Tiny would feel about having his sister's brutal murder highlighted in a book that might sell on a national level. I looked over at him, expecting to see doubt or concern on his face, but instead he looked pleased with the news.

"What if Erik Hermann turns out to be the

killer?" I asked Carter. "What are you going to do then?"

Carter shrugged. "I'll cross that bridge if and when I get to it." He focused on Nick. "Any news about Lewis's case?"

The next few minutes were spent filling Carter and Holly in on the information and cautions Tyrese had delivered to the rest of us moments before. Carter looked disappointed but resigned, at least for now. Holly simply appeared sad.

Tiny seized the moment by gesturing toward a couple of empty chairs beside him. "Okay den," he said. "Let's have a look at dis diary."

Carter and Holly settled into the empty seats and Carter opened the envelope he had and took out a thick sheaf of papers. He divvied them up amongst all of us, handing each person two or three sheets.

Over the next hour or so we read all of the private, intimate details of Anna Hermann's life. Her writing was flowery and the early pages were a bit immature—understandable, given that she started the diary when she was just shy of twelve—but the words revealed a bright, optimistic personality, an above-average intelligence, and a good amount of social savviness. We skimmed through the first year and a half, where the entries were typical for a young girl. A few of the items were so personal and private they made us squirm: Anna's detailing of her first menstruation, the delight and anguish she felt over wearing her first bra, the excitement of her first kiss. But the vast majority of the entries were Anna's surprisingly astute and often humorous thoughts and analyses of the actions, behaviors, and motives she observed amongst her peers,

all of whom other than Lori were referred to by
initials rather than names. The girl had a wry and
critical eye when it came to understanding how
the various cliques, social mores, and peer pres-
sures impacted her life and that of her friends.
In general, her comments were merely observa-
tory, though the girl definitely had a flair for the
narrative. As I read through my portion of the
diary entries, I became convinced that Anna had
been a very old soul inside a young body.

Tiny's sister, Lori, featured prominently in the
diary, particularly in the last year of the writings.
The two girls had obviously been close, tight friends
who spent a lot of time together and shared many
of their innermost secrets. Through Anna's eyes
and words we experienced Lori's first crush and
first kiss with a boy named Brandon Schumacher.
There were a number of other crushes that followed for both girls, but no more kisses appeared in
the diary. It was hard to know if that was because
they didn't happen, or because Anna didn't want to
commit them to the page.

In the last entries, written during the month or
so before the girls were killed, Anna wrote about
her brother's interest in Lori. According to Anna,
Erik spent six months wooing and flirting with
Lori, determined to win her heart. But Lori kept
insisting that the only feelings she had for him
were brotherly in nature and not romantic.

At one point, Anna wrote that her brother's interest in Lori *borders on the obsessive,* and described
how he constantly questioned Anna about Lori's
activities—where she went, what she did, who she
saw—and often spied on the two girls.

Anna mentioned how two girls with the initials

D and B had harassed Lori, calling her names, spreading rumors about her, and leaving nasty notes on her locker, because D had a crush on Erik and was jealous of the attention he paid to Lori. It was classic, schoolgirl stuff, peppered with the high emotions and angst so common to teenaged girls.

In the very last entry in the diary, made the day before the girls disappeared, Anna made mention of the fight between Erik and Lori:

> *I think my brother finally got the message from Lori that their relationship is a friends-only kind of thing. Lori told me he tried to kiss her and stick his hand up her shirt! She rewarded his efforts with a slap to his face. I could still see the red outline from Lori's hand on my brother's cheek when he came home. He looked pretty po'd.*

Based on what Anna wrote, it wasn't hard to see how Erik had become a suspect, but while it was possible to imagine him killing Lori in some failed attempt to seduce her, it was much harder to imagine him killing his little sister. Still, he seemed like a good place to start in the morning, if for no other reason than to get some insight into Anna's life in the days before the murders.

We chatted on for another hour or so about Anna's diary, offering up theories about what might have happened to the two girls. We quizzed Tiny on what he knew about Lori's activities during the days before and the day of the disappearance, but he didn't have much to offer. He knew the girls were supposed to meet up midday to go for a bike ride on the day they disappeared, but other than that, he didn't know much because he was already out on his own at that point, living in an apartment and working during the day. He apologized for not knowing more, stating that because of a ten-year spread in their ages he wasn't always up on his sister's day-to-day life at that point in time.

"All I know is what my parents were told," he explained. "Da cops said dat da girls must have met up in dere secret spot in the park near the Little Menomonee River." Everyone nodded. Anna had mentioned this secret spot in her diary, describing it in vague terms that mentioned a tree and a place where they would sit and talk about school, life, boys, and such. It was where the girls' bodies had been found and if anyone had known where it was, they might have been found sooner.

Throughout our discussion, the letter in my apartment kept intruding into my thoughts, making it hard for me to stay focused. I kept trying to shake it off, hoping I'd be able to put it aside long enough to give Tiny and his sister the attention they deserved. But it wasn't easy. And with every minute that ticked by, I found myself wondering who would be the next person to die.

Chapter 13

As predicted, a couple of detectives showed up around seven-thirty asking to talk with me, my staff, and any customers who knew Lewis. I met them downstairs and talked to them at the bar, making no effort to hide my conversation. I was worried that the letter writer might jump to some wrong conclusions if I was seen talking to the cops and I wanted to make sure everything I did and said with them was up-front and public. I told them what I knew about Lewis, most of which was limited to what he liked to drink, how often he came into the bar, and his involvement with the Capone Club, including the names of other customers he'd had dealings with. It didn't take long—maybe fifteen minutes total—and when they finished with me I told them to feel free to talk to any of my staff as well as the Capone Club members. I instructed both Gary and Billy to help them out as much as possible.

With that out of the way, and knowing that the Capone Club group would be tied up for a while with the cops, I treated Mal to dinner from the bar.

We ate upstairs in the privacy of my apartment, and throughout the meal we discussed and dissected the various suspects in the Gruber-Hermann case. When we were done, Mal headed downstairs and took a turn in my bar kitchen to whip up some homemade strawberry shortcake for dessert, which we shared with the staff. When closing time came around, I helped my staff with the cleanup and closure duties while Mal sat at the bar enjoying a nightcap. Debra kept giving me what I referred to as her wiggle-eyes, letting me know that she was excited for me and Mal. Once the last employee had left for the night, I checked my cell phone, wondering if I had somehow missed a call from Duncan, but there wasn't one.

Mal and I headed upstairs to my apartment and I showed him my Dad's bedroom. "You're more than welcome to sleep in here. I'm sure it will be more comfortable than the couch, and more private, too."

"Thanks, but I don't want to intrude on your father's space. And I'm used to falling asleep with the TV on. Will it bother you if I sleep on the couch and leave the TV on with the volume on low?"

"Not at all. To be honest, my sleep is often noisy anyway because of my synesthesia."

He cocked his head and gave me a curious look. "Interesting," he said. "Your world must be a very colorful one."

"Most of the time it is, though I do have some experiences that are literally black and white."

I grabbed some sheets and blankets from the linen closet and made up the couch for him. But the only extra pillows I had were from my father's bed. When I went back into the bedroom and grabbed one of them, a faint smell wafted up to me, triggering a sensation that felt like a cozy blanket snugged around my shoulders. It overwhelmed me with a flood of unexpected emotion. I knew that sensation well; it was one I used to feel often when my father and I shared a special moment. It was triggered by his smell, a combination of the Old Spice aftershave he always used and the lingering citrus aroma that never seemed to leave his hands because of all the limes, lemons, and oranges he sliced up for drink garnishes. Tears burned at my eyes and my chest felt hollow and cold.

I didn't realize how long I was standing there until a shadow fell over the light coming in through the door to the room. It was Mal.

"Mack, are you all right?"

I nodded, my throat too tight with emotion to speak, the pillow clutched to my chest just beneath my chin.

Mal walked up to me, his eyes and expression sympathetic. "Memory slam?" he said, his voice soft.

I nodded. "I caught a whiff of him when I picked up the pillow."

"Smells are the hardest," he said in a wistful tone that told me he knew what I was feeling.

"You've lost someone close to you, too, haven't you?"

He nodded, a grim expression on his face. "I had a brother named Asher who died when he was eight and I was ten. I tried to save him and couldn't. I watched him die."

He dropped onto the edge of my father's bed

and I sat next to him, momentarily forgetting my own pain when I saw his in his eyes. "Tell me," I said. And he did.

"We were on vacation in northern California," he began, and I could tell from the faraway look in his eyes that he had mentally transported himself back in time. "My father has relatives who live in Big Sur, which is right along the coast, and on the day in question we went to the beach for a picnic. The coastline there is rocky with cliffs that jut out into the water and lots of hidden nooks and beaches. Asher and I loved to climb the rocks along the shore looking for fossils, driftwood, and tiny pools of stranded sea life. Our parents made it clear that we weren't allowed to go into the water because the area was known for having some fierce, unpredictable riptides and currents. Though we thought they were overreacting in typical parent fashion, we had always heeded their warning. But on this particular day, as we scrambled over some boulders at the end of a rocky outcropping that put us out of view of our parents, we came upon a small cove. And in the middle of that cove was a sea lion. It was a small one, a pup, and it appeared to be in distress. We waded into the water, at first only going in as far as our knees, and the creature swam closer to us, or rather it tried to. It couldn't swim very well and, as it drew near, we saw why. One of its flippers had a big chunk missing from it, either from a boat propeller, or maybe an orca. It looked at us with those dark, soulful eyes and let out an odd noise that sounded like a whimper or a baby's cry.

"I remember Asher saying, 'He's hurt. We need

to help him,' and at the time it seemed like the obvious, logical thing to do. I did think about our parents' warning, but I figured as long as we were standing in water that wasn't over our heads and not swimming where it was deeper, we'd be okay. The two of us slowly waded out into the water, moving a little closer to the injured animal with each step, and talking to it in an effort to reassure it. It was wary of us, but either the deeper waters scared it more than we did, or it started to trust us, because it kept doing that awkward wobbly swim in a circle that brought him a little closer to us with each lap. We were probably eight feet away when Asher just vanished. One minute he was standing right beside me and the next he was gone. I later found out that he had stepped into a hole created by the swirl of a rip current and by the time he surfaced again, he was ten feet past the sea lion, and moving out toward the open water. He hollered for help and I could see that he was floundering so I yelled to him to hang on and started swimming toward him as fast as I could. We were both strong swimmers, but no matter how fast I went, I couldn't close the gap. The current was dragging him out at a frighteningly rapid rate. He was trying desperately to swim toward me and the shore, but fighting that current exhausted him within minutes. Four times I saw him go under, though I wasn't sure if it was an intentional act on his part to try to swim out of the current, or if he was going under due to exhaustion. The fifth time he went under, he never came back up."

The rate of his breathing had increased as he told the story until he was practically hyperventilating.

I sat, mesmerized and horrified by his tale, my heart aching for him, knowing how the incident must have tormented him then, and likely still did. I put my father's pillow aside and reached over to lay my hand on top of his. My touch made him jerk, and when he looked at me I saw tears had welled in his eyes.

"I can still see that look on his face," Mal said, his voice cracking. "That primal fear and dread. I was his big brother and I was supposed to protect him, but I didn't. I couldn't."

"God, Mal, I'm so sorry you had to go through that. I can't imagine . . ." I left it at that, truly unable to imagine the depth of his pain and anguish. He began to sob, softly at first, then hard, heaving sobs. I could tell there were years of pent-up emotion behind those tears, emotions that needed to be let out. I put my arms around his shoulders and just held him.

I'm not sure how what happened next transpired; when I try to remember, all I can recall is a blur of emotions, colors, tastes, and sensations. At some point, I realized Mal was kissing me. I liked it, and I kissed him back. One of his arms snaked around my waist and I could feel the heat building between us. Then Duncan popped into my thoughts like a jack-in-the-box, and it made me pull away.

"I'm sorry, Mack," Mal said immediately. "I didn't mean to . . . you made it clear . . . Hell, I'm sorry." He raked a hand through his hair. The heaving, gut-wrenching sobs were gone, but I could still see the fresh, wet tracks of tears on his face. I could taste those tears, and I wasn't sure if the taste was real or synesthetic.

"It's okay," I whispered, laying a hand on his. "You hurt and you reached out. Sometimes we just need a warm body, someone who understands, to comfort us."

I felt him shudder and then his sobs returned, quieter, less desperate, but still oozing with pain. I scooted closer to him and held him as he cried, gently rocking side to side. At some point we lay down on the bed. Neither of us removed our clothes, neither of us got under the covers. There was nothing overtly sexual about the situation at that point, and we stayed that way, spooned together, until we both fell asleep.

I awoke and found myself turned on my side facing a window that allowed bright sunlight to stream in and hit my eyes. It triggered a sensation like fingers walking gently over my face and slowly nudged me from my sleep. I glanced around, mildly confused as to where I was because I briefly saw an image of a large metal door, like on a vault, and beyond that a cozy room filled with warm light and a big overstuffed couch. The vault room image wavered slightly, telling me it was a synesthetic response, and I blinked it away. When I focused again, I recognized my father's bedroom, and it took me a second or two to remember how I'd ended up there. Slowly, the events of the night before came back to me. Behind me in the bed, I heard Mal's rhythmic, soft breathing and knew he was still asleep. The vault room image kept intruding, but it was gauzy and ephemeral, allowing me to see beyond it. I gently picked up the arm Mal had draped over my waist and eased it down onto the mattress between us. As soon as I did this, the vault room disappeared. I slid quietly out of bed and left the room.

It was just past eight-thirty in the morning, meaning we had slept only about five hours. Yet I felt oddly refreshed and energized. Perhaps the emotional purging had something to do with it. *Or perhaps Mal had something to do with it,* an inner voice said. I ignored it, locked the thought away, and busied myself making coffee and breakfast. After starting the coffee, I checked my cell phone and plugged it in to charge it up. That's when I saw that Duncan had called at a little after three-thirty in the morning, right around the time Mal and I were cuddling on my father's bed. I felt a surge of guilt and quickly pushed it aside. I messaged Duncan with an apology for missing his call, excusing myself with a simple I was tired, and a request to call me when he could, preferably before ten.

With that out of the way, I went back to fixing breakfast. Mal appeared, all sleepy-eyed, bed-headed, and boyish-looking, some twenty minutes later.

"Good morning," I said. "I hope you like eggs and bacon."

"I love anything someone else cooks for me," he said with a smile.

"Help yourself to the coffee. The mugs are in the cabinet above the coffeemaker."

For the next half hour, we ate, drank, and chatted about the weather, the upcoming Christmas holiday, and about our plans for the day, beginning with our visit to Erik Hermann's house. No mention of last night was made by either of us. After breakfast, I told Mal he could use the shower in the small bathroom off my father's room while I used the main bathroom. By nine-thirty, the two of us were clean, fed, and ready to roll.

I grabbed my cell phone and saw that Duncan had called while I was in the shower. I checked for a message, but there wasn't one. I cursed his timing and shoved the phone into my pocket, planning to call him back as soon as we were under way.

It was Sunday and the bar wouldn't open until five, so the downstairs was deserted when we left. Once again Mal wanted to drive, and as soon as we were settled in his car I called Duncan back.

"Finally," he said when he answered. "I was starting to feel like the grand loser in this game of phone tag."

"Sorry about that," I said. "Bad timing." _Quite the understatement._

"What are you up to?"

I told him that Mal and I were headed for Erik Hermann's house and why, and then I gave him a brief synopsis of what we'd read in Anna's diary. Then I told him how Tyrese was planning to take us to the correctional facility in Waupun so we could talk to Lonnie Carlisle. "After that, if I have enough time, I might try to chat with one of the other suspects this evening, though I'd rather spend the time taking another look at that last letter, to see if anything occurs to me. Did you come up with any ideas about it?"

"I did not."

"I'm scared, Duncan. What if we're missing something crucial? What if it results in someone else ending up dead?"

"It may happen, Mack," Duncan admitted. "But you can't blame yourself if it does. It wouldn't be your fault. It's the fault of this crazed nut-job who's sending the letters."

"That's all fine and good until someone else ends up dead. You know as well as I do that it isn't that easy to separate yourself from the blame." As soon as I was done uttering the words, I realized how relevant they were to what Mal had shared with me last night. I glanced over at him, but he looked focused on his driving, and if what I had said bothered him in any way, I couldn't tell.

"Why don't we get together tonight when you get back from the prison and put our heads together on it again?" Duncan suggested.

"What about the interview with this Apostle Mike guy?"

"I couldn't set it up for today. Right now we don't know where he is. So that will have to wait."

"Do you think you'll be able to get away later?"

"I've been up all night so I'm taking a sleep break at three this afternoon and plan to return to work at ten. How about I spend the last hour or so of my break with you? I miss you, Mack."

Again I glanced at Mal, feeling suddenly awkward about having this private, somewhat intimate exchange with Duncan in his presence. But he still appeared to be focused on his driving. "That would be nice," I said, avoiding a *miss you, too* comeback and wondering why I was reluctant to make the declaration.

"Meet me at the back alley door at eight then."

"Will do. Sweet dreams until then."

"They will be," he said, his voice suddenly softer, deeper, making me taste rich, dark chocolate, "because I'll be dreaming about seeing you."

I felt myself blush as I disconnected the call and kept my face turned toward the side passenger window.

We rode in silence the rest of the way. Mal didn't ask me about Duncan or the call, nor did he try to make any idle conversation. It should have felt awkward, that silence, but it didn't. When we pulled up in front of Erik Hermann's house fifteen minutes later, he parked and the two of us sat staring out the windows, stretching the silence a little longer.

The neighborhood was one of the nicer ones in the city and Erik Hermann's home was a two-story brick colonial with a perfectly manicured and landscaped yard. The other homes in the area were older, but well maintained and large in size. I guessed Hermann's house had to be well over two thousand square feet inside and guessed it and most of the other houses in the neighborhood would list for four hundred grand and up.

"How does a college professor afford a house like this?" I asked, finally breaking the silence.

"You got me," Mal said. "Maybe he married into money."

We got out of the car and as Mal came around to join me he said, "How do you want to do this?"

"I'm betting his mother told him about Carter's visit, so let's tell him we're part of Carter's research team, and we're hoping to add some more detail and color to the dry descriptions and narratives that we found in the police files. We'll see where that takes us and wing it as we go."

Mal smiled at me. "I like a girl who's willing to wing it. Let's fly, Ms. Dalton."

Chapter 14

We got out of the car and walked side by side to the front door. The air was brisk, signaling an end to our brief interlude with the atypically warm weather, and the neighborhood was quiet. Then the silence was broken by church bells ringing out the hour, most likely signaling the start of the morning service. I wondered if Erik was a church-goer, meaning our visit might be a waste of time. Mal and I had discussed calling ahead, but in the end he convinced me that it would be better to make our visits unannounced. It would lead to more spontaneity, he said, and not give anyone time to prepare a story.

We climbed the front steps to the porch and I rang the doorbell. From inside, a woman's voice hollered out, "I'll get it," and we heard footsteps approaching. The locks—at least two dead bolts—were thrown and then the door opened to reveal a young, dark-haired woman who looked to be in her mid- to late twenties. Her hair was pulled back into a ponytail, and her face was bare of makeup. She was dressed in black yoga pants and a T-shirt, and she had a towel draped around her neck. The faint sheen of sweat on her arms and face made it clear what she'd been doing when we rang the bell.

"Can I help you?" she asked, a little breathless. She had a strong, deep voice for a woman with a pleasant cadence. She oozed self-assurance. But oddly, her voice triggered nothing for me . . . no taste, no visual apparitions . . . nothing, and I noticed the void right away. My mind has become so accustomed to the various reactions my synesthesia creates that they become background noise most of the time, like sleeping with a fan on. The sudden lack of that noise is as noticeable as an unexpected loud noise. I wondered if I'd missed it, or if it really was absent. It wasn't like it had never happened before. There had been a handful of other people over the years who had triggered a similar reaction—or lack thereof—but they were rare. It both puzzled and intrigued me.

"I'm sorry if we interrupted your workout session," I said with a smile. "We weren't even sure you'd be home, given that it's Sunday morning. You know, church and all that."

"Oh, we don't belong to a church," the woman said in a friendly tone, making a dismissive motion with her hand. "Are you selling something? Or are you Jehovah's Witnesses?"

"Neither," I explained. "We're here to talk to Erik Hermann about his sister, Anna. Is he here by any chance?"

The woman frowned and shifted her gaze to Mal. "Are you the guy who's writing the book?"

"Sort of," Mal said. "Mackenzie and I are research assistants for the writer, Carter Fitzpatrick.

We help dig up the facts, and he spins them into word magic."

The woman turned her focus back to me, her eyes doing a quick head-to-toe assessment. I felt sized up and judged, and had no idea what the final verdict had been. Her expression at this point was impassive, and it was as if synesthesia was my superpower and this woman was made of kryptonite.

Curious, I shifted my focus from her face to see if anything else about her triggered a synesthetic response. When I stared at her hair I got a faint whiff of fresh cut wood, a smell I'd experienced when looking at other dark-haired people. Then I focused on the sweat beads on her forehead and felt a prickling sensation along my arms, something I typically experienced when looking at sweaty people.

I was distracted then by a male silhouette that appeared behind the woman, backlit by sunlight coming through windows at the rear of the house. He was tall and slender, but I couldn't tell much more than that because the backlighting hid his features.

"Who is it, Marie?" he hollered. His voice was deep and tasted hot and beefy to me, like a sizzling steak. Clearly my synesthesia was still working.

"Are you Erik Hermann?" I said to the silhouette. "We're with Carter Fitzpatrick and we came to talk to you about the deaths of your sister and her friend, Lori Gruber."

"I have no interest in stirring up any of that again," he grumbled.

"Oh, honey," the woman said, pouting prettily and turning back toward the silhouette. "What can it hurt? You've said a hundred times how much it bothers you that Anna's murder was never solved."

Erik Hermann finally moved toward us and I was able to see his face. He had aged some since the photo that was in the files we had. The planes of his face were sharper, and gone were the downy softness and the slightly pudgy cheeks. Like Marie, he appeared fit, and I guessed that the two of them exercised regularly, but Erik's color was pale and a bit sallow, as if he'd been ill recently.

"My mother mentioned something about some guy who wants to write about Anna and Lori," Erik said. "Is that who you're with?"

I thought I caught a whiff of alcohol on his breath and wondered if it was a true smell or a synesthetic reaction. I made a mental note to ask Mal if he picked up on it, too. If it was a true smell, Erik Hermann was hitting the booze early on a Sunday morning, which to me screamed drinking problem at the very least, and more likely alcoholic.

"Yes, the writer's name is Carter Fitzpatrick," I repeated for his benefit, unsure if he had heard what we told Marie. "May we come in and talk with you?"

Marie looked at Erik and said, "At least hear them out, honey. Maybe this time someone will figure out the truth and you'll finally be out from under that shadow you've had trailing behind you all these years. Doesn't Anna deserve every chance at justice we can give her?"

Erik scowled at his wife and then at us. "I remember all too well what it felt like to be railroaded twelve years ago and I have no interest in resurrecting any of that scrutiny or pain. So you can tell your friend that he'll be writing his damned book without any help from me." With that, he retreated back into the house, disappearing down a hallway. A moment later we heard a door slam.

"I'm sorry about that," Marie said, giving us an apologetic smile. "He hasn't been feeling well lately and he's edgier than usual. And the subject of those murders tends to bring out the worst in him." Her smile faded and she shook her head sadly. "I can't say I blame him. They really raked him over the coals."

"Did you know Erik back then?" I asked her.

"Sure. I knew Anna and Lori, too. We all grew up together. It was a horrible thing that happened to them," she said, looking stricken. "And it was doubly hard on Erik because at one point the cops seemed convinced that he killed them." She shook her head in disbelief and exhaled her disgust over the idea with a sardonic *pfft*. "As if he could do something like that to anyone, much less his own sister."

"Are you and Erik married?" I asked, spying the band on Marie's left hand.

She nodded. "We were high school sweethearts and got married a year after graduation. We've worked hard to put all of that anguish behind us, but it's hard to forget, particularly since the killer was never caught. I've seen the way some folks look at Erik, and I can tell they're convinced he's guilty. Resurrecting it all again is going to cause a lot of pain for him, but if it will help exonerate him once and for all it would be worth it. So while I don't think my husband is going to help you, I'm willing to try, though I doubt if I have any useful knowledge about the situation."

"Sometimes the most insignificant facts can be telling if they're looked at the right way," Mal said.

"The right way?" she echoed with a curious smile.

Mal tried to explain. "Having a fresh eye look at things casts them in a different light, particularly if it's someone with an objective point of view. I'm sure there were a lot of people involved in the investigation back then and that it was a very emotional experience for all of them. Maybe all the bits of information were divvied up among them with no one person having all the pieces, or a grasp of the big picture. Or maybe their emotions colored the way they interpreted things. Who knows? By looking at it again, maybe we can happen upon some bit of information that seemed insignificant initially, but could break the case wide open."

Marie considered this for a moment and then shrugged. "I imagine it can't hurt to try," she said. And then she stepped aside and waved us into the house.

I don't know if Mal felt as uncomfortable as I did about entering the house on the heels of Erik's stormy exit moments ago. If he did, it didn't show. I, on the other hand, felt ready to bolt and had to fight hard not to do so.

Erik had disappeared down a hall off to the left of the entryway. I caught a glimpse of the kitchen straight ahead—Sub-Zero fridge, chef style range, and granite counters—and to the right was a combination dining and living room. The dining table was a dark, polished mahogany centered over a thick Persian rug and surrounded by tall-backed, cloth-covered white dining chairs. A small crystal chandelier hung from the ceiling and at the table's center were three crystal candle holders with long white tapers in them. The living room also featured a Persian rug, and it looked cozy and comfy with a large couch and two chairs done in soft, brown leather with nail head trim. A couple of throws and a variety of pillows added a touch of color. On one wall was a large stone fireplace with a huge wood mantel above it. A coffee table between the couch and fireplace was wood painted a sleek, glossy black and on top of it was a large glass vase with two long calla lilies in it. The place looked like something out of a home design magazine. It also looked unlived-in. There were no personal touches like photos anywhere.

Marie gestured toward the couch and told us to have a seat. As I slipped past her I caught a whiff of something with an herbal smell . . . a shampoo perhaps? It triggered a faint fluttering sensation along my arms, as if a dozen butterflies were hovering above them, flapping their wings. Marie sat in one of the chairs, perched on the edge with her hands between her knees.

"Where would you like to begin?" she asked.

"If you don't mind, I'd like to start with the day of the murders and what you know about Lori's and Anna's whereabouts, as well as Erik's."

"I don't know anything about what Lori and Anna did that day except for what I've learned from Erik, the family, the news articles, and the police. From what I heard, the two of them went for a bike ride and never came back. If I remember right, it was a couple of months before they found the bodies. I do know that Erik had nothing to do with what happened to them because I was with him during the time in question."

Her statement puzzled me. "I thought he was riding out in the country with a friend, some boy named Dylan," I said.

"He was . . . well . . . the riding in the country part. But it wasn't with a boy. I'm Dylan."

I must have looked even more confused because then she added, "My first name is Dylan. My parents were big Bob Dylan fans and thought the name was cute and clever, but I never liked it."

"I see," I said. "I assumed Dylan was a guy."

"A common mistake," she said with smile. "That's just one of the reasons I never liked the name. A few of my friends used it back in high school, but these days the only one who uses it is my brother, and he does it solely to torment me." She flashed an amused, slightly put-upon smile that made me suspect she actually liked that her brother did this. "I prefer to go by Marie, which is my middle name."

"So you and Erik were together during the time of the girls' murders?" Mal asked.

She nodded, looking chagrined. "Erik had just turned sixteen and his parents got him a new car. Not really new, of course, it was used, but it was a car and independence and all that other cool stuff teenagers worship. He wanted to show it off to me so he drove me around town at first and eventually we headed out into the country, parked somewhere, and did what kids do." She paused, looking abashed. "We both lied about what we were doing for a long time because we didn't want our parents to know what we were up to. But when the cops started hinting around that Erik might be a suspect, we realized what the repercussions might be if we didn't fess up. So we finally told the truth."

I said, "We heard that Erik liked his sister's friend, Lori Gruber, and that was why he came under suspicion."

Marie's expression turned hurtful. "I don't know where that rumor came from," she said. "I think Lori might have started it herself because she had a crush on him, though she pretended not to."

"If she did, Anna didn't know about it," I said. "At least not according to her diary."

Marie frowned. "You've read Anna's diary?"

I nodded. "Erik's parents were kind enough to let Carter copy it as part of his research for the book. Anna not only said that Erik liked Lori, she wrote about an incident that happened between the two of them. It said something about Erik trying to come on to Lori and she ended up slapping him to make him stop."

"That's not what happened," Marie said with a dismissive *pfft*. "I asked Erik about it and he said that Lori tried to kiss him and he pushed her away and told her he wasn't interested. That made her mad and that's why she slapped him. I don't know if Anna made the story up on her own—she did have a vivid imagination and used to write stories all the time—or if Lori told her it happened the way Anna wrote in the diary."

I frowned, still bothered by the story. "If that was the case, why did Anna write about how smitten her brother was with Lori before the incident? She and Lori seemed to be very good friends and if Lori had a crush on Erik, I think she would have told Anna."

Marie shrugged. "I know that Lori and Anna

were very close," she said, "but I'm sure they kept a few secrets to themselves."

"Perhaps, but I find it odd that she wouldn't tell her best friend that she liked her brother," I persisted.

Marie shrugged again. "Maybe she did and Anna just never wrote about it. I know that she and Erik used to fight a lot back then, and I heard her accuse him once of snooping in her diary. So maybe she didn't write it down because she didn't want to let Lori's secret out of the bag. Or maybe she intentionally wrote down falsehoods to try to goad Erik since she knew he read her diary."

Knowing how unstable the emotions in teenaged girls can be, I imagined anything could have been possible, so I decided to let the matter go.

Mal said, "Just to clarify, can you remember exactly what time it was that you and Erik were out riding around that day?"

"Like it was yesterday," Marie said, gazing off into space. "It's one of those events that's forever stamped in your mind, like where you were and what you were doing when 9-11 happened. It was the last Friday of Christmas break, right before New Year's Day, and everyone was getting geared up for going back to school the following Monday. The weather was strange that year, with unusually warm temps, kind of like what we had yesterday." She refocused on us for a moment. "Seems like we get one of those every few years, doesn't it? Only, that year we had several days of it. All the snow melted and there were even some crocuses trying to come up."

I smiled and nodded, eager for her to continue.

She did so, once again taking on that faraway expression.

"Anyway, on the day the girls went missing, I went jogging early in the morning and when I was finished with my run I went home to shower. My mom was just leaving for work. She's a nurse at the hospital and there was no extended holiday for her—she's lucky if she gets the actual days off. My dad always went in to work early so he was gone already. I told my mom I was going over to my friend Tina's house later that day, but that was a lie." Again she focused on us, flashing a sheepish smile. "Tina and I used to cover for one another all the time and the real plan was for Erik to come by around eleven o'clock to show me his new car."

"How long were you and Erik together that day?" I asked.

Marie frowned. "I'm not sure exactly. I know it was after three when I got home. I had to be back before my mom got home from work at four."

"Where did you go exactly?" I asked, thinking that the driving time might help narrow down the itinerary.

"I don't know, somewhere north of here. I really wasn't paying attention to anything but Erik at the time, you know? He would know."

"How and when did you learn that the girls were missing?" Mal asked.

"It was that same day, in the evening. Both Lori's and Anna's moms were calling around trying to find them. Someone called my mom and she told me about it to see if I knew anything, which I didn't of course. I really didn't think anything of it at first because I assumed Lori and Anna were like me and my friends, sneaking out to do things, forgetting about curfews, that kind of stuff. I figured they'd be in trouble when they got home but I never figured they wouldn't ever come home, or that they'd end up dead."

A silence fell as Marie once again stared, this time at the floor.

Mal broke the quiet. "It would really help if Erik would talk to us," he said. "We aren't looking to point the finger at anyone, we're just trying to assemble as many facts and details as we can."

Marie nodded but she looked grim. "I'll talk to him and see if I can turn him around for you. But I'm not making any promises. He can be very stubborn when he wants to be, and to be honest, this whole thing has haunted him ever since it happened. He's constantly trying to put it behind him so I don't know how easy it will be to talk him into facing it again."

"Anything you can do will be helpful," Mal said. Then he looked over at me. "Do you have anything else you want to say or ask?"

I shook my head.

"Then we'll be off," he said.

After giving Marie my cell phone number in case she had any additional information to share or Erik wanted to talk with us, she walked us to the door, wished us luck, and asked us to keep her posted. "Even if Erik doesn't want to know, I do, particularly if you are finally able to clear his name once and for all. Living under this cloud of suspicion for the past twelve years has been really hard on him."

We thanked her for her time, got back in Mal's car, and headed for the bar.

"What did you think?" I asked him once we were under way.

He shook his head. "Hard to know. The wife seemed sincere enough but Erik's reluctance to speak to us bothers me. I would think he'd be eager to have someone looking into this again if it might exonerate him, no matter how painful the memories might be."

"Maybe," I said. "But I have to admit that the idea of resurrecting my father's death investigation gave me pause, even though I was desperate to know who had killed him. Those memories can be brutal."

"What was your take on Erik? What does your superpower tell you?"

I laughed. "It's hardly a superpower," I said, recalling how I had thought in those terms myself when we were talking with Marie. "And I didn't have enough time with him to get a sense for how honest he is. Had we been able to ask him some questions about the girls' disappearance, I might have been able to pick up on whether or not he was lying, but we never had the chance. There was something about him though . . ." I trailed off, trying to recall the feeling I had when he had presented at the door. "Something is off with him, but I can't be any more specific than that. Though I did think I smelled alcohol on his breath. I wasn't sure if it was real or one of my responses."

"It was real," Mal said. "I smelled it, too."

"So it seems Erik has lost himself in the drink. I wonder why."

"Who knows? Maybe we'll get another chance at

him if his wife comes through, although if what she told us is true, it doesn't seem likely that Erik is high on the list of suspects. Did you get any sense of her level of sincerity or honesty?"

"Funny you should ask because Marie Hermann is a bit of an enigma to me. Nearly everyone's voice triggers some type of synesthetic reaction in me, and even though I'm constantly trying to tune them out, I'm still aware of them on some subconscious level. And if I focus, I'm very aware of them. But with Marie, I had nothing."

"Nothing at all?"

"Not with regard to her voice. I had reactions to the color of her hair, and some fragrance she had, but her voice gave me nothing at all."

"Has that happened before?"

"It has," I admitted. "It's rare but there have been a few people I've come across in my life whose voice didn't trigger anything."

"Interesting."

"I guess," I said with a shrug. "Anyway, Erik Hermann doesn't seem to offer much promise at the moment, so let's hope we'll have better luck with our next interview."

"Don't get your hopes up too high," Mal cautioned. "Based on my past experience, prisoners don't like to talk much unless you have something to offer them. If they think you're coming after them for something, they won't utter a peep."

Chapter 15

We got back to the bar just after eleven and since the place was closed, we had it to ourselves. I offered to make Mal some lunch but he wasn't hungry enough for an entire meal. So instead I suggested an appetizer and slipped into the kitchen to fire up the deep fryer and make us a batch of fried cheese curds.

"I never had these until I came here," Mal said a short time later as we sat at the bar munching on our curds.

"They're a Wisconsin specialty," I said. "Do you know how to tell if they're fresh?"

Mal shook his head, his mouth full of cheese curd.

"They squeak," I told him. "When you bite into a fresh cheese curd, it should squeak when the curd hits your teeth. It's an interesting experience for me because I can taste both the cheese curd and the squeak. For a long time I thought the squeak was my own unique experience, a synesthetic response to the taste. But then I heard others describe it and realized it's a genuine phenomenon."

Mal looked at me suspiciously. I think he thought I was trying to put one over on him so I told him to sit tight and went into the kitchen to get a fresh, unfried cheese curd. "Go ahead, try it," I said handing it to him on a napkin. "I'll be quiet while you bite into it and listen."

Still looking skeptical, he took the curd, eyed it as if he thought I might be feeding him something rancid, and then slowly took a bite. I heard the squeak, and from the way Mal's eyebrows arched, I knew he had, too.

"See?" I said with a self-satisfied, righteous smile. "Told ya."

"Can you hear my squeak, or is the sound in one's head?"

I took the remainder of the curd from him, leaned in close, and said, "Listen." Then I bit down into the curd, creating an audible squeak.

"Well, I'll be damned," Mal said. "Who knew?"

"Most Wisconsinites," I said. "If you want to stay here for any length of time, you're going to have to learn your cheese stuff. It's Wisconsin state law."

He smiled at that. "As long as I'm not required to wear one of those foam cheese wedges on my head, I'm fine with learning more about cheeses."

"There's a fabulous deli not far from here that has an amazing array of local cheeses. We should go there some day and do a sampling."

"I'd like that."

Once again we found ourselves sharing a moment that felt comfortable and fun one second and awkward the next. This time we were saved by a knock at the front door, though it was more of a pounding actually. We both turned to look and I saw Tyrese peeking in and waving at us through the window in the door. I waved back to let him know we saw him, and then Mal and I grabbed our coats and went outside to greet him.

Tyrese owned a Toyota Highlander, which was double parked in front of the bar. Mal sat up front with Tyrese, giving me the backseat all to myself. As Tyrese pulled out, we gave him a summary of our visit to Erik Hermann's house.

When we were done, Tyrese picked up a folder he had beside him and handed it to Mal saying, "I did a little research on Lonnie Carlisle. Take a look if you like."

Mal opened the folder, scanned the first sheet, and then handed it back to me. It was a rap sheet that showed Lonnie Carlisle's conviction for statutory rape and a couple of DUIs. There were some other offenses as well but they were minor: loitering, trespassing, panhandling . . . typical convictions for someone who was homeless.

"Are you going to get into trouble for showing us this stuff?" I asked Tyrese.

"The arrest records are a matter of public record. You could dig it up on your own if you wanted to. You might find some additional info in there, however, and I'd appreciate you not sharing it with anyone else or saying where you saw it."

"My lips are sealed," I said.

Tyrese nodded and looked over at Mal, who was busy reading whatever was next in the folder.

"Mal won't say anything, either. Will you, Mal?" I said.

He looked up, said, "Of course not," and then went back to reading.

After another minute or two, Mal handed me the second section from the folder. It was several pages stapled together, slightly faded, and dated nearly twenty years ago. It was a narrative summary, typed up by the arresting officer, of the statutory rape charge against Lonnie Carlisle. It stated that Lonnie, who was eighteen at the time, had had sex with a minor girl and that the girl's parents had filed a complaint. The report was written in an objective and unemotional manner until the very end. Then the arresting officer went into an explanation about how upset the victim was over the charges her parents had brought against Lonnie, arguing that the sex had been consensual and the two of them were in love. I got a sense from the wording that the officer had sided with Lonnie on some level and felt the charges were unfair, though there was nothing in the report that explicitly said that.

On the next page there was an addendum to the report written some months later. It noted that the victim had committed suicide by overdosing on a handful of sleeping pills and narcotics, prescriptions the girl's mother had for her severe, crippling arthritis.

Mal handed me another collection of stapled pages that highlighted Lonnie's attempted murder and sexual assault charges from an incident that happened in the summer following Lori's and Anna's murders. The names of the girls who were involved in this incident had been blacked out in the report, and when I mentioned that, Tyrese offered up an explanation.

"Sometimes with minors, the names are excluded, obliterated, or a fake name might be used to protect their identity. The press can get ahold of some of these reports and while some reporters are good about not naming minors, others have no such qualms. Plus one of the girls in this case was the daughter of a prominent local judge at the time."

I read through the report, which included the statement of the girl who had escaped more or less unscathed, the results of the physical examinations of both girls and Lonnie, and a description of some evidence found at the scene. The unscathed girl's physical exam was negative other than some bruises on her arms and some scratches on her legs that were determined to be from running through brush when she escaped. The other girl's exam showed similar leg scratches but it also revealed a huge depression fracture of her skull with bleeding in the brain as a result.

Lonnie had multiple bruises on his body—on his legs, his arms, his head, and his back—most of which he said were incurred when the girls kicked and threw rocks at him.

The statement from the girl who escaped said that Lonnie had jumped out of the woods and scared the girls when they were riding their bikes along a path in the park where the incident occurred. It forced them to stop, and then Lonnie reportedly lunged for the girl who ended up with the brain injury, stating that he wanted to "feel her boobies" and have her "stick your hand in my pants." There was a struggle, and the girl making the statement said she tried to help her friend get away, but after Lonnie shoved the first girl to the ground, smashing her head on a rock, he then grabbed the second girl and started "feeling me up." When the cop asked the girl what that meant, she stated that Lonnie stuck his hand up her shirt and tried to undo her pants.

The unscathed girl said she managed to escape and get back on her bike to go for help. By the time the cops arrived on the scene, Lonnie was gone. They found the wounded girl still lying where she'd been when her friend went for help, and a rock nearby that had her blood and hair on it.

There was no actual evidence of sexual assault on either of the girls, although the shirt of the one who had escaped was torn, and the snap and zipper on the shorts of the girl who had been wounded had been undone. Also noted was the fact that this event took place in the same general area near the Little Menomonee River and the Oak Leaf Trail where Anna's and Lori's bodies had been found.

Lonnie was apprehended a few hours later and his statement was the polar opposite of the girl's. He claimed that the two girls found him sitting on the ground dozing at the base of a tree. The next thing he knew, he was getting kicked. He tried to defend himself, and finally managed to get to his feet and start backing away. He begged the girls to stop, but they started throwing rocks at him so he turned and ran. He claimed he never touched either girl except perhaps in an attempt to ward off their kicks, and that both girls were fine when he left. When asked how the one girl came to be so gravely injured, he claimed not to know.

It wasn't hard to see why Lonnie had been convicted, particularly if one of the girls had been, as Tyrese said, the daughter of a prominent judge. Clearly, Lonnie was a disturbed man and a prime candidate for the murder of the other two girls.

I said as much to the two men in the car. "What I don't understand is why they didn't try to pin Anna's and Lori's murders on him," I concluded.

"Lack of evidence," both men said at the same time, and I saw Tyrese shoot Mal a curious look.

Mal held up the last of the papers from the folder and said, "At least that's what this report says."

This seemed to satisfy Tyrese, who nodded and turned his attention back to the drive.

Mal didn't hand me the next group of papers; he summarized them for me instead. They were reports from the examinations of Lori's and Anna's bodies.

"Both girls' bodies had been in the water, trapped under the frozen ice for a little over two months. Their bikes were found in the river, too, though the one Anna rode actually belonged to her brother. Hers had a flat tire and was still at the house so she apparently borrowed her brother's. The water washed away a lot of potential evidence, but the fact that the water was so cold did preserve the bodies. There were no hairs or body fluids found on either girl, and only Lori showed evidence of sexual assault in that she was naked from the waist down and there was bruising and tearing in and around her vagina. There was also bruising on both girls' necks indicating they were strangled, and the clothesline that was used to do this was still around their necks and tied around heavy stones. While the weight of the bikes and the stones might have kept the bodies under the water for a while, there was enough early . . ." Here Mal paused, bit his lip, and thought for a moment. Then he looked at me. "Basically the bodies would have eventually surfaced due to gas formation," he said with a wince.

I nodded both my understanding of what he meant and his reluctance to relay the grim information, so he went on.

"The rope was eventually traced to a clothesline in the backyard of a house in a neighborhood several blocks away that bordered the park area where the bike trail and the bodies were located. It appeared to have been cut with some sort of sharp object."

"Like what?" I asked. "Were they able to tell?"

Tyrese glanced at me in the rearview mirror. "Darn good question, Mack. You really are starting to think like a cop."

Mal said, "It says the ends of the clothesline were frayed and the person writing the report felt that it had been cut, or gnawed at, with a pair of ordinary household or office scissors."

I opened my mouth to ask another question, but before I could get a word out, Mal said, "And to answer your next question, no, there were no scissors found at the scene or anywhere nearby."

"Did the cops find scissors like the ones described in any of the suspects' houses?" I asked.

Tyrese smiled at me again and Mal looked to him for an answer to this one. Apparently, that information wasn't in the papers he still held.

"They did," Tyrese said. "Scissors were taken into evidence from Lonnie's house, William Schneider's house, Tim Johnson's house, and the Gruber home. None of them produced any usable evidence and they couldn't be connected to the crime, nor could they be ruled out. However, no scissors of any kind were found in the Hermann house even though Mrs. Hermann swore she had a pair on her office desk. She wasn't able to explain why she couldn't find them."

"Wow," I said arching my eyebrows in surprise. "That doesn't look good for Erik, does it?"

"No, it doesn't," Tyrese agreed.

"We really should try to talk to him again," I said. "I hope his wife can convince him."

Tyrese and Mal both nodded their agreement.

That was the end of the papers in the folder and a short time later we arrived at the prison. We checked in at the outer gate and once we were inside the compound, we parked and then Tyrese led the way to the front entrance, where we had to pass through another guarded gate before we were allowed inside the main building. The place had the smell of institution all over it—at least for me—and faded, chipped concrete walls that were painted avocado green. We checked in at yet another gated station, where we all had to offer ID to a guard sitting behind a glass enclosure that sat alongside a barred, floor-to-ceiling wall with a gate. There were two guards inside the enclosure, and the one sitting up front near the check-in spot sported a name pin that said R. DINKLE. Behind him was a series of monitors that showed various areas in and around the prison, and these were being watched by the second guard, who had his back to us. I wondered if the glass of the enclosure was bulletproof. Something about it was different from ordinary glass because when I looked through it, I got a whiff of an acrid chemical scent that faded as soon as I looked away.

Dinkle asked Tyrese who Mal and I were, and why we were along for the ride.

"They're involved with the case I'm investigating," Tyrese said vaguely.

Dinkle frowned, clearly not liking this answer, but he didn't pursue the matter. Instead he slid a clipboard toward us through a slot in the glass and told us to sign in after asking to see our IDs yet again.

Once this process was done he said, "The prisoner has asked his lawyer to sit in on your meeting. The lawyer's name is Philip Longhorn and he's already in the room. If you follow Karl here, he'll take you there."

With that, the second guard stood, exited the enclosure, and came toward us, stopping on the other side of the gate in the barred wall. Dinkle pressed a button and the gate slid open. We followed Karl, who, according to his badge had the last name Houston, down a short hallway, hearing the echo of the barred gate we'd just come through bang closed behind us. It was a scary, creepy sound that made me feel a little claustrophobic. At the end of the hallway we stopped in front of a large metal door that Karl had to unlock. There was a window in the upper third of the door, but it was mesh-filled and triggered the same odd chemical smell the glass in the enclosure had. We all stepped through into yet another hallway, this one much bigger. Along the sides of this hallway were four more windowed doors—two on each side. We waited while Karl relocked the door we had just come through before following him to the last door on the left, which was located near a fifth door at the end of the hallway. The fifth door was windowed also, and beyond it I could see a long open space bordered by prison cells on both sides.

Karl unlocked and opened the door to the room we were entering. "Longhorn is inside," he said in a bored, monotonic voice. "We weren't expecting three of you so someone will have to stand. Once you are in the room, the prisoner will be brought in. This door will be locked behind you but if you need anything, I'll be standing out here. Just knock on the door."

I couldn't help but notice how the guards depersonalized the men by referring to them as prisoners rather than using their names. On the one hand it bothered me, but then I rationalized the behavior when I remembered that some of the men in here had done some horrible, heinous things, and as such, they probably seemed less than human to those who had to deal with them day after day.

"We'll be fine," Tyrese said. He opened the door and we all paraded into the room.

It was a bare-walled, windowless, cinder block structure with a scarred wooden table at the center. There were two chairs on the side closest to us and one on the far side. The door behind us closed with a loud *thunk* and I heard the scrape of the lock being reengaged. I suppressed a shiver and grimaced as I tasted something like dirty potato peels, though I wasn't sure which sound had triggered it, the *thunk* or the scrape of the lock.

Philip Longhorn sat with his back to us but he glanced at us as we approached the table. He appeared surprisingly young; he barely looked old enough to drink. He eyed us with suspicion as Mal pulled out the one remaining chair on the closest side of the table and indicated for me to take it. I did so and smiled at Longhorn, who didn't smile back. Tyrese made the introductions and Longhorn returned the favor by muttering his name. He had an air of disdain about him that gave me the feeling he thought we should simply know who he was, or that he didn't care if we knew.

"May I ask why you want to speak to my client?" he asked Tyrese.

"We're looking into a cold case from twelve years ago, two young girls who were murdered."

"Ah, the Gruber-Hermann case?"

Tyrese nodded.

"The cops tried to pin that crime on my client back when it happened, but it was dropped due to a lack of evidence. Do you have something new to offer?"

"No," Tyrese said. "We're interested in talking to all of the parties who were, or might have been involved back then. Just recovering old ground to see if anything new turns up."

Longhorn narrowed his eyes at Tyrese for a few seconds, then glanced at Mal, and finally settled his gaze on me. "Are all of you cops?"

I answered after deciding to stick with the story we'd been using all along. "No, we're research assistants. We're working with a friend who's a writer, and he's interested in doing a true crime book about the case."

Longhorn arched his brows at this and opened his mouth to say something else. Before he could, we heard noise from the door on the far wall.

We all turned to watch as Lonnie Carlisle was brought into the room.

He was balding and bent over as he shuffled his way to the table, led by a guard. His feet were encased in cuffs with chains that ran between them. Another chain ran from this one up to his waist, where it circled around him. His wrists were contained in cuffs that were attached to this waist chain. The man looked like the setup for a Houdini stunt.

The guard pulled out the chair on the opposite side of the table and Lonnie shuffled over and dropped into it. He took us all in with a sweeping, wary glance and then settled his gaze on his lawyer. The guard retreated through the door he had come in, but he didn't go far. I could see his silhouette on the other side through the small, mesh-filled window.

"Mr. Carlisle," I started. "Thank you for agreeing to talk to us."

"I didn't agree to talk to anyone," Lonnie grumbled. "I said I would meet with you and hear you out." His voice was hoarse and raspy, and it made me taste burnt toast.

"They're here about the Gruber-Hermann case," Longhorn told Lonnie. "Supposedly someone wants to write a book about it."

Lonnie had been leaning forward, arms on his knees. With Longhorn's announcement, he leaned back in his chair as far as his chains would let him, effectively distancing himself from us. "I got nothing to say about that case," he said, his lips set with determination.

With this statement, the taste of his voice changed

from burnt toast to something more like a burnt marshmallow—pasty, with a metallic tinge to it.

"We aren't here to try to pin anything on you," Tyrese explained. "We're simply on a fact-finding mission for the book, as your lawyer said."

Lonnie said nothing. He just sat there, a defiant look on his face.

After many long seconds of silence, Lonnie turned and looked over his shoulder. "Guard!" he yelled. "I'm done here."

The guard who had brought him in reentered and Lonnie stood and allowed himself to be escorted from the room the same way he'd come in.

"I guess this trip is a bust for you," Longhorn said. He looked pleased. I found myself wishing Duncan had been able to come with us because he's good at talking to people and getting things out of them. But he wasn't there and I didn't see much point in dwelling on it.

"He knows something about that case," I said. "Why doesn't he want to talk about it?"

Longhorn eyed me curiously for a moment and then shrugged. "There's a chance he might be paroled soon. I'm guessing he doesn't want to dredge up anything that might risk him being denied."

With that, Longhorn got up, went to the door we had come in, and knocked three times. The door opened a moment later and Longhorn left.

"You folks done here?" Karl said.

Without a word, we all got up and retraced our steps out of the prison and to the parking lot. Once we were in the car, Mal turned to me in the backseat and said, "You sensed something about Carlisle. What was it?"

"He definitely knows something about the girls' case," I told him. "I have a feeling that he's afraid. Maybe his lawyer was right and he's afraid of messing up his chances at parole."

"But you don't think that's what it is, do you?" Mal said, eyeing me closely.

I frowned as I considered his question. "I'm not sure what to think. But I did get the sense that his fear was more visceral than simple worry about his parole."

Tyrese started the car and headed for the exit gate. "I'll make a call to the warden tomorrow and chat with him about Lonnie, see if he can add any insight. I'll find out who's been visiting him, who he talks to, what he's said to the guards and such. Maybe that will give us a clue."

I glanced at my watch and said, "Well, since this trip was a bust, should we try another tack?"

"Have something in mind?" Tyrese asked.

"Yeah," I said. "Let's drop in on the neighborhood weirdo."

Chapter 16

A little over an hour later, we stopped back at the bar so I could grab the information sheet we'd been given the night before to get the address for William Schneider. The bar was empty and the guys waited outside in the car, so I took a moment to enjoy the peace and quiet. Looking at the bar, it was easy to imagine Duncan behind it, mixing drinks, something he discovered he enjoyed doing. I couldn't wait to see him later and the time seemed to be crawling by. Still, it was better that I was busy and distracted, and with that in mind, I pushed Duncan to the back of my thoughts and headed outside.

Twenty minutes later we pulled up in front of a house that had definitely seen better times. There were some scraggly half-dead bushes in the front yard, bare spots in the lawn, and the concrete stoop on the small bungalow was crumbling away, its wrought-iron railings tilting at precarious angles. The paint on the door and window trim was peeling and appeared to have been white at one time, although now the color was more of a dingy gray. Oxidation on the aluminum siding left many of the pieces shiny and metallic along their edges instead of the brown they used to be. The roof appeared similarly neglected and pathetic, with missing shingles, sap stains from a towering pine in the backyard, and a chimney that looked ready to crumble if someone blew on it too hard. Bring on the big bad wolf.

Every window in the front of the house had blinds that were down and closed, but as we pulled into the driveway—which had more grass growing in it than the lawn did—I saw the slats in one of the windows move.

"We're being observed," I said, and Tyrese nodded.

"How are we going to approach this guy?" Mal said. "Same story we've been using?"

"Might as well," I said with a shrug.

We all piled out of the car and headed for the front door, stepping carefully as we climbed the steps to the stoop. Mal raised his hand to knock—there was a hole in the wall where the doorbell should have been—but before he could do anything a male voice hollered out from within.

"Go away! I ain't interested in buying nothing and my soul don't need saving."

We all looked at one another and through some unspoken agreement, Mal took over. "We aren't selling anything and we aren't from any church. We're here to talk to you about the deaths of Lori Gruber and Anna Hermann twelve years ago."

He paused, and when we heard nothing, he added, "We're conducting research for a true crime book. We're hoping we'll finally uncover the real culprit and clear the names of those who were falsely accused."

Another interminable wait and after a minute or so, Tyrese shrugged and said, "I don't think he's going to talk to us."

And then we heard a lock thrown. Then another. And another. Finally, the front door cracked open. Beyond, I could see a grizzled, bearded face, filthy, thick-lensed glasses, and pasty white skin that I guessed was due to an utter lack of exposure to sunshine.

"Mr. Schneider," Mal said with a warm smile. "May we come in and talk to you?"

He stared at us with wild, rheumy eyes, his gaze darting back and forth between the three of us. Something about the way he looked suggested a mind bordering on the edge of sanity, losing its grip on reality.

"You trying to pin what happened to them girls on me?" he said, his voice gravelly and rife with suspicion. It triggered a taste that was like eating a handful of salted nuts and I wondered if the food choice was somehow predicated by my opinion of the man. It didn't last long enough for me to give the idea much thought because a cloud of alcohol-infused breath hit me seconds later. With it came a tinny, tympanic grating sound mixed with the deep bass sounds of a cello, similar to what I'd heard when I smelled the most recent, blank letter. This told me that Schneider's boozes of choice were beer and cheap whiskey. It was all I could do to keep my expression neutral and not back up a few steps.

"No, sir," I said. "We're conducting interviews and

looking into the case for a writer who is working on a true crime book about the case. Mainly, we're interested in getting facts from you as to your whereabouts on the day in question, anything else you saw or heard that day, and any ideas you might have about the case. With luck, we might be able to identify the real killer and figure out what actually happened to those girls."

He narrowed his eyes at me as I spoke and I sensed his skepticism. But after weighing us and our intentions for a few seconds, he apparently decided we were okay, at least for now.

"Come on in," he said, stepping aside and opening the door wider.

We entered the house, which was dark and musty smelling. The windows were all covered with closed blinds and the few stray beams of sunlight that managed to eke their way around the edges highlighted a thick layer of dust atop everything. I was relieved when Mr. Schneider bypassed the living room area and headed for a small table in the kitchen because I sensed that settling into any of the chairs in the living room would have triggered a mini dust storm.

The kitchen was cluttered, but it didn't appear particularly dirty. There were dishes and an assortment of boxed food items covering the counters, but the dishes appeared clean. There were empty beer cans piled high in the trash and a smattering of alcohol bottles on the counter—cheap whiskies, thus proving my nose correct once again. Most of the bottles were empty, though a few had a little left in the bottom. We settled in at the table, a retro chrome and yellow Formica set with matching chairs. The set was in surprisingly good shape, although one of the vinyl seats did have a small tear in it, stuffing protruding. I settled into that chair and the feel of the rip beneath my thigh made me see smooth, rounded pebbles.

"I don't know that I can help you much in figuring out what happened to them girls," Schneider said once we were all seated. "I wasn't anywhere near 'em when it happened."

"Where were you?" Tyrese asked.

"I was home," Schneider said, scowling.

"I understand both girls lived near here," Mal said.

"So? What's your point?" Schneider grumbled. "I was here in my house and I didn't leave it."

"Did anyone see you here?" Mal asked.

Schneider turned his rheumy gaze toward Mal and narrowed his eyes down to a steely glint. "No, and no one seen me anywhere else either, because I was here and never left. I didn't go out much then. Still don't."

"Why is that?" Mal asked.

Schneider looked at him like he was stupid. "People ain't never liked me much. They think I'm crazy or something and the kids make fun of me whenever they see me. They did it back then and they still do. Heartless little bastards!" He spat this out with a surprising amount of venom and the nutty taste in my mouth turned rancid.

I sensed his anger rapidly building and decided to try to defuse it. "You had a child once, didn't you?"

The change in his demeanor was startling. It was like watching a balloon deflate. He sank back into his seat, his face sagged, and his whole body went limp. A devastating silence followed and Mal, Tyrese, and I exchanged worried looks.

Finally, Schneider spoke, though it was as if the flat, tinny voice was emanating from a dead body. "We don't talk about that anymore, understand?"

No one said a word for a minute or so. Schneider didn't move. I don't think he even blinked. My heart ached for the man. Clearly, his daughter's death had been a life-shattering event for him. So I decided to leave that topic alone for now and get back to the case at hand.

"Mr. Schneider," I said in a soft, nonthreatening voice. "Do you have any theories about what might have happened to those two girls, Anna and Lori?"

His head snapped up, he leaned forward again with his arms on the table, and looked me straight in the eye. It was as if some switch had been turned off and then back on again. "How would I know?" he said with an irritated tone. "And why should I care? Ain't like anyone is ever nice to me, or says a kind word."

"That must make you mad," Tyrese suggested.

"Damn right, it does," Schneider said, shifting his rheumy gaze. "Nobody has respect for a man like me who fought for the freedoms these snotty kids these days take for granted. I watched men die, young men, men filled with hope, men cut down in the prime of their lives." His voice and his emotions were both escalating again. "Those men died so folks in this country could live and live well. I almost died, too, and what do I get for my efforts? Gratitude? Hell, no! I get insults. I get rocks thrown at me and my house. I get people looking at me like I'm crazy, and talking 'bout me like I'm something for them to be scared of. Hell, people these days don't know the meaning of scary."

"You were in the military," I said, stating the obvious.

"Damned right," he said, puffing his chest out a little. "I was a Marine and proud of it. Not that anyone respects that anymore." He shoved his chair back and stood up suddenly, startling us all. Both Mal and Tyrese rose, too, and as Schneider spun around and stormed out of the kitchen, they stared after him with worried, questioning looks.

"Maybe we should leave," Mal said.

Tyrese nodded, but I stayed where I was. "Give him a minute," I said.

Seconds ticked by and the two men stood there, twitchy, nervous, ready to jump at the first hint of a problem. I probably should have been nervous too, but for some reason I wasn't. Schneider was a broken, bitter, and angry man; there was no denying that. But my gut told me he meant us no harm. He finally returned from whatever dark recess he'd retreated to, carrying a small wooden box.

"What have you got in there?" Tyrese asked, his voice as suspicious as Schneider's had been moments ago. Tyrese's hand moved to the back of his waist inside his jacket, and I knew he was reaching for a gun. Except I also knew he didn't have one there, because we'd been searched at the prison.

"Sit down," Schneider grumbled.

Tyrese remained standing, as did Mal. Schneider ignored them both and took the seat he had vacated moments ago. He set the box on the table and opened it. Inside I saw a bunch of papers and some old photos. He moved the papers aside and grabbed a handful of photos, tossing them onto the table. Beneath them in the box was something metallic and colorful. He grabbed it and held it out to us in the palm of his hand. It was a round, brass colored medal attached to a gold ribbon with green and red stripes. The medal had the words REPUBLIC OF VIETNAM SERVICE on it.

"This is all I got out of that war," Schneider said. "Wait, I take that back. I also got a chunk of metal in my head, a bum hip, and a whole lot of nightmares." He dropped the medal on the table and grabbed a couple of the photos he'd tossed down. "Even so, I got out with my life, which is more than these guys got." One by one he looked at, and then dealt each picture back onto the table.

He stared off then, and I sensed he was lost in some memory of those times, but whether it was a good memory or a bad one, I couldn't tell. Tyrese and Mal had both relaxed by now, and the three of us watched Schneider in silence, leaving him to whatever tortured reverie he was in. When he finally snapped back to the present he said, "I think kids today are spoiled, disrespectful, and unappreciative, but that ain't no reason to kill them."

Outside a car backfired and Schneider leapt from his chair and ducked beneath the table, knocking into my legs. I scooted my chair back and stood. Mal and Tyrese, both of whom were still standing, stepped back. And the three of us stared at the sight beneath the table. Schneider's face had changed so dramatically that he didn't look like the same person. His eyes were wild with fear and tension. He was squatting beneath the table, arms wrapped around his legs, muttering some type of wartime rhetoric peppered with racial slurs and geographic references specific to Vietnam. I got the sense that he didn't know we were there any longer, or perhaps he didn't know where he was any longer. Then he looked me dead in the eye and stopped rocking. "You can beat me, you can starve me, you can torture me all you want. But I'll never talk. And you better stay on alert because if you turn your back on me I'll slit your throat the first chance I get."

Schneider's eyes were filled with hatred and venom, all of it directed at me, or whoever he thought I was, because I felt pretty sure that his mind was lost in some other time and place. It was sad, but it was also very scary because he looked mad enough to do what he said. Tyrese and Mal must have come to the same conclusion because Tyrese said, "We're outa here." The two men came toward me and quickly escorted me out of the house, never once taking their eyes off Schneider as we left.

Once outside, I breathed a sigh of relief. "That was creepy," I said.

"No kidding," Tyrese agreed. "Now we know why Schneider is called the strange neighbor."

"It's kind of sad," I said, my heart aching for the man Schneider might have once been and could have become if not for his family tragedy and that war. "Clearly his time in Vietnam had a profound effect on his mental health. It sounds like he was a POW or something. That makes his paranoia a little easier to understand. He's probably been suffering from PTSD all these years. And I'm sure the death of his wife and daughter did little to help the situation."

"That may be true," Mal said as we all settled back into Tyrese's car, "and if it is, it is indeed sad. But it's also dangerous. Based on the look in his eyes, the behaviors, and the things he said there at the end, it's clear that the man has a slippery grasp on reality at times. If those two girls were nearby when Schneider went off like he just did, I could see him thinking they were there to hurt him. He might have killed them because he thought they were the enemy."

Tyrese nodded his agreement. "He may not have meant to do it. He may not even remember doing it, or believe he did." Tyrese glanced at me in the rearview mirror. "Did you pick up on any deception with him, Mack?"

I shook my head. "Either he was honest the whole time or lying the whole time, because the basic quality of his voice didn't change significantly except for that one weird episode when he went all limp after I mentioned his daughter. His voice made me taste nuts and the taste turned bitter when his emotions did, but other than that it stayed the same but for that one episode."

"That was a creepy moment," Tyrese said. "It was like the guy had died and then reanimated or something."

We all nodded and then Mal said, "There may be a problem with your lie detecting tricks, Mack. What if Tyrese is right? What if Schneider did kill those girls but has no memory of doing it? If he doesn't know he did it, saying he didn't do it wouldn't be a lie to him, right?"

Tyrese rolled his eyes. "Oh, man, I hadn't thought about that, but you're right."

I shook my head and said, "I understand what you're saying, but I'm not sure it matters because there's another aspect of this that makes me think Schneider didn't do it."

"What's that?" Mal asked.

"The sexual assault. If Schneider killed those girls because he thought they were Viet Cong spies, or soldiers or whatever, why would he rape one of them? And why was Lori the only one who was sexually assaulted?"

Both men thought about this for a moment. Then Tyrese said, "Maybe it started out as a sexual assault but then escalated into one of Schneider's episodes when the girls fought back."

Mal added, "Plus it certainly wasn't unheard of for soldiers in that war to rape young girls in the villages they seized. Maybe the sexual assault was part of whatever scene Schneider was reliving."

Both points were valid, and I cursed under my breath.

Mal gave me a puzzled look. "What? Do you feel so sorry for Schneider that you want to exonerate him?"

"No, but I was hoping we could eliminate someone from the suspect pool. So far all we've done is come up with reasons why any of them could have done it."

"Which, no doubt, is why the case was never solved," Tyrese pointed out.

"I wish we could find out more about Schneider's psychiatric illness," I said to no one in particular. "We should come back and bring Sam with us next time, see what his take on Schneider is."

"Sam?" Mal said.

"Sam Warner. You met him last night. He's one of the Capone Club members and he's also a doctorate student in psychology." Mal still looked lost so I elaborated. "He was the short, kind of pudgy guy with the glasses and longish brown hair who was sitting next to Carter. The two of them have been friends since they were kids."

I saw dawning on Mal's face and he nodded. "Okay, now I remember him. Is he a practicing psychologist?"

"He doesn't have his own office yet or anything like that," I said, "but he does provide counseling services as part of his school clinicals, and he also volunteers at a crisis center. He's a very bright and insightful person, and I'd be curious to see what he thinks about Schneider as a suspect."

Tyrese said, "Just promise me you won't go back to Schneider's place unless you have me, Nick, or Duncan with you. That guy strikes me as a ticking time bomb and you'd be foolish to mess with him unless you have someone there to protect you." He glanced over at Mal with an apologetic look. "Not to say you can't take care of yourself, man," he said, "but I think this Schneider guy is too dangerous to be around without a cop of some type."

"No offense taken," Mal said. "And I totally agree. Mack shouldn't be doing any of this unless she has a cop with her." He shot an amused side glance at me as Tyrese signaled for a turn and looked the other way. "Promise the man," he said to me with a wink.

"I promise," I said dutifully. "And since we have you for the day, Tyrese, let's make the most of it. Who's next on our list of suspects?"

Chapter 17

Our trip to visit TJ, the plumber who had been to Lori Gruber's house the day before the girls disappeared, was temporarily waylaid. Both Mal and I had to pee and neither of us had wanted to use the bathroom in Schneider's house, so we decided to stop back at the bar, both for a potty break and so I could make sure everything was on track for opening at five.

Tyrese parked down the street a ways, and as we approached the bar I saw that the Signoriello brothers and Cora—who as usual was carrying her laptop—were all waiting outside. Since it was only a minute or so before five, I unlocked the doors and let them in.

Cora pulled me aside right away and said she needed to talk to me in my office about a confidential matter. Tyrese took the cue, bellied up to the bar, and ordered a club soda. As I started to head to my office, Cora turned to Frank and Joe and said, "You two come along, too."

"What about Mal?" I asked Cora.

"He can come."

Curious, I led the group into my office. Cora immediately settled into my chair behind my desk and opened her laptop, plugging it into a wall outlet nearby. Frank, Joe, and Mal settled in on the couch while I took the chair opposite Cora.

"What's up?" I said.

"Duncan wants to talk to you," Cora said. She was tapping away on her laptop and after a few seconds she turned it around so I and the others could see the screen. To my surprise, Duncan was on it.

"Hey, Mack," he said. "I had Cora set up a video-conference so we could talk face to face without actually being together."

"You can see me?" I said, amazed by the technology.

"Yes, I can," he said with a smile. "I can see the others in the room, too. Hi, Joe, Frank, Malachi."

The men all mumbled their hellos in return. I saw the brothers exchange perplexed looks.

"Do Frank and Joe know about Mal?" Duncan asked.

"They do not," I said. The brothers turned in unison and eyed Mal curiously. "Mal is a cop, an undercover cop," I explained.

"Hunh," Joe said.

"I knew it," Frank said, elbowing his brother.

"Duncan, I'm not sure this is smart," Mal said, looking uncomfortable. "Bringing in untrained people might place Mack in greater jeopardy. Or me, for that matter."

"Duncan isn't bringing them in, I did. I told them about the first letter and showed it to them before I told Duncan about it. They're trustworthy," I said. "I promise."

"We are," Frank said, and Joe nodded his vigorous agreement.

"I haven't updated the brothers or Cora on the subsequent letters," I added.

"You can bring them up to speed in a minute," Duncan said. "Frank, Joe, it's imperative that no one else know what Mal really does."

"No problem," Frank said. "Our lips are sealed." Again Joe nodded his agreement. Then Frank looked at Mal and said, "I'm glad Mack has someone looking out for her."

Joe said, "So are the two of you really dating, or is that part of the subterfuge?"

"We're not really dating," I said quickly. "And Duncan and I are still together," I added, wondering if it was true.

"Is there a reason for this little party, Duncan?" Mal said, sounding a little irritated, though I wasn't sure what had him riled.

"There is. I've got some more information about those letters Mack has been getting. Let me recap to bring everyone up to speed. I did a little digging into a man who calls himself Apostle Mike. He sent Mack a signed letter that basically labeled her and her curse, as he called it, an abomination and a sin against God."

"Do you think he's the one sending the letters?" Frank asked.

"There is a strong possibility," Duncan said. "This guy is definitely a fringe operator and his church is basically a cult that operates from a compound about twenty miles south of the city. That in and of itself doesn't alarm me all that much with regard to Mack and the letters, but one of the other cops here who has had dealings with some members of the church who left it said that this Apostle Mike has some strong feelings about the occult. Rumor has it he has targeted some Wiccan groups and might have attacked some of their members. He's also spoken out against things like the Harry Potter books because he believes anything that even hints at magic is pure evil. Given the publicity that's been out there about Mack, including some of the hype that called her ability things like black magic, ESP, and such, it's not hard to imagine why he targeted her with the letter he supposedly signed. The question is, has he targeted her with more than that?"

"When you say he attacked some Wiccan believers, just what do you mean?" Mal asked. "Is this guy violent?"

"They haven't been able to pin anything directly on him," Duncan said. "He doesn't commit the crimes himself. He uses his members. But there has been some violence. One woman who is fairly vocal about her involvement with the Wiccan faith had her home broken into and ransacked. There was pig blood splashed all over, the furniture was slashed, that sort of thing. Another woman in the same Wiccan group was attacked while walking home from her job and beaten pretty badly."

"How do you know it's their involvement with the Wiccan faith that made them targets?" I asked.

"Because notes stating so were left at the scene in both cases."

"Notes, letters . . . I'm seeing a pattern here," I

said. "Any similarities between those notes and my letters?"

"Not really," Duncan said, "but that doesn't rule Apostle Mike out. Both the notes left at the scenes of these other crimes and the Apostle Mike letter could have been written by anyone, one of his followers, for instance."

Mal said, "Were they able to determine any identifying information from the notes, or find any trace evidence?"

"Unfortunately, no."

"So where do we go from here?" I asked.

Duncan's gaze shifted from Mal back to me. "Have you had any more ideas about that last letter you got?" he asked.

I shook my head.

"Where is it? What did it say?" Joe asked. "Maybe we should have a look at it, see if we can interpret what it says."

"That's just it; it doesn't say anything," I told them. "All that was on it was a date and time, nothing else. But the paper had been altered."

"Altered how?" Frank asked.

"I smelled champagne and beer on it, and the paper was kind of wavy, as if it had been soaked in the stuff."

"Maybe it was Miller beer," Joe said with a half laugh. "Aren't they the ones who advertise themselves as the champagne of bottled beers?"

"Now it's just the champagne of beers," Frank said. "You're aging yourself, Joe. That ad campaign was back in the fifties."

I gaped at the brothers for a few seconds and then walked over to Joe, grabbed his head between my hands, and planted a big kiss on his forehead. "Joe, you are brilliant!" I said.

Everyone in the room was staring at me with confused expressions so I explained. "Joe is absolutely right that Miller used that slogan back in the day to advertise their Miller High Life and they still use the modified version. I think I understand now why the sheet was soaked in both liquids. The Miller plant here in town offers tours of their facilities free to the public. My dad and I took some out-of-town friends on it a few years ago. It's interesting, particularly if you're interested in beer history, and you get some free beer samples at the end. I'm betting that somewhere along that tour is where we'll find our next clue."

Joe was blushing with pride. Everyone else sat silent, digesting what I'd just said.

Finally, Duncan said, "I guess that makes as much sense as anything else. But I still want to bring Mack down to the station and let her listen in and watch while I question this Apostle Mike guy. I had hoped to do it tonight since the staff around here is bare bones on Sundays, but I couldn't make it happen."

"I still don't like the idea," I said. "If it is Apostle Mike who's behind this, and you bring him in and question him, he's going to know I involved you. I don't want to risk that."

"We'll question him about something unrelated, like these assaults. And I'll have one of the other officers question him rather than Jimmy or me, just to be safe."

"I don't know . . ." I said. "I'm not sure what I'd

be able to pick up if you're questioning him about something unrelated to the letters."

"We can try to bait him into revealing something," Duncan suggested. "In the meantime, I'll see if there's a way we can tie him or anyone in his group to the mailing of those letters."

"Okay," I said, still hesitant. "Just promise me you'll be careful not to show your hand."

"I promise."

"Anything new on Lewis's case?" I asked. "Anything come up on the autopsy?"

"Unfortunately, no. We know he was stabbed to death with a large knife of some sort. He was also beaten about the face."

"That's up close and personal," Mal said, wincing. "Have you found any connection between this Lewis guy and Apostle Mike?"

"Not so far."

"So where do we go from here?" I asked.

"I'm not sure how long it will take to set up an interview with Apostle Mike. I'll let you know when it's set to go, and I'll think up a way to sneak you in here. In the meantime, you might as well do the Miller tour. Maybe it will buy us some time."

I looked at my watch. "I doubt they're running the tours this late on a Sunday. In fact, I think they're closed. So I'll have to try for tomorrow."

Duncan nodded and said, "Mal, what time tomorrow can you be free to go with her?"

"I'm supposed to work all day at the construction site, seven to four."

I racked my brain. "I don't think they do evening tours there, but I'll check the times online once we get done here."

"No need," Cora said, taking out her smartphone and tapping at the screen. "On weekdays they do the tours every half hour between ten-thirty in the morning and three-thirty in the afternoon."

"That explains the deadline," I said. "The tour takes about an hour, an hour and a half with the sampling time at the end thrown in, so if someone did the last one, they'd finish at around five. And that was the time in the deadline!"

Duncan sighed. "I don't want you going there alone, Mack."

"There's a small chance I might be able to go with her," Mal said. "The site I'm at right now is all outside work and if the paper is right, the weather forecast is for snow tonight and tomorrow. Lots of it. And we typically get called off if it's snowing hard."

"Then we need to pray for snow," I said. "Though I have to say, this little warm spell was a treat."

Cora was tapping at her phone screen again. "Mal is right. According to the forecast on one of the local stations, there's a winter storm warning in effect. They're calling for ten to twelve inches of lake effect snow to fall sometime between midnight tonight and ten tomorrow morning."

"Then let's tentatively plan for Mal to go with you," Duncan said. "And if he has to work for some reason, how about the three of you go along? There's safety in numbers."

"Free beer?" Joe said. "Hell yeah, I'll go."

"Count me in," his brother said.

"Me, too," Cora added.

The brothers gave me their home phone number—they considered cell phones "newfangled contraptions"—and made me promise to call them tomorrow if I needed them before the bar opened.

When that was done, Duncan said, "Now that that's settled, I wonder if I could impose on all of you for one more thing. Would you mind stepping out so I can talk to Mack alone for a few minutes?"

"Sure," Cora said, getting up and heading for the door.

The brothers both nodded and followed. Mal lingered for a few seconds, an odd look on his face, but eventually he got up and left, too.

"How are you holding up?" Duncan asked once we were alone.

"Okay, I guess."

He frowned then and said, "About this evening . . ."

"You can't come."

He sighed and I did the same. "I'm sorry," he said. "Things are crazy right now. It was all I could do to get a couple hours of sleep and find the time to chat with you here."

"I understand," I said, wondering if I did. "I just wish you could be here more. Or we could be any-where more."

"Me, too."

"Is there any hope on the horizon?"

"Of course there is."

His placating attitude annoyed me. Not that long ago, I was afraid to speak out and declare my feelings, but I decided that now was the time to do so. I needed to make him understand my stance on things. "I'm not going to lie to you to, Duncan," I said, bracing myself. "This situation has me more than frustrated. I invested my time and money in expanding the bar and hiring on extra staff so I could have more free time, more of a life. And I hoped to be spending a lot of it with you. But I'm afraid that what's going on now is a sign of things to come."

"It won't always be like this, I promise. But there's no getting around the fact that my job is quite demanding at times, as is yours."

"I get it, but I don't have to like it."

"I'm sorry, and I promise I'll make it up to you. Can you hang in there?"

"It doesn't look like I have much choice," I grumbled, hating that I sounded so needy.

"Atta girl. We'll talk again soon." He kissed his hand and then blew it toward me on the screen.

I started to act as if I was catching it, but pulled back at the last second for reasons I didn't quite understand. Instead, all I did was say, "Be careful." Then I reached over and closed the lid on the laptop.

I indulged in a few moments of self-pity, then I straightened my shoulders, unplugged Cora's laptop, tucked it under my arm, and headed back out to the bar. The rest of the group was nowhere in sight, and when I looked over at Billy, who was in his usual place behind the bar, he nodded toward the upstairs.

I made my way there and found the group in the Capone Club room along with Tiny, Tad, Dr. T, Sam, Holly, and Carter. Alicia was there, too, having abandoned her post near Billy for once, and Tyrese had migrated up from his earlier seat at the bar.

"Hey, Mack," Carter said as I walked in and handed Cora her laptop. "Mal was just filling us in on your day."

"I'm afraid it wasn't very productive," I said.

"Did anyone stand out at all?" he asked.

I shrugged and thought back to the day's encounters. "I think Lonnie Carlisle is scared of something, though I don't know what. I think it's more than just a fear of coming under suspicion again, but if he's unwilling to talk to us I don't how we can pursue that angle. Erik Hermann didn't want to talk to us at all either, and I didn't get to spend enough time with him to get a feel for what might be going on with him. His wife said she'd try to convince him to reconsider, but I don't hold out much hope for that." I then told them that William Schneider seemed the most likely candidate at this point, and why. Then I let Sam know that I would like to go back to see the man again and take him along to evaluate his psychological state.

"I'd be happy to," Sam said. "He sounds like a fascinating case. In fact, if he's willing to work with me, I might use him as a subject for my thesis."

"We still have the plumber to talk to," I said. I glanced at my watch and saw that it was almost six in the evening. "Maybe I should try to do that tonight while I have Tyrese to come along."

"I'm game," Tyrese said.

"I'd like to come along, too," Mal said.

"T'anks for doing dis, you guys," Tiny said. "Even if nuttin' comes of it, it's good to know dat we tried."

"I had an idea," Dr. T said. "I know someone who works in the ME's office here, a guy named Todd Bannerman who went to med school with me. I was thinking I might ask him if he could get me a copy of the autopsy reports on the two girls.

Wisconsin has open records policies for stuff like that, so it shouldn't be a problem to get them."

I started to say that we already had a lot of the information, but then I remembered my promise to Tyrese to remain mum about it. Besides, I figured an actual autopsy report might offer more specific details than what was in the summary info Tyrese had.

"That would be great," Carter said to Dr. T, looking excited. "It might help us solve the case and it would be invaluable info for my book. Maybe we could even get Lewis's report at some point."

Everyone nodded their agreement, everyone that is, except Tiny, who looked troubled.

"Tiny, are you okay with this?" I said.

He blushed. "I'm okay wid it if it helps," he said. "But I don't want to see da report on my sister."

"Understandable," Sam said. "It's bound to be very blunt and graphic, and I can't say I'd want to see an autopsy report on someone I cared about."

"We'll let you know before we discuss it so you can step out," Carter said. "Will that help?"

Tiny nodded but he still looked glum and I had a feeling there was something he was holding back.

"Okay, then," Tyrese said, getting up from his chair. "Mal and Mack, are you ready to go see TJ the plumber?"

Cora let out a laugh and we all looked at her. "Mal and Mack," she said. "M and M. From now on, that's what I'm calling you."

"I like it," Carter said, nodding his approval. Others were smiling and nodding, too. I kind of liked the nickname myself, but then I remembered that Mal and I weren't really a couple, which meant M and M would soon come to an end. The thought made me sad. My feelings for Mal were definitely jumbled at the moment, as were my feelings for Duncan.

Tyrese headed for the door and said, "Come on, M and M. Let's hit the road."

Mal pushed out of his chair, walked over to me, and offered his arm, something that was becoming a characteristic trait of his. "It's destiny," he said with a wink. "We were meant to be together."

Chapter 18

Timothy "TJ" Johnson lived in the south end of the city in a working-class neighborhood filled with starter sized homes, postage stamp lawns, and lots of used cars. I expected something a little pricier knowing what plumbers charge, but the reason for TJ being in this neighborhood became clear not long into our visit. His house was made of clapboard that had at one time been painted blue but was now faded to white on the south side and covered with green moss on the north side. The yard had a number of bare spots, spots that would soon be hidden by the snow that was coming. I could taste it and smell it in the air, and the low-hanging clouds that had moved in were pregnant with cold promise.

Compared to the other houses on the street, which were simple but appeared lovingly cared for, TJ's looked neglected. And when TJ answered the door, it was easy to see why. TJ himself was neglected. He was dressed in old blue jeans, a stained wife-beater T-shirt, and his face—at least the part of it that could be seen around the heavy mass of ratty beard he had—was laced with wrinkles and tiny burst blood vessels. The stench of alcohol emanated from his pores and from the house. Issues with alcohol seemed to be our theme for the day.

"What do you want?" he snarled when he answered our knock, making no attempt at pleasantries. His bloodshot eyes looked mean.

Mal handled the introductions this time, something we had agreed to along the way, and he gave TJ the standard book spiel that we'd used on everyone else.

TJ eyed us suspiciously, his gaze fleeting over Mal and me, and settling on Tyrese. "You're a cop, ain't ya?" he said to Tyrese, spitting out the word *cop* as if it tasted bad.

"I am," Tyrese admitted after a moment's hesitation. "But I'm not on duty. I'm simply helping out some friends."

"Bullshit," TJ said, wavering in the doorway and bouncing off the frame. "I knew you was a cop. I can smell 'em a mile away. And I ain't talking to no cops, on duty or off. So if you two want to come in, that's fine. But he ain't setting foot in my house."

We all looked at one another, unsure of what to do. I was trying to think of a way to ask Tyrese if he would mind waiting in the car when he made the suggestion himself. "I'm fine with that," he said. Then he spun on his heel and headed back to the car.

Mal and I entered the house, which was dark, dingy, and musty smelling beneath the alcohol fumes. The living room looked as if it hadn't been dusted or vacuumed in months, maybe years, and there were cigarette butts piled high in two different ashtrays. A fine layer of ash covered the surface of the scarred, wooden coffee table, which was marred by a dozen or more bottle rings and some sort of gelatinous spills that had dried. The furnishings were old and worn—probably gleaned from other people's castaways that were left out for curbside trash pickups—and there were giant gray cobwebs hanging from the ceiling in the corners. Empty beer bottles were strewn everywhere and a garbage can overflowing with them sat at one end of the couch.

My synesthesia was having a heyday in the place. The smells, the sights, the very taste of the air was triggering all kinds of manifestations. I struggled to filter them and quiet that part of my brain down so that I could focus on TJ and what he said, but it was a struggle.

"You can sit if you want," TJ said, gesturing toward the couch.

I didn't want, but I didn't want to offend the man either, so I held my breath and perched on the edge of one cushion as gently as I could so as to avoid stirring up whatever might be embedded in it. Mal perched similarly beside me and TJ grabbed a metal folding chair from the card table in the dining room and set it down on the opposite side of the coffee table.

"You want a beer?" he asked us.

We both declined.

"Well, I'm gonna have me one," he said, disappearing into what I assumed was the kitchen. We heard the sound of a refrigerator door opening and closing, and the hiss of escaping carbonation when he opened the beer bottle. He returned to the living room, drinking as he walked, and plopped down into the folding chair.

"What is it you want to know?" he asked after he had drained nearly half the bottle dry.

Mal said, "We're interested in hearing anything you might remember about the murders of those two girls, Lori Gruber and Anna Hermann. We understand that you visited Lori Gruber's house the day before the girls disappeared, so we're particularly interested in knowing if you saw anything or heard anything that might give us a clue about what happened to her after."

TJ narrowed his eyes at us, nodding slowly for several seconds. "You know them cops questioned me about them girls," he said. "Acted like they thought I mighta had something to do with them going missing."

We both nodded and Mal said, "Why was that? What put you on their radar?"

"How the hell should I know?" TJ hollered, raising his arms and sloshing a bit of beer out of his bottle. "Just because I was at the one girl's house the day before and they found some magazines in my house." He lunged forward, slamming his bottle down on the table and making me jump. "Lookin' at pictures doesn't mean I did nothin', ya know? But those damned cops seemed to think that having them magazines made me some kind of homicidal pre-vert or somethin'." He shook his head, picked up the beer, and took another long swig. "They ruined everything for me. My wife left me, my kids don't speak to me, my business dried up. . . ." He took another long drink, draining the bottle. Then he set it on the table and smiled at us, revealing several broken and missing teeth. "That's kinda funny, ain't it, a plumber whose business dries up?" He laughed uproariously at his own joke, and to humor him and keep him talking, I smiled and nodded.

"So you had nothing to do with what happened to those girls?" Mal said.

TJ's smile disappeared faster than the last half of his bottled beer. "Of course not," he said, grabbing a pack of cigarettes from the table and tapping one out.

As he lit it, Mal said, "But you were in the Gruber house the day before the girls went missing, right?"

TJ sucked in a drag and blew out a plume of smoke. He at least had the decency to turn his head to the side when he exhaled, not that it made any real difference. The entire place was filled with stale smoke. "Yeah, I was there. I was on a job. They had a bathtub upstairs with a leak in the faucet and a drain that was so slow it took hours to empty after a shower. That drain had the biggest damned hair and slime clog I'd seen in a long time. It was like pulling a rotting carcass outa there. I ended up having to replace both the drain pipe and the faucet."

"Did you see the girl while you were there? Lori?" I asked.

"Sure I did," he said, exhaling another cloud of smoke. "The access panel for the plumbing was in her bedroom so I had to go in there to get to it. It was weirdly warm that year and it was hot as Hades in that house, so I took off my outer shirt while I was working 'cause I was sweating like a pig. Kept the undershirt on, but when I left the house, I forgot the shirt I took off in the girl's room. Apparently, to the cops that was a sure sign of guilt."

"Was Lori there when you were working on the tub?" I asked.

He nodded, blowing more smoke. "She was. Nice enough kid. Typical teenager. She was yacking on the phone most of the time with one of her friends."

"Did you hear any of what she said?" Mal asked.

"Some," TJ said with a shrug and another cloud of smoke. He leaned over and stubbed out the cigarette. "It wasn't anything special, just some gossip about a couple of girls, some mooning over some boys, some talk about going back to school, that sort of stuff."

"Did you hear her make any plans, or talk about meeting anyone?" Mal asked.

TJ shook his head.

Thus far, TJ's voice and mannerisms had been consistent. His voice, which was a bit raspy—no doubt from all the cigarettes—tasted like bacon. There was a hint of smokiness to the flavor, but I wasn't sure if that was part of the manifestation or a literal taste I experienced simply from breathing the air inside TJ's house. I wanted TJ to lie to me, to see what would happen with the flavor of his voice. But first I wanted to hear him deny his involvement.

"Mr. Johnson, did you see the girls, either of them, or have any interactions with them after the day you were at the house working on the tub?"

"I already told you no," he said brusquely, reaching for the cigarette pack again.

"Did you have any one-on-one interactions of any sort with Lori Gruber during the time you were in her house?"

He lit his cigarette and blew the smoke out in an irritated puff, this time not bothering to turn his head to the side.

"I never spoke to the kid," he said, his jaw tight. The flavor of his voice didn't change.

"How many beers have you had today, Mr. Johnson?" I asked.

The sudden change of subject threw him. It apparently threw Mal, too, because he shot me a sideways glance, his brow furrowed.

"How the hell should I know?" he said. "I don't count them."

I gestured toward the overflowing trash can. "It looks like you drink a lot."

He dismissed my observation with a wave of his hand and a *pfft*. "I just don't empty that thing all that often."

"Do you think you have a drinking problem?" I asked, trying to keep my tone as nonjudgmental as I could.

He opened his mouth and I anticipated a vehement denial. But something made him pause and after a few seconds he hung his head and said, "Yeah, I suppose I do. But it's the only way I can cope anymore."

I cursed under my breath. I was hoping for that denial. The vast majority of people with drinking problems deny it to others, but deep down inside they know they have a problem. Had TJ denied his drinking issues, it would have been the same as lying and I wanted to see if it affected the flavor of his voice at all. I decided to try a different tack.

"TJ, what day is it today?"

His brow furrowed in thought. "I don't know . . . Saturday?"

I sighed with frustration. "Actually, it's Sunday."

"Whatever. One day is like the next for me.

Don't matter what day it is so there ain't no need to keep track."

I feared his indifferent attitude would interfere with my test—I intended to ask him to lie to me about what day it was—so I decided to take a more direct approach.

"Mr. Johnson, I need you to tell me a lie."

He stubbed out his cigarette, eyeing me like I was crazy. "What the hell is wrong with you, woman?"

"Please, just indulge me."

He stared at me as the seconds ticked by. Then he licked his lips and said, "I need another beer. And I think it's time you folks went on your way. You can see yourselves out." With that, he got up, muttered something about crazy damned people, and headed for the kitchen.

Mal and I got up and left.

The air outside was growing colder by the minute. I inhaled a huge breath of it, filling my lungs with clean air and relishing the stinging freshness of it in the back of my throat.

"Gads, it was awful in there," Mal said.

Tyrese was sitting behind the wheel of his car and as we got in he looked over at us and said, "Well?"

"Well nothing," I said, shutting my door.

"What was all that stuff about the days of the week and his drinking?" Mal said, settling into his seat and shutting his door. We both went about fastening our seat belts and when we were done, I looked up at Tyrese. His eyes were huge and his face was contorted into a grimace. "Damn!" he said, waving a hand in the air. "Nothing personal, but you guys reek."

"I know. You should be glad he wouldn't let you

come in. That place was horrible. I really want to get out of these clothes and take a shower. Can you head back to the bar please?"

"Sure." Tyrese started the car, lowered all the windows a crack, cranked the heat up, and pulled out. "So how did it go? Did he say anything useful?"

"I don't know. Maybe," I said. "We talked about his contact with Lori, the time he spent at the house, and his issue with the porn that the cops found. Not once during all of that did his voice change for me. But it's obvious that he's drinking a ton. I'd bet his blood alcohol is typically four times the legal limit, maybe even higher. And I don't know how that might affect his brain, or his conscience. I tried to get him to lie to me on purpose to see if his voice would change, but he wouldn't do it. As drunk as he is, I'm not sure it would have worked even if he had."

"So we can't rule him in, or rule him out," Tyrese said.

"Pretty much," I agreed. "We've talked to all the suspects at this point and we have nothing. Maybe it's time to think about digging up some other suspects."

"Correction," Tyrese said. "We really haven't talked to Erik Hermann."

"True," I said. "I do want to take another run at him but I want to do it myself this time. I think I might have better luck getting him to talk if he doesn't feel quite so ambushed and outnumbered."

"I don't know if that's wise, Mack," Tyrese said.

"I'll see if he'll meet me somewhere public," I suggested. "That way it will be safe."

"But what if he says something that could be used as evidence?" Tyrese said.

"Can you outfit her with one of those wires?" Mal asked. "That way we can hear everything that's said and kind of keep an eye on her."

Tyrese considered this and then nodded slowly. "That's not a bad idea," he said. "I just have to figure out how to get ahold of a wire setup without going through official channels."

"That's easy enough," Mal said. "All we have to do is hit up the nearest Radio Shack."

"I don't think anything we hear will be usable as evidence," Tyrese pointed out.

"Perhaps not, but at least it will give us a way to keep an eye on Mack."

"Um, do I get a say in this?" I asked, a bit annoyed that they were talking about me as if I wasn't there. I should have saved my breath and indignation.

"No!" they said in unison, and their tones made it clear they would brook no objections.

I did win a temporary stay, however, because the two Radio Shack stores we visited were both closed for the day.

Chapter 19

We returned to the bar and I told the men I was going to head straight upstairs so I could shower and change my clothes. Tyrese said he'd fill the others in on our visit to TJ and he went upstairs to the Capone Club room. Mal said he wanted to shower also, and that maybe he should head home, but I suggested he join me upstairs and use my father's shower.

"Are you sure?" he asked. "I don't want to impose."

"It's no imposition," I insisted.

"Okay, then."

I led him upstairs and once we were in the apartment, I dug out a towel and washcloth for him to use. "Do you have another change of clothes?" I asked him. "If not, I have a few of my father's clothes packed away that I couldn't bear to get rid of. You're close to his size, so I imagine they'd fit you."

"I have another set of clothes left in my go bag, but thanks."

"When we're done with the showers, give me

your clothes and I'll toss them in the washer with mine."

"That would be great. Thanks." I started to turn away but he touched my arm and stopped me. "One more thing," he said. "I planned on staying here again tonight if you're going to be alone. Is Duncan going to come by?"

"No," I said, trying to mask my disappointment. "But I don't think you have to stay. I'm pretty secure up here, between the alarms on the bar doors and the lock on my apartment door."

Mal shook his head. "I promised Duncan I'd look out for you, and that's what I'm going to do."

"Okay," I said with a shrug. To be honest, I didn't mind the idea of him staying over again, though it wasn't just because I was concerned about my safety. I also enjoyed his company.

"This time, I really am going to sleep on the couch," he said.

I felt myself blush, and wondered why he hadn't said anything about our sharing a bed last night. Did he even know? Or had he slept so soundly that he was unaware of my presence beside him?

"You can sleep wherever you want," I said.

His eyebrows arched and he sucked in a little breath.

"The couch or my father's bed," I clarified quickly. Then I turned and nearly ran into my bathroom to escape the awkward moment.

Half an hour later, I came back out into the living room and found Mal seated at the dining room table, writing something down on some paper. His hair was damp from his shower, and as I approached him, the clean smell of him triggered a sensation like a light breeze on my face.

"What do you want to do with the rest of the evening?" I asked him. "I need to go downstairs and see to the bar, do the closing and such. You're welcome to stay here or to come with me, whatever you want."

"I feel like someone needs to keep a close eye on you, particularly when you're in the bar. You're open to the public and while having a crowd around you offers some sense of protection, it can also make you more vulnerable. I noticed that big hulk of a guy you have behind the bar and at the door at times. Is he trustworthy?"

"You mean Gary. Yeah, I'd say he's trustworthy. He took a bullet for me a couple of months ago."

His eyebrows shot up at that, and I quickly filled him in on the story of my father's murder and that of his girlfriend, Ginny, nine months later.

"I feel a little better knowing you have someone like Gary around, especially since Duncan and I can't be here all the time," he said when I was done. "But you still need to be careful until we find out who's behind these letters. If this Apostle Mike is the culprit, it sounds like he has plenty of yahoos who will blindly do his bidding. Not to mention that there might be some fanatics in the group who would take it upon themselves to do something even without Apostle Mike's direction. And that means that being in a public place around a lot of other people may not be much in the way of protection. Maybe we should clue Gary in to what's going on so he can keep a closer eye on you."

I frowned at that. Bringing in additional people

made it more likely that word would spread, and I didn't want anyone else's death on my hands. Yet Mal had a point. He and Duncan couldn't be around all the time and I didn't want to have to hide in my apartment or office all the time, either. But something told me that whoever was behind those letters was more interested in playing with me than killing me, like a cat toying with a mouse . . . taunting, teasing, hurting, but not killing. At least not yet.

"Let me think about it, okay?" I said.

Mal scowled, making it clear he didn't want to agree, but eventually he nodded.

We headed down to the bar and checked in with the group, updating them on the interviews we'd done earlier, though Tyrese had already filled them in on most of it. After that, Mal and I headed back downstairs to the main level, where I chipped in to help wait the tables in Linda's section. She still wasn't very fast, nor did she have many of the drink names down pat. But she was making an honest and earnest effort, and I felt that with a little more time and training, she would turn out okay. While we worked, I found myself constantly looking over my shoulder, staring at unknown customers, wondering if I was being watched, stalked, and hunted.

Mal positioned himself on a stool and spent the time surveying the crowd, both directly and by using the mirror at the back of the bar. I checked in with him periodically, and clued him in when I saw Clay Sanders come in and take a seat at one end of the bar. Clay stayed until closing, so Mal and I put on a good show for him. A couple times Mal put his arm around my waist and pulled me close when I came up to the bar to fill drink orders. Later on, as I was standing at the end of the bar opposite Clay, Mal came out of the restroom. When he saw me, he came up behind me, wrapped me in a bear hug from behind, and kissed me on my neck. Clay definitely got an eyeful, so if he was coming to spy on me, I felt our mission was accomplished.

Had it been anyone other than Mal acting out these moves on me, I suspect I would have stiffened up and looked uncomfortable. But I felt no discomfort with Mal; in fact, I felt we fit together quite nicely.

The forecasted snow started coming down around one. It started with flat, fluffy flakes that drifted down from the cloud cover, but half an hour later they were coming down faster and straighter. By closing time a bitter wind put in an appearance, so I sent my staff home and did the cleanup and closing tasks myself, though I did put Mal to work washing glasses and dishes. We finished up a little before three and by then the wind had sculpted much of the snow into mini peaks and drifts, making the street look like the top of a lemon meringue pie. It gave me a sense of relief, not only because it meant Mal would likely not have to work in the morning, but because heavy snowfalls tend to bring peace, at least temporarily, to the city. No one, not even the most hardened of criminals, was likely to go out and do anything in the midst of a blizzard. Still, I was relieved to be safe behind my locked doors. The emotional tension I'd felt all night had left me exhausted. Mal and I headed upstairs once we were done and, after giving him some sheets and blankets for the couch, I headed for my own bed. My head barely hit the pillow before I was asleep.

As I slowly surfaced from a deep and restful slumber the next morning, I knew the snowfall during the night had been significant. My first clue was the smell of the air, the second was the deep and distant rumble of the plows outside, and the third was the brightness of the light streaming in my window around the edges of the curtains. The light that comes from daylight reflecting off snow has its own unique feel for me.

I sat up and peered out the window. A good foot of snow had fallen and it was still coming down. The plows had been busy during the night clearing the streets, but there was a good two or three inches of newly fallen stuff in many places, waiting for the plows to make their next round. I smelled fresh coffee, and the lure of it pulled me out of bed and out to the kitchen.

Mal was sitting at the dining room table sipping a cup of coffee. "I made a pot. I hope that's okay."

"It's not only okay, it's wonderful," I said. "It's nice to be on the receiving end for a change."

"Well, then, you're going to love it when I cook you breakfast. I hope you don't mind that I snooped in your fridge to make sure you had what I need and that you like French toast."

"I like anything anyone else cooks for me," I said, using his own line on him.

Mal pulled a chair out from the table and waved

a hand over it. "Have a seat. How do you take your coffee?"

"A dab of cream."

He returned a moment later carrying a steaming mug of perfection. My laptop was on the table and I dragged it over and checked out the morning news while Mal occupied the kitchen. I thought he might ask me where certain items were, but he seemed content to hunt and peck and make do on his own. Before long, the wonderful aromas of vanilla, cinnamon, and maple filled the air, and my stomach began to growl. Mal kept sneaking into the room to drop items off at the table: butter, plates, napkins, and two sets of silverware.

I got a text from Cora asking if she was needed for the trip to the brewery and I messaged her back to let her know that Mal was able to go, and to let the brothers know.

As soon as I hit send, Mal appeared at my side and set a full champagne glass beside my laptop.

"What is this?" I asked, eyeing the bubbly drink.

"My personal spin on the classic mimosa," he said. "I make it with peach juice and put half a canned peach in the bottom of the glass as an extra treat."

I took a sip, savoring the flavors of orange juice and peach syrup mixed together with the champagne. "Yummy," I said.

Mal grabbed my plate and retreated back into the kitchen, returning a moment later. On my plate were three pieces of perfectly browned French toast, delicately dusted with powdered sugar. With his other hand, he set down a small gravy boat with warmed maple syrup in it. "There you go,

Mademoiselle," he said with one of the worst French accents I'd ever heard. "Your morning treat." He scuttled back in to the kitchen and returned with a second plate of French toast, which he carried over to the seat across the table from me. "Dig in. Eez best while it's fresh and hot, which is how I like my women."

I laughed, and did as he said. We ate in companionable silence and I scarfed my food down. The tastes in my mouth created a heady combination of sensations that left me feeling warm, safe, secure, and relaxed. When I was done, I set my fork down and ran a finger through a bit of remaining butter and syrup. When I popped the finger in my mouth to lick it off, I caught Mal watching me with an odd intensity. It took him a second to realize I was looking at him, because his eyes were fixed on my mouth. When he did realize it, he blushed and hurriedly looked back down at his plate.

It was a strained moment, and it became only more so when my cell phone rang and I saw it was Duncan calling.

I answered with a cheerful "Good morning!"

"Good morning, Sunshine. You sound like you're in good spirits."

"I am. How was your night?"

"Long, but I'm heading home to bed. And I have some good news. At least I think it's good. One of the other detectives is bringing Apostle Mike in later this afternoon for a little chat about an assault that took place two nights ago. And I think I figured out how we can bring you in to the station without anyone being the wiser so you can listen in and observe."

"How?"

"I know someone who does theatrical makeup. She trained out in Hollywood with some of the best, but then she abandoned the bright lights so she could move to Wisconsin to be with a man she met. Ten years and three kids later she's still here, and she does cast makeup for theater groups in the area, and for the occasional movie set when Hollywood comes to town. She can fix you up so that no one will recognize you."

"So basically you're suggesting I adopt a disguise and come down to the station?"

"You got it."

I looked over at Mal, who was watching me, his brows drawn down to a worried V. "When?" I asked Duncan.

"Is Mal there? Are you two going to do the Miller tour today?"

"Yes, and yes," I said. Mal and I hadn't discussed it, but given the hour and the weather outside, I assumed he wasn't going into work, and that meant our plan to do the tour was on.

"What time?" Duncan asked.

"I don't know. We haven't discussed the specifics yet. We were just finishing breakfast. Let me ask Mal. I'm going to put you on speaker."

I switched the phone to speaker mode and set it on the table between Mal and me. "Duncan wants to know what time we're going to do the Miller tour. He wants me to come down to the station later and listen in on a chat with Apostle Mike."

Mal shrugged. "We can do the tour anytime."

He glanced at his watch, making me do the same. It was after ten already. "I don't think we can make the ten-thirty tour, especially given the conditions outside, but we should be able to do the eleven o'clock tour."

"That will work fine," Duncan said. "We arranged to have Apostle Mike come in at three-thirty, so I'll send Isabel to the bar around two. That should give you two plenty of time to do the tour and get back. Let Isabel work her magic on you, Mack, and when she's done, come on down to the station."

"How should I get there?" I asked. "If I'm being watched and Mal takes me, someone might recognize his car. They might also recognize my car." The idea that the person writing the letters might have police connections had occurred to me, though I hadn't verbalized that thought to anyone yet. If it was true, they might have the ability to run a license plate. "I'm thinking I should take the bus, or a cab," I concluded.

"Whatever you feel the most comfortable with," Duncan said.

Mal said, "I'm not comfortable with her taking some form of public transit alone. She's exposed enough already."

"She'll be perfectly safe because no one will know it's her," Duncan said. "Trust me on this. I've seen what Isabel can do. She's very good."

"Is she someone we can trust?" Mal asked.

"Absolutely," Duncan said. "My mother has been involved with theater groups both here and in Chicago most of her life. That's how I met Isabel. She's a longtime family friend."

"Okay, then," I said, smiling at Mal with more

reassurance than I felt. "Our plans are set. And if we're going to make that eleven o'clock tour, I best get dressed."

"If it's any consolation," Duncan said, "after you get here and listen in on our talk with Apostle Mike, I'll be free to take you anywhere you want. And tonight I'll be able to stay at your place. Mal, that means you're off the hook."

Mal frowned, but said, "Great," and sounded as if he meant it.

I disconnected the call feeling quite chipper after Duncan said, "See you soon, Sunshine. Can't wait."

I dashed off to dress, leaving Mal to his own devices. My spirits were definitely buoyed by the prospect of finally getting some time alone with Duncan, but I was also a little skeptical. I couldn't quite shake the feeling that something would happen to once again quash our plans.

Fifteen minutes later I was ready to go and Mal and I headed downstairs, where my day staff was already on duty, busy prepping for our eleven o'clock opening.

After making sure everything and everyone was on track, Mal and I headed out for the Miller plant, once again taking his car. It was a quiet drive and I felt an odd level of tension in the air, but said nothing. The drive took a little over twenty minutes thanks to the snowy streets and the morning traffic, and when we pulled into the lot of the Miller plant, it was after eleven. We walked inside the tourist area and gift shop, and headed for the podium to register for the next tour. There was a signup sheet, and after a moment's hesitation, I went ahead and put down my real name. I had no way of knowing if a picture had been provided for this latest rendezvous. If someone here was going to find me, having my name on the list would help.

Once we were signed up, we wandered around the gift shop waiting for the tour to start. Mal was quiet and seemed a little sullen, and I wondered why. But I didn't want to be distracted from our goal, so I said nothing. Finally, a young fellow with an acne-stricken face announced to all that the next tour was about to start. We lined up with about fifteen other people—it takes more than a major snowstorm to shut down anything in Milwaukee— and after a brief introduction, we were all ushered into a theater.

For the next twenty minutes we watched a film about Frederick Miller, the story of the girl in the moon, and the history of the Miller Company. When it was done, we were directed to head out a door on the opposite side of the theater. Our guide led us out of the building we were in and into another—the packaging plant. There we were treated to a mesmerizing display of high-speed, modern mechanization. As our guide explained the process and boggled our minds with numbers, we watched from a glassed-in catwalk above the huge warehouse floor as thousands of bottles of beer a minute were labeled and packaged for shipping.

Our next stop was several levels up, where the giant tuns used for fermenting are kept. We learned about malting and mashing, the difference between ales and lagers, variations in the fermenting process, and more. Next we headed out to the street, where the guide gave us a brief history lesson on the architecture of some of the buildings that make up the brewery. From there we entered the underground caves that Frederick Miller used decades ago to store the beer. The last stop on the tour was a Bavarian-style inn where we were seated and given samples of three different beers to taste.

Mal was fascinated by the tour, and his mood had improved remarkably by the time we reached the inn. Because I'd done the tour before, I'd spent most of my time studying the people around us—the others in our group, the guides, the employees, people on the street—wondering if we were being watched, or if we'd be approached. As we sat sipping our beers, Mal was chatting away about what we'd just seen, happy and excited. I, on the other hand, sat disappointed, wondering if we'd made a mistake in our interpretation of the last letter.

As I brooded and Mal chatted on, our acne-scarred tour guide approached the table. "Miss Dalton?"

"Yes," I said, suddenly breathless with anticipation.

"I have something I'm supposed to give you." He reached into his pocket, pulled out a folded, plain white envelope, and handed it to me.

I saw Mal wince and shake his head, no doubt because any evidence that might have been on that envelope—though if history was any indication there wasn't any—was now thoroughly contaminated.

"Thank you," I said, taking the envelope.

He turned to leave, but I called him back. "Wait, I have some questions for you."

He turned back and stood there, shifting nervously from one foot to another.

"How did you get this?"

"It was in a big envelope that was left here at the desk with my name on it."

Clever, I thought. The mode of delivery changed each time. "Was there money in the envelope?"

He nodded, looking about nervously.

"Mind if I ask how much?"

"That's kind of personal," he said in a low voice.

"I know, and I'm sorry to ask. It's just that I'm new to this scavenger hunt game and I'm worried that I'm not paying enough to the people I use to deliver clues. I don't want to look cheap."

He blinked rapidly several times, staring at me with a confused expression. "Scavenger hunt?" he said.

I explained further, using the same story I'd used on the others. When I was done, his confused expression had been replaced by one of dawning understanding.

"It's a game," he said, looking relieved. I wondered what he thought he was getting into. Did he think it was something illegal, like money for a drug trade or something? "That's totally ridic. How did you get into it?"

"It's something my friends and I do for entertainment. So can you tell me how much you were paid?"

"I guess," he said with another lopsided shrug. "There was a hundred bucks in the envelope. But please don't tell anyone, okay? I need this job and I'm not sure they'd like me doing this."

"I won't tell a soul," I promised, thinking, *a hundred dollars for each delivery. Whoever was sending the letters definitely wasn't hurting financially. Someone like Apostle Mike fits that bill.* "And were you instructed to do something to communicate that this delivery was successful?" I asked the guide.

He nodded and flashed a crooked smile. "I'm supposed to post an ad on Craigslist in the lost and found section that says I lost a cell phone with a zebra striped case at the zoo."

"What number are you supposed to list with the ad?" Mal asked.

"Mine." He shrugged again and smiled. "I don't imagine I'll get any calls."

"And what if I hadn't shown up?" I asked.

"If you didn't come in by five o'clock on Tuesday, I was supposed to rip the smaller envelope into pieces and flush it down a toilet along with its contents. Then I was supposed to post the ad on Craigslist but list the phone with a leopard patterned case."

"Do you still have the envelope this one came in?"

He shook his head. "I tossed it in the gift shop trash and the cleaning people came through a little later."

He was starting to look spooked, so I put on my best friendly smile and said, "You did great, uh . . . what's your name?"

"Brad."

"Well, thanks for all your help, Brad. I appreciate it."

He accepted my gratitude with a spastic nod and then hurried off.

I glanced at my watch and then looked over at Mal. "It's almost twelve-thirty, so I suppose we should head back so I can meet with Isabel. Do you think I'd look better as a blonde or a brunette?"

"I think you'd look great as either," Mal said with a warm smile.

And with that, the awkwardness returned.

Chapter 20

The bar wasn't very busy when we got back, typical for a Monday afternoon, not to mention a post-blizzard Monday. I led the way up to my apartment, where Mal and I donned gloves and then carefully opened the envelope the guide had given me, using the same technique as before. There was the usual piece of plain printer type paper, folded into thirds. But there were several other items inside the paper. I unfolded it and let the items drop onto the paper we had on the table: a small piece of green terry cloth, a scrap of some sort of filter paper, a flower petal, three small squares of folded paper, and three tiny pictures that looked as if they had been cut from magazine pages. On the inside of the folded piece of paper, written in the same calligraphic style, was one line:

8:00 P.M., Wednesday, December 16th

"What the . . . ?" Mal said.

His words echoed my thoughts. I carefully arranged all the items on the table, grabbed my cell phone, and took several pictures. Then I sent the pictures to Duncan with a message to call me when he could. I hoped whoever this was couldn't track my calls and texts.

With that done, I focused in on the tiny pictures that had been inside the envelope. The first one I looked at was small, only one inch by two inches, and it showed a faucet with water running from it. The other side of the paper had words on it, some small segment from an article. The second picture showed a marquee advertising the show *Cats,* but unlike the first picture, the back side of it showed no print. Instead it was a plain white expanse. There wasn't a complete sentence to be had in the printed portion of the first picture and the words that were there weren't particularly telling: *next he went to the last,* and *they didn't find anyone who,* and *said he thought it might be . . .* that sort of stuff. I didn't think the words themselves were significant; I felt strongly that the picture was the key. But perhaps there would be a way to trace the words to a specific article and magazine that might provide a lead of some sort.

When I focused on the third picture, which was only one inch square, I realized it wasn't from a magazine after all. It was part of a map. It showed Interstates 94 and 35 meeting at an intersection, and there were other street names visible: Wabasha, St. Peter, and Rice.

I moved from the pictures to the small folded pieces of paper. Carefully, I unfolded one of them and inside I found a tiny piece of plastic wrap that contained a brown, grainy substance. As I looked at it, turning it first one way, then another, a tiny amount of the substance trickled out. I caught a whiff of something and started to tell Mal about it, but before I could he said in a sharp, terse tone, "Put it down now! Very slowly."

He looked panicked and I did as he said, staring at his face. "What?" I said, frightened.

"It might be a poison of some sort."

"It's not. It's cinnamon."

He looked at me with skepticism. "You can't know that."

"Yes, I can. I can smell it, and along with the smell I hear a hollow banging sound, like shells being knocked together. I know what that is. Believe me, it's just cinnamon."

"You're positive."

I nodded, licked a finger, stuck it in some of the grains that had fallen out, and then put my finger in my mouth. I thought Mal was going to faint. "It's cinnamon," I said. "Relax."

I grabbed another of the folded papers and opened it. Inside was more plastic wrap, and inside that was a tiny brown piece of something. I carefully opened the plastic and took a whiff, wrinkling my nose. "This is bread, rye bread."

I set the plastic wrap down with the crumb still on it and went for the third piece of folded paper. A distinctive odor emanated from it even before I had it fully opened. As with the other two, this one contained a small piece of plastic wrap, and inside that were several tiny iridescent, fan-shaped objects.

"Fish scales," I said.

I put the fish scales down and picked up the small piece of filter paper, running it under my nose. "This is from a coffee filter," I told him. "And there was coffee in it at one time."

Mal sucked in a deep breath and said, "This is crazy. What the hell is all this stuff supposed to mean?"

I picked up the tiny square of green terry cloth and sniffed it. "This has been soaked in wine at some point. It's dry now, but at one time it had chardonnay on it."

"What about the petal?" Mal asked. "Anything weird with it?"

I gently picked it up and smelled it. "It's a basic rose petal," I announced, setting it back down.

We stood there for a minute or so, eyeing the items and thinking.

"Any ideas?" Mal said finally.

"Not a clue," I said, feeling my frustration grow.

"Well, at least we have a couple of days to figure it out."

"I'm not sure it will be enough," I said worriedly. "This little game is starting to wear on my nerves, Mal."

"We'll get to the bottom of it," he assured me, though I thought I detected a hint of hesitancy in his voice. He reached over and gave my shoulder a squeeze. "Maybe it's this Apostle Mike guy Duncan is focused on. If it is, we might put an end to this today."

"And if it's not?"

He didn't answer right away. Instead he kept staring at the items on the table. Finally, he said, "There's a lot of stuff here that might produce trace evidence of some sort, that plastic wrap, the pictures, the papers. Maybe the guy behind this slipped up and left something for us this time. We need to get Duncan to have it analyzed."

I realized he was right. This thing was too big for me to handle alone without the resources Duncan could bring to the table. I grabbed my phone again and snapped some more pictures of the items now that we had opened them, zooming in on all of the pictures and the text on the backside of the faucet one. I took a few minutes to send these to Duncan along with a description of the items.

When I was done, Mal said, "Give it time. We'll figure something out."

"I guess I don't have any choice." I thought about my afternoon appointment with Isabel the makeup artist and said, "We need to put this stuff somewhere."

Mal nodded. "Let's bag it all."

I grabbed a box of baggies and we carefully placed each item in its own bag. When we were done, we put them all in a paper bag and I carried them into my father's old office.

When I came out, Mal said, "I'm hungry and that BLT you make is fantastic. Any chance I can talk you into buying me lunch?"

"Sure," I said with a wan smile. "I'm hungry, too."

We headed downstairs into the bar kitchen, where I fixed us both a BLT and some fries. We carried these upstairs to the Capone Club room to check in on the crew. Because of the day, the time, and the weather, there was only a handful of people there: Cora, the Signoriello brothers, Carter, and Tiny. I knew that Alicia and Holly might stop in for lunch since the bank they worked at was walking distance away, and Tad and Kevin might come by after they finished their work days. Dr. T, on the other hand, had told the group last night that she had a couple of twelve-hour shifts coming up, so she might not be back in for a day or so.

Cora eyed our sandwiches with envy. "Those BLTs are making my stomach growl. Is anyone else hungry?" Everyone nodded. Cora nudged Tiny with her elbow and said, "Then I'll tell you what. If you and Carter will run downstairs and order sandwiches for all of us, I'll pay. Just tell Pete to put it on my tab."

Tiny and Carter were more than happy to oblige. I realized as soon as they were gone that the motive behind Cora's generosity was more than simple hunger.

"So how did it go at the brewery?" she asked.

The brothers both sat forward in their chairs, eager to hear the news. I updated them on how our tour had gone and then told them about the items in the letter we received.

"Wow," Joe said. "Whoever is sending these letters is ratcheting things up. That's a lot of clues for one letter. Any idea what they mean?"

I shook my head, as did Mal.

Cora said, "The group is talking about looking into Lewis's case despite Tyrese's instructions not to. His death has hit them hard."

"You guys need to do what you can to keep them focused on something else," I said. "If any of them start poking around they could really stir up a hornet's nest of trouble."

"We can try," Cora said, and the brothers both nodded their agreement. "But a few of them seem rather determined."

We heard Tiny and Carter returning so in a

hushed voice I said, "We can talk some more later. In the meantime, do what you can to rein in the group and let me know if you come up with any ideas on the latest letter."

The threesome nodded their understanding and then switched their attention to our returning duo.

"Any news on the book front, Carter?" I asked as he and Tiny settled back in their seats.

"Not really," Carter said. "But Sam wanted me to tell you that he'd be happy to go and see this Schneider guy either this evening or anytime tomorrow since he's off."

"I think tomorrow would work best for me," I said.

"You should take Tyrese or Nick along," Mal said. "If this guy goes off the deep end I want to make sure you're safe."

"Tyrese said he's on his long stretch off," Cora said. "I'll give him a call and let him know what your plans are."

"Thanks," I said, nodding my agreement. "I have some business stuff to take care of this afternoon, but I'll check in with you guys later this evening."

As I thought, Holly and Alicia popped in for lunch and we all talked about our list of suspects some more. Mal and I finished our sandwiches and just before two, we headed back down to the main area of the bar and settled in on the bar stools. While Mal and my daytime bartender, Pete, started talking football stats, I kept my eye on the door. A short time later, a woman with shoulder-length curly brown hair came up to the bar wheeling a small suitcase behind her.

"I'm looking for Mack Dalton," she said.

"I'm Mack." I hopped off my stool and walked over to shake her hand. "Are you Isabel?"

"I am," she said with a big smile and a firm handshake.

"Let me take you upstairs so we can discuss the plan." I was eager to get her away from prying eyes and ears since I wasn't sure if Duncan had told her that what we were doing needed to be secret.

"The plan?" Pete said, curious, dashing any hope I had for a clean getaway.

"Um, I'm thinking about doing some redecorating in the apartment and Isabel is an interior designer who was recommended to me." I turned to Isabel and gave her a wink that no one else could see. "Would you like a drink before we head upstairs?"

She shook her head. "No, thanks. I just had lunch."

I turned to Mal and said, "Want to come along?"

"Sure," he said with a shrug. "You probably need a man's opinion to keep things from getting too frilly."

I led the three of us upstairs to my apartment and as soon as we were behind closed doors, I turned to Isabel. "Sorry about that, but what we're doing here has to remain a secret from everyone except us three and Duncan. I didn't know if Duncan had relayed that to you."

"He did say that he needed me for a top secret project," she said. "I'm fine with the interior designer story. In fact, I do a little interior design on the side along with some set design."

"Well, feel free to make suggestions," I told her. "I haven't done much with the place. I meant to after my father died, but I've just never gotten around to it." I directed her to the dining room table. "Will this suffice as a work area?"

"It will," she said, laying her suitcase down on the floor and opening it. "Have a seat. This will take a little time because per Duncan's instructions, I'm going to make you unrecognizable."

Chapter 21

"The first thing we need to hide is that hair," Isabel said, eyeing my head with skepticism. "It's like a neon beacon."

I frowned, grabbed a shank of my hair, and held it in front of my face. "My red isn't that bad, is it?"

"No, in fact it's quite lovely, which is why we have to hide it. It draws attention."

She removed a wig from the suitcase—a brunette, chin-length bob—and set it on the table. Next she took out several bottles, each one containing some type of liquid. Most of them were skin-toned, but there was one that was clear, one that was white, and one that was green. She lined them up on the table and removed a small machine that was basically a box with a power cord on one end and some sort of wand that was attached to the other end with a narrow plastic hose.

"What is that?" I asked.

"An airbrush," she said. "I use it to apply makeup. It allows me to be very precise and artistic." She set it on the table and went back to the suitcase.

Out came a plastic container that held a variety of contact lenses: blue, green, various shades of brown, hazel, and a few bizarre ones that looked like lizard or zombie eyes.

As Isabel was assembling her wares, my cell phone rang. It was Duncan.

"Hey, beautiful," he said. "Is Isabel there yet?"

"She is. We're just about to get started."

"Good."

"Did you get the pictures I sent you?"

"I did. It's quite the assortment this time around. Any idea what it means?"

"Not yet," I said. "Mal and I tried to figure it out, but so far we're both drawing a blank."

"Can you bag the items up for me?"

"Already did," I said, feeling a little proud of myself. I was getting to be quite the evidence expert, I thought.

"Bring it all with you when you come down to the station. Given all the items there were in that envelope, our sender might have gotten careless with something and left us a print or some DNA."

"That's what Mal said."

"I know you don't want to involve the lab for fear of our letter writer finding out, but—"

"Save your breath," I said, interrupting him. "Mal convinced me that this is too big for me to deal with on my own. We just have to be careful."

"Well, then, be sure to thank Mal for me." Something in his voice changed with that, turning the chocolate taste a little bitter.

"I better go," I said, seeing that Isabel had her wares ready to go. "Isabel said this is going to take a while. I'll see you soon, okay?"

"Okay."

With that, I disconnected the call and submitted myself to Isabel's administrations. She began by brushing my hair and pulling it into a tight bun on the crown of my head. After that she applied a wide cloth hairband around my head along my hairline. "Have you ever worn contacts before?" she asked.

I shook my head.

"Okay, quick lesson then."

A few minutes later my eyes were a dark brown color, nearly black. At first I kept blinking every few seconds, keenly aware of them in my eyes, but after a bit they became more comfortable.

Next Isabel took some flesh-colored pieces of latex and began putting them on my face, securing them in place with some type of glue. I wished I could see what she was doing, but there was no mirror close by, so I just gave myself over to the process. It took her just over forty minutes to finish, and the last thing she did was put the wig on me. She stood back then and looked at me with a critical eye.

"What do you think?" she said to Mal, who had sat across the table from me in awed silence watching the entire process.

"I think you're a genius," he said, his voice rife with admiration. "If I didn't know that was Mack beneath all that latex and makeup, I'd never guess it. Go look in a mirror, Mack. You truly are unrecognizable."

I hopped up from the chair and went into the bathroom. Looking in the mirror was a shock. It was a strange feeling, both disconcerting and exciting at the same time. Parts of my face felt a little stiff, but after some practice making different expressions, I grew more comfortable with it and felt like I was ready to give it a road test.

"I guess I'm ready to head out," I said, emerging from the bathroom.

"Should we sneak out a back door?" Mal said.

"*We* aren't doing anything," I said. "You can't go with me, Mal. It would be too much of a giveaway."

He scowled at this, but said nothing more.

"I think I'm going to walk right out through the bar. If anyone there recognizes me, we'll need to go back to square one. If they don't, I'll grab a taxi and take it to the police station."

"You can't go yet," Isabel said. "We're not done. You need to change your clothes."

"Oh, right," I said feeling stupid. "I can't be seen wearing the same thing I was earlier."

"And we need to change both your walk and your voice," Isabel said.

Now it was my turn to give her a skeptical look.

"If you're being watched, someone might pick up on something like that. You may not look the same, but your voice is a dead giveaway."

I realized she was right. After ten minutes of voice coaching, I donned a generic pair of jeans, a nondescript navy blue sweatshirt, and a pair of old boots I hadn't worn since two winters ago. I also dragged an old winter parka out of the closet and resurrected a purse I had abandoned four years ago but had never tossed because it was in good condition. I'd simply grown tired of it. Then I went in to my father's old office and put all the bagged evidence into the purse.

"Now you're ready," Isabel said when I came back to the dining room. I put my wallet in the purse, sticking it in a different section from where the evidence bags were. Then I grabbed for my cell phone, but Mal stopped me.

"Silence it first, and whatever you do, don't answer it or look at a text unless you are somewhere alone and private. Easiest way to prove who you are if someone is watching and has a suspicion is to call your cell and see if you answer it."

I hadn't thought of that, just like I hadn't thought about the clothes and speech. My earlier confidence, brought about by the startling change in my appearance, was beginning to fade away.

Mal must have sensed my hesitation because he walked over and gave me a one-armed hug, whispering in my ear, "You can do this, Mack. You're one of the strongest women I've ever known."

His words boosted my confidence and as I went downstairs to the apartment door, I felt energized. I had Isabel go out first to see if anyone was standing in the hallway. I didn't want anyone to see me exiting from my apartment. Once she indicated the coast was clear, I stepped into the hallway, strode down it into the bar, and walked straight to the front door. No one said a word, and no one gave me a second look. I stepped outside and realized I'd been holding my breath. I exhaled a huge plume of relief and walked several blocks away. Then I hailed a passing cab.

I gave the cab driver an address near the police station, using my newly honed Southern accent. He didn't look at me twice. I paid him in cash, got out, and headed in the opposite direction from where I wanted to go. As soon as the cab pulled away, I turned around and went into the police station. At the check-in window, I again used my

Southern accent and asked to see Detective Duncan Albright, giving my name as Susan Smith, something Isabel had instructed me to do. I was told to take a seat, did so, and then got another boost to my confidence when Duncan came through a door, glanced around the room, and then asked the receptionist where Susan Smith was. When she pointed me out, Duncan stared at me, blinking hard several times. Finally, he said, "Ms. Smith, would you please come with me?"

I got up and followed him through the station hallways and into the observation room located at the center of the interrogation rooms. I had been there before, observing Duncan as he questioned suspects in the cases I worked with him several weeks ago. Duncan didn't say a word until we were inside, then he took me by the shoulders and held me at arm's length, shaking his head in amazement. "I knew she was good, but not this good. That is you, Mack, right?"

"It is," I said with a smile, dropping my Southern accent. "Isabel really is amazing. I didn't recognize myself when she was done, and when I left the bar, no one gave me a second look."

Duncan wrapped my face between his palms and kissed me long and hard. When he was done, he leaned back, looked at me for a second, and then started laughing.

"What's so funny? Laughing at a girl right after you kiss her doesn't do much for her confidence."

"Sorry, it's just that I've really missed you and now that you're here, I kind of still miss you because it's like I'm kissing someone else. I feel like

I'm cheating. And in an odd way, that's sort of titillating. Quite the conundrum."

I couldn't decide if I was amused or bothered by this, but when he kissed me again I stopped caring. When we broke apart, I felt breathless and relieved. The magic was still there.

"Okay, much as I hate the idea of stopping, we need to get down to business," Duncan said. "Where is the evidence?"

I opened my purse and took out all the baggies, laying them out on a small counter that ran the length of the walls in the room just below the observation windows.

"How are you explaining all this evidence to whoever is running it?"

"I told her that my sister has a stalker and that I'm trying to figure out who it might be. She understands that I don't want it to be an actual case file and need to keep it private. It hasn't been an issue so far, and I don't think it will be."

I hoped he was right.

"Any more thoughts on this stuff?" he asked me, eyeing the baggies.

"Not really. I thought at one point that it might be some kind of recipe, but I'll be darned if I can think of one that uses fish, cinnamon, water, coffee, and wine. Plus I can't figure out how some of the other items fit in, like the rose petal and that tiny section of map."

Duncan bent down to get a closer look at the map piece. "Do you still have these pictures in your phone?"

"I do."

"Send the one of the map to Cora. I'm betting

she can figure out where it is. In fact, send her all the pictures. Maybe she'll have some ideas."

It was a great idea and I kicked myself for not thinking of it on my own. I took out my phone and did just that as Duncan gathered up all the evidence in a large manila envelope. "I'll take this to Carrie when we're done here," he said. "Maybe we'll get lucky."

I had my doubts.

When I was done sending the pictures to Cora, Duncan said, "This Apostle Mike guy, whose real name is Michael Treat, is due any minute. I seriously considered having Jimmy conduct the interview thinking that the fewer people who know I'm doing something on the side the better, but after thinking it over I decided to let some other detectives do it to make sure there's no connection to me."

"Thank you for that," I said, feeling some sense of relief. "How much of all this does Jimmy know?"

"Very little. It's not that I don't trust Jimmy, but he tends to be a by-the-book guy who doesn't like stepping outside of the rules and regulations."

"Yeah, I got that loud and clear when he was working with me."

"He's come around a lot," Duncan said. "In fact, the other day he said he kind of missed having your input on a case we were banging our heads over."

"Seriously?"

Duncan held his hand up like he was about to swear an oath. "No lie," he said.

"So how much of my situation now is he aware of?"

"He knows I'm looking into a private matter

and doing some stuff off the books, but he thinks it's because I have someone who is stalking me. He has no idea you're involved and I haven't discussed any details with him. Carrie, the lab tech, is trustworthy and she promised she wouldn't share any info with anyone, and I specifically included Jimmy in that request. The less he knows about it, the better for now."

"I agree."

"Now back to Apostle Mike, aka Michael Treat. They'll bring him into room one and talk to him about an assault we're pretty sure his group was involved in. At the end, they'll ask him about Lewis Carmichael's death."

"Do you think that's wise? If he is the one writing the letters that might be just enough to push him over the edge."

"I got it covered. They're going to tell him they found info in Lewis's apartment that suggests he was into the occult. Since Apostle Mike knows we are aware of his hatred of that sort of stuff, it makes sense that we would question him on it. And if he is behind it, the idea that he might have overlooked a connection might rattle him enough to put him off his game. One of the detectives will be wearing an earpiece so I can coach him if need be."

"Do the guys doing the questioning know why they're doing it?"

Duncan shook his head. "I just told them it was for another case I'm working on. I didn't offer specifics."

"I'll need some sort of barometer, a test question that we know is a lie in order to identify any changes in his voice."

"I've got it covered. You remember how this works, right?" I nodded as he handed me the headphones. "You won't be able to say anything to the detectives, but if there's something you want me to have them do or ask, just let me know."

He donned his own headset and a mike, and we both settled in on the stools and waited. Less than a minute later, the door to the interview room opened and I got my first look at Apostle Mike.

I was expecting him to resemble Charles Manson, or maybe David Koresh, but he wasn't close to either. He was tall, lean, bald, handsome, dignified looking. I thought he might be wearing a robe of some sort or some other peculiar dress, but he was wearing khakis and a plain blue dress shirt beneath a gray parka. His feet were clad in black snow boots and his gloves didn't match; one was blue and the other was green. He looked more like your typical downtown cubicle worker than he did the leader of some fanatical religious group.

His nose was red from the cold and he sniffled and swiped at it with the back of one of his hands after he removed his gloves. One of the two detectives who entered the room with him offered him a box of tissues, but he declined with a smug smile and said, "No, thanks. I don't want to provide you with any unasked for samples of my DNA."

I had met one of the detectives before, a balding, overweight forty-something guy named Arthur Cook. He was newly single on the heels of a divorce and came into the bar a couple of nights every week. Based on the flirtatious behaviors he displayed, I guessed that he was using the bar as a hunting ground in his search for a new woman. As far as I knew, he hadn't yet scored.

The second detective was a stranger to me. He was tall and thin—though his arms were well muscled—and looked to be in his mid- to late thirties. Both his haircut and his posture hinted at a military background, and I wondered if that was how he got the scar on his face that ran from his right eyebrow up to his hairline.

Arthur Cook started things off by introducing himself—though he used the name Arty—and his partner, whose name was Doug Farrell. I noticed that Arthur was the one wearing the ear bud, and after the introductions, he got right down to business.

"Mr. Treat, we asked you to come in today because we wanted to talk to you about the recent assault of a woman in a parking garage downtown."

Apostle Mike sat slouched in his chair, legs extended out, wearing an expression of indifference. "You've asked me about other assaults and I keep telling you guys that I follow a philosophy of peace and tolerance, not violence." His attitude made it clear that he wasn't worried about their claims. Either he was a damned good liar, or he was innocent. His voice was an interesting mix of tastes, beefy and spicy hot, like a bite of prime rib dipped in horseradish.

"Yes, so you claim," Arthur said, "and yet we keep finding notes at the sites of these assaults that speak out against certain beliefs, beliefs that you have gone on record as saying are an abomination. Are you telling me it's merely a coincidence?"

"Either that, or an erroneous presumption on

your part." Treat shrugged. "You can pick. But I'm telling you I didn't assault any woman."

The guy was irritatingly smug and that alone made me want him to be guilty. He had a way of getting under one's skin. I cautioned myself to remain objective and not let my feelings get in the way of my perceptions.

Doug took over at that point. "We don't think we're wrong, nor do we put much faith in coincidence," he said.

Treat shifted his condescending gaze from Arthur to Doug and asked, "When, exactly, did this assault occur?"

"Saturday night, around ten P.M.," Doug said.

"Ah, well there you go," Treat said with the return of that smug smile. "I was preaching to a group of my followers that night in the church on my compound. The entire thing was taped. I'll be happy to provide you with a copy if you like."

"The dates and times on videos can be altered," Doug said.

"Yes, I suppose they can," Treat replied in a tired voice. "But the video will also show a number of people who were there at the time, people who can vouch for when and where the meeting took place."

"And why would we believe the word of your zealous followers?" Doug asked.

Treat cocked his head to one side and shrugged again. "You don't have to. You can ask the reporter who was there filming the entire thing. I believe his name was Woods, John Woods. He said he was doing an article for the *Tribune*."

"The *Chicago Tribune*?" Doug asked.

"The one and only," Treat said. He pulled his

legs up and leaned forward, ready to get out of his chair. "So are we done here?"

"No, we're not," Arthur said. "We're also interested in your whereabouts on Thursday night."

"Thursday," Treat said, wrinkling his brow. "Let me think. I believe I was home on Thursday evening."

"Can anyone vouch for that?" Arthur asked.

"No, you got me this time," Treat said, his eyes wide with mock fear. "May I ask what crime it is you're looking into for that night?"

"Murder," Doug said, and Treat's smile faded a smidge.

"Murder . . . that's a very serious claim. Just who is it you think I might have murdered?"

"A man named Lewis Carmichael. His body was found downtown by the river's edge under the *Bronze Fonz*."

"Ah, yes," Treat said, nodding slowly. "I remember seeing something about that in the news. Very sad." Neither his tone nor his expression suggested he believed it was sad at all. "And why would you think I had anything to do with this man's unfortunate demise?"

"We found stuff in Carmichael's apartment that suggested he was into the occult and practiced the dark arts," Arthur said.

"Really?" Treat said, pulling at his chin. His brows drew down in concern, but I got the sense that it was faked. A moment later, my suspicion was verified. "Well, to each his own," Treat said. "Maybe the devil got him."

I saw Duncan shake his head and then he said something into the microphone on his headset that I couldn't hear. Arthur glanced at the mirror in the room, the glass we were watching through, and gave a slight nod to indicate he had heard.

"There's one other thing I'd like to ask you," Arthur said. "There was a double homicide that took place at a home in West Allis on Friday night around nine. Any chance you know anything about that?"

Treat laughed. "Really, gentlemen, you seem determined to lay the blame for every crime in the city at my feet."

"Answer the question," Arthur said, his face dark.

Treat's smile faltered. "No, I don't know anything about a double homicide in West Allis, okay? Now, I've cooperated fully with this inane line of questioning, and my patience is wearing thin. I'm a very busy man with places to go and things to do, so I'm going to leave now." He started to rise from his chair but stopped halfway up and looked Arthur straight in the eye. "That is unless you have something you want to hold me on? Some evidence of some sort?"

The two men engaged in a stare down that lasted a good fifteen seconds. Then Treat straightened up the rest of the way and said, "I thought not. Good day, gentlemen." And with that, he turned and left the room.

I took my headset off and looked over at Duncan. "Well, that was a complete waste of time."

"Maybe," he admitted. "Tell me what your perceptions were, what you heard in his voice during all of that."

"Well, clearly the guy is a smug bastard. He seems very sure of himself."

"What about his voice? Did it change at all while he was talking?"

I shook my head. "No, the taste of his voice remained consistent the whole time. But since the guys didn't hit him up with a known lie, I don't know what his voice would taste like if he was lying."

"Actually, they hit him up with a known truth. That double homicide they asked him about was the case Jimmy and I drew the other night. And we already have the culprit. It was strictly a drug-related thing and we arrested the killer only an hour ago. So we know that Treat wasn't involved in that crime. His denial in that case was an honest one. Did his voice change at all with that answer as compared to the others? Because we're pretty certain he is involved in the assault."

Again, I shook my head. "No, his voice didn't change a bit. Besides, if his alibi holds out, it's clear he wasn't directly involved in the assault."

"But he might have ordered someone else to do it," Duncan said.

I thought back to the discussion that had taken place. "It's possible," I admitted. "He said he didn't assault any woman, and if he had someone else do it, that is essentially the truth."

"So we've got nothing," Duncan said, a look of frustration on his face.

"It would seem so."

"Head back to the bar and do what you would normally do for now." He gathered up the manila envelope. "I'll get this evidence to Carrie and then I have a few other loose ends to tie up. But when I'm done, I'm coming over. Do you mind if I spend the night?"

"Mind? I think I might have to kill you if you don't."

"Dangerous words to say around here," he said, giving me a kiss on the forehead. "Let's use the same plan we did before. Meet me at the back door around ten to sneak me in. And be careful going back. Don't let anyone in the bar see you head upstairs to your apartment in that disguise, just in case your place is being watched."

"I think I'll have Cora do for me what I'm going to do for you later. Though I have to say it irritates me that I've been forced to resort to sneaking into my own place."

"Hopefully, it's only temporary." He kissed me again then, a much deeper, longer, more satisfying kiss. Then he turned me around, patted me on the butt, and said, "Be gone. I'll see you soon."

I headed out of the police station feeling rather chipper despite the disappointing results of the interview with Apostle Mike. As soon as I hit the sidewalk outside, I took out my cell phone and called Cora since I didn't have Mal's number.

"Hey, Mack," she answered.

I'd given Cora a key to my office several weeks ago in case she ever needed to get in there to troubleshoot the Wi-Fi when I wasn't around. I explained to her what I needed, and requested that she turn off the alarm and meet me at the alley door.

"How long will you be?"

"I need to find a cab," I told her. "So I'm not sure. I'll text you once I secure a ride. Stand by the door and let's agree on a secret knock. One knock, a pause, then two knocks, another pause, and then three knocks."

"Ooh, just like real spies," Cora said, sounding excited.

"I hope no one can hear you."

"Give me a little credit, Mack. I'm on the stairs and no one is anywhere near me at the moment."

"Okay, I'll see you shortly." Then I explained to her how my appearance had been altered.

"And by the way, I figured out where that section of map you sent me is located."

"You did? Where?"

"It's in St. Paul."

"As in Minnesota?"

"The very one."

I frowned at this. Was I supposed to go to St. Paul for the next clue? That seemed a bit outrageous. "Good work, Cora," I said. "Now all I have to do is figure out what the hell it means."

Chapter 22

I arrived back at the bar forty minutes later. It took me ten minutes to get a cab after I called for one, and I had them drop me off a block away from the bar. I walked the rest of the way, looking to see if anyone was watching me when I entered the back alley. Minutes later I was at the door and used the secret knock, but nothing happened. I waited for a minute, and then knocked again. This time the door opened before I could finish the sequence.

"Sorry," Cora said. "There was someone in the hallway the first time you knocked so I didn't want to open the door until they were gone."

"Good thinking." I had my key at the ready and I unlocked the door to my apartment and stepped inside so I couldn't be seen if anyone came down the hall. "Can you go turn the alarm back on?" I said to Cora. "Lock my office behind you when you're done and I'll meet you upstairs with the Capone Club group once I'm back to being me."

Cora nodded and shut the door.

Once I was back upstairs in my apartment, it

took me a good half hour to remove all the makeup and latex pieces that Isabel had put on me, and after donning the same clothes I'd been wearing earlier, I gave myself a final check in the mirror and headed back to the bar.

Business was still slow. No doubt the weather had kept a lot of folks busy shoveling themselves out during the day, leaving them too tired to go out and party. It took more than a little snow to slow down the Capone Club members, however, and most of the gang was there: Joe, Frank, Cora, Tad, Carter, Holly, Sam, Alicia, and of course, Mal.

"It's about time, Mack," Mal said, as if he hadn't seen me in forever. He got up, walked over to me, and kissed me on the cheek. "Did you finish up your interior design plans?"

"Interior design?" Holly said. "What are you up to now? Wasn't the bar expansion enough for you?"

I smiled and said, "It probably should have been, but all the new stuff here has reminded me of how old and tired my apartment is. So I've decided to make some changes." Not wanting to dwell on the subject since it was basically a lie—a lie I could hear in my own voice—I switched topics. "Where's Tiny?"

Cora said, "Unlike Mal here, he had to work today because his current job site is indoors. He should be here later."

"Anything new with his case?"

Carter shook his head. "We're waiting to hear back from Tyrese and Dr. T. Tyrese should be here any time, but Dr. T won't be back until tomorrow."

Sam said, "I have no plans this evening if you want to go back to visit Schneider."

"Might as well," I said.

"You should wait for Tyrese to get here," Mal said. "That guy could be dangerous."

As if on cue, Tyrese walked into the room. "Did I hear my name?"

"We were thinking about taking Sam and paying another visit to William Schneider," I told him.

"Sure, I'm good with that. But first let me tell you what I found out from the warden at Waupun about Lonnie Carlisle."

"Anything interesting?" Carter said, scooting up and sitting on the edge of his seat.

"Maybe," Tyrese said. "He's had visits from three people other than his lawyer. One is his mother, who lives in Steven's Point and makes the trip down once a year. Another was a man named Hal Yeager who has visited four times in the past two years, and after a little research I found out he's a law student working on a PhD. According to the warden, Yeager is doing his thesis on Carlisle. The third visitor was a man named Harvey Aldrich who visited two years ago. The warden said Aldrich claimed to be a friend of Carlisle, but he also said that Carlisle was very upset after Aldrich visited, and wouldn't say why. So I did a little digging around. It took me a while because it turns out Harvey Aldrich is dead. He died just over a year ago of a heart attack. But here's the interesting part. Listed among his survivors in his obituary were a wife and daughter, so I looked up the wife and called to see if she could shed any light on the matter. Apparently, she didn't want to talk because she hung up on me. I moved on to the daughter, but it turned out she isn't going to talk either, because she can't."

He paused, apparently for effect. He had the

rapt attention of everyone in the room and it didn't take long for someone to jump in. Frank said, "Why can't she talk?"

"Because she's in a vegetative state and has been for the last eleven and a half years."

Mal was the first one to make the connection. "She's the girl who Lonnie supposedly attacked."

"You got it!" Tyrese said.

Carter said, "No wonder Lonnie was upset after the visit. I can only imagine how that meeting went."

"I wish he had talked to us," I said. "I got a definite sense of fear from him when we were there."

"Well, he is up for parole in a few months, so maybe his lawyer was right and he just doesn't want to do anything that might jinx that."

"Maybe," I said, though I wasn't totally convinced. "Not much we can do about it now anyway. So let's go visit Mr. Schneider again."

It took ten minutes for everyone to fetch their coats and decide who was going to drive. Tyrese ended up behind the wheel again, and this time Sam got to ride in front while Mal and I shared the backseat.

"Tell me as best you can exactly how your first visit went," Sam said once we were under way. And for the duration of the ride, Mal, Tyrese, and I filled him in on what had happened, each of us remembering different parts of the encounter.

When we were done, Sam said, "Here's what I'd like to do this time. Tyrese, I want you to take charge of talking to and questioning the man, and I want you to do it in as authoritative a manner as you can. Act like you're his superior officer commanding him to provide you with intel the way someone in the military might do." He turned and looked at us in the backseat. "Mal and Mack, I want the two of you to hang back and simply observe. Don't say anything."

We both nodded our understanding. "I'm going to act like Schneider's advisor and direct him on what questions to answer and how to answer them. I have a feeling he will react better to a more formal type of inquiry than mere conversational type of talk."

"I'm fine with that," Tyrese said. "Do you think I should word my questions a particular way?"

"Not necessarily. Be firm, but not aggressive. And don't mention the incident with his wife and daughter at all. I want to keep him as focused as we can and on topic."

We arrived at Schneider's house and all four of us piled out of the car. Per Sam's suggestion, Mal and I hung back and let the other two men take the lead. They climbed the porch and rapped on Schneider's door. After waiting a minute or two with nothing happening, Sam nudged Tyrese.

Tyrese nodded and knocked again, harder this time. In addition, he called out to Schneider. "Open up, Schneider," he said in a firm voice. "We need to debrief on an incident."

Sam gave Tyrese a thumbs-up and we all waited for something to happen. When it didn't, Tyrese yelled through the door again "Schneider, your refusal to cooperate in this matter may result in your court martial."

Ten seconds later we heard the locks being thrown. Finally, William Schneider poked his head out. Tyrese didn't give the man a chance to question or object to our intentions. He pushed the door open and marched inside. Schneider looked startled and a little intimidated. Sam extended a hand to him and said, "Mr. Schneider, I'm here to represent and advise you in this debriefing. Let's go have a seat, shall we?"

I half expected Schneider to explode, or at least call foul, but all he did was nod, shake Sam's hand, and head back into his house. Mal and I followed, shut the door once we were inside, and then stood by it while the other three men settled onto seats in the living room.

Tyrese sat ramrod straight perched on the edge of his chair. Sam settled onto the couch beside Schneider.

"Mr. Schneider," Tyrese said, still using his booming voice, "we need to discuss the matter of two girls who were killed. Their names are Lori Gruber and Anna Hermann. Do you recall them?"

Schneider nodded but said nothing.

"What do you know about the incident?"

Schneider looked over at Sam for a second, then back at Tyrese. "Nothing, sir," he said.

"I need the truth, Mr. Schneider," Tyrese said. His tone remained stern, but his expression was caring, understanding.

Sam reached over and put an arm on Schneider's shoulder. "Tell the truth, soldier," he said in a gentle voice. "What happened to those girls?"

Schneider looked over at Sam and tears brimmed in his eyes. "I didn't mean to hurt her, sir," he said.

I heard Mal suck in his breath beside me. The room grew deathly quiet.

"We know you didn't mean to hurt her," Sam said, still talking in a soft voice. "But we need to know the truth."

"It was an accident," Schneider said. His eyes were focused on Sam and his expression was pleading, as if he needed Sam to confirm this for him. "I loved her. I didn't mean to hurt her." Schneider dropped his head and began to sob.

Tyrese started to say something but Sam held a hand up to stop him. "How did you hurt her?" Sam asked Schneider, massaging his shoulder. "Tell us what happened."

Schneider gathered himself and looked over at Sam. "Things got too heated," he said. "But I didn't mean for it to happen."

Mal leaned over and whispered in my ear, "That's it. He went after her and tried to seduce her. She fought back and he killed her."

I shook my head. "There were two of them, Mal," I whispered back. "Lori and Anna."

Sam had apparently made the same connection I had. He leaned in close to Schneider and said, "The fire wasn't your fault."

Schneider looked at Sam with this sad, appealing expression, wanting to believe him. But in the end, he couldn't. "Of course it was my fault," he said in an angry outburst. "I killed her. I didn't know the rags . . . the fumes . . . They said . . ." He buried his face in his hands and started to sob again.

The four of us stood there watching him, and while I can't speak for the others, I know I felt like an unwanted interloper, intruding on this man's private moment, his terrible grief. I felt tears burn in my eyes and Mal shifted uncomfortably beside me.

After a few moments, Sam said, "You knew Lori Gruber, didn't you?"

Schneider nodded, his shoulders hunched, staring at the floor.

"Did you ever talk to her?"

Schneider nodded again. Then he said, "She was nice to me, not like them other kids. She was like Mary. My Mary."

"Mary," Sam said. "That was your daughter's name?"

Schneider nodded.

"Thank you for telling us the truth," Sam said, and then to my surprise, he got up and said, "We're done here."

Mal, Tyrese, and I exchanged puzzled looks. But Sam merely walked out the front door and indicated for the rest of us to follow. We did.

Once we were outside, Tyrese said, "What the hell, Sam? You just got him talking. Why are we leaving?"

"You guys were right when you said he's likely suffering from PTSD," Sam said, "but he didn't hurt those girls. The man is racked with guilt over the death of his daughter. And think about it. His daughter died twenty years ago. I looked into the case and discovered that she was six at the time. Fast forward eight years to when Lori and Anna were murdered and how old would his daughter have been?"

"Fourteen," Tyrese said.

"The same age as Lori and Anna," I said, starting to see the light.

"Exactly!" Sam said. "And look at this." He reached into his pocket and pulled out a printed copy of an old newspaper obituary. Mal and Tyrese hovered around me, looking at it over my shoulders. On it was the name Mary Schneider, age six, along with a picture. I looked at the face of the little girl, saddened to think that her life ended so soon and so tragically. I started to read the article, but Sam said, "Look at Mary's picture and then look at this."

He handed me another page, this one with a picture of Lori Gruber on it. I made the connection right away. "Same hair color, same basic facial shape, same shape eyes," I said. "Lori looked like Schneider's daughter."

Sam nodded. "And you heard what he said in there. Lori was nice to him, not like the other kids. And remember what Tiny said about how his sister was always bringing home strays? To her, Schneider was one of those strays. She was nice to him, and if Schneider is to be believed, the only kid who was nice to him. To him, she was his daughter, reincarnated. There's no way he would have hurt her."

"Are you sure?" Tyrese said. "What if the guy went off like he did on us the other day and thought Lori and Anna were some kind of Viet Cong spies or something?"

Sam shook his head. "His daughter's death and his grief over it are such a huge part of his psyche that he wouldn't do that, especially since Lori looked like Mary and was the same age Mary would have been. Remember how Tiny said Schneider used to try to lure girls inside with promises of cookies and milk? He was trying to resurrect his daughter. The man is ill, I have no doubt. And I plan to speak to a friend of mine at the VA about getting him some help. But I'd stake my career on the fact that he didn't kill those two girls."

With that, we were back to square one, or maybe square two, since we had finally managed to eliminate one of the suspects, assuming we bought into Sam's analysis. I did, but I wasn't so sure about Tyrese and Mal.

"So where do we go from here?" Tyrese said after we had all climbed back into the car and shut the doors.

"I want to take another run at Erik Hermann," I said. "And I want to do it alone."

Tyrese nodded and started the engine. "Radio Shack, here we come."

Chapter 23

Tyrese and Mal filled Sam in on why we needed to go to Radio Shack. When we arrived at the store, I opted to wait in the car while the three men went inside. As the men shopped, I called Cora on my cell and filled her in on our visit to Schneider. Then I told her what we were planning to do with regard to wiring me up for sound.

"That's a great idea," she said. "I can help with that if the guys want."

"Have you had any thoughts about the items that were in the last envelope?"

"As a matter of fact, I have." I detected a distinct undercurrent of excitement in her voice, and that in turn got me feeling hopeful. "You know that little piece of map that showed a portion of St. Paul?" She didn't give me a chance to answer. "I got to thinking that maybe it isn't the city at all. Maybe St. Paul is a reference to something right here in Milwaukee. So I did a little research on my computer and came up with several local churches that are called St. Paul. And that got me to thinking about the other items in that envelope. There are all sorts of religious connections to spices, fish, bread, and wine. And then there is the picture of the water faucet. Maybe it's a connection to holy water, or the idea of Jesus turning water into wine."

"How many churches are we talking here?"

"There are a few, but I have it narrowed it down. Remember the flower petal?"

"Yes. It was from a rose."

"Well, check your messages. I sent you a picture of one church in particular."

I took my phone from my ear and pulled up Cora's message. In it was a picture of a church with a large stained-glass window over the entrance in the shape of a rosette. Under the picture, Cora had typed the name of the church: St. Paul's Episcopal.

"Okay," I said. "But what about the other items in the envelope, like the coffee filter, and the Broadway marquee?"

"I'm stumped on the coffee filter for the moment, though there is a Bible study on Wednesday evenings at seven so maybe they have coffee when it's over? I'm not sure on that one, but the marquee was for the show *Cats*. And guess what the name of the priest is at St. Paul's Episcopal Church?" Again she didn't give me a chance to answer. "It's Father Stephen Manx."

"And Manx is a type of cat," I said, feeling my excitement grow. "I can't think of how the coffee bit ties in, but the rest of it makes sense. Thanks, Cora. You rock!"

"I'm happy to help."

The boys came out of the store a few minutes later and though I was dying to share Cora's brilliant idea with Mal, I forced myself to wait. I trusted Tyrese, but the fewer people who were involved with this thing the better. Within half an hour we were back at the bar and Tyrese headed upstairs to the Capone Club to fill the others in on our visit to Schneider. I took Mal into my office and told him about Cora's revelation.

"It does all kind of fit," he said when I was done. "When are you thinking of going?"

I glanced at my watch, saw that it was almost seven, and said, "Tomorrow I guess. It's too late tonight."

"Speaking of tonight . . ."

"Duncan is supposed to be here at ten. He plans to stay all night."

"Good," Mal said, turning away and heading for the door. "Since you seem to be in good hands, I'm going to head home, replenish my go bag, and get ready for work tomorrow. But call me if anything changes."

He was about to open the door when I burst out with "Wait!" I felt oddly panicked by the fact that he was leaving, but when he did actually stop, I found myself tongue-tied. Then I thought of something. "I don't have your phone number."

"Oh, right," Mal said. He dropped his hand from the doorknob and turned back to face me, but he didn't look at me. He looked at his feet, at the wall, at the couch . . . anything but me. "Give me your phone," he said.

I did so, and he proceeded to punch his number in for me. Then he held it out to me, still not looking me in the face. As soon as I took the phone, he spun around and headed for the door.

"Don't you want to spend some time with the Capone Club?" I said.

He paused, his hand on the doorknob. "I can

catch up tomorrow evening," he said, his back still to me.

And then, before I could think of anything else to say to stall him, he was out the door and gone.

I felt saddened by his departure, but I shook it off, reminded myself that Duncan would be here soon, and headed out to check in with my staff.

Billy was behind the bar so I knew things there were under control. I headed into the kitchen where my newest cook was on duty. My long-term prior cook, Helmut, had quit after Ginny's murder. He was in his sixties and his wife didn't take kindly to him working his retirement years in what she dubbed "a murderous place." With the expansion I hired on two new cooks to replace Helmut. Jon had come on board immediately as a full-time cook and he'd been a good fit. But there were too many hours and too many orders for him alone, so I'd also hired on a part-time cook named Rich Zeigler. He was a grad student at the university, studying sociology, and while he had a passion for cooking he lacked the desire necessary to make a full-time career out of it. He'd only worked a few shifts so far—he had the evening hours Monday through Wednesday—but he'd already doctored up a few of my menu items by adding rich ingredients like heavy cream and butter. Apparently, he felt the need to live up to his name. I balked at his "experiments" at first, but the stuff he turned out was too tasty for me to object for long.

"Hey, Rich," I said as I entered the kitchen. "How are things going so far?"

"Having some fun. Can I fix you something to eat?"

"Yes, as a matter of fact, you can. I really liked

that pizza you made last week with the creamy pesto sauce, sun-dried tomatoes, olives, and prosciutto. Can you whip me up a couple of them for the Capone Club group upstairs? If they like it as much as I do, I'll add it to the menu."

"I'd be happy to."

"Thanks. Just send them up with Missy when they're ready." I started to leave, then turned back. "Rich, any chance you know a professor on campus named Erik Hermann?"

"Sure," he said. "He's the one whose sister was murdered, right?"

I nodded. "Yes, twelve years ago. What do you know about him?"

"I don't know him personally, but a girl I'm seeing does. In fact, he's her advisor. She's a chemistry grad student. Why do you ask?"

"The Capone Club is working on the case involving his sister and her friend. I'm just trying to get a little insight. We tried to talk to him but he refused."

"Can't say I blame the guy for that," Rich said. "I'm sure it's an unpleasant memory for him."

"I'm sure it is." I knew all too well how painful those memories could be. "Have you heard any rumors about him?"

Rich chewed his lip for a few seconds before he said, "I don't like spreading gossip, but I have heard that he might have an issue with the bottle, you know?" He mimed drinking out of one.

I nodded. "Anything else?"

He hesitated again and I got a strong sense there was something else, something he was reluctant to share. I thought about prompting him further, but then decided to just wait and let silence do the work.

"Well, I've heard my girlfriend and some of the other students say that Hermann has been in some kind of a funk lately, more withdrawn, and preoccupied."

"Have they speculated as to why?"

"Not that I've heard."

"Okay, thanks. You've been a big help. Could you do me one more small favor?"

"Okay," he said, but his tone suggested that he was wary of what I was going to ask of him.

"Can you ask your girlfriend what Erik Hermann's office hours are and pass that info on to me?"

"Sure," he said, sounding relieved. "I'll text her and let you know what she says."

I thanked him again and, as he took out his phone, I went out to the main bar area and checked in with Debra, who was taking advantage of the slow night to work a little more closely with Linda. I pulled Debra aside to ask how things were going.

"She's coming along," Debra said. "But she's not a fast learner."

"Give her a little more time. If she doesn't catch on better, let me know. I don't want to let her go, but if I have to, I will."

Debra nodded solemnly and I could tell she had her doubts.

I saw Rich waving at me through the kitchen window and headed back into the kitchen. "Sara says Professor Hermann has office hours on Tuesdays and Thursdays between noon and four. Does that help?"

"Yes, it does," I told him. "Thanks. I don't suppose you know where his office is?"

"I do," he said. And then he gave me directions on how to get there.

With that out of the way, I headed upstairs to join the Capone Club. After telling the group that I was going to provide them with a free meal by using them as guinea pigs for Rich's latest concoction—information that was met with great enthusiasm—I pulled Cora aside and took her into the unused meeting room. I shut the door and the two of us sat down with her computer and did some more research on the church she'd singled out. By the time we were done, I had to agree that it seemed to match up with most of the items in the envelope.

"I'll pay a visit there tomorrow," I told her.

"Is Mal going with you?"

I shook my head. "I don't think he can. He has to work tomorrow, so I'm going to have to handle this one alone."

"I'll go with you if you want."

"I might take you up on that," I said with a smile. "I also want to talk with Erik Hermann tomorrow. I'm going to try to catch him at work at the university, to see if he'll be more open to chatting. He has office hours between noon and four, so I'm thinking I'll try to catch him sometime in the afternoon and visit the church in the morning. Would eleven work for you?"

"I'm totally flexible," Cora said. Then, with a saucy wink she added, "The men like that about me."

We returned to the rest of the group and spent the next couple of hours reviewing the Gruber-Hermann case, discussing the various suspects. Everyone seemed to accept Sam's assessment of

William Schneider, and our focus shifted to the remaining three suspects. Of those, everyone seemed to be leaning toward TJ the plumber and Lonnie Carlisle as the most likely candidates. While everyone agreed that Erik Hermann might have had motive, they had a hard time imagining him killing his little sister.

The pizza was a huge hit with the group, and there was a general consensus that it should be added to the menu and that Rich was a keeper.

A little before ten, I headed back downstairs to my office and turned off the alarm to the back door. Then I went and opened my apartment door the way I had the last time Duncan sneaked in. This time there were no interlopers in the hallway forcing me to stall, and when I opened the door at ten o'clock sharp I fully expected to find Duncan in the embrace of his undercover cop friend. This time, however, he was alone, though well-disguised in snow pants and an oversized parka with a fur-lined hood that made him look like he had gained fifty pounds. Beneath the hood he was wearing a knit cap pulled low over his brow and heavy-rimmed eyeglasses. He was also sporting a mustache. He stepped inside, slid into the foyer behind my apartment door, and headed upstairs while I went back to my office to reset the alarm.

When I got upstairs, he had shucked his outerwear and the glasses, and was in the process of removing the mustache.

"A gift from Isabel?" I said.

He nodded, wincing as the last of the glue let loose. He set the fake mustache on the kitchen table and then went over to the counter. "Mind if I make a pot of coffee?"

"I'll do it," I said. "I should have thought to have some ready for you anyway."

As I went about setting up the coffeemaker and turning it on, Duncan stood nearby watching me, blowing on his hands in an effort to warm them. "Damn, it's cold out there," he muttered when I was done.

I moved closer to him and sandwiched his hands in mine. "I can think of some ways to warm them up," I said. And then I showed him what I meant.

Two hours later we finally got to the coffee, which we drank in bed.

"So how have you spent the rest of your day between now and when I saw you at the station?" Duncan asked as we sat side by side up against my headboard.

I filled him in on our visit to William Schneider, my discussion with Rich about Erik Hermann, the Capone Club's discussion of the case, and Cora's findings with regard to the items in the envelope. Then I told him about Mal and Tyrese's plan to wire me for sound in preparation for my visit to Erik Hermann. "But before I do that, I'm going to visit St. Paul's Episcopal Church to see what I can find."

"Alone?"

"Cora offered to go with me."

Duncan frowned at this. "Cora's a very capable woman," he said, "but I'd feel a lot better if you had someone else with you, someone like Malachi or me."

"Well, Mal isn't available because he has to work. And you can't do it for the obvious reason."

"Can't you wait until later in the day and take Malachi with you?"

He seemed determined to keep putting Mal and me together. "I suppose I could," I said hesitantly, "but . . ." I didn't finish the thought because I couldn't think of a delicate way to put it. I didn't feel comfortable telling him that Mal was attracted me, an attraction that was somewhat mutual.

"But what?" he pushed.

"This thing with Mal and me, it's starting to feel a little real," I said finally, hoping he would get the hint.

"Good." *So much for my hopes.* "The two of you need to be convincing. And from what I've heard, you are. There's already scuttlebutt down at the station about how you've taken on a new beau."

"Maybe we're a little too convincing," I said, trying again. "We've got a nickname for cripes' sake. Folks have started calling us M and M."

"So?"

"So . . . like I said, the whole thing is starting to feel a little too real."

This time my pronouncement was met with a long silence. Finally, Duncan set his coffee mug on the bedside stand and shifted his position so that he was facing me. He looked worried. "What are you trying to say, Mack? Are you dumping me for Malachi or something like that?"

"No, of course not, but—"

He held up a hand to stop me. "I get it. You're feeling neglected, and I'm sorry about that. But such is the nature of my job. I promise to try to do better." He leaned over and kissed me then, and for the moment, my objections were forgotten.

Sometime later I dragged myself out of bed and went downstairs to assist my staff with the closing duties. By the time I got back upstairs, Duncan was fast asleep. Maybe I should have ramped up the caffeine in my coffee.

I sat on the edge of my bed and watched him for a while, listening to the sound of his breathing, which made me see a heart-shaped balloon that inflated and deflated in time with each breath. Eventually I got undressed and carefully slipped in beside him, cuddling up against his back. He stirred long enough to roll over, say "Welcome back," and kiss me. Then he wrapped me in his arms and dozed off again.

I fell asleep sometime later engulfed in a heady cocktail of synesthetic reactions to his touch, his smell, his warmth, his sounds. The last one I remembered experiencing was a visual image of two puzzle pieces, both made out of chocolate, fitting together with exact precision and completing a picture of the two of us.

Chapter 24

I awoke the next morning feeling content, safe, and ridiculously happy. The warmth of Duncan's body behind me was palpable beneath the covers even though we weren't touching. And when I rolled over to look at him, I was surprised to see he wasn't there. The sensation must have been a synesthetic reaction to something.

I sat up, glanced at the clock, saw it was almost nine, and wondered if he had left already. His clothes were gone from the chair where they'd been, but then I heard noises coming from beyond the bedroom door and knew he was still there. Afraid he might be in the process of leaving, I flew out of bed, donned my robe, and hurried out to the main area of the apartment. I found him in the kitchen sitting at the table, eating a bowl of oatmeal.

"Good morning, Sunshine," he said with a smile. "The coffee is fresh and there's more oatmeal in the pan on the stove if you want. I doctored it up with some butter, brown sugar, and pecans."

The kitchen window behind him was frosted

over, but there was bright morning sunshine coming through it, casting a long trapezoid of light on the floor. The tableau seemed so ordinary, and cozy, and domestic. It gave me hope for the future.

I poured myself a cup of coffee, helped myself to a bowl of the oatmeal, and settled in across the table from him. "Did you sleep okay?" I asked him.

"Like a baby. Best sleep I've had in days. Though I'm sorry I gave out on you."

I dismissed his apology with a wave of my hand. "Clearly, you needed the sleep. And you kind of made up for it earlier in the evening."

"Yes, that part was very nice," he agreed with a slightly lecherous smile and a quick game of footsie under the table. "I've missed you, Mack."

"I've missed you, too."

"So are we okay?"

It felt very okay at the moment. "For now, yes."

He reared back slightly as if I'd slapped him. "For now?" he echoed. "You're a hard woman to please, Mack Dalton. I suspect you're going to keep me on my toes."

"I'd rather keep you in my bed," I said with a coquettish grin.

"You'll get no arguments from me on that one."

"Does that mean you'll be back tonight?"

His smile faltered the tiniest bit and I felt my spirits start to tank. "I can't promise anything just yet. I'll have a better idea once I get in to work. I'll let you know. Now let's talk about this trip to the church you plan to make today. I don't like the idea of you going there alone."

"I told you, Cora said she would go."

"You know what I mean."

I sighed. "Duncan, we've been over this."

"I know, but I don't trust whoever is writing these letters to maintain a safe distance. At some point they could decide to kill you, or kidnap and torture you. Cora's a great asset to have on our team, but she's not much in the protection department."

"I don't know about that," I said with a wry grin. "I imagine she could distract any man long enough for me to get away if I had to."

Duncan chuckled. "Yes, I imagine she could."

"Have you made any progress on the items you took to the lab?"

"Some. You were right that the filter had coffee in it at one time, and the green scrap of terry cloth did have wine in it. We also know that the petal was from a domestic pink rose. But in terms of finding any usable evidence such as hairs or fibers or fingerprints, we've come up empty. And nice try on changing the subject."

I sighed and rolled my eyes at him. "What choice do I have, Duncan? If I don't play this game, someone will die."

"And if you do play this game, *you* could die, particularly if you don't take precautions. So if you're going to visit the church, I want you to at least wait until Mal can go with you. He's gone along on the other trips and it hasn't caused any issues or problems, so it makes sense to stick with what we've been doing."

It had caused some problems, just not the kind Duncan was talking about. "Fine," I said, caving to the pressure. Truth was, I didn't mind having Mal along. Not only would I feel safer with him around, his insight might prove critical in figuring things out. "I'll call him and see when he can go with me."

"Thank you." With that, Duncan got up from the table and walked over to give me a quick kiss. "I have to go. Can you come downstairs and turn off the alarm for me?"

"Sure."

I waited while he donned his bulky parka, knit cap, snow pants, and mustache. We went downstairs together and Duncan waited at the bottom while I stepped out into the hallway to make sure no one was in the bar yet.

As I announced the coast was clear, something occurred to me. "How did you get here last night?"

"I drove," he said, stepping into the hall and standing at the ready by the back door.

"What if the letter writer recognized your car?"

"I parked in a structure eight blocks from here. And I know how to watch for a tail. No one followed me." He leaned over and kissed me again, this one lasting a bit longer. The feel of the mustache made me giggle, but as the kiss kept going, I found I didn't notice it as much. When we finally parted, Duncan let out a little moan and said, "Wish I could stay and spend the day with you."

"I wish you could, too."

"It won't always be like this, you know. Have patience. And be careful."

"I will." I went to my office, disabled the alarm and then poked my head back out into the hallway. "You're good to go," I said, and in a flash of morning light and cold, he was gone.

I reset the alarm and went back upstairs to shower and dress. But first I called Mal to ask him when he could come by to get me. He didn't answer, so I left a message that said I wanted to see him, and asked him to call me back.

I went downstairs at a little after ten-thirty to help my day staff get ready. Rich had things under control in the kitchen, and Debra had Linda under her wing, showing her what needed to be done. So I stepped in to help Pete, my day bartender, get the bar set up by cutting fruit for garnishes.

My phone rang in the midst of slicing lemons. It was Mal.

"What's up?" he asked.

I abandoned my fruit-cutting station and slipped into my office for some privacy. Then I filled him in on Cora's idea about the church and my desire to go there. "Duncan insists that I not go alone and he wants you to go with me," I concluded. "So I'm calling to see when you might be free."

"As it turns out, I'm free now. It's too damned cold out here to do much, so the boss is cutting us loose early. Give me an hour to get home and shower, and I can be at the bar around noon. Does that help?"

"It does," I said. "And since I'm also planning to drop in on Erik Hermann at his office today, you can go with me for that, too. In fact"—I glanced at my watch—"let's do that first."

"That's fine by me. I'm yours to do with as you wish."

I smiled, glad that our comfortable camaraderie seemed to have returned.

"Thanks, Mal. I'll see you soon."

We opened at eleven sharp, and as usual, several of my regulars came in within minutes of me unlocking the door: the Signoriello brothers, Cora,

Carter, and Sam. When I took Cora aside and let her know she was off the hook with regards to the church visit, she looked disappointed.

Tyrese popped in just before noon, and Mal showed up about ten minutes after that. I took both of them into my office so we could plan the trip to Erik Hermann's office. I filled Tyrese in on what Erik's office hours were and then said, "I'm hoping he might be more forthcoming if I catch him unaware and it's just me talking to him, so it's important that I do this alone."

"No problem," Tyrese said. "But we'll stand by just in case. I have the stuff we bought yesterday to wire you up out in my car. Let me go get it and I'll be right back."

He headed out, leaving Mal and I alone in my office. "Remember," I said to Mal, "Tyrese doesn't know anything about the letters or the church. So mum's the word."

Mal cocked his head and gave me a tolerant smile. "I am an undercover cop, remember? I know how to keep a secret."

"Of course you do," I said, worried that I'd managed to bring the tension back between us. "I said that as much for my own benefit as yours. I need the reminding."

He nodded and said nothing more.

"So how was work this morning?" I asked, trying for some safe, polite conversation.

"Cold! I wish this guy would get me on a job site with some indoor work. But I have a feeling freezing my ass off is an initiation of sorts. He's testing me, so I don't want to complain too much."

"Want me to get you something to warm you up?" I offered.

"No, I'm fine. I had a huge mug of hot chocolate at home and that got me thawed out enough."

We stood there, looking at one another and then trying not to look at one another, shuffling our feet, feeling the silence wrap around us. I think we both had things we wanted to say, things we were thinking but weren't ready to put out there yet.

Tyrese finally came back and the pressure eased some. He plopped a bag on my desk and removed two packages from it. One was a small, hand-held digital recording device. The other wasn't what I was expecting.

"A baby monitor?" I said. "That's your high-tech listening device?"

"Who said anything about high tech?" Tyrese asked. "This will work fine, though we'll need to be close by in order to hear anything. If need be, we'll stand right outside the office door."

After unpacking the device and doing some minimal setup, Tyrese handed me what looked like a small walkie-talkie. "You're going to be the baby," he said. "I've turned the volume down on it so you won't hear anything on your end. Just clip it to your waist on the side near your back and keep it under your coat. Open your coat when you get in there, but don't let it be seen. In a worst-case scenario, just scream. We won't be far away."

"And the recorder?"

"That you can put in your purse or your pocket. We just need to remember to turn it on before you go in there."

I did as he instructed and Mal helped me position the baby monitor in the waist of my pants. Then we grabbed our coats and headed out.

It took half an hour to get there and another fifteen minutes to find a place to park. Then we had to walk several blocks. When we arrived at the chemistry building, Tyrese stopped to survey the area. The building consisted of two sections: one that was four stories tall and another that was an eight-story tower, both with basements.

"We could try to hang outside since Hermann's office is on the first floor," he said, "but I think it would be best if we just came inside with you. We'll keep the volume low on our monitor and try to avoid anyone seeing what we're doing. Maybe we can find a nearby bathroom to hide in."

We entered the building, found Hermann's office and a restroom that was close by. Tyrese told me to turn on my recording device, and then he and Mal retreated to the bathroom and had me stand in the hall a little ways past Hermann's office but within eyesight of the restroom. Mal then signaled me from the hallway just outside the bathroom and after looking around to make sure no one was close by, I said in a low voice, "Testing, testing."

I watched as Mal disappeared into the restroom and then came back out a moment later. He gave me a thumbs-up to indicate that Tyrese had been able to hear me just fine, and then he disappeared back into the bathroom.

I sucked in a deep breath to brace myself, and then entered Erik Hermann's office. There was a small outer office with a desk, and a young man— a student, I guessed—seated behind it. He was wearing a T-shirt with the word *genius* spelled out across the front of it using element symbols from the periodic table. Behind his desk on the back wall were two four-drawer filing cabinets and a second door with an opaque glass window in the top half. The wall to my left was covered with a floor-to-ceiling bookcase overflowing with books and papers.

"Can I help you?" the young man asked.

"Yes, I'd like to see Professor Hermann."

The kid gave me a quick head-to-toe assessment and furrowed his brow. "Are you a student?"

"No, this is a personal matter."

"Do you have an appointment?" From the slightly smug expression on his face I gathered that he knew I did not.

"I wanted to surprise him," I said.

"Can I have your name?"

"Sure. It's Mackenzie Dalton." I wondered if the name would trigger any recognition with him, but if it did, he hid it well.

"Professor Hermann has someone with him right now, but if you'd like to wait, he does have ten minutes between appointments, assuming the person in there now doesn't stay much longer. But it's the end of the semester and he's pretty busy, so you'll have to be quick."

"That's fine, I'll wait," I said, thinking that Tyrese and Mal were probably cursing me and rolling their eyes about now.

There were two chairs along the wall beside the door and I settled into one of them, feeling the monitor at my waist shift slightly. For the next five minutes, the student behind the desk kept sneaking surreptitious looks at me while he tried to look busy by shuffling some papers around and doodling on the large desk calendar in front of him. Finally, the door on the back wall opened and a young woman came out. Her eyes were red-rimmed with tears and she scurried out of the office without a word.

The kid behind the desk got up and went to the door, which the vacating student had left open. "There is a Mackenzie Dalton here to see you. She said she's not a student and she doesn't have an appointment." His tone—impatient with the vaguest hint of disgust—made it clear what he thought of the situation.

I half expected Erik Hermann to turn me away, but he surprised me by saying, "Fine. Send her in."

The young man looked disappointed as he waved me in.

I entered the back office, which was a larger version of the outer one: desk, chair, overflowing bookcase. Only here there was also a credenza along the wall by the door. The top of it was covered with stacks of papers and books except for an area at the end closest to the door, where there sat a coffeemaker.

Erik Hermann was seated behind the desk, his eyes red-rimmed, his face a road map of tiny veins. I didn't smell booze on him now, but I wouldn't have been surprised to find a bottle in the drawers of the desk or credenza.

"You," Erik Hermann said as I entered and shut the door behind me.

I realized then that the name hadn't triggered anything for him, but my face had.

"You're here to talk about my sister, aren't you?"

I nodded, and then remembering my listening devices, I said, "Yes, I am." I scanned the items on top of his desk and immediately noticed a book off to his right. It was a high school yearbook with the year 2003 stamped in gold on the cover. I did some quick math and realized it wasn't Erik's graduation yearbook, but rather the one from the year when Lori and Anna were murdered. I wondered why he would have it out, but before I could give it too much thought, Erik's objections to my presence switched my focus.

"I thought I made it clear when you came to my house that I have nothing to say on the matter."

"You said that, yes, but I don't believe it. Do you want to know why?"

"I couldn't care less what you believe." He folded his arms over his chest and swiveled in his chair to stare at the credenza, effectively dismissing me.

"I'll tell you anyway," I said. "I, too, lost someone I loved to murder. And while I know how difficult it can be to talk about it, not knowing the truth is even worse." I anticipated another objection, and pushed on before he had a chance to speak. "I'm sure you loved your little sister, and based on her diary you also cared about Lori Gruber. So I find it hard to believe that you wouldn't want to know who did this horrible thing to them."

"The police think I did it."

"I don't." I said this without hesitation even though I wasn't sure. But I knew that if he didn't believe me, I wouldn't stand a chance.

He shot me a look, his expression haunted. After a few seconds he looked back toward the credenza and his shoulders sagged. He looked broken, troubled, and vulnerable. I felt for him, understanding all too well the emotions he was feeling. And in that instant, for the first time, I truly started to believe he hadn't done it.

"I know you didn't do it, Erik," I said, inching closer to the desk. I wanted to get my hands on that yearbook and find pictures of his sister and Lori. Seeing them might trigger a cascade of emotions in him, and get him to open up. "I want to find out who did do it, and see to it that they're punished. I want to see justice for your sister, and for Lori."

He shook his head and ran both hands through his hair. "It's too late for that. You don't understand."

"I understand the pain you're feeling."

He scoffed at that. "The hell you do. You don't know or understand a damned thing."

He leaned his head back against his chair and closed his eyes. Whatever memories he was playing in his mind must have been painful, because tears formed at the corners of his eyes. I was within reach of the yearbook so I went ahead and picked it up. I opened it and saw Erik's name handwritten in the top left corner of the inside cover, and dozens of signatures and notes written below it. I wanted to read them, but felt it could wait. Right now I wanted to get to those pictures. I flipped through some pages and found the start of the freshman class pictures. I was about to start turning the pages one at a time when a noise across the desk distracted me. Before I had a chance to so much as raise my eyes, Erik rose from his chair and ripped the book out of my hands.

"What the hell do you think you're doing?" he bellowed. He stood across the desk glaring at me and he looked angry enough to kill at that moment. I started to rethink my stand on his innocence.

He flung an arm out and pointed toward the door. "Get out," he seethed. And then with the suddenness of flipping a light switch, his arm dropped and his expression softened. "Please," he added.

"Erik, I—"

"Get out!" The switch had flipped again, and I wondered if it had a kill mode.

Chapter 25

The kid at the front desk watched me leave without saying a word, but he looked smug. I hooked up with Mal and Tyrese in the hallway and we formed a silent trio as we left the building. Once we were outside, Mal said, "We were just about to come busting in there. It sounds like you hit a nerve with him."

"Yeah, his emotions were all over the place." I told them about the yearbook and added, "Looking through that book really pushed his buttons. And his pain is clearly acute, almost as if Lori's and Anna's deaths had just happened."

"Guilt, perhaps?" Tyrese suggested.

"I don't know, but to be honest, I don't think so."

"And you're basing that on what, exactly?" Tyrese asked.

"The rawness of his pain, for one thing. His voice tasted like a mix of jalapeño and Tabasco, which suggests to me that he's angry, extremely angry, seething in fact. But there is also a very visceral pain to the taste, and that tells me he's hurting badly. I think that's why he drinks, to dull the pain."

"That's not exactly proof," Tyrese said. "He can still mourn and miss his sister even if he was the one who killed her. In fact, if anything I'd expect him to have stronger emotions if he was the one who did it."

"I don't know," I said. "I think it would take a level of coldness and calculation, a certain degree of detachment to be able to kill one's own sister in the first place. And that sort of emotional mindset doesn't strike me as conducive to the level of pain Erik Hermann has all these years after the fact. He cared for his sister, and I think he also cared for Lori."

"I don't know," Tyrese said. "Guilt is a powerful emotion."

We got into the car and our ride back to the bar was a silent one until Tyrese pulled up out front. "I have some things I need to do," he said, keeping the motor running. "But if you come up with any other ideas, give me a call." He then gave me his phone number, and as soon as Mal and I got out, he drove off.

Mal started to head inside but I stopped him. "Let's not go back in yet. I think it's time you and I got some religion."

As we got out of Mal's car and walked up to St. Paul's Church, we paused long enough to admire the structure.

"This is a fascinating building," Mal said. "It's a great example of late nineteenth-century Richardsonian Romanesque ecclesiastical architecture, built using red sandstone from Lake Superior."

"For someone who has supposedly eschewed religion, you sure know a lot about this church."

"It's not about the religion, it's about the architecture. I've spent a great deal of my time in this city studying the various buildings and visiting places like this. In fact, I've been here before. There's also a building on the grounds made from Cream City brick."

"What is Cream City brick?"

"It's a type of light yellow–colored brick made from clay found in the Menomonee River Valley and along the western banks of Lake Michigan. Quite a few structures in this area were built using it, including a few of the area lighthouses. At one time it was so common that Milwaukee became known as Cream City because so many of the buildings had that light-colored brick. Hence the brick is now known as Cream City brick."

I found it fascinating but also a bit troubling that Mal, a relative newcomer to the city, knew tidbits about Milwaukee that I, a lifer, did not. Maybe my life had been too insular up until now.

We approached the entrance under the big rosette stained-glass window that Cora had shown me in the picture on her phone. Above the window was a sharply peaked roof and standing sentinel on either side of this were two square-shaped towers. The tower on the left, which was taller and had a rounded turret on one corner, appeared to be a bell tower; the one on the right looked more like something you'd expect to see on a Scottish castle.

We walked inside—I half expected the building to be locked, but it wasn't—and stopped just inside the door. There wasn't anyone in the main church area that we could see, and while the interior appeared quite modern compared to the outside of the building, it had that same hushed, slightly hollow feel that many old churches have. The nave featured four columns of pews that marched toward an arched apse. The sanctuary was fronted by a stone altar with a large cross that was suspended from the ceiling behind it. The back wall of the sanctuary featured heavy wood paneling at the bottom, topped off by an array of organ pipes.

We walked down the center aisle until we reached the transept, where I stopped and gawked at the stained glass on either side of me.

"Wow, these windows are beautiful," I said to Mal.

"They should be. Several of them are Tiffany originals."

We stood admiring the windows for several minutes before I remembered why we were there. "We should try to find an office of some sort," I said. "The fact that the coffee-scented filter was in that envelope along with the other clues makes me think that whatever or whoever we're looking for must have something to do with a meeting room or office."

We wandered back out of the church and into another part of the building until we found the church office. Seated inside was a heavyset woman who looked to be in her fifties. She had short, brunette hair streaked with gray, thick glasses, and a pleasant face. The name plaque on her desk said MARY FROMME.

"Hi, how can I help you folks today?" she asked with a smile.

I realized then that I hadn't thought up a cover story for being here and for a moment I was tongue-tied. Mal jumped in to save the day. "We're looking to join a church in this area and wondered if we might get some information, maybe a tour?"

"Certainly," Mary said. "Did you just move to the Milwaukee area?"

Mal nodded and I shook my head. Realizing our faux pas, I jumped in and ran with Mal's story. "Mal is new to the area, though I've lived here all my life. I've never been much of a churchgoer but Mal has convinced me to be more open-minded, so we're exploring the possibilities."

"I see," Mary said. "Well, all comers are welcome here." She shifted her focus to Mal. "Have you been a member of the Episcopal Church before?"

Mal shook his head. "But I attended the Catholic Church a lot growing up. One of my parents was Catholic." I was a little disappointed that he didn't mention how the other parent was Jewish. I imagined it would have made for an interesting and lively conversation.

Mary got up from her seat and grabbed a set of keys. "Let me forward the phones," she said, punching some buttons, "and I'll give you a quick tour."

We followed her out of the office, which she locked behind her, and spent the next half hour touring the building and the grounds. She took us back into the church proper and gave us some of the history of the place, including the Tiffany windows. From there we headed to the basement where there was a meeting hall and a small kitchen.

As Mary filled us in on some of the events and services the church offered, Mal and I poked around in the kitchen area like we were looking to buy the place. There were some coffee urns on a counter, and other coffee-making paraphernalia in some drawers and cupboards, but there was nothing that looked like the next message for me. Mary watched us closely, looking a bit concerned, but she let us explore to our heart's content.

When the tour was done, she invited us to return to the office so she could get some contact info from us. I hoped this might be the moment when she realized who I was and gave me whatever package had been left for me, but after providing us with some brochures and highlighting some of the programs, she thanked us for coming and said she hoped to see us at the Sunday service. It was our cue to leave, but I stood there, perplexed and unsure of what to do next.

After several awkward seconds ticked by, Mary's smile faded. "Is there something else I can do for you?" She sounded put out, making it clear that she had other things to do.

"I don't suppose my name means anything to you, or that you have a package or something like that for me?" I asked her.

Mary furrowed her brow. "What sort of package?"

"Something like an envelope, or a courier package."

"Can't say that I do."

I looked around her office, which was neat and organized, looking for anything that might have been what we needed. There was nothing. So I tried a different tack. "Is there a minister, or priest, or someone like that I can talk to?" I saw Mal bite back a grin.

Mary cocked her head to one side. "Sorry, Father Manx is out making hospital rounds and other visitations. Would you like me to set you up an appointment with him?"

"Yes, I would. Any chance I could meet with him later today?"

After consulting a calendar book, Mary said, "Sorry, he's booked up for today. How about tomorrow at noon? Would that work for you?"

It was cutting things close, but I didn't see any other choice. "Yes, it would," I said. "In the meantime, is it all right if Mal and I go take another look at the church? Those Tiffany windows are so beautiful."

"They really are spectacular, aren't they?" Mary said, bustling with so much pride you would have thought she'd made them herself. "Please feel free, and if there is anything else I can help you with, don't hesitate to ask."

We thanked her and left the office, heading back to the main church area.

"That lady thinks you're a bit off plumb," Mal said in a low but amused voice.

"I don't care what she thinks," I said irritably. "I'm scared, Mal. I'm scared that we have this one wrong."

"I'm assuming you made the appointment with the minister because you think he might have your next envelope?"

I nodded. "I'm hoping so, yes. But in the meantime, I think we need to take another look at the church proper, check out every pew, every book rack, every nook or cranny that might be hiding something."

We spent the next half an hour doing just that, exhaustively searching any potential hiding spots except for whatever was behind a locked door located on one side of the sanctuary.

"That leads to the sacristy," Mal said. "That's the area where the sacred robes and table dressings are kept, where priests and other church attendants vest before a service."

"That would be the perfect place to keep something like one of those envelopes," I said, looking longingly at the locked door.

"We can't break in there, Mack."

I sighed in frustration.

"If Father Manx has the next envelope, you'll get it tomorrow."

"And what if he doesn't have it? What if we're wrong? There won't be much time left."

"Come on," Mal said, taking my arm and tugging me toward the exit. "Let's go back to the bar and think things out. Sometimes it helps to get a little distance or perspective on a situation."

I gave him a halfhearted nod and let him lead me out of the church and back to his car. We rode in silence, huddled inside our respective thoughts to ward off our fears the way our bodies were huddled inside our respective coats to ward off the cold.

Chapter 26

Back at the bar, Mal and I headed upstairs to see who was hanging out in the Capone Club room. A small group—the core regulars—were there: the brothers, Cora, Tad, Carter, and Sam. If past experience was any indication, Holly and Alicia would show up in an hour or so when they got off work at the bank, and Tiny would come in when he finished his construction job to grab some dinner and spend some time with Cora.

We updated those who were there on my conversation with Erik Hermann, and for the next two hours, the group tossed around their opinions of Hermann's mental state, eventually dividing into two camps: those who thought his current emotional state might be due to guilt over killing his own sister and those who thought it very unlikely. Others arrived during this time: Holly, Alicia, Kevin Baldwin—our local sanitation engineer—and Tiny. Each time someone new showed up, there would be a recap and the debate would begin again.

I excused myself a little after five when Duncan called on my cell.

"Hey, Sunshine," he said, making me taste fizzy, hot chocolate. "How has your day gone?"

I stepped into the empty room on the second floor and, after shutting the door, I filled him in on both my conversation with Erik Hermann and our visit to the church.

"You've been busy," he said.

"I guess, but now I feel like I'm stalled on all fronts. I have no idea where to go next with Tiny's case, and I have a sinking feeling that we've misinterpreted the latest letter writer clues. I can't figure out how the coffee ties into the church, so I'm beginning to think we've missed the mark with this one. It makes me nervous because time is running out."

"I have a small tidbit that might help," Duncan said, giving my flagging hope a tiny boost. "Carrie, the gal who's been examining the evidence for me, found a tiny particle of something mixed in with the cinnamon. It turned out to be a bit of pollen from a flower, a stargazer lily to be exact."

"But the flower petal that was in with the other clues was from a rose, not a lily," I said, thinking. "So how did the pollen get in there?"

"That's the key question. Whoever handled the cinnamon must have also handled or been in close contact with a stargazer lily. Given the time of year, it isn't likely that it came from a plant growing outside anywhere."

"That would suggest a hothouse, or a flower shop of some sort. But how does that tie in with any of the other clues?"

"I don't know," Duncan admitted. "Maybe if we

put our heads together we can come up with something." I held my breath, afraid to ask when that might be. "Unfortunately, I can't come by tonight, but how about tomorrow?"

This was shaping up to be a day full of disappointments. "If that's the soonest you can make it, then tomorrow it will be," I said, hoping I sounded more lighthearted than I felt.

"Tomorrow I should be able to come by in the late afternoon," Duncan said. *I'll believe it when I see it.* "And then you can tell me how your meeting with the priest went. In the meantime, keep thinking on it. I'll do the same. Hang in there. We'll get to the bottom of this."

"Call or text me if you have any brilliant ideas in the meantime," I said. There was a long silence that followed and for a moment I thought the call had been dropped, except I still had an image in my mind of multicolored threads running off into the horizon with no end in sight. It was a typical manifestation for me whenever I was on the phone with an open line. "Duncan, are you still there?"

"I'm here. I'm just thinking."

"About what?"

"About you. There's something in your tone that feels different to me. It's almost as if you're moving away from me with every word we speak."

"Now who's the synesthete?" I teased.

"Don't deflect. Are you okay?" He sounded genuinely concerned. "And are *we* okay? Because I really do care about you, Mack. I know things haven't been easy for us here lately, but I don't want to lose you. Tell me we're okay."

I hesitated with my answer and heard Duncan sigh on the other end. "I don't know if I can answer that question, Duncan," I said finally. "Do I care for you? Yes, I do. But I can't deny that I'm feeling kind of lost and lonely here lately when it comes to you. I don't feel like we have much of a relationship at this point and I guess I was expecting something more, something better."

"Damn," Duncan muttered, and I tasted fizzy hot chocolate again. "Look, I promise you that when this thing is over I will make it up to you, Mack. Please be patient with me. I know it isn't easy for you, but it isn't easy for me either. I miss you like crazy."

Now it was my turn to sigh. "I'll try," I said. "And for what it's worth, I miss you, too. Let's talk again tomorrow."

"Okay, but don't hesitate to call me sooner if you need to. Or if you want to, okay?"

"Okay." I had a strong urge to cry so I quickly muttered, "Tomorrow then," and disconnected the call. I just stood there for a few minutes, weighing our conversation, and wondering where it was all going to end.

When I finally headed out of the closed room, I had no desire to talk to anyone about the cases, Mal, or any of the rest of it. I headed downstairs and spent the next few hours burying myself in work. I restocked the beer, inventoried my liquor supply, waited tables, did a stint behind the bar, and helped out in the kitchen. During this time, several of the Capone Club members sought me out to check on me: Joe and Frank, Cora, and of course, Mal.

Sometime around nine, Dr. T came in. She saw me behind the bar, held up a folder she had in her hand, and nodded toward the new section. Then she headed upstairs. Assuming she had finally gotten a copy of the autopsy files on Lori and Anna, I followed. I found her standing in the general area outside the room, looking hesitant.

"Did you get the autopsy reports?" I asked.

She nodded. "I did, but I'm not sure what to do. Tiny's in there."

"Oh. Right. Let me take care of that." I took out my phone and texted Cora. A moment later, she came out of the room, a quizzical look on her face.

"What's up?" she asked. We explained our dilemma and she nodded. "Give me a minute and I'll see to it that he leaves. But you have to promise to share the information in those reports with me later."

"You're leaving, too?"

She winked. "I am. It's time for me and Tiny to have a little R and R, and in this case it stands for romp and roll, if you get my drift." She headed back into the room and after waiting a minute or two, Dr. T and I did the same. Greetings were passed around, and as Dr. T and I settled into some empty chairs, Cora packed up her laptop. Then she made her way over to where Tiny was sitting, leaned down, and whispered something in his ear. Tiny blushed as red as a glass of port, and suddenly the two of them were bidding the others good night. They lit out of there like their pants were on fire, which, if I knew Cora, they probably were.

As soon as they were gone, Dr. T addressed the rest of the group. "I have copies of the autopsy files on both Lori Gruber and Anna Hermann. I'm not supposed to have them yet because I didn't go through the proper channels to request them. I didn't want to get caught up in any delays because of red tape. I didn't make any copies of them so I'll share the information with all of you, but what I'm about to say has to stay between us and within the confines of this room. Understood?"

Everyone nodded eagerly.

"Okay," Dr. T began. "Here's what I found out. Both girls' bodies were reasonably well preserved despite the fact that they had been dead for a little over two months. That's because they were frozen in the river during that time. Whoever killed them tried to weight the bodies down with the bikes and some rocks, but once the spring thaw started and the temperatures rose, their bodies surfaced.

"I'll start with Anna's autopsy." She opened the folder she had and consulted some papers inside. "Both girls had clothesline wrapped around their necks but in Anna's case it wasn't the cause of death. She was hit on the head with some type of blunt object, and hit hard enough that she had a depression fracture in her skull. Basically, that means that her skull was caved in. The coroner's report states that while this didn't kill her right away, it would have rendered her unconscious. It appears she lay that way for a while because by the time the rope was tied around her neck she was already dead. Her clothing was all intact and there was no evidence of any sexual trauma or assault. In fact, Anna Hermann died a virgin."

She tucked the papers she was looking at underneath some others and then continued. "As for Lori, she, too, had evidence of head trauma, but in her case it wasn't a life-threatening injury. Lori's cause of death was strangulation with the clothesline. And she didn't die easily. There were claw marks on her neck, most likely caused by her trying to grab at the rope that was choking her. There was a small piece of skin found under a fingernail, but DNA testing, which wasn't done until five years ago, showed that it was her own skin. Lori was also naked from the waist down. Her pants were found around her ankles. And Lori had evidence of sexual trauma, rather severe trauma in fact. She was a virgin prior to the day in question because remnants of her torn hymen were found. Vaginal swabs were taken but they didn't produce any semen or foreign DNA. However, there was botanical evidence found in her vagina."

"Botanical evidence?" Carter echoed. "Such as?"

"Tree bark. The report suggests that either she was sexually assaulted while lying on the ground and the bark got in there that way, or that it might have gotten in there after she was put in the water. And there was evidence that the sexual assault occurred postmortem."

That triggered some gasps and groans of disgust. We all sat in silence for a few minutes, imagining the horror the girl must have gone through in her last moments.

"The clothesline used was taken from the backyard of a home near the park where the girls were found. The owners were away at the time. It appeared to have been cut, or rather gnawed at with a pair of ordinary scissors that weren't very sharp." She closed the folder and looked around the room at us. "That's pretty much it," she said. "Gruesome, but not of any particular value unless any of you can think of something in this information that points to a particular suspect."

There was a lot of slow head shaking, head scratching, and ponderous looks, but in the end, no one had any new ideas to offer.

The autopsy information proved to be a buzz kill, and feeling a need to distance myself from it all, I excused myself and headed downstairs. For the rest of the night I kept myself busy tasking. One by one the members of the Capone Club headed home as the night wore on, and eventually Mal came downstairs and took a seat at the bar. I didn't speak to him much at all. He was a constant reminder of how unsettled my love life was, and as such, I found myself avoiding him.

By one o'clock the place was nearly empty and I had the bulk of the cleanup done along with the prep work for the next day. I shut down the kitchen and let most of my staff leave early, keeping only Debra. When closing time came around I sent her home, too, telling her I'd do the rest of the closing tasks myself. Mal stayed where he was at the bar, and as soon as Debra was gone and I had locked the front door, he spun around on his stool and gave me a worried look.

"Mack, is everything okay?"

"Everything is fine," I said, wiping down a couple of tables that were already clean.

"Bull. Tell me what's wrong."

"Nothing is wrong," I said. Then, realizing how unbelievable that sounded, I stopped what I was doing, looked at him finally, and said, "Actually, I take that back. Everything is wrong. Everything is unsettled and uncertain, and I feel like all I'm doing is spinning my wheels. I'm just as confused now as I was in the beginning."

"Are you talking about the cases we're working on, or you and Duncan?"

"Both," I said with a pained smile.

"If you're uncomfortable with me staying tonight, I can sleep down here in your office. That couch you have in there will suit me just fine."

Damn the man was so kind and understanding and handsome. I felt inexplicably drawn to him despite my misgivings. Still holding my table-cleaning rag, I sauntered toward him. "No," I said, shaking my head. "You can sleep upstairs. Same as before."

"You're sure?" he asked. I was inches away from him and he leaned back on his stool, looking unsettled.

"I'm positive," I said, and then I closed the last gap between us and moved between his knees. I could tell he was tempted to turn away, but he didn't. Nor did he take his eyes off mine.

My heart was pounding inside my chest, but it was an exciting feeling rather than a frightening one. And before I had a chance to second-guess the impulse, I kissed him.

This kiss was much different than the first one. This time it was Mal who was hesitant and surprised, but that didn't last long. Soon I felt his arms snake around my waist and he pulled me in closer to him. I gave myself over to the feelings and sensations, and there were tons of them! I let myself get lost in the visual display of exploding colors and the wondrous feelings coursing through my body.

And then Mal pushed me away. It was like a bucket of ice water had been poured over my head.

"Mack," he said, breathless, "we can't do this."

I hung my head in embarrassment, though Mal misinterpreted my action.

"It's not that I don't want to," he said, and when I didn't look at him, he tilted my head up with his hand, forcing me to. "Hey," he said softly, "it's not that I don't want to. It's not that I don't find you attractive, because believe me I do. You have no idea how hard it was for me to stop this just now. But Duncan is my friend, and I can't do that to a friend."

He was right, and I felt ashamed. "I know. I'm sorry," I said. "I don't know what came over me. I never should have put you in that position." Perversely, his moral high ground made me want him even more. "It's just that Duncan and I seem to be at a crossroads and I'm feeling a little lost. And I find myself drawn to you, Mal." I sighed and shook my head hard, trying to shake loose the cobwebs that I literally felt there. "I'm so confused right now."

"You're under a lot of stress, what with this letter writer thing and working on Tiny's case. I'm sure that doesn't help. It's hard to think straight under that kind of pressure. You need to give your relationship with Duncan more time. Wait and see what develops when the stressors are gone."

"If they ever are," I said, feeling irritated.

"Things will get better. Give it time. And in the end if you still decide that you and Duncan aren't going to work out, I'll be here."

His words made my heart ache. He was such a thoughtful, sweet, decent man, and that drew me to him even more. "Your kindness and understanding doesn't make this any easier, you know."

"I know. I'm a beast," he said in a joking tone.

Then he reached up and caressed my cheek with the backs of his fingers. "If it's meant to be, it will happen," he said, looking deep into my eyes.

I sighed with frustration. Every fiber of my being at that moment wanted to take him upstairs to my bedroom and seal this deal once and for all. But then, like a jack-in-the-box, Duncan's face popped into my head, and a mini-montage of shared moments with him played in my mind. With it came a longing to be with him.

I cursed under my breath. After years of relationship drought, I'd managed to get myself into a horribly tangled mess. I feared I was falling in love with two different men at the same time.

Chapter 27

In the end, I sent Mal home. It took some arguing, but I managed to convince him, and myself, that I was in no immediate danger. "It's obvious that whoever is writing these letters is toying with me, playing a game," I told him. "If he or she wanted me dead, I'd be dead by now. And to be honest, I need my space, Mal. I appreciate you putting your life on hold as you have for me these past few days, but I don't think it's necessary any longer. I'm quite secure here between the locks and the alarms, and I think it's best if you go home."

It was obvious he didn't like this idea, though whether it was concern for my safety, a desire to be with me, or some combination of these that bothered him, I didn't know. In the end, he called Duncan, explained that I was adamant about being alone for the night, and after some discussion they both agreed. Or perhaps they simply caved. I think both men knew at that point that once I had my mind made up, I wasn't going to back down. Mal left reluctantly, hollering at me through the door as soon as he stepped outside to make sure I locked all the locks and set all the alarms. His concern for my welfare was sweet, and as I watched him turn away, looking sad and disappointed, I almost changed my mind. But I stuck to my guns knowing it was the wisest thing to do, at least until I could get my head on straighter with regard to Duncan and me. I came to regret my insistence. I tossed and turned all night, haunted by dreams of some vague, shadowy shape that followed me everywhere I went, never getting too close, never letting me see a face, but relentlessly there.

My alarm went off at nine, and I dragged my weary bones out of bed and hopped in the shower to wash the sleep off me. After I was dressed, I headed out to the living room and stared at my couch, wondering how Mal had slept. And as I brewed myself a cup of coffee, I realized I missed him.

I shoved thoughts of Mal from my mind and focused on the day ahead. I called Joe, Frank, and Cora, and asked them to please be at the bar by eleven. Then I headed downstairs to start the opening prep work.

Pete and Jon came in just after ten, and Missy showed up at 10:45. We unlocked the doors a minute or two before eleven and, as planned, Joe, Frank, and Cora arrived minutes later. I ushered them into my office, locking the door behind us.

"Did you tell Joe and Frank about the contents of the latest letter?" I asked Cora.

She shook her head.

"Hell, no, she didn't," Frank said. "And we've been dying of curiosity."

I satisfied their curiosity by describing the letter's contents in more detail and showing them the

pictures I had on my phone. Then I told them
Cora's theory about the church and how my trip
there yesterday had been a bust. "I'm meeting with
Father Manx at noon," I concluded, "but I have my
doubts about this church being the right solution.
And if we are wrong, time is running out. So I need
you guys to focus on these items and try to come up
with some alternatives." I told them about the
pollen that Duncan's lab tech had found in the
cinnamon, and how it was from a stargazer lily. "So
maybe think along the lines of florist shops," I told
them.

"Happy to help," Joe said.

"Thanks, guys. And please keep it between yourselves. You're welcome to hang out here in my
office if you want, so you'll have some privacy.
You can use my computer. I'll check back with you
once I get done with Father Manx."

With that taken care of, I grabbed my coat and
headed for St. Paul's Church.

I expected Mary Fromme to cast a dubious
eye my way after yesterday's encounter, but she
greeted me like I was an old friend. "Father Manx
isn't here yet, but I expect him any minute. Would
you like a cup of coffee while you wait?"

"No, thanks."

"How about a cookie then?" She gestured
toward a platter of yummy-smelling, iced sugar
cookies on a plate on her desk. "I went a little over-
board with the Christmas baking this year."

I graciously accepted a cookie and took a bite.
It was sweet, soft, buttery, and had a hint of almond
flavoring that made me hear the faint ping of
water drops.

Father Manx arrived just as I finished my cookie, and Mary introduced us. He was tall, gangly, and like me, a redhead. He greeted me with a warm smile and led me into his office, which was next door to Mary's. Once inside he gestured for me to have a seat in one of two chairs that sat in a corner. I chose one and he settled into the other. Aside from the clerical collar he was wearing, he could have been any guy on the street. He was wearing khakis and a dark blue pullover sweater with a black shirt underneath.

He leaned back, crossed his legs and his hands, and said, "Ms. Dalton, how may I be of assistance to you today?"

I'd thought about how to handle my meeting with him during my drive over and had decided to stick with the story I'd been using all along. "I wasn't totally honest with Mary about the reason I was here yesterday. You see, I'm participating in a treasure hunt with some friends and I received some clues that made me think my next clue might be here in your church."

His smile faltered a little. "I see. So when you told Mrs. Fromme you were interested in joining our church, that wasn't true?"

"It's not the real reason I came here, no," I admitted. Then, feeling like a callous cad, I added a caveat. "But that doesn't mean it won't happen." I tried a smile, but it felt forced and fake to me, so I'm sure it looked so to him.

He nodded solemnly, steepled his hands, and tapped them against his chin. He looked skeptical but indulgent, and his demeanor was friendly, open, and accepting. I felt ashamed for lying to him and I was stricken with a sudden and desperate need to unburden myself.

"Okay, here's the real story," I said, and then I spent the next hour telling him everything, starting with my father's murder, Ginny's murder, Duncan, Mal, my synesthesia, the Capone Club, and finally, the letters and where they had taken me so far. Some part of my mind told me I was being foolish to open up this way to a complete stranger, but I couldn't stop myself. I justified it by thinking that at least this person was someone I could trust to keep the information confidential, and someone I wouldn't be putting in jeopardy by sharing it.

When I had finished my story, I concluded by saying, "So you see, Father Manx, while I may have deceived you and Mrs. Fromme about why Mal and I came here yesterday, our real reason wasn't as frivolous as some fun treasure hunt game. This is a very serious, life-and-death situation."

"I can see that," he said, looking solemn. "And if I understand the situation correctly, you think that this person who is sending you the letters has used me or my church as the next stop in this game."

"Yes," I said. "So many of the clues in the last letter pointed to here: the spice reference, the bread, the wine, the water, the flower petal, the *Cats* marquee, and the map piece. . . ."

"But the coffee?"

"There's the rub," I said, frowning. "I can't figure out how the coffee fits in here."

"Neither can I. We do have a meeting room downstairs with a small kitchenette, and there are coffee urns there, but other than that, I'm at a loss."

"Does that mean you don't have anything for

me? No package that was delivered with instructions and money?"

"I'm afraid not."

I closed my eyes and felt dread settle over me as if a heavy, wet blanket had been dropped on my shoulders.

"I'll be happy to take you downstairs to look around in the kitchen area," Father Manx said.

"We saw it yesterday with Mrs. Fromme, but we didn't search it as thoroughly as we could have. So if you wouldn't mind . . ."

"I'm happy to oblige."

I followed Father Manx back down to the basement kitchen area and he watched as I searched the cupboards, looked at the coffee urns again, including the insides, checked the refrigerator and freezer, and peeked in the oven and microwave. I came up empty.

I remembered the Bible study class Cora had mentioned and asked Father Manx about it, referencing the time deadline in the letter.

"We do have a Bible study on Wednesday evenings that typically runs from seven to eight," he said. "And sometimes they make coffee. But the classes are suspended right now until after the first of the year. We always suspend them during the Christmas season."

"Is there anything else going on here tonight?"

He shook his head.

"Then I'm afraid I've wasted your time. But thank you for being so understanding about this."

"I'm sorry, too. I wish I could help you. Might I suggest something?"

"Sure," I said with a shrug.

"Do you believe in God?"

I sighed, not sure I had the patience for the typical religious rhetoric I was about to hear. "I don't know," I said honestly. "My father was a practicing Catholic before he married my mother, and she converted after they met. But when she died, he seemed to lose all faith in that sort of stuff. And I understand that, because I have to confess, it's hard to believe in some sort of all powerful and loving being who allows people to suffer so much."

"There is a lot of evil in the world, but . . ."

I must have rolled my eyes because he paused, held up a hand, and said, "It doesn't matter who or what you believe, or don't believe. If you have faith in nothing else, have faith in yourself. You were given this disorder you have, this syna. . . ."

"Synesthesia."

"Yes, synesthesia," he said with an abashed smile. "And regardless of what you believe, I believe God gave you this gift for a reason. Sometimes it's hard to understand the trials we face, and even using the most basic, pragmatic, and secular type of thinking, it's hard to make sense of it. So my suggestion is simply that you open your mind to the possibilities. Have faith, Ms. Dalton."

"I'll try," I said with a wan smile. "Thank you for giving me your time today."

I headed back upstairs, and he fell into step behind me. As I approached the exit, he said, "Please come back anytime. All manner of people and beliefs are welcome to worship with us."

"Thank you."

"And remember, Ms. Dalton. Have faith."

I walked back to my car, feeling scared and

worried. With the church idea proving to be a bust in terms of solving the latest puzzle, the clock was ticking, counting down the hours and minutes left to the latest deadline. Time was running out and if it did, someone was going to die.

Chapter 28

As I started my car and pulled out onto the street, a sense of dread filled me and tears burned at my eyes.

My phone rang then, and when I answered it I saw it was Duncan.

"Hey, stranger," I said when I answered.

There were a few seconds of silence and then Duncan said, "Are you okay, Mack? You sound down."

"I am." I then told him about my trip to the church and my failure to find the next clue. "I'm scared, Duncan. I only have a few hours left to figure this thing out. What if I don't?"

He hesitated before he answered. "A few hours are a few hours. We aren't beaten yet. We'll put our heads together and come up with something."

I desperately wanted to believe him, but it was hard, even though I kept hearing Father Manx's words in my mind: *Have faith.*

"If it helps," Duncan went on, "I think we may have solved the case involving Tiny's sister and her friend."

That got my attention. "What? How?"

"Erik Hermann committed suicide last night. His wife found him around five this morning, dead in his car in the garage. He left the engine running and ran a garden hose from the exhaust pipe through a window, sealing it with duct tape. The ME said is looked like a clear-cut case of suicide by carbon monoxide poisoning. He left a note."

"What did it say?"

"He asked his sister and Lori for forgiveness, and then said that he couldn't bear to live with his guilt any longer after twelve years of living in hell."

"Twelve years? He said that specifically?"

"He did."

"Wow. Does Tiny know yet?"

"He should. Jimmy and I told his parents early this morning. They were going to call Tiny as soon as we left."

"Are you sure that the note is legit?" I asked, remembering another case not too long ago that I worked with Duncan.

"Yeah, we had a handwriting expert look at it and compare it to other samples of Hermann's writing."

"How is his wife, Marie, doing?"

"Okay, considering. To be honest, I suspect she wasn't all that surprised. Several people we talked to said that Hermann had a serious drinking problem and has for years, and that he always seemed depressed. If they knew it, she had to know it, too."

I knew what Duncan said was true—I was able to discern as much in the brief visits I'd had with Erik Hermann. Still, I couldn't help but wonder if he would have killed himself if we hadn't come sniffing around to let him know that someone was looking into the case again.

"Can I tell the others?" I asked.

"Wait a bit if you would. We're planning on releasing a statement to the press in about an hour."

"Does this mean you'll have to cancel our plans to get together today?"

"Not at all. We've already cleared the case. I have some paperwork to finish up so I might be a little later than planned, but other than that we should be good to go."

I was glad to hear that Duncan and I would still be able to get together, but when I hung up the phone, I was plagued by an overwhelming sense of guilt, wondering if I had somehow played a role in Erik Hermann's death.

I drove aimlessly for a while, not wanting to go back to the bar yet. Christmas decorations had started springing up around the city, and normally the light displays would have cheered me. But today they only depressed me. What a horrible time of year for a family to lose someone.

I kept replaying my meeting with Erik the day before, wondering if something I had said had pushed him over the edge. Hard as I tried, I still found it tough to believe that Erik Hermann had killed those girls. I recalled the yearbook he'd had on his desk and wondered why he'd had it out. Had he known then that he was going to kill himself? I wished now that I'd had a chance to read some of the things his classmates had written in the book. Would they have provided some extra insight into his character?

Though I wasn't conscious of having a particular destination in mind, I realized I had driven to the UWM campus. The student evacuation for Christmas break was evident everywhere: piles of trash and furnishings along the curbs, parking lots that had once been filled to the brim were now empty, and where once there would have been students bustling back and forth between classes, the sidewalks were now nearly deserted.

I flashed back on Father Manx's words to me: *Have faith.* My gut had led me here, so maybe I'd do what he said and have faith in the idea that it had done so for a reason. I parked and headed for the chemistry building, not sure it would even be open. It was, though the hallways were eerily empty, making my footsteps sound hollow. I headed for Erik Hermann's office.

I wouldn't have been surprised to find it locked, but luck was with me once again. The door was closed, but when I turned the knob it opened.

The outer office looked much the same as it had before except there was a stack of empty boxes in one corner. The door to Erik's office was open and when I entered I saw that it, too, looked much the same.

I looked at the top of Erik's desk and then at the stacks on the credenza, searching for the yearbook, but it wasn't there. I recalled my suspicion that Erik might have a bottle of liquor hidden in his office somewhere, and curious, I searched the drawers of the credenza. They were filled with hanging files and miscellaneous stacks of paper, but no yearbook and no liquor bottles. Next, I moved to the desk and started searching those drawers. The top right one was filled with office supplies: pens, pencils, sticky notepads, staples, extra rolls of tape, paper clips, a staple remover, and bulldog clamps. I shut it and opened the larger drawer beneath it. There it was, a half-empty bottle of vodka. Propped up next to it was the yearbook. I took it out and opened it. This time there was something else tucked inside the front cover: an open envelope with what looked like a folded letter inside. Both the envelope and the paper appeared yellowed with age. I carefully removed the letter and gently unfolded it. It was a letter addressed to Erik, written in a girlish, flowery style with purple ink.

> *Dear Erik,*
> *I'm so sorry about what happened today. When you kissed me, you surprised me and I reacted without thinking. I didn't mean to hit you. If you still want me to be your girlfriend, I would like that a lot.*
> > *With all my heart,*
> > *Lori*

The letter *i* in both Erik's and Lori's names were dotted with little hearts. *So much for Erik's motive,* I thought, setting the letter on top of the desk. Then another thought occurred to me. Had he gotten the letter before or after the girls were killed? Had he killed Lori because she rejected him, only to come home and find the note? That would explain the depth of his pain and anguish.

I picked up the yearbook again and started reading the handwritten notes and signatures on the inside cover from Erik's friends and class-mates. They were the typical stuff: *Good luck. Glad we survived Mr. G's Algebra class. See you next year.* That sort of thing.

I moved on and paged through to the start of the freshman class pictures.

Lori and Anna were in the same grade and given that their last names were close alphabetically, I found both of their pictures on the same page. I recognized Anna's picture immediately—it was the same one that had been in Tiny's file—but when I looked for Lori's picture, I didn't recognize it right away. Had it not been for the name typed beneath it, I wouldn't have known it was her. The eyes had been exed out with a ballpoint pen, and it had been done with such viciousness that the scoring had torn through the page. In addition, a gash had been drawn across Lori's neck with red ink, and devil horns had been drawn atop her head.

Typed beneath both girls' names were brief epitaphs: *Forever in our hearts* beneath Anna's picture, and *Your light will shine forever* beneath Lori's. There was an arrow drawn from Lori's epitaph to the side of the page, and there, also written in red ink, was *Lights out, bitch!!!* I flipped back to the front of the book and looked at where Erik Hermann had written his name on the inside of the cover to identify the book as his. The writing was tight, heavy, and angular with a strong left slant. Then I flipped back and took another look at the writing next to Lori's picture. This writing was round and light, with a right slant and a distinctively feminine style.

An idea came to me. I set the book on the desk next to the letter, and reached into my pocket to take out my cell phone to call Duncan. I felt something else in there and when I pulled it out, I realized it was the recorder I'd had from my visit to

Erik the day before. As I slid it back into my pocket, I heard a voice behind me.

"What are you doing in here?"

I whirled around, and saw Marie Hermann standing in the doorway to Erik's office, holding an empty box. Her eyes and nose were red from crying, her skin blotchy.

"The door was open," I said evasively.

She cocked her head to the side and gave me an impatient look. "I had to go to the bathroom. I probably should have locked the office behind me when I did, but there wasn't anyone around so I didn't see a need. Why are you here?"

"I . . . I felt awful about Erik . . . I wanted . . . I thought . . . I'm sorry."

She gave me a hateful look. "Are you? It's because of you and that stupid writer friend of yours that this happened. You just had to go dredging up painful memories." She set the box atop a stack of papers on the credenza and walked around to see what I was doing behind the desk. When she saw the drawer open, and what was in it, her eyes widened. Then she looked at the yearbook, and the letter and envelope on the desk. Something in her face shifted, and when she looked at me again, I felt my blood literally run cold. It was as if I had ice water coursing through my veins.

"What are *you* doing here?" I asked Marie.

"I'm packing up my dead husband's office," she snapped. Then she narrowed her eyes at the desktop. "Where did you find that letter? Erik told me he destroyed it."

Puzzle pieces in my mind began to slip into place, and the picture they were forming was unsettling. My hand was still in my pocket, still on the recorder, and I fumbled and felt the button to turn it on. "Erik didn't kill Lori and Anna, did he?" I said, slowly sliding my hand out of my pocket.

"Of course he didn't. Erik was a good guy, a sweetheart. He was much too good for that bitch Lori. But it took me to open his eyes to that fact." She turned then, walked over to the door, and closed it. Then she spun around and faced me again, leaning back against it. She smiled, but there was nothing friendly about it.

Chapter 29

"I didn't think Erik killed Lori and Anna," I said. "I wasn't sure who had, but now I know. You did it, didn't you?"

She arched her eyebrows at me. "Why would you think that?"

"It all makes sense. Anna's diary entry about someone she called "D" who had a crush on her brother, someone who spread rumors about Lori, and left nasty notes in her locker. That was you, back when you still used the name Dylan, wasn't it? You were in love with Erik, but he was in love with Lori."

Her smile disappeared. "He never loved her," she scoffed.

I gestured toward the letter on the desk. "That suggests otherwise."

"That stupid note," she said with a spray of spittle. "I went over to Erik's house that morning as soon as my mother left for work and I saw that note on Erik's dresser. I thought he was going to tell Lori to go to hell, but then I realized he was happy about it. I mean, hell, the girl slapped him when he kissed her. *Hmpf!* What kind of love is that? That's not love." She poked herself in the chest, hard, her eyes taking on a steely glint. "I'll tell you what love is. Love is making sure the person you care about stays safe. Love is making sure the person you care about doesn't get arrested for a crime he didn't commit. Love is sticking your neck out and doing whatever it takes to make sure the two of you stay together."

Her expression softened and tears welled. For a brief moment I felt sorry for her, but then she turned her laser focus back on me—cold and brittle—and any sympathy I had for her vanished.

"You and Erik never went riding in the country the day the girls disappeared, did you?" I said.

She smiled. "No, we didn't. I overheard Anna on the phone with Lori, arranging to meet up in their secret place in the park." She scoffed and shook her head. "Afterward I asked Anna about it, telling her some lie about a secret place I had once, and she told me where it was. So I came up with a plan to make Lori go away. I never meant for Anna to be involved, but I underestimated how resourceful that girl was. I found some scissors on the desk in Erik's father's den and used them to slash one of the tires on Anna's bike so she wouldn't be able to ride it. I thought that would keep her home. But after she tried to fix it and realized she couldn't, she dug her brother's old bike out of the garage and rode it instead."

"And you went off to meet Lori in the woods," I said.

"I did," she said with a wistful look on her face. "I still had the scissors with me and when I went past the Andersons' place and saw that clothesline in the backyard, I cut it down and took it with me. I knew they weren't home because they always go south for the winter, and I wanted something to scare Lori with. I really didn't mean to kill her, at least not at first. I just wanted to put the fear of God into her and scare her away from Erik."

Her expression turned spiteful and mean. "But the little bitch told me to go to hell, and no one speaks to me that way! It made me so mad that when she turned to walk away from me, I grabbed a big rock and hit her over the head with it. Then I started to tie her up. She was out for a little while, but then she came to and started cussing at me and fighting. Next thing I knew, the rope was around her neck and I was pulling it as tight as I could to shut her up."

"You killed her in cold blood," I said with disgust.

"It wasn't my original plan, but"—she shrugged and smiled—"shit happens."

"And Anna?"

"She showed up after Lori was dead. I'd already decided I was going to make it look like that creep Carlisle had attacked Lori. I was about to set the stage when Anna showed up. I didn't want to hurt her. I mean she was my boyfriend's sister, after all. But when she saw Lori and realized what had happened, I didn't have much choice."

"You killed them both in cold blood," I said. "Of course you had a choice. Did you feel any remorse at all?"

She ignored my question. "All those *Law & Order* shows my mom and I used to watch finally paid off. I knew I had to put the girls in the water to wash away any trace evidence that would lead back to me." She paused and sighed. "In retrospect, trying to frame Carlisle might have been a miscalculation on my part. I took Lori's pants off and used a stick I found on the ground to . . . well . . . to make it look like she was sexually assaulted, so the cops would think that pervert Carlisle was the one who had killed her. Everyone thought he was creepy. But the rape thing kind of backfired because it made the cops focus on Erik instead."

"So when the police started sniffing around Erik as a suspect, you came up with that story about going for a ride in the country and told Erik you'd provide him with an alibi. And in doing so, you conveniently gave yourself an alibi, as well. Very clever."

"Thank you," she said with a Cheshire cat smile. "But it still didn't work out the way I wanted it to. The cops kept coming after Erik. I thought I could keep him safe by using my father's influence—he was a judge here in the city at the time, though he's retired now. Between his connections and our family money, I figured we could get Erik cleared. But the cops wouldn't let go. So I had to come up with a better idea." That disquieting smile returned. "I think it was a stroke of genius."

"I'm curious. Did Erik know then that you were a coldhearted killer, or did he figure it out later on?"

"He guessed after the second incident with that creep."

"What creep? You mean Lonnie Carlisle?"

She gave me a grudging look of impatience. "I thought you were so smart and had this all figured out. Guess not, eh?" She *tsked* at me.

Marie was right; I hadn't figured all of it out until that moment. With the mention of a second incident involving Lonnie Carlisle, more of the puzzle pieces fell into place. "You were one of the two girls involved with the sexual assault he was arrested for," I said with dawning. "You framed him."

"Just covering all my bases," she said with a smug tone. "He liked Lori, too. Everybody liked that dumb bitch, though I never understood why. After the bodies turned up, Carlisle kept going out to the woods where they were found, so I planned a little . . . intervention for him. I took along my friend Brittany Aldrich after convincing her that Carlisle was the one who had killed Lori and Anna, and that he kept going back to the scene of the crime."

The name Aldrich rang a bell—literally—in my mind and it took me a second to place where I'd heard it before.

"Brittany is the one who ended up in a coma."

Marie nodded. "Yes, very unlucky for her," she said with no sincerity at all.

"Her father visited Carlisle in prison."

"Did he?" Marie thought about this for a moment and then shrugged. "I told Brittany that if we spied on Carlisle, maybe we could catch him doing something, or saying something that would implicate him. We took along a pocket recorder and rode our bikes out into the woods after I saw him heading that way, and we snuck up on him. But Brittany got scared and wanted to leave and I couldn't let that happen because if she blabbed to anyone about us being out there, the cops might start looking at me. So I gave her this rah-rah speech about how we were going to be heroes, save the day, and solve the murders. I told her we should go out and flirt with Carlisle a little, and when he responded, turn on the recorder and get it all on tape.

"Brittany didn't want to do it, but I shoved a rock in her hand, grabbed one myself, and told her if she abandoned me, she was signing my death warrant because it would take both of us to take him down." She paused for a moment looking lost in memory. "Brittany bought it, and it would have worked, too, if Carlisle had done what he was supposed to. But the creep wouldn't play along. He kept backing away from us and telling us to leave him alone. I even went right up to him and started rubbing up against him . . . and let me tell you, *that* was no easy task." She rolled her eyes and grimaced. "That guy didn't look or smell very good. But even then he wouldn't play. He pushed me away and tried to leave. I saw my whole plan falling apart, so I chucked my rock at him and screamed at Brittany to do the same."

"And did she?"

Marie let out a perturbed sigh. "No, she started to cry. That Carlisle creep saw her all sad and scared and everything, and he started walking toward her, telling her it was going to be okay." Marie shook her head in disgust. "Freaking pervert," she muttered. "I yelled at Brittany to hit him, but she wouldn't. She started backing up, heading for our bikes. I had to do something, so I picked up another rock and hurled it at Carlisle. It hit him in the chest just below his neck and that must have scared him because he stopped, stared at me for a second, and then he ran. I started to go after him, but figured I'd better deal with Brittany instead. She was crying pretty hard by then, and she kept saying that what we were doing was wrong and she was going to tell our parents. We argued, and at one point I shoved her. I didn't mean to hurt her, but she fell backward, smacked her head on this sharp-edged rock, and then she just lay there, not moving. I thought she was dead, so I came up with a story to explain what happened. I punched myself a few times so I'd have some bruises, tore my clothes, and then ran for help, telling everyone that Lonnie Carlisle had tried to attack the two of us."

She paused and sighed again. "I admit it gave me a bit of a start when I learned that Brittany wasn't dead, but fortunately, she never recovered enough to be able to talk about what happened. And that pervert Carlisle is right where he belongs—in prison."

"But he didn't do anything."

"The hell he didn't," she snapped. "He was a pervert, a sex offender. Everyone knew it."

"It was a statutory rape charge, and he was only eighteen when it happened."

"What the hell do you know?" she spat out.

"Erik figured it out, didn't he? That's why he felt guilty. That's why he drank. He realized that you killed his sister and the girl he loved, and he was covering for you."

"He didn't love her, he loved me," she snapped. "And yes, he did figure it out eventually. He went to my father to tell him the truth, but my father convinced him that revealing the truth at that point would be disastrous for everyone involved. He told Erik that if he breathed a word of it to anyone else, he would twist the story around to say

Erik had killed the girls and I lied to cover for him. Erik didn't have an alibi without me, and when he said something about leaving me, I let him know I still had the scissors used to cut that clothesline and that I wouldn't hesitate to use them to implicate him. They did come from his house, after all. So he went along with it."

"Your father knew what you did and covered for you?" I said with disbelief.

"That's what family does," she said in a dismissive tone. "I think Brittany's father began to suspect that something was up, too. That's probably why he went to talk to Carlisle in prison. But my father got to Carlisle first. He sent a law student he knew up to the prison under the guise of studying Carlisle for a thesis. And that student told Carlisle that if he kept his mouth shut, some powerful people would pull some strings, help him get paroled, and see to it that he got some financial assistance when he got out. Money and power talk, you see."

"All those lives you ruined," I said, shaking my head.

"Lives *I* ruined?" she said, furious. "What about the life *you* ruined? I sacrificed everything to be with Erik, and look at where I am now."

"You're crazy. That's where you are." I reached into my pocket, pulled out my cell phone, and went to hit the speed dial number for Duncan. Before I could, Marie lunged toward me and knocked the phone out of my hand. It fell to the floor and skittered under the desk, and then Marie grabbed my arm and tried to pull me out from behind the desk. I pulled back and looked around for something I could use as a weapon. I tried to grab the vodka bottle, but Marie yanked so hard on my other arm that I couldn't reach it. Then I saw a letter opener on top of the desk—a long, stiletto-type thing—and tried to grab it, but I couldn't get a grip. I started to lose my balance so I shifted my full body weight toward Marie, slamming her into the credenza. She was extremely fit, and I knew it was unlikely I'd be able to overpower her, so I tried to dash past her toward the door. Her hand grabbed at my collar and yanked me backward. I fell to the floor hard, knocking the wind out of me for a few seconds.

I craned my neck around and saw Marie reaching for the letter opener. She still had a hold on my collar and she was trying to drag me closer to the desk. I shifted my legs and my weight, and pulled as hard as I could in the opposite direction, and it tightened the collar of my coat even more. Marie abandoned her efforts to get the letter opener and switched both hands to my collar. My coat became a noose around my neck, cutting off my breath. I grabbed at it frantically, futilely, trying to loosen it even a little so I could suck some air into my lungs.

The room narrowed and darkened. An explosion of fireworks appeared before my eyes. I knew I was seconds away from losing consciousness so I quit tugging at my coat and made one last desperate grab, reaching for anything I could find. My hand felt the edge of the credenza and after inching up a little more, I found the handle to the coffeepot. I grabbed it and swung it behind me as hard as I could. The glass pot shattered against something hard and with a little *oomph* Marie's grip finally loosened.

I sat on the floor, gasping for breath, welcoming the harsh burn of the air as it entered my throat. My mind was foggy; the fireworks were fading but still there, and my legs felt rubbery. I scrambled for the door on my hands and knees, grabbed the knob, and pulled myself up. I spared a quick glance behind me to see where Marie was, and saw her standing next to the desk, blood streaming down from her forehead. In her right hand she held the letter opener. She positioned it in her fist and came at me.

I knew I didn't have enough time to open the door so I did the only thing I could think of. I dropped to the floor just as Marie lunged at me.

A loud crashing sound came from above me and pieces of broken glass rained down on my head, the floor, and my lap. I closed my eyes and put my arms over my head for protection. I felt the sting of something sharp on one arm and wondered if Marie had just stabbed me. I braced myself for another stab as pieces of glass bounced around me. Then something fell on the floor at my feet with a clatter. I peeked out from beneath my arms and saw the letter opener on the floor, covered with blood. I grabbed it, struggling to get a grip on the blood-slicked handle.

Marie stood in front of me and I backed as far from her as I could, though her attention wasn't on me. She was holding her right arm out in front of her, staring at it with a dazed expression. A huge red gash ran across the inside of her wrist. Her hand hung limp, blood pulsing out of the wound above it at a rapid rate. There was another gash along the front of her neck, this one oozing rather than pulsing, but doing so at a brisk pace.

For two insane seconds I seriously considered trying to help her staunch the blood flow. Then my common sense returned. I stood on shaky legs, opened the office door, and ran the best I could. My arm was bleeding from a big gash of my own, and I wrapped my other hand around it to try and staunch the flow. When I reached the hallway, I looked around for anyone who might be close by, but the place was deserted. I reached into my pocket for my phone and then remembered it was back in the office, under the desk. With a frantic glance behind me, I started toward the exit, half expecting to see Marie running after me. She wasn't, and when I looked forward again I saw the red box on the wall. I went over, pulled the fire alarm, and headed outside as fast as my wobbly legs would carry me.

Chapter 30

Three hours later, I was sitting on an ER bed with my arm and my head—which I hadn't realized was injured until a fireman noticed the blood running down the back of my neck—freshly stitched. A barrage of officers and detectives had been there with me, questioning, taking notes, listening to my recording, and then confiscating it as evidence. I was alone for the first time since the fire trucks, ambulances, and cop cars had arrived in response to the fire alarm, and I was anxious to leave. Despite knowing I was safe and that Lori's case had finally been solved, I felt little relief. I was too keenly aware of the clock ticking inexorably closer to the deadline imposed in the last letter.

The door to my room opened yet again and I sighed with impatience, anticipating yet another inquiry.

"Duncan!" I said, nearly crying with relief. He hurried over and wrapped his arms around me, holding me tight. It felt wonderful, and I indulged myself for a minute or so, not wanting to leave the warmth and protection of his arms.

When he finally let me go, I told him, "You shouldn't be here. It's too risky."

"As far as anyone knows, I'm here with Marie Hermann."

"She's here, too?"

He nodded. "They're getting ready to take her to surgery. That glass cut through a bunch of tendons in her arm. The neck wound is impressive but not life threatening, and she has some other minor cuts that will require stitching. She'll live to stand trial and I imagine she's going to be put away for a long, long time."

"Her father," I said, wincing at the pain in my throat. It felt raw and rough, as if I'd just tried to swallow a cheese grater.

"Judge Cochran," he said, nodding. "Some guys are over there now talking to him. I imagine he'll be arrested, too. You busted this thing wide open, Mack. But going to Erik's office like that was a damned foolish thing to do."

"I know that now," I said, rolling my eyes. "But after I talked to you earlier, I couldn't shake this nagging feeling I had that things weren't right. I acted on instinct . . . on faith."

"And it almost got you killed."

"I'm sorry."

"Don't be. Just don't do anything like that again, okay?"

I nodded. "I need to get out of here. This case may be solved, but the clock is still ticking on our other one. I don't suppose you—"

"No," he said with a scowl. "I haven't had time."

I sat up and looked around for my clothes. "Hand me those," I said, pointing to the chair. He did and I dressed in front of him, not willing to wait any longer.

"Where are you going?"

"Back to the bar for now. Maybe Cora and the brothers came up with something. If not, I want some peace and quiet so I can focus on the items that were in that letter. Maybe something will jump out at me. Is my car here?"

Duncan shook his head. "No, but I can get an officer to drive you back to it. Are you sure you're okay?"

"I'm sure." I had my clothes on and was standing beside my bed. Duncan reached over and pulled me into his arms, giving me one more hug. It felt like I could have stayed there forever.

"I'll call you later, okay?" he said into my ear as he held me. I nodded. "It might be late. I've got a lot of paperwork to catch up on. If you come up with anything before then, you call me."

Reluctantly, I let go of him. "How late do you think you'll be?"

"This evening sometime." He kissed me on the forehead, turned, and was gone.

I stepped out of my room, found the nurse's desk, and announced I was ready to leave. Fifteen minutes later I was in a squad car driven by an officer I didn't know, headed back to the UWM campus and my car. It had started snowing again, and I kept my face turned toward the side window, effectively eliminating any need for chitchat. When we arrived back at my car, I thanked him and hurried off.

I got back to at the bar half an hour later. Pete, Billy, Missy, Debra, and Linda all greeted me with worried expressions, wanting to know if I was okay.

Apparently, someone had filled them in on what had happened, and not just them. The members of the Capone Club who were there came streaming downstairs as soon as they heard I was in the building. Everyone wanted to hear the details but I put them off, saying only that Lori's case had been solved and we now knew that Dylan Marie Cochran was the real killer.

Everyone was shocked to learn who the real perpetrator had been, especially Tiny. "I admit, I believed Erik was behind da whole t'ing," he said.

"Well, in a way, he was," I said. "Clearly, Marie's need to win him over was stronger than anyone realized. One of the cops I talked to called her a sociopath, which might explain why I had no synesthetic reaction to her voice. She was too cold, too emotionless for me to be able to see or taste anything in her voice. It wasn't until we were alone in that office that I tasted her anger and jealousy."

"It will be interesting to see how the cops spin this one," Carter said. "Given the publicity storm triggered by your involvement with those other cases, I can't imagine they're going to be very happy to announce that you were the one who figured it out and caught the killer."

He had a point, and it made me think that I might have to go back into hiding again for a while, which wasn't likely to help my relationship with Duncan any. It was a sobering thought.

Joe must have sensed what I was thinking because he sidled up to me and said, "Don't worry, Mack. Whatever happens, we all have your back. You can count on us."

"Thanks, Joe," I said. Then I looked at the rest of them. "Thanks, all of you."

They smiled, nodded, gave me *pshaw* waves of their hands, and looked generally pleased with themselves and the outcome. While it felt good to have the attention of everyone, and to know they were watching out for my welfare, I was also impatient to move on from them and get back to trying to solve the puzzle of the letter. I could feel the pressure of time weighing down on me. It was after six already, which meant I had less than two hours left.

I told the group I was tired and sore and needed to rest for a while, but promised to fill them in on the details of what had happened later. Then I pulled Joe, Frank, and Cora into my office.

"Please tell me you guys came up with something," I pleaded.

The disappointed looks on their faces told me all I needed to know.

"We started to look into it," Frank said, "but then we heard about what had happened to you, and that you were in the hospital, and we got kind of sidetracked."

"I did look for florists in the city that might somehow fit in with the clues," Cora said. "I found one that is on St. Paul Avenue but other than that, nothing else fit. But that did get me to thinking that maybe what we're looking for is on St. Paul Avenue. Then we heard about you, and I didn't look into it any further."

Something glimmered at the back of my mind. I tried to visualize it, but it was there and gone in a flash.

"Sorry, Mack," Joe said.

"Has anyone heard from or seen Mal?" I asked. I couldn't help but notice his absence.

"Oh, yes," Cora said. "I almost forgot. He called a while ago after he heard about what happened. He wanted us to tell you to call him when you got back here."

Someone knocked on my office door then, and when I went to open it, I found Carter standing there. "We're going to have a little celebration upstairs in the Capone Club room," he said. "Do you guys want to join us?"

I could tell that the brothers and Cora were so distracted by recent events that they would be of little use to me right now, so I told them to go ahead.

"Are you sure?" Cora said.

"Yes, I'm sure. You need to be with Tiny. And you guys"—I looked over at Joe and Frank—"shouldn't miss out either. You all had a role in solving this thing. I'm going to go upstairs and lie down for a while. I'll come and join you later."

My helpers left and joined the rest of the group for the celebratory dinner. I headed upstairs to my apartment. I thought about calling Mal right away, but I wanted to stay focused on the task at hand, so I decided to wait.

Instead, I pulled up the pictures I had on my phone of the items that had been in the envelope. I felt like I needed a stronger visual cue, so I e-mailed the pictures to myself, printed them, and then spread them out on my dining room table. At first I lined all of them up in a row, but something about the way they looked felt wrong, so I started shuffling them around. First I arranged them in a circle, then in a boxier pattern. Something about the boxy arrangement felt right to me and I left them that way and stared at them for a while hoping for a *eureka* moment.

It didn't happen. Remembering what Cora had said about St. Paul Avenue, I grabbed my laptop and pulled up a map of Milwaukee. St. Paul Avenue was a huge street that ran east and west for miles. I had no idea where to begin looking. Frustrated, I banged a fist on the table. Then I heard Father Manx's words again: *have faith.*

A crazy idea popped into my head, and I tried to dismiss it, but it persisted. I glanced at the clock, saw that I had less than an hour left, and figured I had nothing to lose. I went into my father's office and headed for the bookshelves. It took me a minute or so to find what I was looking for, but eventually I saw it: his Bible. I took it down and felt a flood of memories overtake me. Despite my father's disillusions with religion after my mother's death, he'd still kept his Bible, and I'd even caught him reading it on occasion.

I held it in my hands, closed my eyes, and said a silent prayer, though I had no idea who I was praying to. Then I opened the Bible to a random page and started to read.

The section I landed on was 1 Corinthians 10. It cautioned the faithful to avoid idolatry, sexual immorality, and other temptations. It also encouraged them to eat, drink and be merry, but to do so at the Lord's table, not the table of demons.

It was all very moral and righteous, but not particularly helpful. I was about to toss the Bible aside when I read 1 Corinthians 10:25: *Whatever meat may*

be had at the public market, take as food without question
of right or wrong. . . .

It was like a lightning bolt to my brain. I mentally envisioned the items from the envelope
again, and this time in my mind, each one was surrounded by a faint halo of color. At first the colors
seemed wrong, somehow incongruous with one
another. But I started mentally rearranging them
and slowly but surely, it began to feel right. I
dropped the Bible and hurried back out to the
dining room table.

First, I grabbed my laptop and did a quick
search. I found what I wanted quickly, and when I
saw a map insert in the search listings, things fell
into place. Two more clicks and I knew it had to be
right. Excited, I grabbed my phone and dialed
Duncan's number. It went to voice mail, so I left a
quick message: "Call me back as soon as you can. I
figured out the envelope clue!"

I disconnected that call and dialed Mal next. He
answered on the first ring.

"Mack, are you okay?" he asked, sounding frantic.

"I'm fine. Mal, I figured out the clues in that last
letter. It wasn't the church, it's the Public Market."

"The Public Market?"

"Yes! I'm sure of it," I said, talking fast. "It's
located on St. Paul Avenue. There's a bakery there,
a coffee shop, a wine shop, and a florist. And
Duncan had one of his lab techs look at the stuff
that was in the envelope and she found some
pollen from a lily mixed in with the cinnamon.
And there's a spice shop at the Public Market,
right by the florist. There's also a fish market, and
a shop called the Green Kitchen, which explains
the green scrap of terry cloth."

"What about the water, and the marquee?"

"The cross streets that border the sides of the Public Market are Water Street and Broadway."

I paused and heard nothing but silence. "Mal, are you there?"

"Sorry, yes, I'm here. I was just checking it all off in my head."

"I need to go there now," I said, glancing at my watch. "The deadline was eight o'clock because that's when the place shuts down. I've only got about half an hour."

"Want me to come and get you?"

"No, it will be quicker if I just drive myself there. Meet me there, okay?"

"Okay."

I disconnected the call, grabbed a coat and my keys, and ran downstairs. Billy hollered at me as I flew by, but I waved him off and kept on going. "Be back in a bit," I yelled over my shoulder.

I hurried to where my car was parked but the sidewalks were slick with the new snow and I had to slow down after slipping and nearly falling once. By the time I got to my car, my nerves were on fire and my hands had started to shake, so I took a deep breath and tried to center myself. The engine signaled its reluctance to start by cranking over slowly a few times before it caught. I knew I should probably give the engine a chance to warm up, but I didn't have the time.

The Milwaukee Public Market was located in the Historic Third Ward and was less than half a mile from my bar as the crow flies. But snow and traffic made the drive a slow one. Twice I became impatient with drivers in front of me and honked at them, only to be rewarded for my efforts with some unfriendly sign language. And when I went around a double-parked truck, my car skidded and began to slide, forcing me to slow down. I cursed as I came up on the intersection of Wisconsin and Water Street because the light turned red before I could get through. I inched up to the intersection and stopped, one foot on the gas, the other on the brake. The second the light turned green, I hit the gas. My car fishtailed, but I was able to get it under control. Unfortunately, the car coming up on my left wasn't as lucky. Later I learned that the driver was going too fast for conditions and when the light turned red, he was unable to stop. He hit his brakes, but his car just kept going, hurtling into the intersection and colliding with my driver's side door.

After that I don't remember anything except the explosion of stars and lights, followed by a brief but all-encompassing darkness that was rapidly replaced with a knifelike, searing pain.

Chapter 31

It was Friday night, and I was seated at my dining room table with Cora, Joe, Frank, Mal, and Duncan. Under any other circumstances, it might have been a fun gathering of good friends, but the faces of everyone around the table were glum and all too serious.

My left leg, which was in a cast that went from my foot up to my knee, was throbbing with pain. There was a little red light in the periphery of my vision—a synesthetic light—and with every pulse of my heartbeat it turned on, then off, on, then off.

"Are you okay, Mack?" Joe asked, giving me a concerned look.

I nodded. "I'm fine. The leg is just throbbing a bit."

Duncan, who was seated next to me, scooted his chair back and said, "Put your leg up on my lap. It will feel better if you elevate it."

I used my good leg to scoot my own chair back and turn it toward him. Then, with his help, I managed to get my leg up and position it in his lap. It did ease the throbbing some and I leaned back in my chair with a sigh of relief. "Thanks. That is better," I told him.

Cora, who had taken on the role of nursemaid over the past two days, glanced at her watch, frowned, and then hopped up from the table. "It's time for one of your pain pills," she said.

While she went to fetch my medicine, Frank said, "Good thing you only broke the bones in your lower leg. Breaking that big old femur bone is way worse."

Joe nodded. "Yeah, I broke my femur years ago in a skiing accident and I can tell you, it was no picnic. Good thing I did it when I was young, though. It's the kiss of death when it happens to old guys like us."

The mention of death made everyone at the table wince.

"Sorry," Joe said, realizing what he'd done.

Cora returned and handed me a pill, which I swallowed down with the water I had on the table. "Thanks," I said.

Cora settled back in her seat, and for the next few minutes an awkward silence hovered over the table.

When I couldn't stand it any longer, I said, "I'm so sorry I let you guys down."

"Don't be ridiculous," Mal said. "You didn't let anyone down. You are not responsible for what happened, Mack, any more than you'll be responsible for what may happen. Don't let this guy get to you that way."

The others all nodded and murmured their agreement with this statement.

While I appreciated their support, I didn't agree

with them. "I should have figured out those clues sooner than I did."

Everyone started to object at the same time and as the clamor of their voices became an undecipherable jumble of noise and synesthetic responses, I held up a hand to stop them. "Let's move on," I said when they quieted. "We need to figure out what to do from here on out. Should we warn the others?"

"You can't protect everyone you know," Duncan said. "And if another strike occurs, we have no way of knowing who will be targeted."

"I realize that," I said, "but I think it's only fair to give them a heads-up. At least then they can be more careful."

"And if they are, and the letter writer is watching, don't you think it will be obvious that you've told them?" Joe said. "That alone may trigger an attack."

"I think Joe is right," Duncan said. "As it is we had to work hard to spin your involvement in the Gruber investigation so that it didn't look like you were working for the police."

"Little good it did me," I grumbled. "I'm still fodder for the news and that's likely to only fan the letter writer's flames."

Despite efforts to keep my involvement in the case under wraps, too many people knew about my encounter with Marie Hermann, and the reporters had run with it. Clay Sanders had latched on to it like a rattlesnake, injecting his story with just enough venom to make life painful for me once again. In the paper yesterday, he had an article about the crime-solving savant barkeep that had used her "special skill" to solve a twelve-year-old murder. He hadn't gone into exactly what my special skill was, mainly because he didn't know. But he had spun the story in a way that made the police look bad, writing about how a not-so-ordinary citizen had solved a crime that the police were too bumbling to figure out on their own. The end result of that was I once again persona non grata with the department.

The upside of this was that business in the bar was teeming. The downside was that I was once again forced into hiding. This time it was a little easier, since negotiating the stairs to my apartment was quite the challenge, thanks to my cast and crutches.

Heaven knows what the press and others would have thought and speculated if they knew about the other situation. My frustration with the letter writer had reached its peak. And I was scared about what might happen next. Duncan had gone to the Public Market on Thursday while I was still in the hospital and had questioned all of the various shop owners and employees, all of it unofficial and off the record. But either no one there had been tagged by the letter writer and I had the answer wrong yet again, or they were too intimidated by Duncan's questioning to admit to it. Given that the prior recipients had received instructions to destroy the contents of the envelopes once the deadline had passed, it probably wouldn't make a difference. But now I would never know.

I felt as if I had the sword of Damocles hanging over my head, ready to drop. I was seriously considering heading to the Public Market myself tomorrow to see if I could get the answers Duncan didn't. I knew Duncan wouldn't approve, so I hadn't mentioned the idea to him yet, and had more or less made up my mind that I wasn't going to.

My cell phone rang, and when I saw that it was the main bar number, I answered it.

"This is Mack."

"Hey, Mack, it's Billy. I just wanted to let you know that Gary hasn't shown up for work. I tried to call him but I didn't get an answer."

My spine suddenly felt as if it was encased in ice. "Keep trying," I said to Billy. I looked at the others and knew from their expressions that my own had given away the fear I felt. "In the meantime, call Pete and see if he can come in and help out for a few hours."

"Will do."

"And if you hear from Gary, let me know right away, okay?"

"Sure."

I disconnected the call and looked at Duncan. "Gary didn't show for work and he isn't answering his phone," I said.

"It's probably nothing," Duncan said. "He doesn't have a cell phone, does he?" I shook my head. "So maybe he's stuck in traffic somewhere. Last night's snowstorm has made a real mess of the streets."

I nodded, but I couldn't shake the feeling of dread that had come over me. "I think we need to tell the others," I said. "At least that way I'll feel like I've done as much as possible to help keep them safe." No one said anything. "Let's put it to a vote," I suggested. "Cora, should I tell the others or not?"

Cora frowned and stayed silent for several

seconds. Finally, she said, "I appreciate knowing it myself and I have to admit that I've been extra-cautious lately about where I go, when I go, and who's around me. So I guess I'd have to say yes."

"Frank?" I said.

"I think you should tell the others and let them decide how much of their fate they want to risk."

I shifted my gaze to Joe with a questioning expression.

He gave his brother an apologetic look. "I usually agree with my brother," he said, "but in this case I don't. Don't give the bastard the satisfaction of setting fear into everyone."

"Mal, what do you think?"

"I think you should shut the bar down for a while and let the cops investigate this thing. Maybe if we talk some more to the people who got those packages, we can figure out how the letter writer targeted them. And that might lead us to the culprit."

I shook my head. "I can't afford to shut down," I told him. "I just invested all that money in the expansion. I have enough left over to survive a while if things slow down, but to shut down altogether would be too big a hit. Besides, my employees are depending on me for their paychecks."

"Then sell the place," Mal said.

I gaped at him. "Sell my father's bar?"

"It's your bar now," he said. "And you can move away and start over somewhere else. Open a new Mack's Bar."

"This is her home," Joe said. "If she gives it all up, this letter writing bastard wins."

"Joe is right," Cora said. "Besides, even if she put

the place up for sale, a business like this doesn't sell very fast. It could be months or even years before someone buys it. And that leaves the letter writer plenty of time to wreak more havoc."

Mal threw up his hands and sighed. "Then I'm out of ideas," he said.

"But you didn't answer the question," I persisted. "Should I tell the others?"

He looked at me for a long time. His eyes softened and then he dropped his gaze to the table. "I think you need to listen to me and go somewhere safe," he said. He pushed his chair back and stood. "I'm not going to play roulette with the fates of the others." He looked at Duncan and his expression turned angry. "I can't believe you're just standing by and letting her deal with this." With that, he walked into the living room, fetched his coat and hat from the closet, and left the apartment. The door below slammed closed as he exited.

Another awkward silence fell over the group and once again I was the one who broke it. "Well, I know where you stand on this question, Duncan, so it appears I have a stalemate and the decision is up to me."

Cora's phone chirped, and she picked it up and read a message. "Tiny's downstairs," she said, getting up from the table. "So I'm going to head out." She looked at me with a sad, sorrowful expression. "I'm sorry you have to deal with this, Mack. Let me know what you decide. And let me know if you need anything."

Joe and Frank both got up from the table as Cora turned to leave. "Time to call it a night," Frank said. "Thanks for the dinner."

"Yeah, and what Cora said goes for us, too," Joe added.

Minutes later, Duncan and I were alone. "So what are you going to do?" he asked me.

"I don't know," I said with a frustrated sigh. "But I do know that I hate being in this position."

"I think Mal is sweet on you."

"What?" His sudden change of subject threw me.

"He's fallen for you," Duncan said.

My face felt hot.

"Don't tell me you didn't notice," he said.

"I noticed," I admitted.

"Should I be worried?"

I stared at him, debating my answer. Before I came up with one, his phone rang. He glanced at it, frowned, and answered. "Albright."

I watched his face as he listened, saw his expression change from one of worry, to frustration, and then something akin to fear. He said very little, just the occasional "I see," and "uh-huh," and some one-word questions such as, "Where?" and "When?"

Finally, he thanked the caller and said he would be there soon.

"That was Jimmy," he said as he disconnected the call.

"You have to leave?" I felt my heart sink.

"I do. I'm sorry."

"I thought you were off tonight."

"I was. But something has come up."

"Can't the guys on duty handle it?"

He shook his head. "I have a special interest in this case." Then he leaned over and took both of my hands in his. "I'm really sorry, Mack. Gary Gunderson isn't missing anymore."

I pulled my hands loose of his and leaned back away from him in a futile effort to distance myself from the news he was about to deliver. "Is he . . ." I couldn't finish the question.

Duncan nodded. "They found his body an hour ago. He was in his car, parked in the lot by the Public Market."

I squeezed my eyes closed as my heart tightened with pain. The location was no coincidence, I felt certain.

"He was shot," Duncan continued, "and no weapon was found in the car."

"No," I cried. A tsunami wave of anger surged though me and I pounded my fist on the table. "Damn it, damn it, damn it!"

"There's something else," Duncan said in a soft voice.

I stared at him through my tears, afraid of what he would say next.

"They found something stuffed in his mouth."

"A note?"

"Not exactly." Then he frowned and added, "Well, maybe."

I held my breath, waiting. His next words took my breath away.

"It was a cocktail napkin, one of yours with the Mack's Bar logo on it."

Recipes

IRISH COFFEE

6 oz. hot coffee
2 tsp. brown sugar
1.5 oz. Irish whiskey
2 oz. cold heavy cream

<u>Directions</u>: Stir the coffee, sugar, and whiskey together in a glass mug. Pour the cream over the back of a spoon so that it layers on top of the coffee mixture. Do not stir. If desired, it can be topped off with a light sprinkle of cinnamon or nutmeg.

For a yummy cup of virgin Irish coffee simply leave out the whiskey.

CHOCOLATE COVERED CHERRY MARTINI

1.5 oz. chocolate liqueur
1.5 oz. cherry liqueur
1 oz. vodka
1 oz. crème de cacao

½ oz. grenadine
1 oz. cream or half and half
Maraschino cherry

<u>Directions</u>: Fill a shaker with ice, add all of the liquid ingredients, and shake vigorously. Strain into a martini glass. Garnish with a maraschino cherry. Cherry flavored vodka can be used in place of the cherry liqueur, if desired.

For a virgin version, mix 2 oz. of half and half or milk with one Tbsp. of chocolate syrup, ½ oz. of grenadine, and one oz. of juice from a jar of maraschino cherries.

FRUSTRATION

1 oz. cherry liqueur
1 oz. of triple sec
1 oz. of vodka
3 oz. pineapple juice
3 oz. of sour mix
½ oz. grenadine

<u>Directions</u>: Put ice in a shaker, and add all the ingredients except the grenadine. Shake well and then strain into a large glass with ice. Pour the grenadine on top and enjoy.

For a nonalcoholic alternative, use one oz. of cherry juice from a jar of maraschino cherries in place of the cherry liqueur, use one oz. of orange juice in place of the triple sec, and omit the vodka.

MAL'S MIMOSA

1.5 oz. of champagne
1.5 oz. of orange juice
1 splash of triple sec
1-2 slices of peach canned in heavy syrup
1 oz. of the peach heavy syrup

<u>Directions</u>: Place 1-2 canned peach slices in the bottom of a champagne flute and slowly pour in the champagne. Add the orange juice and the peach heavy syrup. Do not stir. Top it off with a splash of triple sec.

To make this as a mocktail, use a nonalcoholic sparkling wine or apple juice in place of the champagne and leave out the triple sec.

FRENCH TOAST

½ oz. Bailey's Irish Cream
½ oz. cinnamon schnapps
½ oz. butterscotch schnapps

<u>Directions</u>: Put a cup of ice in a shaker, add all the ingredients, and shake. Pour into a chilled shot glass.

For a nonalcoholic treat, make real French toast!